I0770078

Also by Fae

SPOOKY BOYS SERIES

Bite Me! (You Know I Like It)

Possess Me! (I Want You To)

Hunt Me! (I Crave the Chase)

There's a Monster in the Woods

PNR/OMEGAVERSE

The Devil Takes

CHRISTMAS DADDIES

Let Your Hearts be Light

You Can Count on Me

TALES FROM THE TAROT

King of Hollywood

Hunt Me!

(I CRAVE THE CHASE)

BOOK THREE

Spooky BOYS

FAE QUIN

(I *CRAVE* THE CHASE)

SPOOKY BOYS #3

Copyright © 2024 by Fae Quin

WWW.FAELOVESART.COM

This book is a work of fiction. Names, characters, places, and incidents are either products of the author's imagination or are used fictitiously. Any resemblance to actual persons, living, dead or otherwise, events, or locales is entirely coincidental.

Cover Art and Interior Artwork by Fae Loves Art

WWW.FAELOVESART.COM

Typography and Interior Formatting by We Got You Covered Book Design

WWW.WEGOTYOUCOVEREDBOOKDESIGN.COM

Editing by Angela O'Connell

Dedicated to my husband,
my fated mate

for anyone that wants to escape for a while

Author's Note

HELLO EVERYONE! THANK YOU so much for picking up this copy of *Hunt Me*! I am so incredibly excited to dive back into Elmwood with all of you. This book was so much fun to write! It took a lot longer than I anticipated to complete it, but I am so incredibly proud of what the story evolved into and it means the world to me that I am in the position to share it with all of you. This book made me laugh, cry, and giggle like an absolute dork. While Mutt and Jeffrey as a whole are adorable, precious beans, this book does contain some darker elements. You can find a full list of the content on my website faelovesart.com. Stay safe, my loves. Happy reading!

Chapter One

Jeffrey

THE DAY I was taken, it was sunny out. It'd been raining all week and I'd been so incredibly excited by the warmth. Richard, my older brother by less than a year, was scrambling eggs in the kitchen while my oldest brother, Christopher, yelled at someone from work on the phone. I was nine. I thought I had the world figured out.

Mom and Dad were gone, but they were always gone so that wasn't new or surprising. Maybe a small part of me had hoped that they'd be there on my last day—that I'd get to say goodbye, even though they wouldn't have known that's what I was doing—but their absence didn't change my plans.

I wore white sneakers, because they felt like new beginnings.

I wore white sneakers, because Lydia's favorite color was white. Because she'd told me she was going to be my new mom now, and I needed to start acting like I belonged with her.

Lydia was sugary promises and visions of the future.

Her clothes were never dirty.

She laughed at all my jokes.

Brought me gifts.

Told me I was special. I was perfect. That I should've been hers all along.

At the time, I hadn't seen her for what she was. She had seemed so pure. Kind. No one had ever treated me the way that she did. I thought she saw something in me, something my parents never had. I thought she'd take me away to somewhere brighter and *better*. Somewhere where the monsters couldn't find me.

Somewhere I'd be needed and loved.

I was a dumb kid—most kids are.

But *I* was exceptionally stupid. Because it took losing everything I'd ever known to realize that snow can cover spilled blood. That monsters sometimes wore Gucci slides, smelled like cinnamon-flavored gum, and promised happy endings.

If Lydia was a spider, I was the fly that flew willingly into her web.

I'd paid the price for my stupidity the second I climbed into her car that sunny day and realized the truth. I wasn't the only person who had been affected by my choices. I was innocent, naive. I hadn't realized what I'd done, or who had been hurt.

It'd been sixteen years since that sunny day from hell. Sixteen years and nearly every night, I'd lain awake, replaying that memory over and over. Replaying the year that led up to it. The gifts, the cookies, the lies. The doubts she whispered in my ear till my thoughts were hers.

It'd been sixteen years, and despite the fact she was in prison now—I was still trapped in Lydia Evan's web.

Jesus fucking Christ, could this room get any more crowded? At twenty-five, with eyebags dark enough a customer at work that morning had asked me, "Who won?" I wasn't sure why I was torturing myself.

Because you're a glutton for punishment.

I should've gone home after open-mic night ended, before the horny crowds rolled in and the bass dropped low. But, like the sad sack I was… I'd stayed.

Stop acting miserable and fucking do something.

That had been my mantra when I'd texted Blair and found out he was heading off on a date with Richard. Don't get me wrong, I didn't resent him for that. In fact, I was proud of him, honestly. Happy that Blair and my brother had found each other.

Part of me was even relieved.

An ugly, bitter part of me that I tried not to acknowledge.

Because the truth was, now that I'd moved across the country to Elmwood, Maine to be with Blair like we'd planned, there was no buffer to protect me. And without Lydia around to distract him, he kept giving me those sad green eyes and asking me, "How's therapy going, dude?"

And I'd lie and pretend, like always.

"Soooo great. I'm not a basket case at all. Thanks for asking."

"I don't think about the fact I had to use bleach to clean your blood from the kitchen tile only a few months ago or anything."

"Or the fact that I thought you were dead for a while there. That Lydia had

finally snapped and killed you.”

“I’m just fucking dandy, really.”

Our relationship over the last month had been, frankly…*awkward.* He felt it. I felt it. We all fucking felt it. But I couldn’t seem to make it stop, no matter how many well-meaning, “Can I help you with anything?” texts I sent. Or how many, “I’m good! Can I help you with anything?” messages I got back.

An endless fucking loop of us being weirdly nice to each other.

It was uncanny as hell.

But neither of us seemed to be able to figure out how to make it fucking stop.

The last thing I need right now is to accidentally activate Blair’s sad Pikachu face.

Especially when I keep doing that exact fucking thing.

Haven’t I put him through enough?

Which is why I—wisely—kept the true extent of my fucked-up-ness to myself, like a good big brother. Also, why I was *here*—brotherless—sitting on a sticky barstool while flashing neon lights at a club an hour away from my new apartment blinded me.

Because I was *maybe* a bit delusional, I’d convinced myself that sitting alone in a room full of people would be less pitiful than sitting alone at home. That it was better than lying in bed and making shapes out of the popcorn ceiling while I over-thought what I’d say at my next therapy appointment.

I’d gotten it into my head that an excellent way to not spend the night by myself would be to get laid.

Part of me wanted to prove to myself that I still could, even though it’d been ages.

My seat squeaked as I pushed a twenty across the bar and ordered my sixth mocktail for the night. I'd be driving home, so alcohol wasn't in the picture for me, even though I kinda wanted it to be. Liquid courage and all that.

Don't get me wrong, I was no stranger to sex. To seduction.

I'd fucked my way through the graduating class at my high school in Oregon because it was something I was expected to do. Virile young male, family with money, golden-boy, star-of-the-baseball-team.

Getting my dick wet was pretty much a requirement to maintain the persona I'd created.

In public, I was untouchable.

Behind closed doors? Not so much.

But this was also my first time chasing tail since arriving in Elmwood, and I wasn't sure how to feel about it. I mean, sure, I was horny. I'd been horny for weeks. Been horny when I drove across the country, ditching my old life for a town I wished I didn't remember.

But mostly, I was *tired*.

Hence the eyebags.

And if there was one thing that helped me sleep, it was having sex.

Which was why I'd come back in instead of heading home after all the performers had finished. And why I was doing my damndest to ignore the weird prickle at the back of my neck that meant someone was watching me.

People were always watching me.

Peeking through my lashes, I scanned the crowd, but no chick jumped out at me. There was a shadowy man in the back corner of the room, though. His eyes flashed as the strobes hit him. His dark hair pushed back.

I could feel the weight of the stranger's gaze like a brand on my skin— but just as quickly as I'd spotted him, he disappeared.

When I'd first sat down at the bar I'd been hit on a few times, but I'd been too tired to mask my apathy as efficiently as I usually did, and the women hadn't stuck around. I didn't blame them. I was poor company when I wasn't trying to be someone else.

I should go home.

But wouldn't that be a waste?

I'm already here.

I should at least get my dick sucked, right?

It will help me sleep.

As I twisted the maraschino cherry stem from my drink into a knot in my mouth, I scanned the room for potential fuck-buddies. Unfortunately for me, all of the women who'd talked to me before (there were three of them, not millions) had managed to disappear, and the weird, massive stranger I'd seen was gone too.

Not that *that* would've gone anywhere, seeing as he was a dude and I'd never been interested in one before, but still.

It was weird.

The guy looked…familiar.

Not in the way most people in Elmwood did—because they were from my past life. But because I swear to God I'd seen him pretty much everywhere lately. Always at the back of a room, always watching.

The throbbing bass shook my stool as the sweaty bodies on the dance floor moved to the beat. Back and forth, twisting and writhing. Couples that wore matching, flickering grins. Some handsier than others. The two exits were both partially blocked. One near the front, and one back by the coatroom. And there was a rowdy bachelorette party that had set up shop in the back corner of the room beside one of them.

I should go home.

I pulled the twisted cherry stem out of my mouth and dropped it into my cup.

"Neat trick," a cheerful voice beside me spoke. I perked up, though my stomach simultaneously filled with dread as I twisted in my seat to take in the flushed face of a petite woman wearing a shiny white silk sash that declared her as "bride to be."

Oh thank God.

Is it bad I'm relieved she isn't hitting on me?

"Thanks, dude," I ducked my head to indicate the sash, tacking on a *dude* so she'd know I knew she wasn't flirting. "Congrats."

"Thank you!" She beamed at me, practically vibrating with energy. Before I could blink, Bride-to-be climbed onto the empty seat beside mine and waited for the bartender to acknowledge her.

My shoulders relaxed.

Tracing a cool drop of perspiration on the outside of my glass, I tried to muster up the energy to socialize.

I didn't really *want* to, but I didn't want my new "friend" to think I was an asshole, either.

It wasn't her fault that sometimes I felt like I was on one of those merry-go-round things they have at the fair. Just spinning, and spinning, and spinning. The world this big confusing blur around me. *Watching.* On the outside, looking in—because I'm not real.

Not really.

At least, not in the ways that count.

I'm not sure *when* exactly I stopped being a real person. Maybe it was when I was a snot-nosed kid and I stepped foot in that car with Lydia. Or when I found out *the secret.*

Or maybe it was after my first kill.

Or my second.

Or my third.

They started to blend together after a while.

Scars on scars on scars.

Kill after kill after kill.

The world spun, and spun, and spun.

Maybe this is karma for what I've done.

"Hey," the girl waved her hand at the bartender with a big grin when he glanced our way. She wore the kind of smile that looks like it hurts, all wide and innocent and vulnerable. The kind of smile that belongs in a sitcom because it's pure.

Her nails were done. Her makeup too. Probably professionally, because judging by the brand of her bag, she had money. Sheltered. It was obvious in the way she carried her body—and also because geographically speaking, that made sense. This was a bigger city than Elmwood but still small. Tight-knit.

Young girl meets the love of her life at college in Ridgewood, experiences a whirlwind romance—the kind of thing you hear stories about but never seen in real life.

The *perfect* couple.

Until you look behind the masks ten years later and realize he's fucking his secretary—like a fucking cliche—and she copes by spending his money on more designer bags and vacations with the friends that feed her constant platitudes that "at least it could be worse."

I'd seen worse.

And I could attest that even a life like that was better than half the shit out there.

Less blood too.

Her smile didn't falter, and because of that, I knew it was genuine.

Put that thing away before you blind somebody.

"What you lookin' to drink?" the bartender asked, finally approaching.

Jolted out of my thoughts, I found myself suddenly back in the club, surrounded by people and not memories. There was no blood on my hands— at least not visibly. I was *okay*—or as close to it as I ever got nowadays.

"Another sex on the beach for me, and a refill for my friend," Bride-to-be beamed. Her tiny hand lay on my shoulder, and I *ached.*

Because it was *warm.*

And it felt so *good* to be touched without a price tag attached.

It was something I'd never known how to ask for. I hadn't thought I'd receive that simple kindness tonight. Historically, Blair had been the only person that touched me like that. Richard too, more recently, but he was awkward and weird about it.

I could understand why.

We were supposed to be brothers, after all, and neither of us knew how to fix what had happened between us.

"You didn't have to do that," I said to the bride, though I accepted the new drink with grace when the bartender sat it down in front of me with a *clink.*

"You looked sad," she shrugged, and I laughed, even though it hurt.

"It's the lights," I waved to the flickering blue lights above, then pulled an exaggerated dopey sad face. "See?" She giggled and shook her head. They turned pink right after, and I grinned just to watch her roll her eyes. "They're unflattering."

She blinked at me like I was stupid, but her smile grew softer. Then she withdrew her hand from my shoulder.

Stop shaking.

Stop it.

She'll notice.

"I don't think anything could be unflattering on you, but okay." She wasn't hitting on me, so I didn't get why she was being nice. It wasn't my first time being complimented because of my looks, but usually the compliments weren't free. "No one's allowed to be sad during my bachelorette party," Bride-to-be took a massive swig of her drink, burped, and thumped her hand against her chest. "Sorry."

"I'm not here for your party," I replied, though she already knew that.

"Still."

I didn't know what to do with her kindness.

Or the fact that I was apparently so shit at masking nowadays that even a stranger could see I was cracked down the middle.

I felt bad immediately for over-analyzing her the way I had.

I really hope her husband isn't a dick.

In an effort to prove to myself—and her—that things were fine, I spent the next twenty minutes trying to teach her how to tie a cherry stem with her tongue. Maybe I also kinda hoped she'd pat my back again? But I refused to admit that, even to myself. *Shit.* I just did.

She didn't.

Pat my back, I mean.

And when she left me alone at the bar, I felt lighter without the weight of having to pretend. The smile I had pasted on dropped as soon as her back was to me as I threaded my fingers around my half-empty glass and let the world spin again.

I should go home, I told myself again as I watched the crowd. *I don't belong here.* The minutes on my phone ticked by as I waited for something, anything to happen—I wasn't sure what. A spark. I don't know. Something cosmic.

Like magic, a few minutes later, my wish came true.

Though not in the way I had hoped.

I could feel the prickle of eyes on the back of my neck again. The hair on my arms stood on end and goosebumps shivered up my body. Four guys sat on the other stools at the bar beside mine. A crowd of people danced to my left, dressed in skimpy but tasteful clothing. No one was looking at me. No one.

And yet…someone was.

Someone I couldn't see.

I could feel it as easily as I felt the throb of bass from the DJ.

Maybe it was the guy from earlier?

Or maybe it was one of Lydia's hunter buddies?

Hello, paranoia, my old friend. Nice to see you haven't abandoned me.

You're fine, Jeffrey.

You're fine.

Somehow, the reassurances didn't help.

They never did.

Around two a.m. I decided it was time to stop pretending I was trying to get laid and get my ass in bed. I had work in the morning, and it seemed pretty self-explanatory that I should not be nodding off on the job. I was lucky enough that Avery had hired me in the first place, considering my background.

He insisted it was a plus, but I knew better. There was a reason no one in my life but him knew what I'd done. They'd run. I wouldn't blame them, either. The blood on my hands was as red as my hair. But Avery was a bleeding heart. That was the reason he'd hired me at his magic shop. Not because he found my skill set useful, or that he didn't care about what had happened to me.

I was a charity case.

I climbed from the stool, limbs creaking, ass numb. As I wobbled my way through the crowd I shook the pins and needles out of my legs, and swiveled my torso from side to side to pop my back. Simultaneously, I patted my pockets to make sure my wallet was still there.

You can never be too careful.

Some dude jabbed me with his pointy ass elbow, but he apologized, so it was fine.

The sugar in my stomach swam around in circles as I flicked the guitar pick I kept in my pocket between my fingers. Flick, flick, flick. It was warm to the touch from sitting against my body. I traced the smooth surface with my thumb the way I always did, letting it dig in for just a moment, the pain centering me.

"Someone forgot to shower tonight," I muttered under my breath as I dodged between sweaty bodies, avoiding as many lethal elbows as I could. One elbow to the gut was enough for me, thank you very much.

I was almost to the exit when I heard it.

A familiar voice.

Syrupy and slow, obviously intoxicated.

It only took a second to recognize it as the bride-to-be from earlier, and the moment I did, my blood ran cold. I scanned the room for her, immediately spotting the dark hallway I'd nearly passed on my way out the door.

My hands clenched into fists as I slowly approached. Lights continued to strobe behind me, painting the walls in splashes of color as I stood at the open end of the hallway, horrified.

This hadn't been what I meant when I'd said I wanted something to happen.

Bride-to-be was pinned to the wall by a big nasty dude wearing a muscle tank and probably no deodorant, if the smell was anything to go by. I could smell him from ten feet away, and man, the guy was rank.

He looked like the kinda dude who snorted cocaine and Kraft mac and cheese on the weekends, thought onions were spicy, and spent every second he could futilely trying to convince everyone at work that he wasn't a wife-beater—even though the string of exes he left behind said otherwise.

In other words: dude was a grade-A asshole.

I didn't have to smell him to know that.

Though that didn't help.

He smelled more like an asshole than he looked like one—and that was saying something.

The closer I crept to the two figures, the easier it was to parse out what had happened. The women's bathroom was just behind the bride-to-be, like she'd been exiting when he grabbed her. He'd probably been waiting in the hallway like the creepy opportunist he was, ready to pounce on his next unwilling victim.

I was exhausted, but not dead. There was no way in hell I was going to leave her alone with him. For the first time in months I wished I had a weapon on me—though realistically that wouldn't do anyone any good.

Wasn't like I could slice the dude's throat or shoot him.

Not in public.

And even if I could, I wasn't sure I had that in me.

My heart raced as I watched her struggle for the moment it took me to cross the remaining distance between us. Her eyes were droopy and her protests were feeble.

She's wasted.

The thought made me sick. Even if she hadn't weighed a pound and a half, soaking wet, she'd still be no match for this dude—not at that level of intoxication.

Asshole hadn't noticed me, even though I was right behind him, but Bride-to-be had.

Her eyes widened, her mascara smudged, and I shoved aside the last dregs of my exhaustion to answer the call for help in her gaze.

I could still feel the weight of eyes on the back of my neck, but I ignored the sensation, certain it was still paranoia. *Thump, thump, thump,* I focused on the beat of my own heart as I took a steadying breath, centered myself, and leapt into action.

Asshole was big, bigger than I was, but all that meant was that I had to push at the right spots to get him moving. His bulk could be used against him as easily as it could be used in his favor.

"Hey, fuck face." I grabbed the nape of the dude's shirt, kicked the back of one of his knees, and used his falling momentum to pivot him away from my wasted buddy. Surprise was a useful tool. And it came in handy now more than ever.

"Wha—" He slammed into the wall the second I released his shirt, stumbling a little as I put myself between Bride-to-be and his bulk, ready to fend him off the second he retaliated.

Which he did.

Because he was big, and dumb, and predictable.

"I'll kill you." Asshole's nostrils flared like a bull.

"Uh-huh, sure, dude-wipe," I beckoned him forward, just glad he had his sights set on me and not my new friend. I'd fought things far larger and deadlier than a drunk dude with bad hygiene, so I wasn't scared.

Because I knew I could take him.

It would be easy.

He didn't have fangs, or claws, or supernatural strength. He wasn't faster than I was. He didn't heal more quickly than I did. He may be big, but he was a human. A *stupid* human. I could fight him. I could fight him and I'd win.

But that didn't mean that I wasn't...*tired.*

Tired of the fight.

Tired of being strong.

Tired of holding the world together when it didn't feel like I belonged in it in the first place.

It would be nice if someone else stepped in for a change.

It would be nice if I could rest.

Distracted, I could blame no one but myself when Asshole's fist connected with my shoulder. It stung, and I gasped—which was a mistake. Big fucking mistake. Jesus-god. Fucking, fuck. *The smell!*

Acrid and thick. Greasy hair. Potato chips.

"God, you are *rank*," I managed, trying to breathe through my mouth, though that wasn't any better.

"Fuck you, princess," his nostrils kept on flaring.

"It's Prince, actually." I shrugged. "Jeffrey Prince."

"Fuck you, *princess*," he repeated, like he thought he was being clever.

"You're really not my type." I twisted to avoid a second punch, fingers bunching in his shirt for the second time that night as I shoved him deeper into the hallway. It was a bit of a struggle, I'll admit that. Harder than I'd thought it would be. I wasn't really in peak form at the moment, but I managed to hold him off long enough that the girl I'd saved could hurry back to the safety of her bridal party.

My shoulder throbbed.

It was going to bruise.

Up close and personal with my chest against his, I couldn't help but gag a little when his breath filled my nose. "Ever heard of a toothbrush?" I couldn't help but ask as he struggled, then roared, his steel-toed boot stomping down right where my foot had been. "It's this really cool invention—revolutionary, really."

Hopefully someone would call security so I could go home.

I really didn't want to deal with his stench for longer than I had to.

"Shut the fuck up, fire crotch," he hissed, stomping at my feet again, his fists swinging. However, before one could connect with my body for a second time that night, he was suddenly gone.

Gone.

What the fuck?

"What—"

Chapter Two

Jeffrey

"THE FUCK?" I stared at the spot where the asshole had just been, my empty hands shaking. Stumbling as his weight disappeared, I was forced to find my balance. The sugar in my stomach churned.

Whipping my head around, alarmed, I observed that there was no one to my left, or right—the hallway completely empty.

Except that it *wasn't*, because before I could take another breath, a low, menacing growl filled the air.

Mean and *deep*, the sound quaked through my bones. It set my teeth on edge. Made it feel like electricity was zapping through my body, the hair on the back of my neck standing on end.

It was the kind of sound I heard in my nightmares.

The kind of sound made for creaking woods, starry nights, and blood-splattered leaves.

It had no place here, in a town like Ridgefield, where the population was normal and humans were unaware. In fact, the sound was so out of place that when it stopped as abruptly as it had begun, I was nearly able to convince myself that I'd made it up. Hallucinated this entire encounter.

That this was just another nightmare.

Fuck, I really need sleep.

Maybe I'd spent so much time around monsters I was seeing them in places they weren't.

I wasn't hallucinating though.

I just needed to turn around.

Because the growl had very clearly come from behind me.

It was quieter here in the hallway, just the echo of the music from the main room glancing off the walls. Quiet enough it made it easy to catch the wet gasp that left Asshole's lips, confirming that he was, in fact, also behind me. I almost didn't want to look. It felt like Pandora's box. Nothing good could possibly be waiting for me.

Buuuut I looked anyway.

And as I twisted my body entirely around to see where the hell Asshole had gone, it became clear that there was no monster lurking in the dark. At least, not in the way I'd expected.

Pressed against the wall, with his arms twisted behind him, the douchebag wheezed in pain. His mouth opened and shut, sputtering like a fish outta water, his eyes wide with fear. Even in the dark I could see that his face was red. Redder than the sunburn I'd gotten when I was twelve that'd made my whole face peel.

But as ugly of a sight as he made, he wasn't the thing that caught my eye.

Nope.

Nuh-uh.

My full attention was reserved for the man restraining him.

The very muscular man.

The very muscular man who had *werewolf* practically written all over him.

The very muscular man who towered over the douchebag—despite the fact that he was a massive man himself.

Holy shit.

My savior was huge. Absolutely fucking *huge*. His body loomed behind the man he had pinned, the low menacing noise I'd heard having clearly come from him. Maybe I'd imagined how *terrifying* it had sounded. But then he made the sound again—and nope.

I definitely did not imagine that.

My pulse thrummed and my skin felt hot and cold all over as I stared. I couldn't help it. I wasn't used to staring at men and thinking about their biceps. Especially not men I highly suspected to be supernatural. But when faced with a specimen like *that*…well… Even a straight man couldn't deny he was gorgeous.

Thick thighs.

Broad shoulders.

Veins beneath the dark hair that coated his ropey forearms.

A statue of him belonged in a museum—that's how chiseled his physique was. Or maybe he should've starred in an action flick, all oiled-up muscle and corny dialogue. He belonged on the big screen, blasting through buildings with his laser-beam eyes, or stopping trains one-handed, not… saving *me*, of all people.

Especially when I could've—probably—saved myself.

The electricity I'd felt in the air was still there. It trembled, making me feel shivery and scared and excited all at once. There was no denying that something was happening here. Something huge. I felt like I'd just woken up.

The merry-go-round stopped spinning.

Distantly, I recognized that this was the same man who had been staring earlier. I wished I'd paid more attention to him then because…holy fuck. Wow.

My toes curled in my Converse as I stared at the muscles rippling in the stranger's back. He barely had to move to keep Dick-face in check. That took a shit ton of power. I would know, seeing as I'd just barely restrained him myself.

He made it look easy.

Effortless.

"I'm sorry, I'm sorry, I'm sorry—" the asshole chanted in a panicked, quaky voice as his arms were twisted tighter and tighter behind his back. "I'm sorry—" Sexy-strange-probably-a-werewolf-man's forearms flexed, and my stomach went funny for a second—because *woah.*

I didn't need to see his eyes to know what he was.

But I knew, the second I did, every doubt I had would disappear.

"*Security,*" I stammered toward their backs, still shocked. "I'll, um. *Yeah.*" I jerked my head toward the end of the hallway. "I'll be back. In a sec. Yep."

I raced the fuck out of there.

When I returned with two bouncers and my heart in my throat, Mr. Savior was gone. Asshole was on the floor, tied up with his own nasty t-shirt, shivering and scared, snot running down his face like he'd been crying the entire five minutes I'd been gone. He didn't put up a fight as he was ushered out of the club to the front where the cops that had been called were no doubt waiting. When his gaze caught mine, one last, final time, the whites of his eyes flashed, and he quickly ducked away.

Like it was *me* he was terrified of.

Weird.

Weird, weird.

I made my way outside in a daze, using the back entrance because it was closer to where I'd parked. Ignoring the weight of eyes I still felt on the back of my neck and my aching shoulder, I couldn't help but feel disappointed.

I didn't know what I wanted. Maybe to say thank you to the wolf that had saved me?

It's for the best.

He probably doesn't want your thank you anyway.

In a weird way, I felt like a little kid. Like I'd just seen my hero in real life—and before I'd gotten a chance to get his autograph he'd fucked off back to saving Gotham or whatever.

Disappointed and paranoid was a new combo for me.

But so was the flip in my belly and the flush to my cheeks.

It was pretty outside. All glittery stars and warm breezes. Summer was my favorite time of year. I liked the heat and the way the night sky seemed to stretch on for miles. Figuring I'd do my best to enjoy it on the walk to my truck, I tipped my head toward the clouds, my shoulder aching, and my teeth on edge.

Halfway through the parking lot, things took a turn.

"Jeffrey Prince," a voice said, and I jolted, spinning around, ready to face another threat. Only it wasn't. A threat, I mean. Or at least, I *hoped* it wasn't. Because it was…yeah.

It was him.

Mr. Savior Hottie McMuscle Pants.

My disappointment bled away as I ran my fingers over the guitar pick in my pocket and swallowed the lump in my throat.

Respond, dumbass.

He's waiting.

"That's your name, isn't it?" Big-and-handsome asked. His voice was soft, and low, and *sweet.* Cheerful and careful, like he didn't talk all that often and wanted to get it right. There was an uptick to his tone that reminded me of a dog—all hopeful and puppy-like. "I heard you say it. Earlier. He called you a princess. You said "It's Jeffrey Prince actually." It was very heroic!"

So, he'd seen me fight the guy before stepping in. That tracked.

But he was the heroic one, not me.

"Uh, yeah." I squirmed, not really sure why I was squirming. "Thanks for um…" I jerked my thumb back toward the club. "All of that. Not that you needed my help…because obviously you didn't. I got security to come but by then you were—"

"Had to get out." His eyes flickered in the dark, almost like a cat's.

Fucking knew it.

Werewolf.

This was…my first actual encounter with a werewolf as an adult, despite my unorthodox education.

"Had to…get out?" I repeated, taking a half step toward my truck, my pulse thrumming. "Why?"

His entire face scrunched up, expressive brows drawing low, and his teeth baring as he shook his head. "He was…*awful.*"

"Yeah, he was," I agreed, because duh.

"No—" the man shook his head again. "He *smelled* awful," he explained.

"Oh," I couldn't help but laugh. The sound startled right out of me. "Fuck yeah. I was thinking the same thing!"

"Really?" Big dude perked up, taking a half step to meet me. There were barely two feet between us, but it felt like it was closing with every second. It was weird being smaller than someone else. I was tall. I'd always been tall. Plus I'd grown up with Blair, who was practically a goth dwarf. So this feeling of…oh-my-god-I'm-*tiny* was as unfamiliar as looking at forearms and thinking, *fuck, that's hot.*

Mr. Savior's chest was right in front of my face. And he didn't have tits, but he may as well have, his pecs were so fucking round. I swear to God I expected them to bounce when he stepped closer. My dick twitched.

I swallowed, taking another half step back, laughter forgotten.

"You are not angry I stole your kill?" he asked, following me again. There were street lights throughout the parking lot—for safety reasons— and I was suddenly grateful for them as his shadowy figure became clearly illuminated the moment he stepped into a puddle of light.

If I'd thought he was handsome before, cloaked in shadow, it was nothing compared to him now that I was seeing him clearly for the first time.

He was *striking.* Vivid blue eyes. Dark, warm brown hair that flowed jaggedly to his collarbones. Almost like a mullet, but less on purpose. Like it had simply grown that way, and he'd let it—no styling necessary.

His lips were perhaps on the thin side, but that only added to his rugged appearance—made his jawline look wider, made the cleft in his chin more biteable. The slope of his nose. His sharp cheekbones. His heavy brow.

In contrast with his more classically masculine features, there was something soft about him too. Boyish and innocent. I couldn't help but wonder if this was his first time outside his pack entirely.

Maybe it was the flutter of his lashes. Or maybe it was the way he was looking at me, not an ounce of guile in sight.

"Stole my…what now?" Dammit, he'd distracted me with his face.

"Your kill," the man replied. *Boy?* Because he was obviously younger than me, maybe eighteen, nineteen? So…six years? Fuck. "I would not want to anger you."

"Ummm, no. Nope. I am not angered." I could only assume he was talking about jumping into my fight with Douche-canoe. "It was…" I was so distracted by his pecs I forgot to lie. "It was nice not to have to fight for a change."

"Do you often fight?"

"I guess?" I took another step back and my shoulders connected with the cool metal of my truck. I should get in. I should drive off. I should leave this weird growly guy behind and forget about my fucked up night. I should try to sleep—however unsatisfying and brief it would be.

But I didn't.

"You attract trouble." It wasn't an accusation so much as it was an observation.

An observation that was true, so I didn't bother denying it.

There was something about the way the stranger was looking at me that made it impossible to leave. His gaze pinned me in place. Hungry. Not in a lustful way, the way I was used to people looking at me. But like my presence alone was enough to sate him.

There was no denying that I was standing in front of a predator.

I should've been scared.

But I wasn't.

"Sometimes." I hoped he wouldn't ask more questions I wasn't ready to answer. My keys were a lead weight in my pocket, my belly full of butterflies.

"He smelled awful," the man repeated his earlier words, changing the subject. I nodded, because we'd established this, and I wasn't sure where he was going with it. "But *you* don't. You smell like *happiness*."

Oh.

Oh no.

Is he coming on to me?

I should turn him down, shouldn't I?

I'd just spent all night kidding myself that I was ready to get laid, and I very clearly was not. I should've been disappointed that he wanted something from me, after all, but I wasn't. There was just…something about the way he was staring at me that felt different.

Let him down gently, Jeffrey.

Don't crush him.

He seems like a nice guy.

Shit.

I probably shouldn't have kept staring at his pecs. That was probably why he was confused.

I was throwing off mixed signals.

"*Please*?" the man asked, his voice low and needy. It was such a *polite* request. "Please can I?"

I wasn't really sure what he was asking for, but he was being so sweet about it I couldn't help but agree. A people-pleaser to the core. "Sure, but what are—*oh.*"

His skin was hot but his breath was even hotter as he pushed against my body. Electricity zapped through me where our thighs touched as the stranger pressed in close and *inhaled.*

Is he smelling me?

He's totally smelling me.

"Oh fuck." My dick jerked, immediately recognizing the presence of another person.

"It's not enough—" Handsome's voice was a muffled whine, his nostrils flaring. And then, before I could even react, his large palm sunk into my hair. Gently, but firmly, he grabbed a fist full, then tugged my head to the side. Straining now, I sucked in a ragged breath, eyes wide, as the werewolf closed the last few inches between us and snuffled greedily against my throat.

It was kinda innocent. In a sexy way. Like he was literally just breathing me in. His nose skimmed against my sensitive skin, making my toes curl, and I held impossibly, obediently still.

"I have waited *so* long," he murmured, confusing me once again. Waited so long to sniff someone? Weird kink, but hey. I wasn't judging. So long as we didn't go further than this I would— "*Please* let me taste you. I will be good. I will be so good for you."

"T-taste me?"

"You are everything I've ever wanted." *Damn, okay.* "Your skin is sugar." A hot wet tongue swiped across my jugular and my eyes rolled back. "Your scent is…" he growled, low and needy, hips jerking against my own. "Ugh, I don't know—" he whined. "It is heaven. It is everything—it is—"

I should definitely push him off.

Definitely.

I should definitely let go of his t-shirt and stop pulling him closer.

I should do that.

Otherwise this was going to get very gay very fast, and I wasn't sure how I felt about that. I'd never looked at another man before and wanted him to touch me. Sure, I'd stolen glances at the guys on the baseball team in high school but that was different. I'd had a girlfriend then, and I wasn't looking. At least…not really?

One time, I'd caught Ian Kelley jerking off in the showers and he'd smirked when he saw me looking.

But that was it.

It wasn't that I was homophobic, because I wasn't. It was just…Blair was the gay one, not me. He should be the one pressed against a pickup truck with a big beefy dude chomping at his neck. I had a PhD in tits, this should not be turning me on.

Except that it was.

And fuck.

Okay.

Maybe I wasn't as straight as I'd thought. Because…damn.

Handsome needed to stop whining or we were going to get caught. The cops were just around the front, probably still dealing with Asshole. We could get arrested for public indecency.

He was being way too loud. I clenched my jaw a little when he dug his teeth into the tendon on the side of my neck, and the whining stopped.

Okay, I'll admit it. The one whining from a little neck stimulation? That was me. Apparently I liked being chomped on.

He was just so…big.

So big.

And he'd *saved* me.

And with him towering over me there was no one to hide from. It was dark, and warm, and safe. And he smelled as good as he claimed I did. Musky sweet, with a hint of spice. His hand in my hair slid down, cupping the opposite side of my neck.

He could kill you.

Snap the bones easier than you can blink.

That thought somehow only makes this hotter.

I could stay. I could stay and get laid.

He obviously wanted it, if the bulge of his cock pressing into my abs was any indication. This was why I hadn't gone home, wasn't it?

Did it really matter if it was with a dude or a chick?

No.

Feeling rejuvenated, I stopped scratching at Handsome's back—because I'd been doing that too, along with the whining—and gently pulled on his hair to get him to stop chewing on my neck. Damn, his hair was soft. Way softer than any dude's hair had any right to be. Did he condition?

He didn't look like the kind of guy who conditioned.

"One second," I breathed out, unable to help the way I fingered his feathery locks with one hand as I pulled my keys out of my pocket with the other. When I looked up, my stranger's big blue eyes searched mine. Sad, needy, almost like he couldn't fathom why I'd forced him away from his new favorite treat. "Just getting the car open, buddy," I laughed.

"So it is not over?" He perked up again, like an overgrown puppy, and I snorted out another chuckle and grinned.

"Nah." I shook my head, jerking the door open the moment it was no longer locked. "But I'm not touching your dick. I've never… I mean, I'm not—I don't…I'm not comfortable with that. So long as you're cool with that, then yeah, we can keep…doing whatever it is we were just doing."

Maybe more too.

"That is okay," Handsome-and-handsy immediately replied. "I would not last if you did. Looking is enough."

"If you want, you can do a hell of a lot more than look." I pulled the door open to the back seat with a flourish, and then hopped inside, grateful for the length of my legs because they made it easy.

"*Really?*" If he'd had a tail, I swear it would have been wagging right about then. The second I was in, my stranger climbed in after me. The hot flicker of his breath on the back of my neck sent a shiver down my spine as I turned my body around to face him. Without preamble, he jerked my legs open, and pinned me against the seats with his bulk.

The door slammed shut behind us with a final sort of sound, and my belly flipped as Handsome loomed over me. He was between my legs now, his mass squashing me, my back to the opposite door.

I swear to God he was staring at my pulse.

All thoughts of cops and decency fled my head.

"Really," I managed. "Touching is good too—"

God, had my voice always gotten all pathetic and breathy like that when I was turned on?

"You sure you're okay with this? I was um…Mmmm…" He licked his lips, his hips rubbing against mine in an entirely distracting way. It was unpracticed but enthusiastic. Like he wasn't sure how to make this work, but sure as fuck wanted to. "Mmm, fuck." My stranger ground down *harder,* and I couldn't help the way my hips jolted up to meet him. "*Shit,* I can't think when you do that."

His eyes flashed again.

"I don't want you to think."

My dick was now fully hard, straining against my jeans as he fanned his large, molten hot hands along my hips and squeezed tight enough I was sure I'd bruise.

With a frown, Handsome seemed to decide the angle was not, in fact, good enough.

Because a second later, he yanked my pelvis up, easy as flipping a goddamn pancake. His tongue poked out of the corner of his lips as he concentrated, a needy rumble building in his chest as he grabbed one of my thighs, forced my legs wider, and lined our dicks up.

And that was…fuck yeah.

Fuck.

Handsome rutted me hard against him, like I was a fucking toy for his pleasure. Like I weighed nothing at all, not six-foot-something and two hundred plus pounds of muscled jock.

"No thinking," Handsome moaned, sweat beading at his temple, his hips jerking into mine in an uncoordinated rhythm that made me feel half-drunk. "If you think, you might make me stop."

"Not likely," I could hardly get the words out, my earlier bravado gone as he fucked me through my clothes with my ass off the bench, his big hands clenched around my body. I should not have liked being manhandled like this. It was wrong. *I shouldn't.* But I did. I really fucking did.

All my life I'd been the strong one.

I was supposed to be the one doing the manhandling, not the other way around.

So why did this feel so good?

Why did it feel like for the first time in my life I wasn't *pretending* during sex?

I spared one last second to think about how bad of an idea this was—but ultimately—my dick decided for me. I may not have known what my limits were before we'd gotten into the truck, but now that we were here, I was finding I was a lot more flexible than I'd ever known. In more ways than one.

Because the truth was, while I'd never thought I'd have sex with a man, that wasn't the shocking part of all of this. It was what he was that made all the difference. A wolf.

Lydia would've made me shoot him on sight.

And that, somehow, only made me more sure that I was making the right choice.

"Please let me taste you," Handsome murmured for a second time. I wasn't sure if he was asking my permission or not, so I figured I'd just give it to him anyway.

"*Yes.*"

He licked his lips, our cocks aligned, the hard length of him rub, rub, rubbing against mine. His was larger than mine, even through denim, a frankly monstrous dick rutting against my own. I tracked the movement of his tongue before my gaze snapped to the heave of his pecs as he took a shuddering breath, squeezed his eyes shut, and *groaned.* Almost like he was holding back. Like he had to center himself. Like there was something about the way I was looking at him that was really fucking doing it for him.

Or…like he'd just come.

My eyes widened.

Wait.

Fuck.

No fucking way.

"Did you just come?" I asked, aiming for incredulousness but landing somewhere around amazed. "Just because I said you could suck my dick?"

"It is a nice dick," Handsome released my hip, pressed the length of his massive hand against my still-clothed dick, and *squeezed.*

"Hnnnn," my cock spurted a little, precum slicking the inside of my boxers. Hot and sticky, and unfamiliar. I'd never felt this way before. Not with any of my hookups. Ever. My lashes fluttered and I watched through hazy lust-filled goggles as Handsome undid the button on my jeans, then my zipper, and pulled my pants down my legs.

Still clothed in boxers, I felt like an idiot with my jeans dangling around my ankle for all of two seconds before I was distracted by him again. God, his shoulders were big, and round. This was a big vehicle, and yet, it totally shocked me he could fit inside it. That we both could.

He ducked down, soft brunette hair tickling my hips as he buried his face in my crotch and sniffed. I had no idea how he squashed his body to fit, but I was too hard to care.

"Fuuuuck," I gripped onto his head, terrified by how fucking turned on I was. "Are you *smelling* me?" I was probably sweaty. Which was gross. *Did he think I was gross?* Did he think—

"You smell *delicious*," Handsome growled, rubbing his lips and nose up and down my length, before diving down to suck through cotton at the secret space behind my balls. I wanted to tell him to back off, that back there was strictly off limits. "You *are* delicious. Do not worry."

But it felt good.

Way fucking good.

Maybe too good.

No girl I'd been with had ever told me I was *delicious* before. No girl had ever left bruises on my hips. None of my girlfriends had ever slurped wet kisses up my thighs and scratched me up with stubble. Handsome bit greedily at the sensitive squishy skin on my inner thighs, and I hissed out a breath, pulling hard on his hair to remind him where his mouth should be.

Which was on my dick.

My very needy, very *hard* dick.

The red tip had poked out of the slit in my boxers, and I nearly came when I saw Handsome open his eyes and spot it for the first time. He growled, low enough it rumbled my entire body and made my hair stand on end again.

He sounded *ravenous*.

"You are better than a daydream," he told me, breathlessly before leaning over and taking my tip into his wet-hot-wet-hot oh, oh, *oh*. He did something with his hands, but I was too distracted to tell what it was. Only that my skin felt colder, and his mouth felt hotter, and—

"Oh," I shuddered, beginning to whine again as he flattened his tongue and slurped. It was unpracticed. I'd certainly had more expert head in the past. But no one had sucked me like they'd die without my cock down their throat before. No one had dug their tongue into my crown to taste every drop of precum that slipped out.

No one had buried their nose in my balls and pulled, and sucked, and *sampled* the sweat sticky skin like I was a fucking delicacy.

I felt decadent.

Desirable.

Wanted.

Needed.

Loved.

Like a daydream.

"Wider, my prince," Handsome crooned. He shoved my thighs open before I could, pinning my leg against the back seat with one hand. *My prince? Huh.* That was new. I wiggled a little, just to see how hard it would be to break out of his hold—and was quickly rewarded with a quiet warning growl and the answer that—yes, in fact, it would be quite impossible to get out of his grip.

He was too fucking strong.

Way stronger than me.

Faster.

Better.

That should've scared me.

But it didn't.

Wait…when had he taken my underwear off? I blinked down at my naked cock with confusion. A fresh drop of precum slipped down my shaft as I watched, the vein throbbing, my balls drawing tight, and releasing—over and over as Handsome stared, enraptured.

He looked like he wanted to *eat* me.

And then he did.

His mouth was liquid heaven as he slurped me down again, hot and messy, his drool slipping down my shaft, my balls, and tickling my taint till it slicked my hole. He was enthusiastic and unabashed, and I had to bite my arm hard to keep my whining quiet enough we wouldn't get caught.

"Did you know you have spots here?" Handsome asked, pulling off my dick with a wet popping sound that had my eyes nearly crossing. My hips jolted toward his lips and he chuckled, like he thought my desperation was cute. The hand he had on my thigh squeezed. Tight.

"S-spots?"

"Mmmm," Handsome leaned down, rubbing his nose up and down the sides of my dick till I stared down at him through hazy eyes to figure out what the fuck he was talking about.

"I don't have—oh." I blinked as he fluttered a kiss against the freckles decorating my shaft. "I guess I do."

"Where else do you have them?"

"Where else do I—" Then my eyes really did roll back. Because he was slurping around my balls again, and one of his fingers was rub, rub, *rubbing* at my asshole. I opened my mouth to tell him to knock it off, but all that came out was a pathetic little mewl as my hips pressed against his fingers invitingly, and he leaned down to spit—almost lovingly on my hole.

"I have always wanted to do this," Handsome said, his voice almost giddy. I was too shocked and turned on by the spit in my ass crack to properly reply. Why did that feel good? Why did that feel so fucking—

"Ahhh," he rubbed some more, my ass fluttering and sucking at his finger tip as he slurped my cock back into his throat—like it was nothing, Jesus—growing more practiced by the minute. It didn't take long for me to want more. "Fuck yes."

I mean really, who could blame me?

It wasn't often I felt good. And this was…this was light-years better than good. This was like if amazing and awesome fucked. A new feeling entirely.

"You are so soft here," Handsome murmured when he popped off my dick again. I wasn't sure how I felt about the fact he was staring at my asshole, or commenting on it. So I just closed my eyes and enjoyed the way he tugged at my rim. This was nice. *It was nice.* "Such pretty, copper hair."

This was *definitely* nice.

And it wasn't so scary—I mean, he wasn't going in or anything—

I spoke too soon. I spoke too soon. Jesus Lord Almighty.

"Ugh," I hissed out, clenching hard around his finger to try to force it out.

"Relax," Handsome murmured. "I have not done this before, but I am sure it will go better if you relax."

"Wait, you haven't—oh shit. Fuck." Deeper he pressed, and I thrashed a little, only to discover that was futile because Gigantor still had me pinned. "Fuck. Shit. I-I-I can't. I've never—you're too big."

More, more, more.

"Breathe, sweet one," Handsome murmured, kissing the tip of my cock to distract me. "Let me in. I know you want this. I can smell it all over you."

I hated that he was right, because he was. I *did* want this. Weird-but-hot comment about my smell, aside.

I needed this man inside me so fucking bad I could hardly breathe, I just–fuck. I had never known that was something I'd want.

"I'm not sure I—" my words were cut off the second he popped deep enough inside me I could finally, properly squeeze around him. It was a weird feeling. Strange. I'd never had anything up there before, and I wasn't sure I liked it. At least…not at first. The longer his finger wiggled though, the more I grew accustomed to it. "Oh fuck yes."

Admittedly…being full *was* kinda awesome.

Comforting, almost.

Was this why girls liked it?

Because for those few seconds you knew you held someone's entire attention. That they were focused on you. That they *wanted* you, *needed* you. It sounds bad but…I'd never liked putting in the work that was necessary for sex. The chase. The seduction. The fuck. Everything fell to me, the responsibility of both our pleasure, my responsibility.

But right now…

Now it wasn't.

I could just lie back.

I could lie back and I could take what Gigantor wanted to give me.

All I had to do was breathe.

"*Breathe*," he repeated. This time, I listened. Immediately, there was an improvement. Instead of *too full* the width of his finger was…*not enough*. I shuddered, squeezing around him to test the new sensation before relaxing once again as his knuckles brushed against my ass. Handsome grinned up at me from between my legs. "You like it," he blurted, excited.

"I…" *Did I like it?*

Yes.

Yes I did.

"I like it," I squeezed around him a second time and he groaned.

His eyes flooded black with lust, his chest heaving, as he nosed behind my balls and inhaled greedily. "When you are being fucked your scent grows stronger," he murmured, rubbing those soft-soft lips all over my perineum. "Your eyes beg me."

That was such bullshit, but it was hot bullshit, so I didn't call him out for it.

He pulled his finger halfway out and I hissed, having just gotten used to it. When he pushed back in he crooked his knuckle experimentally and—

"Oh fuck, shit, god, damn, fuck, yes." My eyes rolled back, my cock jerked, and my ass ground down hard on his fingers. Stars burst behind my eyelids as pleasure exploded through my body unlike anything I'd ever known.

"So pretty," Handsome groaned, pulling his finger out only to shove back in and rub that spot inside me for a second time. "So pretty when you take what your alpha gives you."

"Jesus fucking Christ on a cracker, my god." I ground my ass against his fingers, looking for more, which he happily gave me. In and out, wiggling curiously. He spat on my hole several more times to keep it slick, but I liked the burn of it. I liked it so goddamn much. Maybe that made me fucked in the head. That the pain was half the pleasure, but I didn't care.

I'd have to invest in some lube if I—

No.

No.

What the hell was I thinking?

This was a one off. A one time thing. That was it—that was—oh. "Please, please," I found myself chanting, spreading wide and writhing like a total slut. This was the exact kinda shit I used to get my girlfriends to do—and yet, here I was, on the receiving end. "Need it—I…" Handsome growled, low and throaty, pleased with himself as he shoved his finger back in at the same time he sucked my cock deep down his throat.

I came the second he glanced against that special spot inside me again. Stars swam in my head, my body a floaty, buzzing mess of endorphins as I gasped and shuddered my way through orgasm. When I glanced down, Handsome was hard again, straining against his jeans. His eyes were bright, excited, like I'd just given him a fucking gift.

When he stuck his tongue out and I caught sight of my load, I nearly came again.

"Turn over," he commanded, voice sounding funny with his mouth full. And then, just like before, he manhandled me onto my belly before I could comply.

My ass felt twitchy and empty now that he wasn't in it. I wasn't sure what to do with *that*. Wasn't sure what to do with the way I whined and swore when I felt him spit my own cum onto the small of my back, then rub it down my crease and all over my still twitchy asshole.

"Why did you—" There was a weird rustling noise and when I glanced over my shoulder, Handsome had his hand down his pants. He made this *wounded* sort of sound, animalistic and mean, his teeth bared as he jerked himself off almost violently.

The rosy head of his dick peeked out of the top of his pants—uncut, his foreskin pushed back. The slick *shh, shh* of his fist moving was almost as filthy as the cum I could feel clinging to my hole. When he was close, he aimed at me, eyes practically glowing as he spilled his load all over my messy ass and thighs.

Hand still on his cock, ringing the last few drops from his tip, my stranger grinned.

It was brighter than sunshine, and warmer than the summer.

I wanted to keep it forever.

And that—yeah.

That was the gayest thought I'd ever had.

Ass messy and sticky with cum, I struggled on wobbly legs. It was tricky, but I managed to flip over, hurriedly tugging my pants back up, mess be damned. Handsome had been polite. He hadn't asked for more than I wanted to give, but still, my mind was reeling.

Exhausted, hyped up on adrenaline, and sated for what felt like the first time in years, I stared at Handsome for what felt like a lifetime, trying to figure him the hell out. He licked his lips, staring back at me like I was still naked. I had to glance down to make sure I wasn't.

"You smell like us," he said, looking proud of himself. "Like you should."

"Okay…that's…" Yeah. And that was officially enough of that. "Thanks for, you know…saving me." I told him again, insides shivering, my hole twitchy. I swear I could feel his cum inside it. Though I knew that wasn't physically possible. My stranger sat down, his cock still peeping out, legs spread as he settled in the seat beside mine.

"You will be safe while I'm around," Handsome promised. Which again—I didn't know what to do with. Felt random as hell, and not at all sex-related. "Trouble will not bother you."

"Yeah, okay, buddy." I leaned over the empty seat and patted his chest, but he caught me by the wrist and yanked me across the seat and into his lap. Nuzzling behind my ear, lips greedy and slick, one of his big hands began kneading one of my ass cheeks.

And then he began his sniff-kissing game again.

I should've pushed him off.

But I didn't.

Because if Bride-to-be patting me earlier had felt good, this was like fucking nirvana. By the time he was done, I was a dazed, sated mess. Fuzzy and soft on the inside as he murmured against my skin, lapped away the salt, and helped me out of the car and around to the front seat.

My truck smells like sex.

"You will be safe," he promised again in parting, beaming at me as he reached over to buckle my seatbelt in a clear dismissal.

I wished I could believe him.

I *wanted* to believe him.

I really did.

I was sure I'd have a proper freak-out in the morning about all of this, but for now I was content to ride my high all the way through the spindly, winding roads home. Eyes burned on the back of my neck the entire drive, even after I watched Handsome's silhouette disappear in my rearview mirror.

Maybe my head didn't believe him, but my heart kinda did. Because when I pulled into my shitty apartment complex, ninja-d myself up the stairs, and fell into bed—cum covered and hazy—I couldn't help but feel safer than I had since I was a snot-nosed, naive kid.

No one had ever saved me before.

No one.

And for one night, I let myself relive what that had felt like.

Chapter Three

Jeffrey

YOU KNOW THAT saying, "There ain't no rest for the wicked"? Well, that turned out to be true for me. Because not twenty minutes after I'd passed the fuck out I received a surprise visitor at my front door.

I don't know why I was surprised that my night could get weirder than it already was.

The building I lived in was shitty. Not like, *the shittiest.* But shitty. It was a few blocks from Spruce, the street that housed all the refurbished—but ancient—buildings that had made up the original town of Elmwood. The halls were drafty. The carpet was stained. And the back of the parking lot led directly into the woods so it was always full of pine cones, leaves, and other debris.

It was the only place I could afford on my limited budget, since I made a point of ignoring the bank account my mom had set up for me when I came back to town. She hadn't asked for anything in return yet, but it was only a matter of time. Nothing in life was free. I knew that better than anyone. So the money rotted, and I was happy to let it. That had been my one and only interaction with her. A letter she'd left with one of my brothers.

She clearly cared…a lot.

Yeah the fuck right.

I'd lucked out with one of the nicest units in the building, but still, the water heater was always on the fritz—either blisteringly hot or ice cold. My oven smelled like gasoline sometimes. There were stains in the carpet. The walls were yellow. The AC unit only worked twenty-five percent of the time. And every doorway was covered in at least fifty layers of flaky white paint.

And I loved it—every last flaw.

Pine cones and all.

Because it was *mine.*

That didn't mean it was perfect though, or the safest place. It was drafty and the walls were thin—and as I startled awake, I couldn't shake the feeling that something was here.

Something was here.

Waiting for me.

Just outside the front door.

As my thoughts filled with memories from the club, I very quietly, sleepily padded toward the front door to soothe my anxiety. Realistically, this was Elmwood. There was bound to be people out and about at this time—it was a fucking given when more than half the population was nocturnal. But still.

There was no way I'd be able to go back to sleep unless I listened to my gut.

The slight twinge in my ass made me grin as I strode down the hallway, happy memories assaulting my senses for once, rather than the bad ones that usually kept me up at night.

Just thinking about my stranger made my blood sing and my pulse thrum.

I should probably be freaking out more about this.

But I wasn't.

Because for the first time since I'd moved here, I felt like I'd actually be able to get a decent night's rest.

That was, until I looked through the peephole on my door and realized something really was waiting out there.

There was a dog lying right on my stoop. His ass was plopped down on the welcome mat Blair had bought me as a housewarming gift. His head was on his paws, and his eyes were closed, like he was resting. Like he was…guarding my door.

He was…*beautiful.* Massive and shaggy, his fur a warm deep brown. I gasped—and that ended up being a mistake, because he woke up immediately. Jerking to his feet, the large creature moved like he was about to make a run for it. I fumbled with the bolt locks, scrambling in a panic.

Before he could leave, I managed to yank the front door open, heart in my throat.

He looked familiar.

He looked so fucking familiar.

"Wait!" My voice was panicked, my mind reeling.

Surprisingly…the dog listened. Halfway down the open hallway, he hesitated, wavering between running away now that he'd been caught and coming back. "*Please*," I managed. Once again, shocking me, the dog turned back, padding in close and sitting on my welcome mat with a nervous wag of his tail.

He had these adorable big blue eyes, framed by ridiculously long eyelashes that fluttered with each pitiful blink. The poor thing was soaked to the bone, his massive body squashed down into a small little ball like he was worried he might scare me.

Which was fair.

Because even sitting, his head easily came to my stomach. Maybe even my ribs. Oh, and he looked like a giant fucking wolf. Pointy ears. Long snout. Long fluffy tail.

It hit me all at once why he looked so fucking familiar.

Familiar because I'd met this very fucking dog before. At a gas station… somewhere in Colorado probably? Holy shit. *Had he followed me all the way here?*

"Oh shit," I stared at him, honestly flabbergasted. If I'd been less exhausted I probably would've seen the similarities sooner, but I was operating on less than one brain cell, and as it was, I was just fucking shocked to see a dog at all, especially one I'd met before. "Hi!"

And then he was diving forward, shoving his face into my crotch with a needy, deliberate sniff.

"Fuck." I shoved his head away, laughing a little as I shook my head. Fucking dogs. For real, man. "You came a long way, buddy," I murmured, in awe, squatting down so that we were at eye level and no longer crotch level. "Fuck. That's…fuck. How the hell did you manage that?"

Why would you follow me, of all people?

He whined, and I sighed, curling my hands into fists, unsure if touching him would be welcomed. His head butted against my hands, however, so that question was quickly answered. I scratched along his back, rubbing the downy soft fur behind his ears as he stared up at me beseechingly.

Fuck.

Should I take him in?

I should take him in, right?

I could go to the vet tomorrow. Get him checked out. See if he had a microchip or try to see if anyone was looking for him. But for now it was…what? Three in the morning? And I was dead on my feet.

"Okay, sweetheart," I murmured, petting him as he practically purred, his big heavy head butting into me again—thankfully not my crotch this time—as his tail *thump, thumped* against the ground. "Okay. You're gonna come in, alright?" He woofed happily, and I laughed, finding it more than a little adorable that he'd responded. "We'll get you sorted, I promise."

There was no way he knew what I was talking about, so clearly the dog was just a vocal guy.

"Let's get you all cleaned up," I urged, rising and stepping back into the house.

He followed after me dutifully. I shut the door behind us, twisting the lock—and then the five bolt locks I'd installed when I moved in. When they were all in place, I could finally breathe again. With a wobbly smile, I stared down at the furry beast, heart fluttering.

It was late, and I was exhausted.

I should've felt awful.

But I didn't.

I'd wanted companionship and I was about to get more than I'd bargained for.

There were muddy footprints down my hallway. The air smelled like damp fur. And the dog splashed like hell when I got him in the bath. I snorted out a laugh, blocking my face as his big, fluffy body sloshed water over the sides of the tub.

"Dude!" I snorted, falling on my ass when his heavy, soggy tail whacked me right in the ass. He leveled me with a look. A look that said he was over my shit. I didn't blame him. I bet with all that fur baths were not fun. "You were soaked—and covered in mud. You needed a bath. Don't look at me like that."

The dog woofed, unamused.

"Fuck," I giggled, unable to help myself. I couldn't remember the last time I laughed like this, carefree. Soaked myself, I rose, grabbing the hem of my shirt and tugging it up and over over my head. In my peripheral vision I could see my torso in the bathroom mirror, covered in the scars I avoided, and freckles that barely outnumbered them.

Don't think about it.

Before I could get sucked into my head, the dog's cold, wet nose pushed into my abdomen. He snuffled, and I laughed, nearly slipping and falling on my ass again when he stared up at me, giant head right by my bare belly. His blue eyes practically glowed.

His eyes seemed to say, "What are these?" while nudging at my scars.

"It's nothing," I hummed, surprised by how easily he'd been able to pull me out of a flashback. Then I shook my head, focusing on him and not my own spiraling thoughts. He looked like a soaked rat. A giant soaked rat. Even worse than before. "Towel," I reminded myself, reaching for one of the two towels I'd bought when I moved in.

Only the towel barely covered part of him and he was still fucking wet.

So I grabbed the other one too—figuring I could dry myself off in the air. Or with an old t-shirt or something. As I ran the fabric over his fur, the dog glared at me, though his tail wagged—so I knew he wasn't all that annoyed. When I started drying his belly I was able to confirm that he was, in fact, a boy dog.

"Put that thing away," I laughed, grimacing when his cock began to unsheath, his blue eyes boring a hole into mine. "Fuck. Definitely a guy. Congrats, I guess. That's one…yep. Uh huh. Okay. That's one angry-looking *thing*."

I avoided his dick, because I could only handle a certain amount of weird and that was definitely past my limit. "You'll thank me later when I let you into my bed," I informed him as I scrubbed over the wet fur on his head. His ears went back, big eyes blinking up at me. "Clean dogs get more privileges."

He stopped grumbling, and for a second it was almost like he really did understand me. Maybe I was being paranoid, but part of me felt there was something…human about him. But I figured I was imagining things. Especially after I'd spent an hour having sex with a werewolf.

Supernatural shit was always on the brain. You'd have to be *insane* to pretend to be a dog, and while this regal beast bore a lot of similarity to the man I'd let have my ass virginity, even I knew I had a tendency to catastrophize.

"Tomorrow we're going to the vet," I informed him after I'd broken out my blow drier and gotten him from sodden to damp to dry.

The dog gave me the stink-eye again, and I laughed for the second time that night. I scratched behind his ear and smiled. "You're a good mutt, aren't you?" He wagged his tail in response.

After texting Avery that I couldn't come in after all, I invited my new pet into bed, and with his large furry bulk crowded behind—and on top of me—I was finally able to rest. No nightmares awaited me. I felt safe.

The vet in Elmwood was a witch, like Avery, my boss. She was soft spoken and wore glasses that made her eyes look three sizes smaller than they were, and she smelled like pineapple.

Because I was worried he'd have a bad reaction to the other sights and smells, I'd left my dog in the running car while I got all his information down. Not that there was much I actually knew. I wasn't sure what breed of dog he was, and there was no "wolf" option, so I'd just written "big" there instead.

"If he's not chipped I can run some more tests if you want me to? Blood tests, stuff like that," she offered. I'd gotten lucky as she was out front when I arrived, so the process had been easier. Surreptitiously, I glanced through the large front window, checking that the truck was secure. When I could see the dog's silhouette in the front passenger seat, I relaxed.

"Do you think we need to?" I didn't like the idea of poking him.

"It's a good idea, yeah," she agreed, writing something down on her notepad with a soft smile. "I recommend it for all strays that come in."

"Okay." I didn't know shit about owning a pet—Lydia had abhorred animals—so I decided to just defer to her.

"Go grab him, sweetheart. I got you taken care of," she hummed softly, grabbing the clipboard I'd filled out and reading through it while her receptionist clacked away at the computer.

He's going to hate you if you do this, I fretted as I headed outside and crossed over to the passenger side of my truck.

You're just being a responsible pet owner.

But needles, Jeffrey.

Needles.

"Okay, buddy," I hummed, smiling and projecting calm-calm-calm as the dog's giant head pressed to the glass, watching me. In the light of day he looked even more like the wolf I'd hooked up with the night before. It was kinda hard to ignore the similarities. "We're just gonna pop in for a minute, okay? It'll be fine." I wasn't sure who I was trying to convince, him or me. Either way, I pulled the handle to the door open, leash in hand.

I'd bought him a collar right before this—and a few essentials in case I got to keep him. A dog bed. Some matching sweaters for us. Food. Like fifty toys.

I had a hard time thinking a dog this well-behaved and beautiful didn't already have a family though, so I wasn't getting my hopes up. But…he had followed me here, hadn't he? And that meant something.

It had to.

Maybe it was fate.

I was fully prepared to clip the dog to the lead, and carefully lead him inside—

Only.

That didn't happen.

Because the second the door opened, the beast barreled through it. My jaw fell open as I reached for him immediately, fingers barely skimming his soft fur. He'd been so calm and slow last night and this morning, always careful not to be rough with me. But now, all that flew out the window as his shoulder clipped my side and I stumbled a little, shocked, as he bolted away from me.

"Hey!" I jolted, already moving to chase—but he was too fast.

Too fucking fast.

His brown furry body disappeared around the corner and a little part of me died the second he was out of sight, because I got the feeling this was the end.

I still chased him, because of course I did.

I spent an hour searching the area for signs of the dog that should've been mine. Because—*fuck me*—he was nowhere to be found. Eventually, I somewhat convinced myself I was better off this way. Swallowing past the lump in my throat, I returned to my truck and let his leash drop to the front seat.

"Right," I said simply, hands shaking. "Of course he left the second he could." A sick, devastating weight crushed my heart as I leaned my forehead against the shell of my truck and tried to breathe.

"Why would he stay?" My heart hurt.

It hurt, it hurt, it hurt.

"You didn't want a dog anyway," I reminded myself—but even I knew it was a lie. Somewhere between the bath and our night together—and our trip to the pet store this morning, I'd grown attached.

We were supposed to wear matching sweaters in the fall, dammit.

"He doesn't need you," I murmured to myself.

You're just a pretty face, darling.

Who would take you seriously?

I didn't want to look at my truck and its seats full of dog stuff, so I went to the one place in town that didn't feel claustrophobic. It was a short walk, and the heat was welcome as I stepped around the cracks on the sidewalk, my head spinning.

Shaking and sick, the moment I arrived, I called Blair.

I just…I guess I just needed to hear his voice.

He picked up on the second ring and my heart was in my throat as I spoke. "Blair?" I tucked the phone between my shoulder and ear as I fiddled with the joint I'd stashed in my pocket this morning. "How you doin', bud?"

"Jeffrey!" Blair's voice was only somewhat muffled, but then the sound cleared, like he'd stepped outside. "I'm good. What's up?"

Play it cool.

Don't let him know how fucked up you are.

"You wanna smoke?" My heart thumped unsteadily. "I still have one of the joints you gave me."

Please say yes. I don't want to be alone.

"Oh hell yes. Where are you at?"

"Our spot."

Elmwood's graveyard had quickly become our favorite hang out spot. It was peaceful here in a way most places weren't. The quiet helped. And aside from the occasional caw of a crow, or *chirp, chirp* of a chickadee, the only thing that could be heard here was the whisper of the wind. Trees blocked the entrances, overgrown and unkempt, dripping needles to the ground and offering privacy.

The tombs felt like friends.

Sometimes I felt like I had more in common with the corpses than I did the living.

Blair and I had been here a grand total of two times since I'd moved back, which may not have seemed like a lot, but it was.

"I'll be there in…" I heard more rustling, like Blair was checking the time. "Five minutes."

"Cool."

Ten minutes later—because Blair sucked at being on time—my wayward adoptive brother finally showed up.

"Surprise, motherfucker!" Tiny but solid arms wrapped around me from behind, pushing me out of my morose thoughts as the scent of apples filled my nose along with…I sniffed. *Cheese?* He nearly knocked me off of the tombstone I was sitting on, and I laughed, sliding to the ground with a thump, before twisting to greet him properly.

"Blair." I gave him a tight squeeze at the back of his neck like I always did, before pulling back to beam at him. Already, I felt better. Things had been awkward between us, but so far this had been the best interaction we'd had since I'd joined him all the way across the country.

Blair took a step back, grinning wide and bright, the way he never used to before. He was dressed like he always was, head-to-toe black, though today he sported a floor-length vintage vampire cloak and the giant platform combat boots Richard, his boyfriend—my blood brother—had bought him.

He was more muscular now, though still bite-sized. He looked like an adult. Not the punk-ass kid I'd spent half my life protecting. He didn't need that from me anymore. Though apparently he still wanted me around, despite that fact.

Blair looked good.

Full of life.

Way different than he had when we lived together in Oregon. Elmwood had done him a lot of good, even though he hadn't had the scar across his nose and temple before coming here. It sucked honestly, that no matter how hard I tried I hadn't been able to protect him from Lydia.

Each of his scars was a failure on my part, so looking at them hurt probably more than it should've. I could remember how he got each one. The days she'd grabbed him by the face, her nails biting in—and I'd bandaged him up and prayed they wouldn't scar.

"I brought pizza," Blair shoved the box at me with a grin. "It's a new flavor. I'm calling it…claw-sauge and pepper-moon-ie." He blinked. "Damn. Didn't realize how much that sucked till I said it out loud."

"Vegan?" I asked curiously, climbing back onto my favorite headstone. Blair struggled up beside me, watching closely as I pulled the box open.

"Nah," Blair kicked his feet against the stone we sat on in excitement, practically bursting at the seams. "I already finalized the vegan portion of the menu. Which is why I need you—"

"And me!" a familiar voice popped up from behind us. I jerked in surprise, twisting to see that Collin, my youngest brother, had apparently come with him. Immediately, my calm melted, nerves fluttering around in my belly.

"And Collin," Blair rolled his eyes fondly, nudging me till I finished pulling the box open. "To taste test."

There was a nervous flip in my belly as I tossed Collin a smile over my shoulder and reached for the first slice. It was hot to the touch still. Not surprising, since Blair had bought the building across the street from Avery's magic shop and was turning it into a restaurant. It was only a few blocks from here, which meant the pizza was probably fresh out of the oven.

He'd hired a whole bunch of staff members already—thankfully—since no one we knew had any idea how to run a business. Blair took great pleasure from the planning side of things and the aesthetic of it all, even if he wasn't the one that actually rolled out the dough—or whatever pizza places did. Or the one who knew how to fill out paperwork.

They weren't open yet, because Blair was one goth motherfucker, and was quite stubbornly waiting till Halloween.

It was amazing how quickly something could come together when you had money, and Blair…well. He had a shit ton of money. At least—*now* he did. It was weird that the kid I'd grown up pilfering pennies from my allowance for, could now afford to buy my entire apartment complex on a whim, if he so chose.

Lydia had stolen a lot from him, just like she'd stolen from me. But at least she hadn't been able to take his fortune—despite doing her damndest to steal just that.

How the tables had turned.

Collin reached past my hand and snagged a slice of his own, groaning happily as he stood sentinel behind Blair's shoulder, watching me.

I liked Collin.

He was supposed to be my kid brother, after all. Supposed to be— because, even though he was, he felt more like a stranger than the rest of the siblings I'd left behind. He'd been born after I was taken, after all, and at fifteen years old with his gangly boy-feet and pointy knees, he might as well have been an alien for all I knew how to talk to him.

He was my only brother that was still human. Since the other three had transitioned to vampires while I was living with Lydia.

But I got the feeling Collin saw through me better than everyone else did, and that made me wary. Something about being the youngest made him have this *super* sharp bullshit radar. He could smell my lies from a mile away—and he always looked at me like he knew I was hiding something.

I didn't know what to do with him.

Especially because looking at him was just…weird.

Because he looked just like me.

Well…

Just like I'd looked at fifteen. Minus all the scars I hid under long sleeves, and the weight on my shoulders. But unlike me at that age, Collin's smiles weren't fake. They were *genuine*. He wasn't faux sunshine, he was an actual summer day. He was *everything* I tried so hard to be, only he wasn't pretending.

How the hell are we gonna smoke a joint with him here? I tried to convey to Blair, but he was too distracted by pizza to read my eyeballs.

I swallowed the lump in my throat and took a bite of the pizza to appease the both of them.

Salty, cheesy deliciousness burst across my tongue.

"Shit, fuck." I groaned, shoving more inside my mouth. My tastebuds danced and I sighed, eyes pinching shut. "Shit, that's *good*."

"See?!" Collin nudged Blair. "I told you hiring me would pay off."

"Yeah, yeah," Blair nudged him back, his green eyes bright with mischief. "Collin's helping with the non-vegan items."

"And the names," Collin added. "Because you're horrible at them. The pepperoni is imported," he added in a British accent, looking self-important.

"I want them all to be puns," Blair glared at him. "Sue me."

"No one argued with that," Collin shrugged. "I'm just saying. Zom-beef is way better than Peppermoonie."

"Yeah okay, but that doesn't even make sense. We're not even talking about a beef option."

Collin gave him the stink-eye. "I don't see why not."

"Because it's weird?"

"Weirder than catering pizza to supernatural creatures?"

"You're a little shithead." Blair turned to me, ignoring Collin completely. Clearly this was a sore subject for the both of them. "So…yeah?" Blair waited for my approval, his painted fingernails tapping nervously on his knees.

He'd taken to painting them different colors since he'd moved here. Always goth. But sometimes green. Purple. Red. Like he was experimenting with them as much as he was with the other aspects of his life.

I blamed Richard and the fact that Blair had never had actual freedom or a home to go back to before. Richard supported him and his colorful nails far better than I'd ever thought he was capable. Though to be fair, the only Richard I'd known had been nine-years-old, scared of tetanus—and definitely not the vampire he was today.

But he made Blair happy.

Elmwood made Blair happy.

And happy was a good look on him, even if I didn't recognize him sometimes. Even if it hurt to know that he was moving on, and I was still stuck.

Always stuck.

The pizza turned to lead in my stomach.

"It's good, dude," I said, because he was still always looking for my approval, even now. And this was our sweet spot. The only time I really felt like I could be who I was supposed to be. "Definitely the best pizza I've ever had." Better than the one last week, that's for sure. I don't think I ever wanted to try asparagus on a pizza ever again. That had been a failed experiment I was more than glad Blair had tossed to the trash.

Asparagus belonged uhhhh—

Somewhere.

But it definitely didn't belong on pizza.

"What are you doing tonight?" Blair asked, leaning back as he watched me eat, his shoulders flexing while he picked absently at the chipped polish on his thumb. "Rich bought us tickets to go to the movies in Ridgefield and I thought you might want to come?" He peeked up at me through his lashes, always a worrier, that one.

Worried I spent too much time alone.

I'd only been here a month and he'd tried to invite me out with him and my brothers at least three times a week. I was running out of excuses, and we both knew it.

"And watch you guys make out? No thank you." I frowned. "Didn't you go out last night?"

Blair laughed, his cheeks pink. "I'll keep the PDA to a minimum. And yeah, we did."

Good for him.

"My dog'll get lonely if I'm gone too long," I lied. And then was struck with loss so visceral I nearly threw up. Because I didn't have a dog anymore. He'd run off. He hadn't wanted me. Hadn't needed me, the way I needed him.

"You have a dog?" Blair cocked his head, eyes wide. "Really?"

"Um. Yeah." Lies, lies, lies. "Except, he kinda ran away."

"Oh, shit."

"I'm gonna…yeah. I'm gonna look for him later," I pretended like I hadn't spent an hour hunting for him already. Like the dog hadn't fucked off as fast as he possibly could the second he had a chance to get away from me. My stomach churned.

"You want help?"

For a second I considered it, but then I remembered Blair had just told me he had plans. And my gut told me hunting for the dog would be fruitless. He'd followed me all the way from Colorado. If he'd wanted to find me, he would've by now.

"Nah, you enjoy your movie."

"You sure?"

"I'm sure."

Blair nodded seriously like I wasn't totally blowing him off. Like he didn't even *get* that I was blowing him off. "I'm a phone call away if you change your mind about needing help."

"Yeah," I grimaced, flicking my gaze to Collin who was staring at me with those *all-seeing* eyes. Like he saw right through my bullshit. He arched an eyebrow, and I cringed. "I know." I projected confidence, smiling at Blair, then Collin, trying not to get caught when thoughts of my missing dog made me want to punch the nearest surface till my skin looked like ground beef.

I'm just your strong, solid older brother.

Not a train wreck.

I didn't call you here because I was two seconds from beating a brick wall with my fists.

I didn't call you here because I wanted to cry.

I don't cry.

I can't.

Not anymore.

"You're coming to the beach though, right?" Blair confirmed, eyes narrowed at me. He waggled his brows a moment later, a wicked grin lighting up his face. It was a weird expression on him. Not because it looked bad or anything, but because he'd never really made faces like that before.

Like a fucking stranger had inhabited my little brother's body.

"Right," I agreed, because there were only so many times I could say no before he started noticing something was actually up.

"Sunday," Blair reminded me, and I nodded, knowing full well I wouldn't be fucking going.

"You can ride with us," Collin added. I snagged another slice of pizza and shoved it into my mouth, smiling around the mouthful so I wouldn't have to respond.

"Thanks," my voice was muffled as I continued to project confidence.

"Collin," Blair pointed at him. "Go away."

I blinked, surprised, twisting to look at the both of them again, brow furrowed in confusion.

"He was only supposed to say hi," Blair frowned. "I'm not about to smoke with him around."

"I'm practically an adult," Collin huffed, arms crossed.

"*I'm practically an adult,*" Blair mirrored back in a nasally voice. "Yeah, right. Go take your pre-pubescent ass back to the pizza joint. Your shift's not over."

Collin snorted, but then smiled at the both of us, obviously not all that annoyed. Even though he did walk off muttering, "prepubescent ass," under his breath.

When he was gone, Blair snorted out a laugh, shaking his head. "I love that kid," he said simply, nudging his shoulder against mine.

Thank fucking God he didn't smile again.

"So. Joint?" He held a hand out, and I pulled it out of my pocket, handing it to him. Blair pinched the joint between his fingers, loosening up the bud so it wouldn't clog, and I snorted, amused. Because for most of our lives he wouldn't have known how the fuck to do any of this. Then he pulled out a lighter—a ridiculous fucking thing that looked like it weighed forty pounds, all ornate spooky-looking metal.

"The hell is that?" I asked, because that shit was ugly as hell.

"My new lighter."

"Lemme guess," I cocked my head, lips pursed. "Richard?"

"Yeah," Blair flushed, eyes dancing. "He bought it for me." He blinked, flabbergasted. "For no reason. Told me…it reminded him of me or some romantic shit."

"Disgusting."

"I know," Blair countered, laughing, though his cheeks were pink so I knew he was a lying liar who lied.

"So fucking weird you're dating my brother," I managed, watching as he lit up and took a long, happy drag.

"So fucking weird you *have* a brother, or brothers," he countered, blowing smoke in my face. "Other than me, I mean." I set my pizza slice down and took the joint, sucking a drag myself. Bitter smoke filled my lungs, and I held it, lashes fluttering, then released, the tension bleeding from my body.

"Yeah," I said softly, handing it back with a sigh.

That was fair. I'd never told him about my family. Never told him shit, if I was being honest. Lydia hadn't wanted me to and I'd been so fucking scared of her I hadn't dared. By the time we'd gotten old enough for me to feel slightly less terrified, it was too late.

"What other secrets have you been keeping from me?" Blair asked, and even though I could tell he was joking, it still made me tense up. Because my secret family wasn't the worst secret I still kept. *Maybe he had a right to know?* But I wasn't…ready to talk about it.

So I just shrugged and he nodded, accepting my silence as the answer it was.

"How's therapy going?" Blair asked, keeping his tone light, even though I could feel the weight behind it.

Because of fucking course he asked about therapy.

"It's…going." I'd been going pretty much since I'd moved here. But the first two appointments hadn't really done much? Other than make me rehash shit I didn't want to talk about. "She asks way too many questions."

"That's her job," Blair snorted, taking another drag before passing the joint back.

I stared at it, the cherry red tip, brought it up and sucked in. Already a sense of calm was settling over my body as the high hit and my lungs opened up wide. When the end burned unevenly, I licked my finger and gently tapped it so it would even it out.

"I know," I exhaled, low and slow.

"Is it helping?" Blair asked, still trying to pretend like he wasn't worried about me. *Blair used the sad pikachu face, it was mildly effective!*

"I dunno," I answered honestly, hunched over. I hadn't invited him out to get grilled, and I was kinda regretting this choice—but that wasn't new. I regretted a lot of things nowadays. "You need help at the pizza joint?"

"Don't change the subject," Blair laughed. "And yeah, man. That would be nice. I got a shipment coming in later that's gonna be a total bitch to move. Rich'll probably be busy with council shit—some treaty, negotiation, I dunno, whatever. For a wolf pack? Thing? And Collin's starting public school so he's no help."

The idea of being useful made me perk up.

"I got your back, man."

"Thanks," Blair grinned, eyes crinkling at the corners. Then, he sobered. "Look. Just let me say one last thing—then I *promise* I won't bring any of this shit up again," Blair blurted before I could distract him successfully. I sucked in a breath, wanting to say no—to deny him this—but I was officially too high and sad to argue.

"Fine," I sighed, smiling at him because I figured he needed reassurance.

"You…" Blair sucked in a breath. He'd been going to therapy too. Same building, different therapist. It was why he'd invited me there in the first place. He said it was helping him. He wanted to help me too. And what was I supposed to say to that?

I'd told him I was fine, and he'd leveled me with a look that had silenced every last one of my protests.

I didn't interrupt, because I knew sometimes it took him a lot of courage and thinking to figure out what he wanted to say. Especially when it was dark or shitty.

I'm not ready for this.

Don't do this to me.

I can't handle it.

Don't, don't, don't.

"Never mind," Blair smiled at me—and it was as fake as my own. But I was grateful. Grateful because it meant I wouldn't have to deal with this. Wouldn't have to add something new to my already full plate.

But…Blair looked *disappointed* in himself.

That he'd chickened out at the last second.

And I couldn't stand that.

"No," I said softly, shaking my head, blowing smoke up toward the cloudy sky. "Say what you were gonna say. It's cool." *It hurts, it hurts, it hurts.*

Blair waffled, but when I flashed him another smile—this one apparently more convincing than the last—he was able to move forward.

"You know I don't blame you, right?" Blair said softly, and ice filled my veins. Immediately, revulsion burned through my body. The pizza in my stomach threatened to come up. But still, I smiled.

"Of course."

You should blame me.

It was my fault.

It was all my fault.

"I think…it's time to move on," Blair said softly, reaching out and squeezing my shoulder, his grip tight. "Don't you?"

"Yeah," I agreed.

I can't, I can't, I can't.

I deserve this.

I deserve this.

I can't.

"Okay," Blair blew out a breath, grinning at me, the tension in his shoulders slipping away. "Good." He leaned against my shoulder for a second, the warm heat of his body lending me strength as my thoughts spun out of control. "You deserve to be happy."

I don't.

I don't.

I don't.

"I know," I bumped him back and he snorted out a laugh. "Fuck."

"Corny as fuck," Blair shrugged, "but…I dunno. I thought maybe you needed to hear it."

"Thanks," I took another bite of pizza so I wouldn't throw up. Blair put the joint out, and we sat in silence for nearly twenty minutes before we'd calmed down enough to leave.

And then I went hunting again. First for my dog. And after that, for somewhere quiet to fall apart. Somewhere with a brick wall, and only one exit, so I wouldn't have to worry about watching my back.

Chapter Four

Mutt

THE DAY MY moon mother betrayed me I was sixteen. The full moon was supposed to rise the following night and my skin itched and itched and itched. Pain ached in my veins, poisonous and all encompassing, and the world felt foreign—full of shapes I didn't recognize, visions through unfamiliar eyes.

That's how I knew something was wrong.

Because the moon had never hurt me before. She was my constant companion, hanging high or low, watching over me as I pranced through puphood to adolescence. Her steady glow had lit my fondest memories—nights rolling around in the leaves with my brothers. Hours chasing and running, with the scent of wet dirt in my nose, and pine needles beneath my paws. She had lent me light when I needed it most, lit my way when

I was lost and lonely. Given me a family, a community, a home.

She was soft, cool blue edges—a second mother who looked down on me from the sky.

It had never occurred to me that she could turn her back on me.

The full moon had brought comfort before.

It meant time with my family when we were all one. Four paws, our instincts, and fur—the rest of the world forgotten as we became, for one night, what we were meant to be.

Those nights were pack-family-solace.

Safe-safe-safe.

But apparently that was over.

I'd felt no comfort then, as I'd laid in my bed and the sun began to shrink.

Because I could feel the moon before I even saw her—and I burned.

I burned.

I burned.

And as I burned and itched and itched, alone, sick, scared-scared-scared, I knew nothing would ever be the same again. Because I may be a wolf, but I was also an alpha, and like all young alphas, my timer had begun to tick. Before the sun had even sunk below the mountaintops I knew my second mother had forsaken me.

I shifted before the moon ever rose.

And it was fire.

And pain.

And black.

Black.

Black.

When I came back to myself I was in the basement of the main lodge at the compound. My mouth was dry, my paws ached, and I'd been lying on the cold concrete for so long I felt bruised. Or maybe that was the shift? Because this was my first alphashift—and I knew, before I'd heard my father enter the basement that something had gone wrong.

His eyes glinted in the dark as he stood at the top of the stairs.

When he descended, careful as ever, his scent was sorrow-loss-worry.

He loosened the manacles on my ankles and wrists, silent.

Dad was hardly ever silent.

But he wasn't my dad right then.

No.

He was my Pack Alpha.

And he knew…as well as I did, that my clock had just started ticking. And one day—in the near future—I was going to lose myself, unless I found a mate.

PRESENT DAY

"I need your pants."

"You need my—"

"I need your pants," I repeated, staring at my brother, Butters, with what I hoped was a convincing expression. To his credit, he didn't question me a second time. Didn't even blink, despite the fact I'd yanked him off the street into an alley and I was currently standing naked in front of him, smelling like distress-need-help.

"Sure," Butters shrugged, his big shoulders going up and down as he began tugging his clothes off as directed. *God, could he be any slower? I asked for your pants, not your whole wardrobe.* My hands shook, clenching into fists as my heart thumped unsteadily.

C'mon, c'mon, c'mon.

Butters shucked off his pants last, and I snatched them up, yanking them on—and then his shirt, because he had been kind enough to give me both. I hadn't been thinking properly, but he had. Humans were weird about nudity. He stared at me all the while, as his phone and the keys to our shared home rattled in his—now my—pocket.

He didn't ask for either item back, and I didn't think to give them over—my head was too tangled, thoughts of Jeffrey spinning, spinning, spinning.

He needs me.

Hurry, hurry.

"Thanks," I grunted out before I dove out of the alley and ducked down the street, back the direction I'd come from.

I wasn't sure why Butters was out and about. Probably out on a snack run, or doing…Butters-y things, like hunting squirrels (a hobby we both shared) or trying to wrestle the biggest men he came across. He preferred his wolfskin like I did, so it had been more than a little lucky that he'd been out and about wearing clothes at all.

Jeffrey needs me.

Jeffrey needs me.

Jeffrey needs me.

Too slow, too slow, too slow.

I picked up the pace, bare feet pounding the pavement as Butters clothes clung to me like a glove. We'd always been similar in size. Similar in appearance too—though he was broader faced, and blonder than I was.

It made sense, as we shared blood—but still.

So close—

Just gotta round this corner and then—

There.

There.

He was still there.

Suddenly, I could breathe again.

Jeffrey was where I'd last seen him, in an alleyway several blocks away from where I'd hunted Butters down. His broad shoulders were curled in, tight with tension, his body minutely quaking. If I was human, I probably wouldn't have been able to see it. But I wasn't human.

I saw the way he was holding himself together as tightly as he could.

Saw his cracks and splinters.

My beautiful love who reeked of anguish-lonely-scared, though his body language projected nothing but calm to the untrained eye. The coppery bright scent of blood filled my nostrils, and I scanned him quickly for injuries, standing like an idiot in the mouth of the alley, terrified.

He's hurt.

He's hurt.

He's—

There.

My eyes narrowed when I saw the state of his hands.

Knuckles bloodied, scraped raw.

A wounded sound escaped me, unbidden—and Jeffrey startled, twisting around to look at me as I stood motionless, shocked. I took another sniff of the air, certain I must've missed something, only to realize that I had not. The only person that had been in here aside from Jeffrey was me.

So why…were his hands like that?

It didn't make sense.

There had been no foe he was fighting, not like the other night when I'd broken my own rule and approached him. How could his hands be so torn up, unless—

Unless he…

Unless he—

Oh.

He'd hurt himself.

It was the only logical conclusion, but one that was illogical all the same.

Normally, I knew better than to approach a wounded animal if it could still move on its own. They could smell what I was from a mile off and though I'd always been gentle with my paws, and hands, I knew what sort of effect my bulk and overall essence had on creatures smaller than I was.

I was frightening.

I knew that.

But still—I approached, unable to help myself as Jeffrey continued to stare at me, and my heart threatened to beat right out of my chest.

I knew this was my fault.

I knew he'd been looking for me.

I just…hadn't known what to do.

He wasn't supposed to find me at all. Last night I'd been there to protect him, as promised, but when he'd opened the front door it was like every plan I'd had melted away. He'd welcomed me in, because of course he had, and like an idiot, I'd thought things would be fine.

That I'd leave the moment I could, and go back to watching over him from the shadows.

But then he'd looked for me.

Even now, he was looking for me.

And I couldn't do this to him.

Which was why I'd enlisted Butters and his pants for help, and why I was here—now, hunting him back, even though it was stupid. So fucking stupid. And he couldn't help me. Couldn't save me. Couldn't be what I needed.

But maybe I could be what he needed.

At least, today.

"Fuck off," Jeffrey's voice was rough and quaking as I slowly, carefully crossed the empty alley. When I stepped into his space, close enough our chests brushed, his nostrils flared. His mouth said "fuck off" but his eyes said, *help me.* They said, *I'm lost, lost, lost.* And his scent was relief-please-lonely-lonely-lonely.

I had never met anyone in my life who needed an alpha more than Jeffrey Prince.

The tremors in his body were more obvious up close. As was the haunted, wild look in his eyes—like there were demons flitting behind them. Beneath the riot of emotions that flooded the air, I caught his comforting musk, the salty burst of sweat, the effervescent bubbly orange of his natural scent.

I wanted to roll around in it.

To lick and rub and stick my dick inside it.

I wanted to bite and nip and lick and suck—to taste and smell, and feel every inch of his body. But I didn't do any of those things. Because it wasn't what he needed. And once was already more than I'd told myself I could have.

"It is okay," I reassured. And then I wrapped my arms around Jeffrey's body and pulled him in tight. He didn't go willingly—stiff as a board at first, his bloody hands hanging limply at his sides. "I am here."

For ten agonizing seconds I worried I'd gotten this wrong.

That he didn't feel the same relief I did when we were together.

That while I knew he was my fated mate, to him, I was a stranger—and a scary one at that. Someone who had taken him, then disappeared, only to corner him in an alleyway when he was alone.

It didn't matter that the moon had played a trick on me. That his soul should not have called to me the way it did. It didn't matter that this was not something I had planned. That I had intended to protect him from a distance, and not up close. Because at that moment, I couldn't think.

I could only act.

I worried I'd gotten this wrong—

But then…like a brittle twig during dry season, Jeffrey snapped. Bit by bit, he melted into my embrace. His fluffy orange hair tickled my nose as he tucked his face inside my neck and the minute tremors in his body vibrated against me.

Relieved it no longer felt like he was about to run, I rubbed a hand up and down his back, nuzzling at his temple, a pleased rumble bubbling up inside my chest.

I wanted to ask him what was wrong—but I already knew what was wrong.

I'd left him.

And yet…here I was. Beside him once again, like I hadn't decided to stay away for both of our own good. Mama had raised me on fairy tales. Stories of princes and knights, of happily ever afters. It didn't feel natural to leave Jeffrey, even though it was the smart choice to make. Especially when it was my fault he was hurting in the first place.

Ever since I was a pup, I'd dreamed of the day I'd pick my mate and we'd rule the pack together. I would glance through the catalogs Dad brought home, hearts in my eyes, my tail wagging.

I knew that was my destiny.

Because that's what alphas have to do.

And yet…here I was. Wrapped around my very human fated mate. A man who should not have made my heart sing, but did. A man who was confusing, arousing, and mine-mine-mine in a way that nothing ever had been before. A man that I could not keep, no matter how badly I wanted to, because keeping him would mean my death.

I'd promised myself I was only here to protect him.

That watching from afar would be enough.

But it wasn't.

It wasn't.

Because there was no way I was giving this up—at least…not until I had to.

Eventually, Jeffrey's arms curled around me in return. His grip was weak—especially for a man of his size—but it was welcome all the same. He may have been muscular himself, large in all the ways that counted, but my mate was prey, and there was no denying that. And he seemed to know that too if the plume of near-constant fearscent that exuded from him was an indicator.

We hugged for a long time.

For long enough the sun sank low and the moon began to climb high into the sky.

He didn't cry.

And his bloody knuckles left smears on the back of my borrowed shirt.

When his stomach growled, I gently peeled my head away from where it'd been buried in his hair for the last hour. For so long I'd avoided speaking, it felt unnatural and odd—but when I was with Jeffrey my words came easy.

"Are you hungry?" I asked, shocked by how low and rough my voice sounded.

Jeffrey shook his head, but his stomach growled, betraying him again. "I'm not hungry." I could hear the lie in his words.

"I am," I said, because it was true. I was always hungry.

"Oh…" His voice was quiet. Like he was terrified of taking up too much space. Like he wasn't sure who or what he was—lost as his eyes told me he was. "You can go if you want to."

Why would I—

Oh.

It took me a second to replay the conversation and realize what I'd said and what it might imply. Damn. Humans were tricky. He couldn't smell my intent, or hear my heartbeat. Which meant I had to be as literal as possible, and even then, I might mess up—like I just had.

"I am hungry and I am feeding you." There. That was better.

"You…are?" Jeffrey blinked up at me, those lovely eyes searching mine like I was a beacon on a stormy sea. Dark brown. The color of freshly turned soil. My favorite color probably—in all the world. Wolves did not have brown eyes. I was used to blues, purples, gold—variations, yes, but the same three shades.

Brown was foreign.

But it was lovely too.

Unable to help myself, I curled a hand around the corner of his jaw, tipping his head up so I could see him better. His scent shifted then, turning musky and sweet. My cock jerked, immediately rising to the occasion. Unable to help myself, I licked my lips.

He likes being touched.

"You are so pretty," I murmured. "Pretty, pretty, sweet Jeffrey."

It wasn't the first time I'd called him that, but he wasn't cum-drunk and bitch-hazy this time, so he didn't react the way I'd hoped.

Jeffrey scoffed and his scent soured. He jerked his head out of my grip, though I smelled the loss he felt the second we no longer touched. So I grabbed him again—maneuvering him back into place. When I had him under control, I released a pleased rumble. Immediately, he settled for me—and his scent became musky sweet all over again.

I was glad then that I hadn't given Butters his wallet back.

I didn't carry money of my own—I felt no need.

The land had fed me all my life, and I hardly partook in human things like restaurants. For most of my life, the compound hadn't had anything of the sort. And even if it did, I never would've gone there. I'd never in my life walked up to a counter and ordered a meal. But I would today. For Jeffrey.

Using Butters money.

I sniffed out the diner before I saw it, tugging Jeffrey along the night-dark street as the residents began to wake up. During the day, Elmwood was a ghost town, as most of its inhabitants were fanged-ones. They smelled off. A hint of smoke and bitterness that masked the usual heat-musk-salt that humans exuded.

Still, I ignored the unpleasant odor, keeping my touch gentle as I steered Jeffrey toward the scent of grease, and my own stomach growled.

He was quiet again.

And I let him be.

After leaving him alone and frightening him earlier I didn't deserve his sweet words—even though his voice was music, and every time he opened his mouth it made my heart sing. I would have to do better.

I *would* do better.

Even if it meant rethinking my master plan.

Because doing better was a choice I could make—even if keeping him wasn't.

When we pushed into the diner an awful jingle sounded. I jolted, immediately yanking Jeffrey behind me, a menacing growl escaping as I scanned the room for threats. It only took a second to recognize the awful cling—and see that it had come from a bell above the door.

Relaxing, I twisted to make sure Jeffrey was alright—more than a little surprised to find he was staring at me.

Staring at me and *smiling*.

My tail popped out. I couldn't help it. It *thwapped* happily as I beamed back at him, just as brightly. My pants, as always, slipped down to accommodate its length. Not that I was used to wearing pants, because I was not. I hated them actually. With a burning passion.

"You are safe," I told him proudly.

"From the door," he echoed, the iciness in his voice melting away.

"Yes."

"…Thanks?"

"You are welcome!" When I sniffed him, his scent told me he was *amused.* I didn't mind being the butt of a joke if it meant I had made him happy. Even though I didn't understand what about protecting him he'd found so funny. It was still success.

My tail continued to wag as I cut through the line of people gathered at the front and pulled Jeffrey with me.

"Hello. I would like food," I told the colorful woman at the counter after shoving a man aside. "Here is my wallet." I pulled out the wallet, leaning against the counter and exuding as much confidence as I could muster as I passed her the…very beat up—I squinted at it—leather rectangle.

She was tiny and her hair was blue.

Which was odd.

Was that normal?

I cocked my head at her, though most of my attention was still on Jeffrey who was—laughing at my side. Laughing. *Again.*

"Thank you," the girl said gently, accepting the wallet—like she should—*I think.* She opened it up, then frowned at me. "Was there a certain kind of food you wanted?" She *also* smelled amused.

There was silly paper money inside, which she counted as she waited for me to speak.

The man I'd shoved, that stood behind me, huffed something about cutting a line, but I didn't know what that meant—or care about him—so I pretended not to hear.

The blue-haired girl passed me a large rectangular…paper thing that was sitting beside her on the counter. I opened it, scanning it and recognizing some of the pictures on it as food items I'd had before when Harry brought take-out home.

It reminded me of the catalogs I'd looked at back home with wolves on them. Like you could just flip through and pick what you wanted—and that was that. Or the rectangular paper thing the funny man with the mustache and the pink shirt had placed on the table in *Lady and the Tramp* before the dogs had kissed.

Recognizing what the itemized list of food was, however, didn't mean I knew what anything was called—or how to read it. So I closed the damn thing and handed it back.

"I want something good," I told her seriously. "Do you have squirrel?"

"Do I have…squirrel?" she repeated, her eyes dancing. She turned her attention to Jeffrey and I growled, side-stepping in front of him to block him from view.

"Yes," I repeated, frowning when I realized by putting myself between Jeffrey and the girl I'd forced him right next to the disgruntled man behind us. So I jerked him in front of me again, figuring she was the lesser of two evils as she would have to climb over the counter to reach him and I could incapacitate her before that happened.

Jeffrey's scent was amused-happy-pleased, so I couldn't have been getting this entirely wrong. His eyes were crinkled at the corners, and his spots looked particularly fetching in this light. I hadn't seen him up close like this in bright light. At least…not in this form. It was different.

"He is pretty," I explained to her dreamily because it was true, still blocking Jeffrey from view of the rest of the restaurant with my bulk. "And must be protected."

"I don't have *squirrel*, unfortunately. And yes, he is, and should," she agreed, eyes crinkling. She was agreeing with me, but I wasn't sure I liked that. Was this a flirt? *I* was flirting. She should not be flirting. That was my job.

Jeffrey was *mine*.

I growled at her, "No." I frowned. "You don't get to say that too. Only I do."

"Ooookay," she hummed, twisting to look at Jeffrey again. "Jeffrey," she said—and I jolted, rigid, when I realized they knew each other. "What do you want to eat, baby?"

Baby?

He was not an infant.

I glared at her, but my gaze softened when Jeffrey began to speak. The haunted quality to his tone was missing, and his voice was warm. His fingers wrapped around my wrist where I bracketed him against the counter.

"How about two cheeseburgers?" he said, voice soft. "You know what," he glanced at me, gaze traveling from head to toe. His tongue flickered out to wet his lips and his scent was hungry. My cock jerked, and I clenched my hands into fists, using all the self-control I possessed so that I wouldn't pin him to the counter so he could feel it. "Make that three."

The blue-haired woman pulled several paper moneys out of Butters's wallet and handed the rest back to me along with a few coins. "Here's your change, baby," she said, addressing me this time.

"Th-thank you." I pocketed it again, frowning—confused. I didn't understand why she'd given me money back? I thought I was paying for dinner.

I suppose I must've done it right though, because Jeffrey didn't look offended.

He picked us a booth—and because he was smart-good-strong he chose the booth that would offer us the best room of the diner and all its exits. With our backs to the wall, we settled into our little corner to wait.

Jeffrey picked at the peeling linoleum on the table, his eyes on me—but he didn't speak. His knuckles had crusted over, the blood no longer fresh. I was tempted to lean across the table to lap at them to help them heal, but he looked so serious I didn't want to break his focus.

He watched me.

Like he was trying to figure me out, and he wasn't certain how.

I sat up straighter, my ears and tail perking up as I puffed up to my full height so he'd have something to look at. He snorted in amusement, like he somehow knew what I was doing. Then he cocked his head to the side, and leaned his chin on his palm.

"What's your name?" he asked, voice soft.

"Mutt." I jolted a little, tail thumping as my hands grew slick with nerves as I revealed to him the name I'd chosen.

"Mutt, hmm," he repeated, his brow furrowing a bit in thought. Just hearing my name on his tongue sent me spinning. It sounded like *music*. Jeffrey had the kind of voice that was prettier than bird song. Smooth, melodic, natural in the way only a rushing stream or tinkling waterfall could be. "You got a last name, Mutt?"

"Last…name?" I blinked, not sure what he meant. "I guess I don't… like it when my brothers call me stupid."

"Wh—" Jeffrey snorted out a laugh. "That's not what I—You know what? Never mind." He grinned and it sent butterflies rioting in my belly. His shoulders flexed as he moved, and my mouth went dry. "I don't like being called stupid either."

"That is why it is the name I like last," I explained, in case that was why he smelled and looked so amused. "It is awful."

"Yeah, it is." Jeffrey agreed, because he was smart and good and lovely.

A lock of his copper hair fell across his brow, somehow only managing to make him look even more handsome. Like a prince in one of the fairy tales I used to watch.

He was a prince in a tower built from his own fear, and I wanted to save him.

He moved gracefully, like a dancer. There was power in each flick of his wrists, in each twist of his powerful upper body. Though leaner than I was, there was no denying the muscle that was packed tight to Jeffrey's body. It was the kind of muscle that took years to build, especially on someone like him who—while tall—had a more willowy figure.

Despite this…he was self-conscious.

He held himself now, like he was frightened of being seen.

And I ached for him.

Ached for what had to have happened to him for him to feel this way.

"Why are you sad?" I blurted, even though I knew. I just…maybe I needed to hear it confirmed? Or maybe I wanted to offer solutions. I don't know.

"My dog ran off," he said, picking at the table, eyes downturned.

"W-why?" God, if he were a wolf I'd have been so screwed. He'd have been able to sniff out my deception in a heartbeat.

"I…don't know," he said softly. "Well," he amended, shrugging. "The vet maybe? I dunno. Not like he could know that's where we were going. Dogs don't read."

"Smells," I offered immediately—because I couldn't help it. "He could smell it."

"He could…smell it," Jeffrey repeated, frowning. "Huh. That's what I worried about."

"Vets smell like chemicals," I offered helpfully. "Very bad. Gross. Awful.

And all the different animals. Maybe he got overwhelmed?" The smells hadn't been what had overwhelmed me. But I just…I wanted to give him something. Something that would help him feel less alone.

"Too bad there's no such thing as an at-home vet," Jeffrey huffed, scrubbing a hand over his face, looking dejected. "Could've avoided this entirely."

"I could help," I blurted out. Jeffrey's eyebrows shot up. "Not me," I amended quickly. "I know…a vet. Or at least—someone who works with animals."

"Huh." Jeffrey eyed me warily.

"When your dog comes back I could send him over."

"You mean *if?*" Jeffrey sighed, the weight of the world on his shoulders. "*If* my dog comes back."

"No, I mean *when*," I corrected, voice soft. "He'd be stupid not to."

Jeffrey's cheeks flushed and he ducked his head, obviously pleased. "I dunno about that."

"I'll send help over," I blurted, heart thumping.

"But—"

"If the dog is not back, you can send him home."

"…okay," Jeffrey looked pensive, but somewhat cheered up. And that was good. I'd fixed it, hadn't I? At least a little.

I shouldn't have run.

"Tomorrow at eight," I said, heart thumping.

"Yeah…I guess," Jeffrey relaxed a little, obviously less worried.

"Why a vet?" I asked, because I couldn't help it. "Does your dog not look healthy?" I was more than a little curious, and that probably showed.

Jeffrey shook his head. "No, I just…I mean, I've never had a dog. I thought it was the right thing to do, you know? Gotta take care of him."

I nodded, heart thumping harder. This made sense. The Jeffrey I'd met at the gas station when he'd been passing through Colorado had been a caregiver. Of course he'd be immediately concerned.

"You are noble," I told him. "A good man. Very good."

"I dunno about that," Jeffrey shook his head, but he looked…pleased, and his smell was happy-satisfied-grateful.

Things were going…well.

Far better than I had even hoped.

Jeffrey may have been human, but he carried my favorite wolf traits. He was observant. More observant than most of my brothers. A very attractive trait.

"That man has refilled his fizzy juice—"

"Seven times," Jeffrey finished for me, staring at the same man I was. I laughed, because he was right. "He's only been here twenty minutes. Dude's chugging that shit." I grinned at him, eyes narrowing as he covertly tested me. "And that woman—" Jeffrey jerked his head toward a woman all the way across the restaurant. "She—"

"Has sneezed six times." She sneezed again. "Seven."

Jeffrey grinned. "You think she has allergies?"

"Allergies?" I squinted at him.

"You know, like…when your body reacts badly to something. Usually flowers and shit."

"Humans are allergic to flowers?" I asked, aghast.

"Humans are allergic to a lot of things," Jeffrey replied sagely.

With every mutual observation we made, the space between us lessened. Jeffrey grew more animated, more warm. Like he was incredibly excited to have finally met someone as judgy as he was.

"I mean…ten times. Ten times by the time he left," he giggled to himself, shoveling food into his mouth. "Who needs that much soda?"

I shook my head, because I did not know. But I loved the face he was making and did not want him to stop making it.

The food was good. Surprisingly so. And Jeffrey was far more astute than I'd given him credit for because he had been correct, one burger was absolutely not enough. I plowed through the first in a matter of seconds as we sat in our little diner booth, knees bumping, elbows on the table.

Jeffrey ate like a bird does. Little tiny bites. Like he was worried about making a mess.

Which made me slow down a little, because I didn't want to finish way before he did. When he grabbed a napkin and dabbed at his mouth, I frowned, then mimicked him, pleased when his scent shifted again. Happy. As he looked at me.

My napkin was a lot dirtier than his.

"So," Jeffrey said after he'd neatly wiped his mouth. I chewed my newest bite eagerly, eyes lighting up as I waited to see what he was going to ask. "You're from Elmwood?"

I frowned, confused. "No."

"No?"

My tail thumped against the seat as I shook my head. "I am from Colorado. The mountains. It is green and good. There are many plants and animals. It is safe." I wasn't sure why I was trying to hype up my home, as Jeffrey would never visit it—despite how badly I wanted him to—but I couldn't seem to stop. "You would like it."

"So why are you here?"

"Business." I felt very important telling him that, my chest puffing up. I wanted to tell him that I was here for *him*. And only him. That was why I'd convinced Dad to let us set up a compound here. But…even I knew that would be too much too soon.

I couldn't tell him I'd wanted to protect him.

To watch over him from afar.

It might frighten him.

Like a forward thinking chipmunk, I would keep some nuts in my cheeks for later.

"Business?" Jeffrey frowned at me, taking another bite of his food as he mulled this over. He dabbed his mouth again when he was done. "Business like…werewolf business?"

I was relieved then, to know for certain that he knew what I was.

"Yes," I told him, heart dancing.

"Like what?" Jeffrey arched an eyebrow, his scent skeptical. "What kinda business does a werewolf from Colorado have in Elmwood, Maine?"

"We are setting up a new compound," I told him. "A home for our pack," I added, because I wasn't certain he knew what I was talking about. "We are growing too fast for our current space. There are negotiations that need to be finalized with the local pack and council, but soon things here will be more permanent. Right now, it is just me and my brothers, but one day soon it will be half our pack. And it will be *beautiful*."

That was the most I'd ever talked all in a row.

It was *exhausting*.

"So…you're staying here?" Jeffrey peeked up at me through his lashes, an almost shy look on his face. It was so different from the flirty apathy I'd seen on him at the club—or the blank-faced sadness I'd seen in the alleyway. "Like indefinitely?"

I swallowed the lump in my throat, suddenly at a loss for words all over again.

Because I knew what he was asking.

And I couldn't give him the answer we both wanted.

"Till January," I said instead. The truth. "Then I'm going back home."

"Oh."

Jeffrey was silent the rest of the meal.

When we walked out onto the night-dark street his scent was murky enough I couldn't recognize the emotions. He did, however, smile at me. And it was summer soft—his dark eyes full of warmth as he gently bumped our shoulders together before twisting away.

"Thanks for dinner, man. And the hug." His cheeks went bright red. "It was good to see you…you know. Without bumping uglies." He bit his lip, then added, almost bashfully, "you're cool."

"I am not cool," I frowned. "It is very hot outside."

"Too true," Jeffrey laughed, like I'd said something funny. "You said tomorrow at eight, right? For your vet friend?"

I nodded, my heart in my throat. He was gorgeous, glittering beneath the streetlamp, that lovely bright hair practically glowing.

"Sweet. I guess I'll…um…see you around?"

"You will," I promised.

And I meant every word.

Chapter Five

Jeffrey

IT WAS DARK.

It was dark.

It was dark.

I was back home. Ten years old and hiding from my demon as I crept down the dark, empty hallway of Lydia's home, my heart in my throat. It had been sixteen hours, four minutes, and fifty-three seconds since she'd locked Blair in the closet again.

Sixteen hours, four minutes, and fifty-three seconds since I'd felt my stomach drop, and watched horrified as she dragged him down the hallway. I'd felt powerless, but that wasn't a new feeling nowadays.

I couldn't do anything.

I'd tried before, and all it had gotten him was more time locked up.

I hated when she did this. I hated it more than I hated anything else. More than I hated this home and its mausoleum-like rooms. Hated it more than my weekend lessons at the hunter lodge. Hated it more than I'd hated my old home, my old parents—the ones who thought I was dead.

The plate in my grip shook as I took a steadying breath, using the training Lydia had given me against her, silent as a specter.

When I reached the hall closet I felt two seconds from throwing up.

This could go so wrong. This could go so, so wrong. But…I couldn't just let him go hungry. Blair was only a year younger than me. Smaller than me—even though when we'd first been taken we were the same size. Still, his stomach was like a cavern. The kid could put away more food than I could—and he wasn't the one with the "extracurricular activities."

He had to be starving.

He had to have been starving for *hours*.

I hadn't been able to manage much. It'd taken a lot of distractions at dinner, twiddling my thumbs, sneaking rolls and carrots into my pockets, trying to pretend like everything was normal. Like I wasn't dying inside. Like I wasn't completely attuned to the kid who was locked only fifty feet away from where Lydia, her husband, and I sat like a picture-perfect family.

Lydia had asked to hear me play my guitar after dinner.

It had taken every ounce of strength I had in my body not to bolt into my room where I could hide the rolls before she could find out about my deception. Somehow I'd gotten lucky. Because she let me go.

And now…hours later—well after she'd gone to sleep—I was finally able to deliver my gift.

My heart was pounding as I fiddled the key out of my pocket one handed.

It'd been tricky sneaking it out of her room. Especially because I knew for a fact she was a light sleeper. One time, Blair had sneezed too loud, and she'd shown up inside our room at three in the morning—a demoness in a white nightgown.

"Be quiet," was all she'd said.

And Blair and I hadn't dared breathe the rest of the night.

Still though, luck had been on my side. Or maybe it really was my lessons. At least they were good for something, right? Other than giving me nightmares.

As I'd snuck the key into the lock and twisted the door open my palms were sweaty. It was hard to get a good grip on the door, but somehow I managed. The second I'd pulled it open, something settled inside me. Something that had gotten knocked loose the second Blair had been out of my sight.

He sat in the dark, huddled in a sad little ball, his mop of black hair hanging over his face.

I had swallowed the lump in my throat, falling to my knees and pressing into the tight space as much as I could.

"Blair," I'd said as quietly as I could. "I can't let you out."

Blair made a broken sound. He lifted his head, looking at me with these devastated green eyes—and I just...I just wanted to die.

I wanted to die.

I could hardly breathe.

Everything hurt, hurt, hurt.

"I'm sorry." My eyes burned. I'd tried to make my hands stop shaking but they wouldn't listen. Especially as I reached out with my free hand and squeezed Blair's knee tight. It was bony—like mine were. His lips were chapped. Dry.

I should've brought him water.

But who knew how long it would be till she'd let him out to pee. Maybe it was better I hadn't.

"I brought you food." It was hard to get the words out when my throat felt like it was going to close up entirely. "You have to be quiet though." He didn't need the reminder, not really. We both knew about Lydia and her games. But still, I felt better getting the words out. "And you can't make a mess."

Blair nodded and my heart had lurched as I offered him the plate I'd brought. He eyed it like I'd gathered up a gourmet feast, and not a shitty pile of carrots and rolls. He licked his lips. I nearly threw up.

Don't.

Don't, Markus—

Jeffrey, Jeffrey, Jeffrey—I corrected myself. My new name is *Jeffrey*.

Blair's hair looked indigo in the moonlight as he latched onto one of the rolls with vigor. He tore through it, careful of crumbs just like I'd begged. There was something wild and ravenous about him. Like he wasn't human at all.

Something had settled inside me as I watched Blair eat. Sure, he was miserable. Heck, so was I. But at least I'd been able to do something about it. However small it was. Three rolls and carrot sticks. It wasn't much, but it was enough.

He clearly thought so too, because the way he was staring at me made me feel like I'd done far more than feed him table scraps.

Blair may not have been my blood brother, but after spending the previous year in hell with him, I felt closer to him than I had with my real brothers. I tried not to think about them often. It just made me feel guilty—a sense of loss so all-encompassing it threatened to choke me.

I tried not to think about the past at all.

I'd learned all it did was make me want to die.

Because we were in this mess because of me.

And while I was getting laptops, an Xbox, and guitars—Blair was getting locked up in closets, beaten with belts, and called enough names I worried he'd start to believe the words were true.

Blair's hands were trembling—almost as much as mine. He didn't try to hide them. Because of course he didn't. As fucked up as we both were, Blair was the braver of the two of us. I'd always envied him for that. He hadn't let Lydia defeat him. Maybe that's why she was so determined to flay him every opportunity she got.

She could see the spark in his eyes.

Blair had been almost through the plate when I spoke again. "I'm sorry," I bit my lip, a raw feeling of inadequacy sitting like a pit in my stomach. "I would've brought more but I had to sneak it into my pockets from my plate." Maybe TMI. Probably shouldn't have told him how exactly I'd managed this.

At least I hadn't told him that I'd stolen the plate we were using a couple weeks ago in fear that this would happen again. Because I was less scared of getting caught with a stolen plate than I was of Lydia finding crumbs on the closet floor.

If she found them, I didn't know what would happen to Blair.

Stop thinking about it.

Don't cry.

Don't cry, don't cry, don't cry.

Blair nodded, though he'd looked about as depressed as I felt. Guilt ate at me, acidic and heavy. Because it wasn't fair. Here I was—outside—and he was locked up. I knew I wasn't the one that had put him here, but I might as well have.

It's my fault, it's my fault, it's my fault.

I reached for him, needing his touch probably more than he needed mine. My hand found the back of his neck—the same way Richard used to do to me—and I pulled him tightly into a hug. He was warm, at least. Though he felt so fucking small. His bony shoulder jabbed into my chest but I didn't let him go.

Part of me hoped it would bruise.

I deserved it.

When Blair started to cry I'd nearly lost control myself. He shook. He shook and shook and shook. His normally in-your-face attitude was missing. Like he'd been whittled down to nothing. *Don't let her change you, please, please, please*—I begged silently, curled around him for as long as I could get away with.

All the while, I kept one ear on the hallway—always aware that we were on borrowed time.

Any moment Lydia could wake up.

Any moment she could find us.

And then where would we be?

Eventually, I'd had to let him go. He clutched at me when I did, and pulling his fingers from my pajamas was the hardest thing I'd ever done. Harder than stealing the key. Harder than my lessons. Harder than dealing with Lydia's attention.

"I'm sorry," I managed, voice rough. "I'm so sorry." His nails bit into my hands as I peeled myself free, carefully sliding out of the closet. "I'm so, so sorry. I'm sorry, I'm sorry, I'm sorry."

Blair didn't hear me. He was too lost in his own tears. He curled up into a little ball again, and I'd carefully slid the plate out into the hall before shutting the closet and locking it up again. This wasn't over. I still needed to return the key to where I'd found it.

I still needed to climb into bed before Lydia discovered I was missing.

But I couldn't leave him.

I couldn't.

I stayed by the door all night long.

I cried.

I couldn't seem to stop.

And all the while, I'd shoved my fist in my mouth and choked on every sound. Terrified that Blair would hear me. Terrified that he'd know I was crying too. Eventually he quieted down, having likely fallen asleep. And still I cried. Though the sobs grew softer, and I was left feeling like an empty husk as I listened to the hallway for threats, my heart sawed in two.

When the sun threatened to rise, I rose from my spot by the door.

I returned the key.

I fell into bed.

And I cried again.

I searched for my dog, just like I told Blair I would.

I searched for him and found jack shit except for a place to fall apart, and apparently a nosy werewolf. To say I'd been surprised to be cornered by my hookup in an alleyway would be the understatement of a century.

But I could admit now, I was really fucking grateful.

Sure it'd been weird at first, but his odd brand of awkward earnestness had quickly won me over. Also…his hugs were kinda fucking awesome. Warm and the right amount of sweaty, his arms tight and greedy, his body solid.

The cheeseburger had helped, but the hug and the laughter he'd caused had helped more. Like medicine injected directly into my veins. But I'd still ended the night alone, dogless, friendless, wishing I'd had the courage to ask Mutt to come home with me.

I quickly became grateful that I hadn't, however, because there was a surprise waiting for me on my welcome mat.

The whole drive home I'd felt eyes on me. They crawled and crawled, coating my body in spiders as the moon sunk between the branches that lined the roads. Soon it would be fall, and half the leaves would rot and fall off.

When I pulled into the parking lot, the crushing sense of loss I felt nearly made me sick. It was well past midnight, and I felt about a thousand years old. Like my eyebags had bags, and my heart weighed a hundred pounds. Exhausted, vision bleary, my movements sluggish, I almost didn't notice the hairy figure sitting on my welcome mat when I trudged up the stairs.

Dusty, fluffy, and happy.

My dog had returned.

"You came back." I paused at the end of the hallway, staring at him, worried I was hallucinating. He took pity on me, crossing the distance between us. When his cold nose bumped against my fingers, the shock was enough to center me.

The dog woofed as if to confirm that he had in fact come back for me.

"You…" I fell to my knees, dropped the pizza box Blair had given me, and wrapped my arms around his neck. "I thought I'd never see you again."

His eyes were blue. Mutt blue.

And my heart fluttered—fluttered—fluttered.

Mutt.

It suited a dog more than it suited a man.

And after spending more time with the werewolf, I had my suspicions that the oddly convenient reappearance of my dog was not a coincidence at all. *If I end up being wrong, I'll give him a new name,* I decided. But for now, I knew just what to call him.

The dog—Mutt—snuffled at my neck, huffing in big breaths like he'd missed me as much as I'd missed him.

"What the hell happened earlier?" I asked him, my eyes wet. "I thought…"

He pulled back a little, staring at me with those big, sad blue eyes. His tongue flicked out, swiping at my cheeks and I laughed, shoving him off. "Never mind. You're right. Doesn't matter." I sucked in a breath.

"Let's get some rest, bud."

And we did.

Mutt had promised me a vet would show up at my house at eight the next day. And while it felt like it was too good to be true…I chose to believe him. So I didn't book another appointment at the clinic, and instead decided to wait.

If I was being honest…the part of me that was paranoid and young—stuck at nine years old with monsters not only under the bed but walking the streets of my childhood hometown—suspected my late-night suspicions about Mutt-the-dog were correct.

That he was not a dog at all.

But Mutt the werewolf.

Normally…that thought would piss me off. Terrify me. All that. But… we'd been completely alone twice now—four times, if you counted what I suspected was one of his shifted forms—and all he'd done was call me pretty, make me laugh, and get me off.

There were so many dark things in my life.

I didn't want to throw away the only light I'd seen for a long-ass time.

But that didn't mean I wasn't curious to see how this "check up" with Mutt's "vet friend" would go.

Mutt couldn't come—he'd made that clear, looking shady as hell, and not nearly as sneaky as he thought he was.

Which was again, very convenient.

Amused, but still full of trepidation, I sunk my fingers in Mutt-the-dog's fur, stroking through it as I waited for the vet to arrive.

Me: That vet guy is showing up soon

Blair: Fuck yeah. You want me to come over?

Me: Nah. I'm good. I'll let you know how it goes.

Blair: You sure?

Me: Dude. It's just a vet. I'm fine. Not like I'm selling my kidneys or something.

I put my phone away when I heard the knock at the door. "Stay," I commanded Mutt-the-dog, before heading toward the front door with what I hoped was a friendly grin.

It was time to figure out the truth.

The man waiting on the other side of the door when I pushed it open was seriously fucking stunning. He exuded calm, his very energy infecting the air around him as I relaxed and stared up at him—and up—and up—because holy shit, the guy had to be seven feet tall.

I had never met a person that big.

I'd thought Mutt was massive—but fuck, he had nothing on this guy.

His dark skin lit up orange as the light from the complex hallway hit him from behind. His smile was pearly white, and his gold eyes glittered as he shifted his armload over and offered me his now free hand. I shook it, still a little shocked by his size.

"I'm Theo," he said, eyes warm. "It's nice to meet you."

Werewolf. Definitely a fucking werewolf.

I wasn't sure why I was surprised. Of course the only people Mutt knew were werewolves.

"Thanks for coming on such short notice," I said, releasing his hand quickly so I wouldn't look like a total weirdo before shifting to the side to invite him in. "You want a drink or anything?" *Holy-shit-he's-big.* As he passed by me, I couldn't help but stare.

Mutt-the-dog hopped off the couch, his tail wagging, his head cocked to the side as he stared at the visitor.

"What's his name?" Theo asked curiously, smiling down at the dog as he knelt on the ground—obviously not worried about getting dirty. He was barefoot. I stared at the bare soles of his feet, eyes wide, cheeks a little flushed. I hadn't expected that.

The bare feet.

Maybe it was a werewolf thing?

Or maybe…a Theo thing.

He seemed very down to earth. Perhaps that was part of it.

He was either a really good liar, or simply too fucking chill to give himself away.

"Mutt," I answered automatically. And then I flushed even redder, because even I knew how that sounded.

Shit.

Don't give yourself away.

"Huh," Theo held a hand out, gently stroking along the dog's head. He woofed softly, butting into the palm, his blue eyes warm. I stared at the two of them, something settling inside me as I sucked in a breath.

"He looks like—you know," I shrugged a shoulder, shutting the door behind us, and doing my damndest to force down the need to bolt all five of the locks. *He'll think you're a freak. Don't do it. Don't do it.*

I did one—and then another.

But was able to force myself not to do the last three.

Though that was difficult.

"He does look like Mutt," Theo agreed simply. "He must've made an impression if you're naming your dog after him." He was gentle as he pulled out his supplies, and I knew jack shit about dogs or exams—or anything like that—but Theo looked like he knew what he was doing.

Mutt didn't seem scared of him either, and that had been my biggest fear if he actually was a dog—and not a werewolf pretending to be one.

"So," I said, chewing on my lip. "Drink?"

The big dog was docile as a bunny now as he let Theo begin his examination. He checked his ears and his fur, carding through it with large, gentle hands. I took a seat on the couch, watching him curiously. "A drink would be nice, yeah." Theo smiled at me, his tone gentle.

Immediately I hopped to my feet and scurried into the kitchen. I had a few orange sodas in my fridge for when Blair came by, so I snagged one of them. And then I paused, stock still—because I could hear Theo talking and I…yep. Okay. I had not been paranoid after all.

All my suspicions were suddenly made reality.

"Mutt. You owe me for this," Theo's voice was soft but amused. "I don't know what—but you definitely owe me."

Mutt whined.

"This is weird, even for us," Theo added with a chuckle. "I get that you want to protect him, but there's gotta be a limit to that."

A growl.

"Fine."

I pushed out of the kitchen, soda in hand, a smile on my face. Offering it to Theo, my heart thumping, I pretended like I hadn't just overheard their entire muttered conversation. I took my seat on the couch again, leaning over the back of it, watching Mutt with curious eyes.

Huh.

So he was…

I mean—

I'd have to react properly to this later, but for now, I needed to keep my poker face on so neither of them would know what I'd heard.

"So…how do you know Mutt?" I asked, playing dumb. I was curious. Well…more than a little curious.

I could admit I had a bit of a crush.

I mean….

Who the fuck asks for squirrel at a *diner*?

Mutt.

That's who.

He was weird, and cute—and he liked to stick his fingers up my butt. So like…that made him kinda perfect? Lying about being a dog, aside.

"He didn't tell you?" Theo arched a dark brow, looking amused.

"Uh. No."

"Not surprised." Theo nodded and then…frustratingly kept silent. He continued to check Mutt-the-dog, and I watched, though my skin was itching for more information. After what felt like a zillion years, Theo finally answered my question. "He's my brother."

"Your brother?" I blinked, surprised.

"One of five pups," Theo hummed, eyes twinkling. "Adopted," he added, looking amused. "Aside from Mutt and Butters."

"Butters?" I squinted. I'd thought the name Mutt was ridiculous. Butters was somehow worse.

"Mhmm," Theo scratched behind Mutt's ears in a way that looked way too familiar, like he'd done it a thousand times, and Mutt woofed good-naturedly, his tail wagging. "Blond as his name suggests."

"I don't mean to be insensitive," I blurted out, fingers slipping into my pocket to play with the guitar pick I kept there. The hard edge dug into the pad of my thumb, soothing me. "But what's up with the names?"

"The names?"

"Yeah." I frowned. "I mean…Mutt and Butters—those are…kinda weird, right?" Fuck, I was not saying that right. "But Theo's a normal name. Is that a wolf thing?"

Theo snorted out a laugh. "Butters and Mutt are the youngest."

"Oh." I blinked, frowning—because that didn't exactly answer the question.

"They're the cutest too," he added, eyes dancing. Mutt-the-dog woofed, baring his teeth when Theo dug his finger in too hard along his ribs. He did not look amused. "When Butters was little he'd zoom around fast as a bullet—looked like a butterball flying around with all that blond fur."

"Right." Huh. So werewolves really did stay in their four-legged forms. I wasn't sure if that was the proper term, but figured I'd have time to figure that out. Might even be something Avery knew about. I'd have to ask him on my next shift at work.

"Plus his name is Buchanan, and that's a mouthful. Hard when you've got fangs especially. Most of us can't manage a full humanskin shift till we're preteens."

Welp. That answered that question.

If this form was called humanskin, I could easily infer that the wolf form was called wolfskin.

I nodded, because that made sense. "And Mutt?" I asked, because realistically I didn't give a fuck about Butters. Not to be rude—but I'd never even met him, and my curiosity was really reserved for his brother.

"Matthew," Theo laughed. "When he was little he had a hard time saying it." He shrugged. "You'd think our parents would've learned with Butters, but they didn't. Besides, Mutt's always preferred his wolfskin. Not much of a talker." Dude talked my ear off every time I was next to him. Huh. "Not sure how Matt got changed to Mutt though. Seems like a more recent development." Theo seemed to eye Mutt-the-dog curiously.

"That's…cute." My heart fluttered, picturing Mutt as a tiny, hairy little werewolf kid.

"Anyway," Theo shrugged, a fond look on his face. He pulled away from Mutt-the-dog, already packing up the kit he'd brought with him.

"So, Mutt…" I wasn't sure how to phrase this, once again getting stuck. "He's not been…" *Fuck, this was tricky.* "Integrated into society long?" There.

"I dunno if I'd say that. He's plenty integrated back home." Theo shrugged again, rising from the floor with a gentle smile. "Just not in the way *human* society would expect," he said gently. "It's different."

"Different how?" Fuck, my cheeks were burning. This felt so invasive, but…I just…I just wanted to understand. If I understood better, maybe I'd be able to navigate this easier.

Maybe I could understand him?

"He's a hunter," Theo explained. "Brings food back for the pack. Spends weeks out in the woods. One day he'll be Pack Alpha, but for now, he's content to provide." Mutt-the-fake-dog woofed at Theo, and the large man huffed out an amused smile, folding over and gently stroking his head. "He's a sweetheart," he said to me, not answering my question—but giving me the information I wanted anyway. "But he's stubborn. Dumb too, sometimes."

Mutt-the-dog woofed, and I laughed. I'd never seen him look so disgruntled.

"We're all dumb in our own ways," Theo added, tone softening. "Mutt doesn't understand humans because he's never had to be around them. Me, on the other hand…well, I've had a lot more experience. The pack I was in before Mom and Dad adopted me was full of humans. I spent a lot of time with them. It's how I learned what I know about most things."

Like being a vet. Was easy enough to connect the dots.

"A hunter," I repeated, oddly charmed. No wonder why he'd wanted to eat squirrel at the diner. If he spent a lot of time out in the woods he probably ate that shit all the time. Ew.

Seriously.

Ew.

Theo flashed me another smile, and his golden eyes were knowing. Almost like he knew what I'd overheard, and was trying to reassure me. "If you're asking me questions because you wanna know if you can trust him, you can."

My heart ached.

I pressed my thumb hard enough into the guitar pick it made me feel like I was about to bleed. "Right," I said, voice hoarse. "Of course."

"There's a lot of scary things out there," Theo said, his voice low and sweet, like he was talking to a frightened animal. "But Mutt's not one of them."

My heart fluttered, cheeks still flushed as I nodded. I wanted to ask more questions, but it didn't feel appropriate. I'd already been nosy enough. So I cleared my throat. "Is he chipped?" I asked, shifting the conversation back to my dog.

"Nah," Theo replied. I wasn't sure if he'd actually checked, but figured we were past that now. "Healthy looking guy, though," he shrugged. "Nothing to worry about."

"Do you think we need to run blood tests or anything?" I asked, cheeks still hot. "Google said that might be a good idea." Had to keep up pretenses.

"I'll do whatever tests you want me to do," Theo said good-naturedly, taking on a more serious air as his eyes crinkled. "You just say the word."

"Do you think neutering is an option?" I asked, because even though I'd decided to play this by ear, I figured I deserved a little fun along the way.

Theo laughed his ass off. "You wanna snip his balls?" he asked, more than a little amused. I had a feeling he'd said it that way because Mutt wouldn't know what the hell "neutering" was.

The dog's eyes widened, and he barked in alarm.

"Neutering strays is always the best option," Theo hummed, messing with his brother. Mutt barked again, tail between his legs.

"I'll think about it."

I decided I liked Theo.

A lot.

But not as much as I liked Mutt.

Chapter Six

Mutt

IN MY DEFENSE, I've never been the best at forward thinking. Hell, if we're being really honest, I'd never been the best at thinking in general—despite the fact that my thoughts were all I had most days, and that's how I liked it. Which was why…I'd now been parading as a dog for almost an entire month.

My first moon had passed, and while it had been difficult—it always was—it'd been easier than usual. Like the calm before the storm. Jeffrey hadn't batted an eye when I'd disappeared for several days, just simply let me back inside his home and offered me more of the awful round brown pebbles humans thought were food.

Fall had come with a vengeance.

And with it, came the cold chill of reality.

Because I didn't know what the fuck I was doing. And every day that passed dug me deeper in that hole. But I couldn't seem to stop.

I just…*couldn't.*

Dad warned me about hunger once.

He told me it would eat me alive if I let it. I listened, yeah—I had always listened. But I'd be the first to admit that I didn't understand. I didn't know there were two kinds of hunger. The kind that's easy to sate with a warm meal, or a warm bed—and the kind that tears you apart from the inside out.

One was predictable.

One was ravenous, and all-encompassing.

Dad had warned me but I didn't understand.

Not till the day I'd met Jeffrey.

Till the day I saw him standing there, looking prettier than sunshine, and I knew as surely as I knew the moon had forsaken me that I couldn't have him.

He'd been dappled with rain water, dressed in a hoodie pulled low over his face. Shadows hid his eyes from view, but it only took a single sniff to know he was human. The only feature on his face that I could see clearly were his lips. Soft. Pink. Relaxed into a gentle frown. There were spots that dotted his creamy, lovely skin. Freckles. That's what humans called them. A few of them crept onto his lips from where they splattered his jaw, and I was…lost.

I knew hunger then.

Unquenchable.

A thirst that burned me from the inside out.

As I stood on the edge of the parking lot, hidden inside shadows of my own, I ached. I ached because I couldn't do what I wanted. Couldn't cross the asphalt and push him to the ground like I wanted. Couldn't take him, then and there, like he needed to be taken.

Because if he was my fated—and he was, it only took one sniff to confirm that—he needed me as much as I needed him.

It'd seemed only logical to follow him then.

To approach, to taste that smell up close.

To sate the itch beneath my skin and the ache in my very bones.

But that had only been the beginning.

Then, just like now, I hadn't thought through my actions. Hadn't thought ahead to what obstacles might fall along my path. Planning was not my forte.

Case in point.

I was locked inside Jeffrey's truck in the middle of a busy parking lot full of humans. The tall building that rose high above casted shadows, and the brisk fall chill made the temperature inside the vehicle rather pleasant. Being left behind shouldn't have been a big deal.

It wouldn't have been.

Except for the fact that the building I was currently stuck outside of was apparently a head doctor. I wasn't sure what it was called. I'd heard a few whispers from other occupants of the building, something about therapy—a new word for me—or psycho-lo-gi-sists. Something like that.

I hadn't been alarmed at first, because I hadn't known what any of those words were.

I hadn't been alarmed till I heard Jeffrey greet a woman he called "Doctor Mason" and suddenly realized I was privy to a conversation that I should not be hearing. I couldn't see him. Obviously. Super hearing did not mean I could see through concrete. But no matter how hard I tried, I couldn't block out his voice coming from a cracked window on the second floor. Couldn't shift and force the door open either—not with so many humans present.

I was stuck.

I was stuck.

And I could only blame myself.

"How are you this week, Jeffrey?" an unfamiliar woman's voice asked.

"Fine," Jeffrey replied immediately. I heard the skip in his heartbeat though, and I was suddenly sick with the need to comfort him. To lap at his fingers the way I had the previous night when he'd had a nightmare.

"How are you really?" The woman, "Doctor Mason" probably, asked.

"I…" Jeffrey's heart thumped unsteadily for a moment, betraying his nerves. "I'm…okay. Better. Kind of?"

"What's caused the change?" she asked, her voice light and soft. The kinda voice that reminded me of cinnamon rolls and women who smelled like happy-mother-calm. Like my own mother.

"I found a dog?" Jeffrey answered, then laughed. "I mean… More accurately, he found me."

"Good for you, having a pet is a lot of responsibility," she hummed, and she truly sounded like she meant it. "I remember you mentioning last session that you never had a pet growing up."

"Lydia doesn't—*didn't* like animals," Jeffrey agreed and his tone was sad-sad. "She said they were messy." *Who is Lydia?*

"This must be exciting for you," she asked, voice still gentle. "That you have something you've always wanted? Something you were denied. How does it make you feel?"

"Good…I think?" I hated how nervous Jeffrey sounded, like he wasn't quite sure what words to use. It was different from the way he talked to me. Different from the way he'd talked to the short one who smelled like apples. Because obviously, I'd been eavesdropping after I left him at the vet's office, trying to make sure he was okay.

The short-apple-one had said, *"You know I don't blame you, right?"*

He'd said, *"You deserve to be happy."*

He'd said, *"It's time to move on."*

And Jeffrey had agreed but his scent was sour, sour, sour, and his heart was full of lies.

There were no lies in his words now. Not when he was talking to this doctor person. Like she'd gotten beneath his shell and to the doughy soft bits inside.

I didn't know why Jeffrey felt he didn't deserve happiness.

Didn't know why he smelled like guilt-love-protect when he was with the short-apple-one.

But I had the feeling…I was about to find out.

"How's Blair?" the doctor asked.

I didn't need to see Jeffrey's face to hear the tension in his voice. "He's good. Happy."

"And that makes you…" she waited until he answered, a few awkward beats passing.

"Scared."

"Right," the doctor agreed, like they'd talked about it before. "We've touched on that before, but you weren't ready to talk about it. Are you feeling more ready now?"

"I…" Jeffrey sucked in a breath. "No." His heart was galloping. I ached for him. I couldn't leave the cab, but I paced as best I could across the seats, restless. "Can we talk about something else?"

"What would you like to talk about?"

"I don't know. Just not…*that*. I'm not…I just. I can't. Not yet."

"That's perfectly fine," the doctor's voice was gentle. "We've got time."

Jeffrey laughed, but it was a bitter sound. "Do we? Because I want to get better. Like…yesterday. I'm so fucking tired of feeling like this. I'm sick of coming here—and talking about things I hate talking about. I'm sick of the fact that I have shit I need assistance working through."

"You resent therapy."

"I resent needing *help*." His voice was tight. "I'm…not used to it." His voice cracked at the end.

I thought of how good he'd felt in my arms. How right. How his scent was happiness-mate-home even when he was hurting. How he made my skin feel too tight, and my blood sing.

How desperately he'd needed comfort that day, and how glad I was that I had been there to give it—even though it was my fault he'd needed it in the first place.

"Why is that, do you think?" the doctor asked.

There was a long pause, and I knew—I *knew* there was no going back from this. There was no forgetting these words. No forgetting the raw honesty that fell from Jeffrey's tongue. No forgetting the acid in his tone and the fear that quaked within every syllable.

"I…" Jeffrey sucked in another breath. "I'm just…*not*." He sounded so small. So very small.

"Because of Lydia?" Doctor Mason guessed.

"Yeah." Even that single word sounded painful.

"You're used to being the one who is needed," the doctor sussed out. "It is difficult for you to accept a role that isn't protector."

"…yeah," Jeffrey agreed, voice still rough. "I think so. I…" Jeffrey paused for a second, gathering his thoughts. "Do I have to talk about this?"

"If you have something to share, it might help me understand how to help more."

Jeffrey blew out a breath. "Right. Okay." He was silent again for a few seconds, and when he spoke my heart ached anew. "For so long…looking after Blair was all I had. It's the only part of myself I still like—and doesn't feel totally foreign."

"Having crises of identity is understandable given what you've been through."

What had he been through?

"When Lydia…kidnapped me—"

My thoughts screeched to a halt.

Kidnapped. *Kidnapped? What did he mean kidnapped?*

"As a kid," Jeffrey continued as if he hadn't just shattered my brain into tiny little pieces. "There were all these…rules." He spoke slow and soft, as if he was far, far away—trapped inside his own head. "I wasn't allowed to talk to Blair about who I was before. I had to wear the clothes she picked out for me. Had to use the name that she'd given me. Had to pretend like Oregon wasn't a new and…scary place."

"That must've been frightening, especially when you were so young."

"It was." Jeffrey's voice wavered. "She promised me…a lot of things. So I went with her? And it was a stupid choice—and I get that now, I *really* do. But at the time, I just wanted someone to care about me. To *need* me. To…love me." The doctor was silent, like she didn't want to interrupt when he was finally opening up, and I was grateful. Because Jeffrey's words were spinning around inside my head, and my stomach was churning—and I…

Didn't.

Know.

What.

To.

Do.

This was a private conversation, and one I shouldn't be listening to. But there was nothing I could do but wait.

"To…think I was special."

"Those are normal things to want," the doctor said softly. "There is no shame in that."

"Yeah, there is," Jeffrey's voice wavered. "Because she never gave me any of them."

"But Blair did," she murmured.

"Yeah," I could hear the tears in his voice, but knew already none would come. Jeffrey didn't cry, even when his body wanted him to. Even when his body shook and shook and shook. Like it had been trained out of him. "Blair became my little brother. I did everything for him. My entire life revolved around trying to keep him out of harms way—or…or cheering him up after another fight with Lydia. He *needed* me. And we survived her together." He sounded hoarse. Quiet. "But now she's gone—and we're here and I—"

"You're afraid that if *you* are the one that needs help, you'll no longer be of use."

"Right." Jeffrey's voice was choked. "Can we…please just…can we just—"

"Why don't you tell me about your dog?" the doctor asked, and I sagged in relief, grateful she'd stopped pressing so hard at a wound he so obviously still had. My thoughts continued to spin, my tail still.

"I think my dog is really a wolf," Jeffrey managed.

I jolted, alarmed. My ears flattened, then perked back up so I could hear better, my own heart pounding. *Had he already figured me out? Fuck. Was this a good thing? A bad thing? I didn't know.*

"Interesting."

"But…" Jeffrey trailed off. "A small part of me is worried that I can't trust myself, that I'm just being paranoid."

"Do you often suffer from paranoia?"

"Yeah," Jeffrey's voice was tight again.

"Would you mind sharing some examples?"

"I don't…know." Jeffrey sounded ashamed, and I hated it.

"I think you do know," her voice was gentle. "There's no need to be embarrassed. This is a safe space, and none of this is going to leave the room. I'm here to help you, not judge you."

"I know," Jeffrey snorted out a laugh.

"I'm not your enemy here."

"I…know." That was more reluctant. "It's just…I'm not used to admitting any of this. I try not to think about it."

"Maybe that's part of the problem." Her voice was still gentle—which I was realizing was important. Jeffrey was a cornered animal, his hackles raised, and she was approaching with her hands out—surrender already evident. It was the only way to get him to relax. "Acknowledging what's going on is half the battle, sometimes even more than that."

"Oh." Jeffrey sucked in another ragged breath. "I…"

"Take your time."

"Easy for you to say," Jeffrey joked. "You're not the one that has to get brain-fucked for an hour then figure out how to survive after."

"Is that how this feels for you?"

"I…guess." Jeffrey obviously hadn't meant to admit that. "Fuck." He sucked in another breath, obviously gathering strength. My tail wagged, pride thrumming in my body. My smart, resilient, wonderful Jeffrey. *Brave. Brave. Brave.* "Okay. I…feel like people are following me."

Guilt churned in my stomach.

Because I was most definitely the person that had been following him.

I only left his side to interact with my brothers and the pack we were setting up an alliance with. Other than that, whether I was in humanskin or wolfskin, I was always beside him. Even if he didn't know it.

I figured we didn't have much time. And I'd spend all I could with him, protecting him.

I'd *promised.*

"Is that a constant feeling for you?" she clarified.

"Yeah," Jeffrey sighed, sounding exhausted. "It never turns off."

"What about at home?"

"That's the only place I feel somewhat safe."

"Why do you think that is?"

"I…" Jeffrey sighed, struggling for a minute to find his words again. It was odd. Over the last couple months, spanning both before and after we'd officially met, I'd noticed he had a silver tongue. He always knew exactly what to say—and how to say it to get the desired result. This stilted, awkward conversation was completely out of character.

Or at least…I'd thought it was.

Now I was starting to wonder if the smooth-talking, flirty version of my mate was the fake one. He certainly lied more.

"I guess it's because it's mine?" Jeffrey's voice was quiet. "And I've put locks up and shit, you know, to keep myself safe."

"Locks?"

"Bolt locks."

"Right." There were a few scratching sounds that I figured were probably a pen on paper.

"And you feel like your paranoia is affecting how you feel about your dog?" Doctor Mason cycled back. Jeffrey made an affirmative noise. "Perhaps…this is an opportunity for you to practice trust."

"I…"

"Sometimes a dog is just a dog, Jeffrey," the doctor continued, voice gentle. "Sometimes we feel eyes on us, not because we're being chased or stalked but because as humans it is natural to simply attract attention. You've mentioned that your looks have often affected how you are perceived. That you receive more attention than you are comfortable with because of them. Perhaps the eyes you feel are because of that. I know that is hard to believe because of your background and the fear that has been instilled inside you from a young age."

Because of Lydia.

"But this could be an opportunity for you to let loose a little. Let go of those reins you've had to hold on so tightly to."

Jeffrey was silent for a few minutes. A couple passed by the truck, and I barked at them to scare them off, their chatter interrupting my eavesdropping. I wasn't supposed to be listening in. But now that I'd heard what I had—there was no going back.

I might as well commit.

The couple scurried off, eyeing me warily as I settled down and Jeffrey started talking again.

"Maybe you're right," Jeffrey finally said, his voice quiet, contemplative—still turbulent, but softer somehow. "I…" he sucked in another breath. There had been a lot of that today, and I was starting to realize it was a tell of his. When he was frustrated, scared, or uncomfortable, he could hardly get a full breath in. His beautiful lungs grew too tight. "I've had a hard time breaking those habits. They're what kept me alive."

Kept him alive?

What the fuck?

"Then try this," Doctor Mason said gently. "Let loose a *little*. Do one thing you wouldn't normally do, simply because it makes you happy. It might do you some good."

"Okay," Jeffrey sighed, but even I could tell some of the tension in his voice was gone.

Relief filled my body.

Relief that I'd somehow…maybe gotten away with my accidental espionage. I didn't want him to know. Not after this. If he had such a hard time trusting, I didn't want him to find out that I'd deceived him.

Maybe I could keep this up till the day I left?

Or maybe after a few more weeks, I could get him to become sick of me to the point that he'd not miss me if I disappeared. Though…I didn't see that plan going well. I'd have to do something truly nefarious—like eat all his underwear.

That thought was not…unappealing.

My cock twitched.

"How are you sleeping?" Doctor Mason asked, gently segueing into a new line of conversation before the silence could get awkward.

"I'm not," Jeffrey admitted, and it was easier this time.

Last night he'd had a nightmare.

I'd woken him, pushing my nose against his face till he stopped whimpering. He'd been drenched in sweat. So much sweat that his t-shirt clung to him and the mattress. For a second he'd stared at me and his scent had been scared-hurt-help-help. But then he'd recognized me, and the wild look in his eyes faded away. His long fingers had tangled in the fur at my throat and he'd *sagged*, as a broken sort of gasp escaped from him.

Easily, as if he'd done it a thousand times before, he pulled his sweaty shirt up and over his head and tossed it across the room.

"S-sorry," he'd managed, like his nightmare had inconvenienced *me*. I'd licked his face till he laughed, and he curled up in a miserable sweaty ball. "Guarding me even when I'm asleep, huh?" he'd asked, and it felt like a loaded question.

That morning Jeffrey peeled the sweaty sheets off the mattress, and I'd nearly balked when I saw just how stained the mattress was beneath its covers. A physical representation of the long, sleepless nights he often battled. The scent of fear sweat wafted through the air as Jeffrey calmly deposited his sheets in the clothes-washing machine and pulled a new set from the closet. It was full of sheets. All fresh, but mildly scented with fear. Like he'd had to buy so many of them because sometimes he'd have to replace them more than once throughout the night.

Though eavesdropping on this conversation was wildly invasive—even if I hadn't had a choice—I was grateful as it gave me the opportunity to learn what I needed to help him.

I'd never been the best with people—I preferred four paws to two legs, and conversation had never come easy, even when I'd tried my hardest.

As I'd aged and began fearing the moon, *that* had only gotten worse.

I'd spoken more to Jeffrey the two times we'd met in my humanskin than I had—probably since I was born, and that was the truth. Which meant I wasn't necessarily the best at understanding how I could help him, especially if words and communication were what he needed. I'd simply have to learn.

Simply protecting him, my ass.

This was going to tear me apart, and I knew it.

But more than that…I knew that getting close to Jeffrey and then leaving him would hurt him even worse. But I couldn't seem to stop. Not when he was so sweet and he reeked of need-alpha-hurt-please.

I couldn't leave him.

I needed to help him.

I wanted to help him.

I wanted *him*.

"Having a dog helps with sleeping," Jeffrey admitted, voice ashamed as he broke through my turbulent thoughts. "And sex does too."

"Did you have sex?" the doctor sounded surprised. "The last time we spoke you mentioned you were having a hard time initiating intimacy, despite it being a big part of your past."

"My man-whore days are over, yeah. Hard to feel sexy when you don't… feel sexy," Jeffrey grunted, voice bitter. "But yeah, I did. Have sex, I mean. A couple weeks ago."

Me.

He had sex with me.

I helped him.

Pride buzzed through my veins. Inappropriate yes, but brilliant all the same. The hunger that ached inside me roared to the surface. I had provided for him. Had provided comfort and release. He had struggled with sleeping and sex, and I had managed to help with both.

"What changed?" the doctor asked, keeping her voice calm.

Surprisingly, it took hardly any prompting at all to get Jeffrey talking this time. About me. *About me!* My heart thudded and my tail thumped happily against the car seat as my ears perked up and I cocked my head to the side.

Tell me, pretty one.

Tell me what I did so that I can repeat it.

Tell me how to help you.

"He was a dude," Jeffrey laughed, and his surprise was apparent. "A really…big dude."

"Was this your first time with a man?"

"Yes." Jeffrey laughed again, and this time it was lighter. "It's weird…I mean, I never thought I'd be interested in that? But he…"

"But he?"

"I dunno. I guess he was special."

"Are you going to seek him out again?" Doctor Mason's voice was warm. "You're smiling. That's the first time you've smiled since you walked in here."

"I am?" Jeffrey startled. "I mean. Yeah. I am. Smiling. I uh—I dunno. It feels weird to do that. He hasn't approached me—at least not in a way I can like…reciprocate? It was just a one-night stand at first. But then he bought me dinner and I…guess maybe…it could be more? He's a werewolf." Jeffrey laughed, like that was the weirdest part of all of this.

"We're not even the same species."

It wasn't fair.

Not for him, or me.

If he had been born a wolf, there would've been no room for this insecurity. Through my scent, my heartbeat, my actions—the very bond that tied us as fated mates, he would've known immediately how important he was.

If he had been born a wolf, I could choose him. He could mate with me and keep me from going feral. But he wasn't—and he couldn't.

Fate had turned its back on the both of us.

"Do you want it to be more?" the doctor asked, and my heart pounded as I waited to hear his answer.

"I don't know if I'm ready for more."

"But do you want it?"

"I…" Jeffrey sucked in another breath, and my tail beat a happy *thwap* against the car seat. "I think I do?" He laughed again, and this one was more brittle. "Lydia would hate it."

"Lydia hated a lot of things."

I hated her. I hated her. I hated her.

A blinding, wicked hate that made my skin burn beneath the surface of my fur. Made my teeth snarl, and my head fill with visions of blood. I hated her, because I may be dumb—but even I could connect the dots. Even I could see what effect she'd had on my pretty, perfect mate. Jeffrey's voice was small and shaky—childlike almost.

"I guess I'm just trying to figure out who I am without her pulling my strings."

"She's had a big influence on you."

"Yeah, no shit." Jeffrey snorted. "Sorry. *Sorry.* Didn't mean to be rude. That's just…yeah. Yeah. She has."

"And you miss her."

"I…don't know if I miss her so much as I miss knowing what to expect. She was predictable. At least…until the end. I knew what she wanted from me, and who she wanted me to be. It was hard at first, but over time it got easier to be the Jeffrey she wanted."

"And not Markus."

"I stopped being Markus the day she faked my death," Jeffrey answered easily. Somehow that sounded less painful than his other truths. Like this was something he'd come to terms with a long time ago. My thoughts spun. Like seeds in the dirt, the truth of what I'd learned began to bud. "I don't even…I don't even know who "he" is anymore."

"He, as in Markus. You view him as a separate entity."

"He is. Was. I am." Jeffrey obviously tried to backtrack, but failed. "I just… Behind the person I built to survive Lydia I don't really know… who or what I am anymore. The only part of me that ever felt good or real, was the part of me that was Blair's big brother. But even he doesn't need me anymore."

My heart ached for him.

"When you had sex," the doctor started, "did you feel as unsure as you do now?"

Jeffrey was silent once again.

Silent for so long I wasn't certain he'd answer her at all.

"No," his voice shook. "That was the first…first time in a long time where I just felt like…me?"

"Were you paranoid?"

"No."

"And you were present, in the moment."

"Yes." Jeffrey's voice was soft as hummingbird's wings. "I felt…real."

"You felt real," she repeated. "That's good. That's very good."

He felt real.

He felt real.

He felt real.

Did that mean he often didn't?

The thought saddened me. Especially because, to me, he'd felt larger than life since the first moment I met him. He was real in a way nothing ever had been.

The hunger I'd felt for him all these weeks suddenly softened. From lust, it morphed into the need to see him whole. To see him happy. To soothe him, to love him, to protect him till the day I couldn't anymore.

"Did the date make you happy?" she asked in a gentle voice. "Does your dog make you happy?"

"Yes," Jeffrey replied immediately.

"I think…you haven't devoted enough of your new life to discovering the things that make you who you are," she said. "You need to spend time pursuing the things that make you feel happy. I'm not saying, go out and have a bunch of riotous sex—but I do think you should take some time to really figure out who you are, and self-discovery is a big part of that."

"Okay," Jeffrey sucked in one last, broken breath.

"I also urge you to do your best to rely on someone else this week. Even if it's just something simple and small. Try to let yourself go a little. Test your own boundaries. You might like the man you discover you are. And the people you love might surprise you."

"Right," Jeffrey laughed, letting out the breath he held in a quiet swoosh. "Rely on someone. Ha. Okay."

"*Try*," she said softly. "And if you don't, we'll try again later."

"Okay."

When Jeffrey left the building, his hair was a floppy, sweaty mess. It stuck out all over, like he'd been running his hands through it the entire time he was inside. He grinned and waved, flashing a flirty wink at the people he passed on his way to the car, shining brighter than the sun above.

Even from a distance, he smelled like other people and Lysol. His hands had the acrid scent of hand sanitizer clinging to them as he pulled open the driver's side door and slid into his seat.

As soon as the door shut, Jeffrey leaned his forehead against the steering wheel, his hands flexing. He gripped it tight enough the leather squeaked, and then he just...*sagged*. Like all the energy in his body had been completely drained.

He reminded me of a deer I'd found in the woods last spring. She'd been shot in the leg and limping—for God knows how long. I'd caught her scent combined with copper-blood from a mile away and chased her down. It took a good hour to find her, as she had kept moving, and by the time I finally did, I'd expected to find a corpse.

But I didn't.

Instead, I watched as the deer continued to limp. She was in a meadow, dappled wildflowers crushed beneath her unsteady gait. She pushed through the woods and the pain, moving forward, away, away, away from the danger that had hurt her, even though there was no way she could survive her wounds on her own.

Resilient.

Stubborn.

She collapsed as I approached, and I shifted to my humanskin so that I could bring her home where I could get her help. As I'd carried her through the forest, past my favorite set of boulders and the main hall where my concrete prison sat beneath the dirt—I'd prayed to the moon mother to give her strength.

She survived.

Somehow.

And that was how I knew Jeffrey would too.

Jeffrey was limping and injured. He'd been hurt badly. He was bleeding from a wound I couldn't see. But the drive to survive still flickered in his eyes. Like the deer, he pushed forward—bleeding but stubborn.

Stubborn, pretty man.

Perfect, perfect, perfect.

For a second, I didn't know what to do.

Didn't know if he needed space or if I should approach like I had with the deer, careful and quiet, and gentle. Like I had that night that I'd found him in the alley, wounded and lost, his eyes full of demons.

I knew he couldn't smell my scent, but I exuded as much strength-love-calm as I could anyway, an alpha rumble bubbling up inside my chest to soothe him.

His scent was sad-lonely-tired.

He was shaking again, minute little tremors. His knuckles had healed, though for weeks the skin had been broken and brittle.

I wished the doctor had asked about them. I hadn't known how to—but I desperately wanted to understand why a man like him, all sunshine, would hurt himself. Did new pain distract him from the wound that wouldn't heal?

I wished I was in my humanskin, because while the question was invasive and would more than likely be awkward coming from me and my disjointed communication—I still wanted to understand.

To know him.

To love him as he was, broken bits and all.

I hope I get this right.

Taking a leap of faith, I crossed the seat, my paws digging into the fabric, and pressed my head against Jeffrey's bowed shoulder. He sucked in another quaking breath and the action was somehow more devastating up close. I could hear his lungs wheeze. Hear the stutter of his throat, see the tremor in his body, like he was barely holding himself together, even now.

I woofed softly.

Jeffrey's head tipped to the side, one lovely brown eye peeping at me as he held incredibly still. There was no trace of tears on his speckled cheeks, but that didn't make the way he shook any less devastating.

"You want a cheeseburger?" he asked, voice wobbling. "You look like the kinda guy who needs a cheeseburger." I huffed in amusement, tongue lapping at his cheek till he ducked away with a startled squawk and pushed me off.

We got cheeseburgers.

Cheeseburgers were officially my favorite food.

Jeffrey ate his while he drove, blasting music as loud as he could. He tore the wrapper off mine for me, then left it on the seat for grease to seep into the fabric. Yelling along to the music, he tapped his fingers on the wheel, shoving food into his mouth as he sang about love, and loss, and things I couldn't understand but wanted to—because he clearly did.

His voice was like magic.

A warm bath, twinkling and soft.

Melodic and sweet as honeysuckle.

I listened, enraptured.

And by the time we returned to the apartment together I came to the conclusion that Jeffrey was the strongest person I'd ever met. I had a feeling the more I learned about him, the fiercer my feelings of admiration would grow.

Hunger for him burned beneath my skin as he walked up to the steps to the apartment, his ass muscular and bouncy—and right in my face. An ass I'd *touched*. Been inside of. I knew how velvety slick it was and I wanted *in* again, so very badly. It had been too long. Too fucking long.

I'd never resented my wolfskin before, but these last few weeks had been agony. To see and not touch. To not hold him the way I'd grown to crave.

I whined, unable to help myself as I pressed my snout between the round globes the second he paused to put his key in the lock. His sweet, lovely musk filled my nose and my tail began to wave as I inhaled.

"Hey!" Jeffrey laughed, startling a little as I growled against him. I couldn't help it. I didn't even mean to do it in the first place—he was just…right there. And he smelled so good. And I wanted *inside* where he was slick-hot-pink so damn badly. "*No*. Bad boy." Jeffrey tried to wag his ass away from my face but I chased him greedily. "No!" He laughed, batting at my head—though not hard enough to hurt—as he got the front door open. I let him go—but it was hard. So was my cock as I followed Jeffrey and his delicious ass down the hallway, all the while muttering under his breath about "dogs being disgusting."

He had bowed legs.

Perfectly spaced so that there was room for his alpha between them.

Later that night, Jeffrey caught me rolling around in his underwear.

I hadn't even done it to push him.

It'd just been sitting in his laundry basket. And the idea had gotten into my head earlier—and god. Fuck. He smelled like heaven. Like oranges and happy and *mate-mate-mate*. And his boxers somehow smelled even stronger—more concentrated, the mix of sweat with his natural man-musk sending me floating.

I'd told myself I'd only sniff the first ones.

He won't even know.

Jeffrey was in the bathroom showering off the day's funk. That's what he'd called it. His delicious, musky scent—"funk." And he was about to cover it up with some awful artificial soap scent. I hated it.

I'd have to figure out how to introduce him to scentless soap. The kind that wouldn't cover up his natural scent.

I pressed my face against the fabric, huffing greedily, my cock perking up immediately. My wolf itched beneath my skin, a feeling of rightness buzzing through my body, warm and fuzzy and lovely-lovely as I stuck my tongue out and—yes. Oh fuck. I lapped at the fabric, soaking it in spit as I tried to taste him through it.

I sucked at it till his flavor disappeared.

I couldn't stop my tail from wagging.

It thwacked against the bed as I dug around for more. Because while I'd promised myself only one pair…I…yeah. I had very little self-control when it came to Jeffrey. Just one more, I promised myself. Just one, Mutt. And then you'll be done before he can catch you.

This was wrong, even I knew that.

And that somehow only made me need it more. Made my fur puff up and my cock threaten to spill from its sheath.

Just one—I promised, sucking the second pair of boxers into my mouth, a needy growl escaping as my tail *thump, thumped.*

And thennnnn, I discovered another pair of boxers hidden within the pile beneath that one. And then another. And then another. And then another—and then, because I was horny and needy and fuck-fuck-fuck, I decided enough was enough. And I dumped the basket entirely.

Jeffrey, Jeffrey—

Mate-mate-mate.

My cock ached, my head full of thoughts of creamy freckle-covered skin. Of his smile—the quake of his shoulders. The way he looked at me with those dark, needy eyes. My cock slid from its sheath, achingly hard as I gave up all pretense and started rubbing my scent all over the dirty clothing till Jeffrey became Jeffrey-Mutt and my wolf preened happily beneath my skin. Our combined musk was even better. It was *right*. My cock jerked when it pushed against the pile of fabric. I growled softly, the friction sending my head spinning.

In my defense…I hadn't actually meant to fuck the pile of clothes.

I just…got carried away?

Thoughts left the building, the parts of me that were human slipping away as I jerked my hips again, then again, then again. The friction was good but not enough—not enough, not enough. *I need more. More taste, more smell—more Jeffrey.* I sucked one of the new pairs of boxers into my mouth till the fabric grew foamy wet, tongue laving over the fabric, my body buzzing with need.

So close—just a little—

Just a—

That was, of course, when Jeffrey walked in.

He'd taken one look at me rutting into his dirty laundry, with his boxers in my mouth, and immediately started laughing his ass off. That was fair. I wasn't sure how I'd gotten into this mess, but I was glad he found it funny, rather than disturbing.

Perfect mate.

So sweet.

So kind.

Stop calling him that—stop.

It hurts, it hurts, it hurts.

"Dude!" Jeffrey gasped out, amused and horrified in equal turn. His scent was happy-confused-shocked. "*Gross!*" His hands moved to his hips as he huffed down at me. But my gaze snapped to his very naked, very spotted chest, and I was…*fuck*. Couldn't stop my hips from moving.

This was what I'd needed.

Just looking at him was enough.

Hungry, hungry, hungry.

"Fuck, I don't even know what to do with this." Jeffrey pinched the bridge of his nose as I panted up at him, unable to help myself. God, his scent was even better like this—with only a towel to cover it.

I so badly wanted to cross the room and tear the towel off. To snuffle and lick where he was soapy clean and soft. Would've been better if he was still sweaty. If his musk had been stronger—but this was good too.

So good.

So so so good.

So—

Uh.

Fuck.

Fuck, that felt so good.

I whined, and Jeffrey shook his head, still horrified-amused.

"I'm going to leave," he said simply, talking to me like he expected me to understand. "And when I come back, you're not going to be doing… whatever it is you're doing right now."

My tail wagged, ears flattened, and Jeffrey nodded to himself.

"Yeah. Okay." He stumbled back, and my gaze snapped to his long muscular legs. Then back to his torso, because the scars that littered it were beautiful. Wolves didn't have scars. We healed far too quickly for that. They were as foreign as his culture was. "No more…whatever this is. Okay?"

I woofed in ascent, and Jeffrey shook his head again, laughing to himself. "What the fuck? You give a dog a cheeseburger, and he thinks he owns the place."

I *did* own him.

But I didn't say that.

I couldn't.

Because I couldn't keep him.

You can't, you can't, you can't.

I had never hated being an alpha more than I did in that moment.

Because Dad was right.

He told me the hunger would eat me alive, and I was going to let it.

Chapter Seven

Jeffrey

"I'M STARTING TO think you're stalking me." My voice was a little hoarse, as I'd just finished my fifteen-minute set at the club in Ridgefield. It was open mic night again. Though I'd been attending religiously, tonight was my first time actually performing.

It felt weird to see Mutt in his humanskin. But right too. He looked guilty, curled in on himself like he hadn't meant to get caught—a naughty puppy—and my heart did a weird flip-flop thing in my chest.

As much as I liked his furry form—and I did—there was just something about all that muscle and those damn blue eyes that made me weak.

"Did you think I wouldn't notice?" I asked, voice low and soft. Unable to help myself, I took him in. All six-foot-six of his gorgeous, wide form. He filled out his height in a lovely way, all long thick thighs, broad shoulders, and full pecs.

I'd never seen anything like Mutt's chest—and though it was new and foreign, it was exciting too. Everything about him was exciting. I'd played our nights we'd spent together with him in this form over and over in my head—convinced I had made up the raw chemistry that buzzed electric between us.

But…I hadn't.

Because all it took was one glance across the dance floor during my set tonight for my cock to perk up and all the hair on my body to stand on end. Like Mutt's heady gaze had a direct connection to my nerve endings, and just looking him in the eyes was enough to make heat pool low in my belly.

Still though, the fact that Mutt was here was more than a little… obvious, right?

I'd only been partially joking about the stalking thing—but his reaction had solidified the truth.

He really was following me. In dog form. In human form. All the fucking time.

You will be safe.

Mutt took his promise pretty fucking seriously. Almost obsessively so.

That should've freaked me out.

But it didn't.

I knew what it felt like when someone was going to hurt me. I'd been manipulated enough times that I could recognize the signs. And Mutt had…none of those. I didn't think he had a single manipulative bone in his entire body. That was part of what attracted me to him in the first place.

Mutt was a good person. Not very sneaky, but a good person all the same.

I could tell he felt bad about lying to me, and that made all the difference.

In fact, right now, he looked like he was two seconds from bolting.

And I didn't want him to.

"You…" I reached out, looping my fingers around his wrist. My guitar hung loose in my other hand, easy as though it was a second limb. "Did you like the music?" I hadn't meant to ask that. I'd meant to ask him if he wanted to come home with me. Because that first time had been fire—and the second had felt like a balm on my weary soul. And I'd had a month of his fur, but not his dick, and I was kinda starved by this point—not that he knew that.

He made me feel like…me?

Not like Markus Prince. Not like Jeffrey Evans—Lydia's heir. But like *me*…the messed up mish-mash of a man who hadn't had solid footing since the day he sold his soul to the devil and traded his training wheels for a gun.

"I loved the music," Mutt blurted immediately, and his voice was so *loud* and jerky with excitement I couldn't help but believe him. "Your music. You. Your—voice. You are just! Wow!" He didn't have his ears and tail out—which was probably wise, as Ridgefield was not a sanctuary like Elmwood was. I kinda missed them, if I was being honest.

"Thank you." I flushed, heart thumping. And then because I missed his voice, and kinda desperately needed him to keep talking, I asked, "What was your favorite song?"

"All of them," Mutt blurted immediately again, blue eyes bright. "You are an *angel*."

I balked, shifting awkwardly and dropping my hold on his wrist. "I dunno about that."

You're my angel, Jeffrey.

My precious little boy.

You're so good for your mommy, aren't you?

You love me so much.

You'll do what I ask of you, won't you? You won't embarrass me.

"No." Mutt grabbed my face.

I jolted, jerking out of my thoughts with a gasp like I'd just been dragged out of deep water.

"No sadness," he commanded, his palm big and scratchy and warm.

"O-okay," I managed, though weirdly enough…his words worked. It was a direct approach, yeah. But it was hard to be sad when a huge sexy man was grabbing you and demanding you be happy about it. "Yeah."

"You do not like the word *angel*," he said simply, like it was that easy.

"I don't."

"What else?"

"I don't like compliments in general," I admitted, my skin crawling. Mutt nodded, though he didn't release me. He looked like his brain was breaking though, like he physically could not comprehend a world where he was not whispering sweet nothings—or in his case, sometimes *yelling* them—my way.

Maybe it was that honesty that made it different.

I wasn't sure.

Or maybe it was just him?

"It's fine though," I said, surprised to find that I meant it. "If you do it. It's fine."

For the same reason sex with him felt natural and good, when it didn't with anyone else anymore.

He was just…different.

Simple as that.

Mutt nodded, relaxing. His eyes danced and he leaned down, the hand on my face sliding low to gently cup my throat. He pressed into my personal space, his nose brushing mine. "If you were stuck in a tower I would save you," he said softly. "I would hear your voice, and I would chase it, no matter how far away you were. *That* is how beautiful it is."

My music had been my only source of true joy for as long as I could remember.

And his words meant…well, a lot to me.

A lot.

I swallowed the lump in my throat. "How romantic," I teased, though I kinda meant it.

"I *am* romantic," Mutt proudly proclaimed. "I am romantic for you. Because you are so very precious. The most precious. The smartest, most lovely man in the whole world."

"Yeah, okay." I waved him off, ducking away from his hand even though that was the last thing I wanted to do. "How about a drink, Casanova?"

"My name is not Casanova," Mutt followed after me excitedly like I'd offered him my left kidney, not a shitty cocktail at a shittier bar. "It is Mutt."

"I know, baby," I snorted out a laugh, signaling the bartender with a grin and a head nod. I'd been here a couple times now, and he was starting to recognize me.

"I am not an infant," Mutt huffed as he slid into the seat beside me. He kicked a leg out, hooking his foot between my legs and pulling on the stool. An awful screech sound filled the half-empty bar as Mutt yanked me close enough the heat of our thighs bled together.

"Believe me, handsome," I hummed, shivering as he stared down at me, his brow scrunched. "I know."

The bartender winked at me as I leaned my guitar against my thigh, making sure it was secure. Mutt stared at it like it had personally offended him. Like he was the only thing that should be allowed to touch my thighs.

Fuck.

That was hot.

"The usual?" Bartender asked, his eyes dancing. His name tag read John. I made a point to remember it later.

"Yeah. Mocktail for me," I shrugged with a grin. "I dunno what he's having, but you better make it strong."

"I like strong," Mutt stared at my biceps.

"Me too," I agreed, licking my lips as I looked him over again. "A lot. Apparently."

When we got our drinks I spent way too long teasing Mutt by tying my cherry stem in knots. He chugged his whiskey in two long gulps, and I tried not to find that hot. Even though everything about him kinda was.

Thinking a dude was attractive was new to me—but it didn't bother me. It was just another thing I hadn't allowed myself to explore when I'd been living under Lydia's roof. I had no doubt Blair would freak out when I told him I was maybe, probably bisexual.

He'd probably throw me a party—with confetti canons or some shit.

The girl that was up for her set was singing a little too loud—and slightly off key—and Mutt kept flinching, but he didn't seem to notice he was doing it. So I decided to distract him. His gaze was trained on my lips, and when I stuck my tongue out and he saw the twisted stem that sat there taunting him, he whined, *low*.

The sound sent a shiver up my spine and heat pooling between my legs.

That was not the kind of sound a man made. It was animalistic, and needy—and primal.

"I want you to do that to my dick," Mutt said immediately. The bartender choked—as he'd been walking right by us when Mutt spoke—and then he strode twice as fast to get away. My heart fluttered and my cheeks flushed—but not because I was embarrassed. Mutt was just…yeah.

He was cute.

Dopey cute.

Unlike anyone I'd ever met.

I laughed. "That's the point, dude," I hummed, winking at him. "Why the fuck do you think I keep doing it?"

It felt weird…this *confidence.*

Not manufactured like it usually was—or a front, hiding what was beneath it. But *genuine.*

"That is very naughty." Mutt stared at my mouth, eyes wide.

I tied another stem. When I stuck my tongue out and waggled my eyebrows, heat burning beneath my skin, Mutt had to discreetly adjust himself. Well…discrete is a stretch. He full on—very obviously—placed that gorgeous as fuck, *massive* hand on his dick and squeezed—right out in the open where anybody could see.

And with the way he was looking at me—like he wanted to bend me over the bar and stick his cock up my ass—there was no denying who exactly had caused him to act so lewdly.

That was when I broke.

I was only human, after all.

And while I was still dealing with all the new shit in my life—including the fuckload of info my therapist had given me, and my were-dog—my dick still knew exactly what it wanted.

I was supposed to be trying new things, right? Things that made me happy. And while the dildo I'd received in the mail that morning was *intriguing*—and I fully intended to use it when Mutt-the-dog wasn't around—there was nothing quite like the real thing.

I'd never thought I'd be the kinda guy who thirsted after a throbbing, warm cock. Who thought about foreskin and imagined licking beneath it. Who wanted to twist and suck and slurp. Who wanted to be forced onto his knees and fucked raw.

But…

Apparently I was.

And sex with a real person was way better than masturbation.

At least…if tonight ended up half as good as the last time, who cared if my one-night stand became more than that?

My dick definitely didn't.

Didn't mean I had to be ready for a relationship, right? Or ready to face the fact that I didn't deserve a guy like Mutt. A guy who was pure, and honest. Who wore his emotions on his face as plainly as if they'd been written in Sharpie.

I was turbulent lies, dark twisting vines, and thorns.

But…I could still have sex. It wasn't like I'd hurt him either—so my past didn't matter. At least, not here. Not now. When the only thing I could think about was touching his cock and seeing if it felt as soft as it looked.

I licked my lips, dragging my gaze over Mutt's body. Across his broad shoulders, his biceps and the way they bulged with muscle, the hair that decorated his forearms, down to the hand that held his cock captive behind denim. He looked uncomfortable in clothes—like they didn't fit quite right, even though they did.

I could feel eyes on me—but now that I knew they were Mutt's I was able to force away the paranoia.

When I flicked my gaze up to his face, I groaned, unable to help myself. His nostrils were flaring, like he was scenting me and fuck…his eyes were black with lust. Fangs had popped out, filling his mouth like he was so turned on he hadn't been able to control his shift fully.

"Hey, Mutt?" I asked, voice low. "How would you like your dick sucked?"

Imaginations were great but reality was trickier.

By the time we arrived at my apartment—I'd given Mutt a ride in my truck—he'd sniffed me about a hundred times, his face shoved against my neck at every red light like he couldn't get enough of it.

Sex was on the horizon, and I knew that.

My dick did too—and it was happy as fuck, lemme tell you that much.

I didn't feel the trepidation I had earlier when I'd tried to go out and get laid. This was…smooth sailing. I, oddly enough, didn't have walls up with Mutt around. Even though I liked him, a lot. So you'd think I'd have more—on account of wanting him to like me back.

He was just…immune, I guess? To walls.

Maybe it was his honesty. The way he usually didn't lie to me. The way he was sweet and dopey—and so open with his affection that I never needed to guess if he liked me or not.

At first, I worried that when we got inside my apartment that I'd have to pretend to be surprised my dog was gone, but Mutt didn't ask—so I didn't say anything either.

"I'm gonna shower," I blurted, instead of going for his belt buckle as soon as we pushed through the front door like I'd planned.

I hated feeling the cling of sweat after a long day and sometimes I needed the heat to reset my mind. Plus, if I was going to ask him to put his fingers up my ass again, I kinda wanted to be squeaky clean.

"Do not use soap. I do not like soap," Mutt said happily, his tail thumping against the door as he crowded behind me. His breath tickled the back of my neck. I shivered as he leaned down, nosing at the fuzzy hair at my nape.

"I kinda need to use soap." My brow scrunched—but I was distracted.

Especially when he parted his lips and started mouthing at the skin he'd been nuzzling. I shuddered. My neck had always been one of the most sensitive parts of my body. In high school, when I'd fuck my way through parties, all it would take was a single kiss at my throat and I'd be hard enough to fuck for hours.

This was no different.

Maybe it was even better? Because I could feel the prickle of Mutt's stubble rubbing against my skin and fuuuuck, that was nice. Different, but nice.

"No soap." Mutt huffed against the back of my neck. The hot tickle of his breath made my knees weak. "I will buy you new soap. Better soap."

Why were we talking about soap?

Also, his dick was pressing into me. Perky and hard, pushing obscenely through the fabric of his jeans and against my lower back. He kept doing these little forward rolls of his hips, rubbing it against me—almost like he didn't realize what he was doing.

Hell, knowing Mutt, he probably didn't.

Probably just wanted to fuck me so bad he couldn't control it.

Oh god, that's sexy.

Fuck, fuck, fuck.

"Um."

Get in the shower so you can get on that dick ASAP. The fuck are you waiting around for?

"It will be okay. You will see." Mutt grinned at me. He stayed pressed to the front door, watching me as I shuffled down the hallway in a daze, pretty sure I must've fallen and hit my head when I was restocking the magic books Avery had gotten in earlier that day.

His dick was a hard line in his pants, staring at me as it lay long and thick and trapped against his thigh.

Would he have a knot?

Fuck.

I should've researched that before inviting him over.

I knew werewolves were real.

Of course they were.

This was just…my first time trying to seduce one. When we'd hooked up the first time, I hadn't even gotten to see his dick—at least, not much of it. Sure, I'd seen the rosy pink head, and the fact he was uncut. But that was hardly enough. And also…*huh.* That was fucking unfair actually—when I thought about it. He'd been all up on my grill, shoving his fingers in me, and his mouth had been *everywhere* all at once—and I'd barely even gotten a peep show.

Never mind the fact I'd told him at the time that I wasn't ready for that.

Because now I was. Very ready, I mean.

And now my thoughts were spinning back to knots.

Like…how would that *feel*? And what would one look like? And did all male wolves have them, or just alphas? And how big did they get—and did it hurt when they pushed in? And how long did they last—would it pulse? Would it force me open wide? Would it burn and ache, and make me sob into the mattress?

Would I feel *full*?

Too full…or…just right?

Fuck.

I didn't have anyone to ask. Blair had only been with a vampire. And it wasn't like I could ask Avery. I doubted there was a book about how to bang shifters in the shop—and even if there was, Avery was my *boss*. Asking him about wolf penises would be totally inappropriate. Fucking sucked that my background didn't help in this situation either.

Every weekend for sixteen years, Lydia had forced her twisted teachings down my throat. She'd tortured me in the way only she knew how. Taught me how to kill, to stab, to maim where it counted. Made me read libraries worth of information about creatures she expected me to know how to murder—and yet…

I *still* had no idea whether or not I was about to touch a knot.

Though I suppose Lydia wasn't entirely to blame. At least not for this.

Werewolves were private people—and didn't write about their dicks.

They had always been tight-knit creatures. Their secrets were kept close. There were records of the basics, sure. Shape-shifting. Three possible forms. The clusters of communities that lived off-grid. The eye colors that showed rank. Blue for alphas, purple for omegas, gold for betas. Their main weaknesses were silver and wolfsbane—and fire.

I knew all of this.

Buuuut, that was about it.

That was as far as Lydia's mentorship had gotten me. Apparently, even with all of the Evans's years of monster hunting they'd never managed to gather more than a few sparse details. Maybe because—and I realized this belatedly—a lot of the werewolf population apparently preferred to live their lives as large fluffy were-dogs.

As I pushed into the bathroom and stripped off my clothes quickly, I lamented my life.

You'd think the fact that I was born in Elmwood would've helped things, considering it was supernatural central for the Northeast. But it hadn't. Probably because I had been a snot-nosed brat who had no business asking about genitals.

When our parents had broken the secret to us, I'd been the only kid who freaked the fuck out. Everyone just took it in stride. Vampires? Oh yeah, those bad boys were real. Werewolves too. Ghosts. Witches. Demons. All the creepy little things that kept nine-year-old me up at night were apparently hiding in plain sight.

I'd avoided them as covertly as I could.

Until I couldn't anymore.

Until Lydia's training forced the monsters under the bed in front of my bullets.

Swallowing the lump in my throat, I pushed away the memories as I pulled the shower door shut behind me and turned the water as hot as it would go. Naked and vulnerable, my skin crawled. At least...until I remembered Mutt was still here, guarding the front door.

He'd promised I'd be safe.

And I…believed him.

The water was blistering as it pelted against my back, the now-familiar numbness that had crept inside my mind settling back into place. It'd been easy to push away my metaphorical demons when Mutt was with me, but now that I was alone in the bathroom, memories—writhing, twisting, serpentine memories—crept to the surface.

My arousal dimmed.

Thoughts of knots and fucking drifted away as I tried not to fall into the trap my mind had laid for me. *Focus on the water. Focus on Mutt. You're safe, you're fine, you're—*

So alone.

So alone, alone, alone.

I shut my eyes and the world was dark. There were no monsters. There was no werewolf waiting to have his dick sucked—standing like a wet dream—in my stained front room.

I wasn't Markus, the kid who'd been kidnapped.

I wasn't Jeffrey, the chosen keeper of the Evans family legacy.

I was just…

I was…

Lonely, lonely, lonely.

Without thinking, I reached for the bar of soap and—

"No soap," a familiar cheerful, rumbly voice echoed from behind me. I startled, slamming against the cool tile as I whipped around to face my intruder. The room was impossibly bright for a moment, blinding me before my eyes refocused.

"What the—"

"You smelled lonely," Mutt said, shattering me open. My heart pounded, and the hot water burned and burned and burned. *I smelled…lonely?*

Could he *actually* smell emotions?

How—

Uncaring of my nudity or how invasive this was, Mutt yanked the shower door open and stuck his head inside the shower.

He stared at me.

His eyes were so fucking blue.

Blue as the ocean during the summer. Blue as my first car. Blue as I felt sometimes when the days were long and I was lost, lost, lost.

Mutt's warm chocolate-colored hair was unevenly cut and styled haphazardly, if it had even been styled at all. Which I doubted. He probably rolled out of bed and called it good. He was that kinda guy. I, on the other hand, spent at least half an hour every morning styling my hair so it looked effortless.

"*Are* you lonely?" Mutt asked, voice soft. I could see on his face that he already knew he was right. Which was just…unfair. Because apparently he could smell emotions, fucking fuck. That was…not cool.

But at the same time…it was kinda nice?

Meant he was perceptive—and as a person who struggled with honesty, it was nice to know someone would know my truths without me even having to say them.

Water droplets sprayed him but he didn't seem to mind. Didn't seem to notice, really, aside from blinking them away, his big blue eyes soft as he regarded me. Felt like he was looking right through me.

"I'm not lonely," I said automatically, because it was a habit to deny the things that made me hurt. My voice wobbled and I moved to cover my junk, not really in the mood to be ogled by someone right now. Mutt didn't notice my scars. Either that, or he didn't care.

His eyes were far more intelligent than they had any right to be. "Lie," he said, calling me out with no judgment or accusation in his tone at all. "Why do you lie?"

"What?"

It didn't escape me how bizarre all of this was.

Like a fever dream.

Here we were, getting pelted by hot water. A werewolf and a human. Two entirely different species. This wasn't a fairy tale, or a horror story. More like one of those absurd *Reddit* threads that pops up when you least expect it.

Help: I'm dating a werewolf. He's nosy and stalks me. And also apparently a human lie detector.

"How did you know?" I asked before he could answer my previous question.

"Know what?"

"That I lied?" I reached for the soap again, just to spite him, and Mutt growled, his fangs flashing. I put the soap down. His expression smoothed. Water droplets spilled down his cheeks, splattering against him. He blinked them away, like he was used to water hitting him in the face.

"Your heartbeat," he answered simply.

Oh.

Yeah.

Okay.

That made sense.

I'd just learned two new things about werewolves today—but not the one I wanted to know most.

Just ask him.

Just do it.

Like ripping off a Band-Aid.

"I…" I shook my head, still covering my junk with one hand, the other one clenching into a fist. "I would really appreciate some privacy right now." I still needed to clean my ass. That was non-negotiable. And I didn't really want Mutt watching me while I did it.

"But you are lonely," Mutt argued, attempting to shoulder his way further into the shower, despite the fact he was still clothed. It was odd. His clothes didn't suit him at all—almost like they were borrowed and not his own. Today's outfit was a ridiculous gray t-shirt with a wolf head on it. Very on the nose, if you asked me. Looked like the kinda thing you'd buy at a gas station while on a road trip.

I pushed the sliding door shut with my hip, struggling against it as Mutt huffed out an annoyed little breath. It pinched his shoulder.

"Yeah, okay." There was no point lying. I wheezed a little as he fought the door again. "But showers are not cuddle time."

"Any time is cuddle time," Mutt told me sagely. He fought back against me and I couldn't help but laugh. Mutt huffed again in annoyance. "Let me in."

"No."

"Why?" Mutt demanded, holding the frame in one hand, half of one of his big bare shoulders still inside along with his now soggy head. The triangular wolf ears on top of his head flattened unhappily.

Fuck.

My cheeks felt hot and I shivered, embarrassed and weirdly…turned on.

Apparently fighting with him did it for me. Because my cock began to fill despite how awkward and uncomfortable I felt. I didn't know how to get him to go so I could do my business—so I just…decided to tell the truth.

Since apparently he could sense lies, anyway.

"Because I wanna wash my ass, dude." Ew. *Did I really just say that?* "Hole," I corrected myself, though that didn't feel much better.

"Why wouldn't you want me here for that?" Mutt narrowed his eyes at me. Then his gaze flickered to where my dick still lay out of sight. It twitched, and he licked his lips, like he could sense it somehow. Like he could smell it.

Oh fuck.

He probably could.

Aroused, annoyed, and irritated, I shivered.

"Did you forget that I have already been inside you?"

My nipples perked up, achy and pink as I licked my lips and stared back at him—my desire probably written all over my face. I shifted, uncomfortable—turned on, and more than a little horny.

Mutt looked hungry.

His eyes were blown black with lust, his delicious cock a greedy line where it lay trapped against his thigh. Fucking huge cock. Monstrous really. I hadn't remembered it being that big last time—but I'd also been distracted.

"Fuck," I shuddered, half of me offended, and the other half needy as hell. "I just…need five minutes. I'm showering, man."

"I could be showering too." Mutt's nostrils flared and he inhaled greedily, his tail wagging as he forced the rest of his upper body inside the shower stall.

"No," I shoved at his meaty shoulder, removing the hand I had covering my dick to do so. His grin was *feral*—like that was what he'd wanted all along. His eyes flashed—glowing for a second as my heart stuttered. "You can fucking wait."

"Okay," he conceded for once, not pushing back. He didn't leave though. He stayed halfway inside the shower, growing soggier with each passing second as he stared at me in all my freckled glory. His eyes slid down my heaving chest, over my hard nipples, to my belly button, and then my cock where it stood in a nest of copper curls.

My dick flexed, and Mutt rumbled, pleased.

"Good bitch," he said softly, and I jolted, heat coursing through my veins and lighting me up from the inside out.

Suddenly, it didn't matter if he had a knot or not.

My shame didn't matter.

Only his voice, and its husky rumble.

And my new name.

A name no one had ever called me—that should've been mean and degrading but wasn't. Because I knew Mutt didn't mean it that way. When he said "good bitch" it was because I was meant to lie down, ass up, and let him take me. Being a "good bitch" simply meant I was his.

I'd never been a self-conscious dude. Not with hookups or at the school gym, or anything public. Sure, I hid myself from Blair, but that was out of a sense of duty to protect him from the truth, and not because I was ashamed of my body and what I'd been through.

We both had demons.

We both had scars.

But I'd also never willingly let someone into the shower with me knowing they were about to watch as I cleaned the most private part of my body. I shuddered, hot all over—these delicious, wonderful hot flashes burning through me.

"If you really want me to leave," his eyes flickered with something like understanding. "I will sit by the door and stand guard."

He was giving me a choice.

I knew the right answer.

The answer I should pick.

The socially acceptable one.

But…if I'd wanted to date a normal dude, I wouldn't have taken a werewolf home. And though this was weird as hell, it was also…fuck. It was the hottest thing I'd ever done.

"I will give you time," Mutt generously promised. "But…."

"But?"

"If you need help…"

"Help…" I sucked in a breath. "Cleaning my ass?" Mutt grinned at me, this wide feral thing, his ears perking up as his tail smacked against the shower door. *Thwap, thwap thwap.*

"It is mine to care for," he hummed, eyeing me with liquid heat. "Isn't it? That is why you brought me here. You have been smelling of need, need, need."

I wasn't sure when I'd become his property—let alone my ass, but… fuck. It was really doing it for me. My cock jerked, a drop of precum sliding down the tip, trickling down the freckled skin as I sucked in a needy breath.

"I will guard the door," Mutt repeated. "You will be safe. I will not be angry if you do not choose the correct option."

The correct option.

He hadn't even realized what he'd said.

His words were innocent and yet…he was right.

What the fuck was I doing? I'd wanted to fuck, hadn't I? That's why I'd brought him home. I was supposed to be chasing happiness. What was happier than sex? Than getting touched when I so desperately ached to be touched.

Sure this was weird and embarrassing, but it was also…

So fucking sexy.

It took a lot of trust. Trust I'd never given another person. Trust I'd never even been tempted to offer to someone else.

And yet…here I was.

"Yeah, okay. You can stay."

It had been a long time since I wasn't lonely.

It had been a long time since I wasn't scared.

And I felt neither of those things as Mutt stepped into the shower, fully clothed, and in one swift movement, grabbed my cock and my throat and shoved me playfully into the wall.

Chapter Eight

Mutt

JEFFREY'S AROUSAL WAS heady. It filled up my lungs, made me ache and shake, my cock weeping into wet denim. His skin was hot to the touch, the lovely flush on his cheeks climbing down his throat, splotchy and gorgeous, betraying his arousal.

His face looked apprehensive, nervous—

But his scent was needy-hot-lust.

He wanted this.

He wanted this but he didn't know how to ask for it.

"Hold still," I murmured against the shell of his ear, shivering when he released a ragged little whimper.

"Mmmnn," Jeffrey gasped out, obediently frozen, his bowed legs trembling as I reached for the soap. Because he was playful, as well as delicious—he did manage one last barb. "I thought you said no soap."

I snorted out a laugh, coating my fingers with the substance, before sliding a soapy hand down the broad line of his back. "That was before I knew what you were doing with it."

Jeffrey shivered, and his nipples rubbed up against me and I was…fuck.

I was lost.

My hips jerked, pushing up against him, but I ignored my own very real need as Jeffrey laughed, low and throaty.

"You get this is weird, right?"

"Is it?" I asked, mouthing at his ear, sucking, licking the shell of it before nuzzling his throat where he was most sensitive. Earlier when I'd touched it, I'd scented the spike of arousal in the air, and it was easy enough to replicate the nibble-sucking he seemed to like so much.

He melted a little, still rigid, but twitchy soft now too. Like he couldn't decide whether he wanted to be offended or melt into me.

It made sense.

After what I'd learned about him, I knew how difficult trust was for him to give.

"I mean…" Jeffrey managed, voice throaty soft. "I…"

"It's not weird," I countered, even though it probably was. I was certain, however, that touching him like this, taking care of him like this, was not as odd as he thought it was. I may have been a virgin before we met, but that didn't mean I was an idiot.

I had instincts.

And my instincts were telling me that Jeffrey wanted this.

When my soapy fingers ran over his ribs and his hips, he wheezed, his cock leaking a steady stream against my thigh. He jerked his hips forward a little, looking for friction. His sweet bitch-cock left a sticky trail along the denim of my jeans and I growled, teeth digging hard into his throat so that he would be still so I could work.

"Oh fuck," Jeffrey sighed, sagging the moment I bit down.

I rumbled my pleasure, unwilling to release him yet as I soaped up his cock and gave it a few, sudsy strokes. His hips stayed submissively in place, despite the pressure, but he still whined, his sweet little knees quaking like he was having a hard time standing up. Which was incredibly flattering—especially from a man who was so terrified of being vulnerable.

I held Jeffrey still with my teeth, his body lax and sweet as I teased and trailed my fingers over him, soaping and sudsing his lovely balls, then back behind them. By the time I pressed a finger to his pucker, he was panting, his chest jerking with each ragged breath.

I pulled back to check on him—and what I saw made my knot swell and my cock jerk inside my jeans.

Jeffrey was…a mess.

His eyes were glazed over, dark with heat. He was shaking and trembling—this time from pleasure. There were no demons in his eyes, there was no murkiness to his scent.

Simply put, my freckled prince was entirely focused on me.

His soapy cock pushed against my thigh again and I grinned, staring down at him through my lashes as he made a hurt little sound. Lost. Like he was begging his alpha to help him find his way home.

"Such a pretty bitch," I said softly, voice low and crackling with heat. "Such a pretty, pretty bitch. Aren't you, sweetheart?"

Jeffrey whined and I gave his hole another tap before withdrawing my hand.

His eyes widened—alarmed—like he thought the fact I was moving was a punishment for not agreeing outright. "Yes," he gasped, ever the people-pleaser. "Yes—yes. I-I am."

I'd never heard him so eager.

I liked it.

Maybe too much.

"Yes you are, *Alpha*," I corrected him, stroking up his inner thigh and across his hip to his ass so I'd have a better angle. I hadn't meant to punish him—I'd simply been moving so I could reach better—but his response to what he perceived as punishment was more than a little telling.

"Yes, I am, Alpha," Jeffrey echoed, voice quaking.

"You're what?" I asked, groaning as I fondled one of his thick ass cheeks and the muscle gave beneath my fingers.

"I'm…a pretty bitch." Jeffrey's voice quaked. His scent was happy-good-need, and I groaned, diving into his throat again, my teeth digging in hard to reward him as my fingers found his twitching entrance. It gave beneath my touch, like it was trying to suck me inside, and I rubbed and rubbed and rubbed—softening the muscle.

He'd need to be relaxed if he was going to take more.

Fantasies danced behind my lids.

Fantasies of the day I'd have him whining and wet, sobbing as he rode my knot. Fat with my cum and leaking, my pretty, pretty bitch.

If he had been a wolf I would've mated him already. He would wear my mark on the back of his neck, and our bond would've been tightly knotted. He would be back home in our pack, and I wouldn't be playing here— pretending like he wasn't everything I'd ever wanted. Like he wasn't it for me.

I forced those thoughts aside, instead focusing on the beautiful man in my arms. On the way he scratched at my forearms, raking trails up them—trails that healed the moment they rose. His legs were quaking, his hole sucking at my fingers.

When I pushed inside, he gasped, shame coloring his scent.

So I bit down harder on his neck. Hard enough I felt the skin begin to give. He was human. We couldn't bond—so I didn't worry as my teeth marked him, my index finger sinking in to the first knuckle.

"F-fuck," Jeffrey hissed out, his back arching toward my hand, his voice quaky and soft.

I growled in agreement.

Because yes.

I wanted to fuck as much as he did.

His ass gave beneath my fingers easily. I knew it was because he played with himself—when I was here in my wolfskin I could often hear him in the shower, whining into the tile while he fucked himself. The slick slip-slide of fingers tucking into all that warm-wet-pink.

The same warm-wet-pink that I was currently stretching.

"M-Mutt," Jeffrey managed, his voice low and husky. "Please, Alpha."

He begged so prettily, so I had no choice but to give in. I knew what he wanted even without smelling him. So I pulled my fingers free, my teeth too. Lapping at the bruise I'd made, I grabbed on to his hips and jerked him around so he was facing the tile wall. The bow of his hips was gorgeous from the back, as was the curve of his ass.

I licked my lips, dropped to my knees, and pulled his cheeks apart. Water slid over the long line of his gorgeous body, cascading between his ass cheeks and washing the soap away.

"Oh fuck," Jeffrey's voice cracked as I grabbed a cheek in each hand

and spread them wide. The pink of his hole winked at me, and I groaned, diving in tongue first. I ate him with a ferocity I'd never felt—not even when shifted. Long swipes, rough rubs, twisting, pressing, sliding in.

And when his little hole twitched and clenched around me, and his hard nipples were pressed against the chill tile, I reached up to slide a finger in alongside my wriggling tongue.

"Oh fuck," Jeffrey repeated, lower this time, his hips humping back against my face. "Just like that—yeah—" he gasped. "Just—mmm. Deeper, I need—" I pushed in deeper and he sobbed. Then he fumbled for something on the shelf. A bottle of something I didn't recognize.

He jerked it back toward me, and I growled at him, my tongue vibrating inside his ass.

"Fingers, lube. Fuck. Please—" Jeffrey managed.

I didn't know what a lube was, but I didn't like that he was bossing me around with it.

"Mutt," Jeffrey quaked. "Trust me. Please. Put this on your fingers, and then you can really fuck me." His voice was thready and low. "Fuck me hard enough I'm sore and thinking about you tomorrow."

He was my good, clever mate so I trusted him. I took the bottle, pulled my fingers free—despite his whining—and coated them in the odd slippery substance. When I pushed inside next he howled. It was easy. Too easy. I slipped further than I had before, and my cock jerked as I stared at his sweet pink rim spreading for my finger.

"Oh," I said simply, my soggy tail whipping against the lip of the tub.

"Oh," Jeffrey repeated, reverent, his back bowed as he pushed back against me.

And then I fucked him.

I fucked him hard. One finger, two, my tongue—then all three. Eating him the way he deserved to be eaten. His sweet little cock leaked uselessly against the tile as he humped my face, scratching at the tile with blunt nails.

It was difficult to hold back, to not pop my claws, but I managed.

Grunting and growling, I slurped and sucked, pushing a third finger into him till he was howling.

"Fuck, fuck, fuck."

And then he came.

Untouched.

His freckled, pretty dick spilled as he grabbed my hair and ground his ass back against my tongue and fingers. He was a sweaty, shaking mess as I softened my sucking, releasing his hole with a slick little pop, but leaving my fingers inside as I rose from my spot on the floor and crowded behind him.

With my free hand I grabbed his face, jerking it till I could see one of his eyes, and the dazed, fucked-out expression on his face.

"*Mine*," I growled, jerking my fingers inside him again, enjoying the way he sobbed and his lashes fluttered in surrender, probably way too much.

"Y-yours," he replied, voice hoarse. "Yours, Alpha."

"You are so good," I told him, because he needed to hear it. Even if he didn't believe it. Even if he hated compliments—he still deserved them. "So pretty, so sweet, so noble. Perfect, perfect."

Jeffrey whined, clenching around my fingers, his body lax as I kissed his parted lips. When he didn't open as quickly as I wanted him to, I licked them, just to feel their softness. He groaned, opening wider—wide enough I could slip inside. I explored then, toying with his useless blunt little teeth. Rubbing along his tongue, enjoying the texture and shape of him. Eating him here as eagerly as I'd eaten his ass.

His hole clenched around my fingers every time I twisted my tongue against his, so I did it again. And again. And again.

When I pulled out of his mouth, a slick trail of saliva connected us, and my wolf crowed in triumph, burning right at the surface.

"Do you have a knot?" Jeffrey asked me, his voice fucked-out and soft. There was nothing behind the words, no fear, no revulsion, no shame. He was fuzzy and sweet, my perfect, pretty mate-mate-mate.

His scent was aroused-sated-happy.

My cock jerked and I groaned, the combination of how docile he was and his filthy words sending me spinning.

"Yes," my voice was hoarse and low, my knot burning with the need to lock into something tight and hot and wet.

"Can I…lick it?"

And then it was my turn to burn.

Because Jeffrey was reaching for my wrist, gently pulling my fingers free. And he was twisting around and falling to his knees. And then his hands were at my zipper, and I was—Oh.

Oh.

Oh.

Oh.

My head tossed back as that slick, hot little mouth wrapped experimentally around the tip of my cock. Precum leaked onto his clever tongue, spilling wet-hot-salt as I forced my head down to stare so I wouldn't miss a single moment.

No one had ever touched me before.

Ever.

And it was…

Oh fuck.

Oh fuck.

"You're big," Jeffrey said around his mouthful of my dick, still hazy, his lashes fluttering. "I like big."

I whined, claws popping free as I scrambled at the wall for purchase. I knew if I reached down and grabbed him I'd likely break him—so I didn't. Didn't want to scratch up his pretty scalp, or crush him as I found pleasure inside his mouth.

This was better than anything I'd ever done to myself.

And trust me…since we'd met—I'd done a lot.

Spent any night he wasn't around me with my hand down my pants and my cock wet, slick, needy.

"Oh." Jeffrey's voice was surprised, but not in a bad way as he peeled the pants lower and off and he caught sight of my knot for the first time. The water had run warm, and I was grateful—because my body felt overheated as it was. "It's kinda…"

I whined as he traced a single solitary finger around the engorged ring at the base of my dick. "It's kinda pretty," he said softly, mouthing at the root, as he toyed with me curiously. His tongue flattened, tasting it like he'd promised. Then he slid up again, far too soon.

"Squeeze it," I begged, hips jerking. "Please—" Apparently it was my turn to beg. "Please," I repeated, voice low and rough. "Please, please—"

Jeffrey squeezed my knot, his long, lovely fingers wrapping tight. I whined, rutting forward, my eyes rolling back as hot slick cum spilled all over his lovely face. That was all it took. One tight squeeze from his sweet, big hand and I was—

"Oh, oh—" I sobbed, rutting against his face, pushing my cum into his hair and over his cheek, my balls emptying for what felt like centuries. He hadn't needed to lick it, after all.

By the time I finished, Jeffrey was coated.

My wolf rumbled his approval, and I groaned, staring down at my mate with rapturous amazement as he lapped at the tip of my cock, pink little tongue teasing beneath my foreskin like he wanted to taste.

I wasn't sure when I'd stopped trying not to call him my mate in my head, but I had.

"Not bad," he said softly, voice low and rough. "Kinda messy but—"

I yanked him up to his feet, shoving him into the wall, my claws pricking at his hips as I bit and licked and sucked my way into his mouth. My spent cock pushed against his belly, our half-limp dicks pressing together as I devoured him.

It felt natural to eat him.

To taste our flavors together.

To mingle our scents like I did when I was in my wolfskin.

I swiped my fingers through my cum first, then his, then rubbed it over his skin. Over his cock and balls, down to his taint. Over his nipples— which I plucked till they were swollen—and then up to his lips.

I fed the last precious drops of our pleasure to him, and Jeffrey simply groaned.

His eyes were as dark as ever, his long lashes fluttering.

"Taste it," I growled, jerking his jaw open and pressing my cum-covered fingers against his tongue. He lapped at them obediently, eyes rolling back as he whined.

He liked this.

He liked this as much as I did.

My perfect match.

My mate, mate, mate.

I had been naive to think I could leave him alone.

That I would survive with only one night of this.

I'd been wrong.

So wrong.

And as Jeffrey lapped at our combined cum, I knew there was no giving this up. I'd rather be put down than live my life without him.

Chapter Nine

Jeffrey

Trevor: Hey man, I'm going to the bar tonight. You wanna come?

Becky: Martha misses you, you should text her back. I know it's been a while…but you were so good together. It's silly to throw that away, you know?

Martha: How are you?

Richard: Stir fry at eight pm next week. Tuesday.

Richard: Bring your dog.

Blair: Who do you think would win in a fight? Gomez Addams or Herman Munster? Enquiring minds need to know.

Blair: Also come Tuesday!

Blair: Seriously!

Blair: My apartment.

Blair: It'll be awesome.

Avery: Don't forget the shipment of frog warts is coming in Wednesday. Needs temperature controlled ASAP, please and thank you. I have to do lunch with Violet so I won't be in. I'll bring you back a sandwich. I'll love you forever if you head in early. I'm not sure when the delivery will arrive.

I STARED DOWN at the steadily growing pile of unanswered texts in my inbox, turned my phone off, and spat the rest of the toothpaste in the sink. Even my orgasm—which had been fantastic— couldn't block out my rising panic. My hand shook as I set my toothbrush down, closed my eyes, and tried to breathe. The cold counter bit into my palms as I squeezed it tight, looking for balance.

I just want to be left alone.

Why can't I be left alone?

My therapist had told me to try to rely on someone else. And part of me was tempted to ask Mutt—who I'd left in the other room, naked on my bed—to crush my phone.

Did that count?

Fuuuuck.

What was wrong with me?

"Jeffrey," Mutt's voice was soft where it echoed in the crack beneath the door. "You are upset." Apparently he hadn't stayed where I'd left him.

"No shit, Sherlock," I muttered under my breath—but that felt mean. It felt *really* mean, and I hated that I'd said it immediately.

"Let me in."

For a guy who's here on "business" he sure doesn't have much to do.

Exhibit A: Every day this week, Mutt-the-dog had been waiting outside Avery's shop for me to finish work. He'd nap or chase butterflies, his thick chocolate brown coat flickering in the weak autumn sunlight. He was always there, standing sentinel in my peripheral vision. No matter what Avery and I were doing, I could always see him. And that comforted me in a way nothing else ever had.

What I didn't understand was *why* he'd go to such lengths to stick around me.

Sure, we'd met in Colorado.

Sure, we had this kinda…freaky sort of connection. And he was hot like fire and made my blood sing.

But there had to be some other motivation, right?

He couldn't simply be here because he wanted to keep me safe.

Except that he probably is.

Dude doesn't have a nefarious bone in his entire Gigantor body.

All my life I'd been the solid one. The dependable one. The one that laughed in the face of danger—not because I wasn't frightened, but because you either laughed or cried, and I was sick and tired of being weak. Was it still bravery if you felt you had no choice?

I don't know.

Either way, I'd always known my place.

But now…now I was skittish and lost. I wanted to hide behind Mutt's bulk and never come out again. Either Mutt, if I was being honest. Hairy or…slightly less hairy. I wasn't picky. And having a second set of eyes watching my back at any given time helped soothe the part of me that was still a lost little boy, just waiting for the monsters to hurt him.

Alright.

That was a fucking lie.

I had a preference.

Of course I fucking did.

Mutt the dog offered comfort, yes, but he didn't laugh at my jokes. He didn't tell me I sang like an angel, making me rethink that word entirely and what it had used to mean to me. He didn't stare at me like I'd hung the fucking moon—okay yeah, maybe he did—but still.

There was something about warm arms and Mutt's sunny grin that settled me in a way nothing else ever had. If I decided to hide in his arms for the rest of all time, I got the feeling he wouldn't mind. Not that I could, mind you, because he'd already told me he was only here until January.

He just liked being around to protect me. I could see it on his face. See the way he puffed up with pride, like simply providing a buffer between me and the world gave him purpose.

But accepting that was…hard.

I had a nasty tendency to look for the worst in people. And I knew that. But still, it was difficult to turn that off. To ask for help. To believe what

I already knew instinctively to be true, when my mind was full of traps.

Even now, when Mutt was sitting outside the bathroom door waiting for me, I struggled crossing that metaphorical distance. Admittedly, I wanted him to push inside the room and wrap himself around me. I wanted to be crushed against his chest. Held close and tight, until all I could smell was him. Until all I could hear was his heartbeat.

I needed him, but I couldn't bring myself to ask for help.

Maybe it was Lydia's training.

Or maybe it was the fact that no one had ever helped me when I needed it before.

Asking for help felt like trying to speak a foreign language.

"Fine, I'm coming—" The door pushed open and I jolted the second hot arms curled around my body, just like I'd hoped they would. *Mind fuckery.* Mutt's nose pushed into the soft hair at the nape of my neck. Exactly the way I needed, like he was a fucking mind reader. He squeezed and squeezed, tight enough I could hardly breathe.

Still standing at the sink, frozen, I let his bulk protect me from the door and the world it led to. I couldn't stop shaking, but like usual, no tears accompanied my panic. They never did. Not anymore.

"You did not answer me," Mutt accused, gently, an explanation for why he'd barged in, no doubt. "Who hurt you?" he asked so softly I wasn't sure it wasn't my imagination. "My sweet, pretty, *perfect* Jeffrey."

I shook my head, the words too choked to rise, even if I had wanted to talk. Which I didn't. I never did. It didn't help. But Mutt's arms did. They did. And I fell into them easily, curling tight inside his grip as I took a shuddery sob in, trying my hardest to stop the tremors.

I looked stupid.

In the mirror.

My hair was a goddamn mess and there were hickeys on my neck. The dark circles beneath my eyes were somewhat better, but there was no denying the fact I looked like a fluffy-haired trainwreck.

I could hardly recognize myself.

Pretty and perfect were not words I embodied. Not right then, with my lungs seizing, and Mutt's giant body curled over mine. His eyes flickered in the mirror, staring at me—not my reflection, like he hadn't noticed it was there at all—he was so engrossed in making sure I was okay.

"No one hurt me," I said, but that was a lie. A lie he could easily see through, wolf or not.

"Shhhh," Mutt rumbled against the top of my spine, his hands hot and gentle as he rubbed over my heart, my arms, across my body. I hadn't realized how cold I'd gotten till then. Till his heat bled into me and he pulled me tighter against him.

His attention was everything I needed and too much all at once.

"Shhh, it is *hard* what you are going through." There was so much compassion in that statement. Too much. I couldn't help but react, because he was right.

It was hard.

And it fucking sucked.

And all I'd done was brush my goddamn teeth and check my goddamn phone—and look what a mess I'd made.

"It is," I bit out, telling the truth for once.

"*It is,*" he agreed. "But you will survive it."

I laughed, because I wasn't sure if he was right or not. But hearing those words out loud? Yeah. It helped. It helped so much.

"You will survive," he said again, pulling me away from the counter, though my fingers didn't want to let go. He gently removed them, one hand at a time, before he swung me to face him, so I could no longer judge my own reflection. His massive palms scrubbed across my cheeks, fingers tangling in my hair, covering my ears. His hands blocked out the buzzing from the light overhead, and the swoosh of cars out on the street. One of my neighbors was blasting music above us, loud enough the ceiling vibrated, and even that disappeared.

The world was quiet.

And his eyes were *blue*.

So, so blue.

Like the ocean view off our balcony in Oregon. The apartment Blair and I had shared when we'd become adults. He'd filled it with plants, and I'd often catch him sitting out there staring at the water.

I hadn't understood until now.

Because blue was calm, steady, and loyal.

I just hadn't seen that before.

"Today is hard," Mutt repeated gently, ducking his head till our noses bumped. "But one day, it won't be. There will be a day when you forget the pain. When it is simply a memory. Wounds heal, Jeffrey."

I wanted to believe him.

So badly.

I squeezed my eyes shut again, because looking into his gaze made me feel raw. "You are tired," Mutt stroked over my shoulders, before one heavy palm slid back to squeeze my nape tight. The bruise on my neck that he'd left stung, but it was a welcome pain. This was the same thing I'd always done to soothe Blair, even when we were tiny.

I saw now why it worked.

Why he melted, every single time.

My body felt like putty as the tension seeped away and Mutt rumbled his approval. He pinched harder, and finally, I began to relax. "It has been a long day, hasn't it? You are tired, and have given so much to me already. You need to rest."

Every day was a long day, but I didn't tell him that.

I nodded, still refusing to open my eyes because everything was too bright, too much, too-too-too. I wished the tears would come, but they didn't. I couldn't remember the last time they had.

Maybe it had been when I was nine? When I realized my mistake and that no one would be coming to save me. That because I'd left my family behind in Elmwood and gone along with Lydia, it had facilitated her plan to frame Blair's parents for my death and allowed Blair to be kidnapped too.

People had *died* because of me.

That it was my fault.

Or maybe…

Maybe it had been the first time Lydia had taken me monster hunting. After I'd stared at the carcass of the goblin I'd killed and promptly thrown up all over my new white sneakers.

No…no.

I remembered now. It had been when I'd come home that night this last spring to the blood smears in our kitchen. When Blair's car had been gone. When I'd called him, and called him, and called him, and he hadn't picked up the phone—and I'd thought—

I'd thought she'd finally killed him.

That he was gone.

That I'd never see him again.

"Oh my, sweet one," Mutt's arms shifted, his hands sliding away. For a moment I was weightless as he pulled me up easily, my legs automatically wrapping around his waist. "You are *hurting*."

I was.

I was.

I was—

And I couldn't seem to stop.

It wasn't fair. I should be basking in my orgasm. I should be snuggling him because it had been what I'd wanted for weeks now, not because I was falling apart at the worst possible moment.

"Sweet, sweet Jeffrey." I did not feel sweet, I felt *wretched*. "So good, so perfect." I did not feel perfect. I did not feel good. I did not— "It will be okay." My heart ached and I shuddered, dropping my head against Mutt's shoulder as he pushed the bathroom door open, somehow, and we made the journey down the small dark hallway to my bedroom. "You will see."

I didn't understand why he was here.

Why he'd stayed after the sex was done.

I didn't understand *him*.

I didn't.

But I was grateful all the same as he laid me on my bed and tucked the blankets around me. The window was cracked open and the wind whistled through it as Mutt climbed onto the mattress behind me and curled himself around my body like a giant hairy cocoon.

He held me.

No one had ever held me before.

He was a man. He was a werewolf. I shouldn't feel the way I did about him. I shouldn't—I shouldn't—but I did. I pressed into him, I buried my shame against the sheets, and he kissed the back of my neck over and over and over again.

Patient.

I had never known patience like his.

A soft howl echoed through the crack in the window the moment my shaking had become nothing more than a tremor. It was a mournful sound, wicked and as spooky as a town like Elmwood promised. A place full of impossible things.

Mutt groaned, squeezing me tighter. "I must go," he said, his voice hoarse and almost…*angry?*

I'd never heard him angry before.

"Please," I said, surprised when the word burst out without permission. He had to go. What was I doing? Asking him to stay?

"I would not leave if I had a choice," Mutt said quietly, squeezing me even tighter. "You have to know that by now."

I didn't understand it. But I supposed he was right.

"I guess I'll…see you around?" It was the second time I'd said that, and I hoped next time, I wouldn't have to accuse him of stalking me to get him into my bed.

"Soon," he promised, kissing the back of my neck one more time before he stroked a hand through my hair and rose from the bed. His movements were jerky and angry, nothing like the normal, casual sway of his athletic body.

Mutt was *agitated*.

Another howl echoed through the window and I pulled my blankets tighter around me as I watched him jerk his still wet jeans on before he turned to face me one last time. His eyes flashed, his fangs elongated, his broad body lit up by moonlight.

He looked ethereal.

Every inch the supernatural being that he was.

"Rest," he commanded, and I nodded.

And then—he pulled the window open and leapt out of it. There was a quiet thump as his feet met the ground outside. Casually jumping down two fucking stories like it was nothing. My heart raced as I shucked the blankets off and dove toward the window to make sure he was okay.

His half-bare body was already bounding away, loping between cars in the parking lot before he launched himself over the back fence with a graceful ease that left me breathless. When he landed, Mutt stood on the other side of the fence, moonlight lighting his tan skin as he twisted back to look at me, blue eyes flashing.

Another howl rang out, this time closer, and Mutt tipped his head back to answer, low and throaty. A haunting sound that had my heart racing and my hair standing on end, just like it had the first night we'd met when I'd heard his growl and realized what he was. The moon in the sky was nearly full again, and the way it glowed only added to the eerie feeling that settled like fog in the air.

And then Mutt was gone.

Gone.

Again.

And I was alone.

Just the unanswered texts on my phone for company, and the empty warmth of the space he'd vacated in my bed.

Chapter Ten

Mutt

"WHERE THE HELL have you been?" Harry, my older, tinier brother asked with his severest expression. It was the one he used when talking about taxes, pack finances, and *Godzilla* movies, so I knew he was being extra-serious. His scent was calm-soothe-annoyed, but his heartbeat was steady. Which meant, while irritated, I didn't need to start panicking immediately. This was a personal problem.

A personal problem that I had caused—and therefore should listen to.

Harry liked to think he was the boss of me because he was older. He did have a whole three years on me, and at the ripe age of twenty-two was therefore much wiser than I was—at least, according to him. Despite the years he had on me, I was the one who was going to be the alpha of our clan one day, which meant the way he talked to me half the time—

now included—was what most would consider inappropriate. Not that he cared, or I did.

It was just how we were.

The day Harry stopped talking to me like I was a naughty, dumb kid would be the day the world ended.

He had flaws, sure. But he had strengths too. Truthfully, Harry was more suited to the role of Pack Alpha than I was. He had that whole "bossy" air about him, despite being reed thin and an omega.

"Out…" I hummed guiltily, doing my best not to accidentally crush the Pop Tart in my hand. *Think gentle thoughts, gentle thoughts.*

Harry made an annoyed sound, tapping his foot with his hands on his hips. "Out *where?*" The fact his eyes were wide betrayed him, however—making it obvious how surprised he actually was. He probably hadn't expected me to reply at all, let alone with a whole-ass word.

Which was fair.

Normally I wouldn't.

Normally I'd shred my clothes—because I hated them—and shift into my wolfskin to avoid conflict just like this. But…for some reason, I didn't. Maybe it was because I'd already made my choice, and I knew in light of that, communication was important.

Harry had always been nosy, but ever since we'd started negotiations with the pack outside Elmwood he'd been kinda…insufferable? Always asking me where I was and why I wasn't home. I felt bad for saying that about him, seeing as he was my brother—and he was technically doing *my* job, but still. Two things could be true at the same time.

Or was that three?

There was a weird snapping sensation between my fingers and—

Fuck.

I broke the damn Pop Tart.

Fuck fuck fuck.

Oh well.

Tasted the same way like this, right?

Crumbs fell to the floor, and I eyed the exits, trying to figure out if I could sneak out without Harry catching me first. I caught the pieces before they could fall, huffing in annoyance. Surreptitiously, I edged toward the front door to our small house, broken Pop Tart in hand.

This place wasn't half bad. Reminded me of our childhood home, but smaller, and smellier because we were all adults now. Jules had an unhealthy obsession with Kimchi, and the scent of Theo's lemon bars mixing with it in the air was less than pleasant.

"Out *where*, Mutt?" Harry repeated.

"Out…?" I tried to come up with something plausible, but couldn't. "*Out.*" Harry raised a perfectly manicured dark brow, his scent sparking with surprise a second time, though his face never stopped looking annoyed. I offered him the crushed pastry in my hand, at a loss for what else to do. "Pop Tart?"

Distract him.

Escape, escape, escape.

"I don't want a Pop Tart. I want answers." Harry pinched the bridge of his nose like I was the most frustrating person he'd ever talked to—which was fair. He opened his mouth like he was about to speak—probably to say something smart and cutting, or worse—point out the fact I still smelled like sex.

I shoved the pastry in my mouth, cheeks puffed up, eyes wide.

Don't do it, don't do it.

"For example…why exactly do you smell like *sex*?" Harry asked. *Dammit.* "Where have you been going? Why are you acting so sneaky? *Who* are you sleeping with? Are you okay? Do you like him? You can't like him, Mutt. Fuck. Does Dad know? Does *Mom* know? Are you using protection? I know you don't need it—but humans expect you to be prepared. Does the human know *what* you are?" Harry's eyes widened with fear. "Did you tell him? You *can't* tell him. Oh my god. Do we need to have the talk? I am not prepared to have the talk. I left my binder at home."

So many questions.

Too many questions.

I could barely keep track of the first one. Partly because there were too many, and partly because I didn't want to. I didn't intend on answering any of them. Denial was the name of the game, after all.

I shook my head, flushing bright red, the Pop Tart growing pasty inside my mouth. I didn't swallow, for fear that the second I did he'd start interrogating me again.

Save me, Butters. Save me—I pleaded at my other brother, who was sitting on the couch playing some weird matchy-matchy game on his phone. He'd been sitting there since I'd left to follow Jeffrey to open-mic night, and I wasn't certain he'd ever moved. Not even to pee. All six-foot-something of his massive frame was sprawled out, one hand tucked inside the hem of his sweatpants, his shirtless chest on full display as he played on his phone.

Save me, save me.

I edged a little closer to the door.

Harry had called me home, but I officially realized what a mistake this had been.

"Why *do* you smell like sex?" Butters repeated, throwing me under the bus curiously as he twisted to look at the both of us, his lavender eyes wide. He set his phone down, clearly more interested in Harry's interrogation than he was in his game. He stared at me, then my clothes—eyes narrowing. "Hey, aren't those mine—?"

This was not the first time I'd borrowed his clothes. And it wouldn't be the last…and I just—

Oh fuck.

That was when I broke.

And the growling started.

I couldn't help it.

I was caught in a lie I was not equipped to keep. I was surprised Butters hadn't figured it out already—but then again, he was Butters—so actually that made sense. He was connecting the dots as we spoke, eyes widening as he no doubt remembered the frantic way I'd stolen his pants right off him weeks ago.

He wasn't the only one that knew, either. Theo obviously did, because he'd already helped me out once before. He was a secret keeper. Giant. Soft-spoken. Trustworthy. Despite being close to Harry, I knew he wouldn't say anything.

I probably should've anticipated this.

But I was still reeling from comforting Jeffrey and the fact I'd had to leave him alone when he so obviously needed me just so I wouldn't get us caught. And I had not been prepared to be outright called out and questioned. It was hard enough keeping quiet about Jeffrey in general, when all I wanted to do was tell everyone how pretty-perfect-lovely-sad-sweet-brave he was.

And also see what they knew about Lydia, the woman who had hurt him, so I could hunt her down and snap her head off with my teeth.

If I'd been in my wolf form my hackles would've raised—but as it was, all I had was soggy pastry-filled cheeks and subvocals that rumbled loud enough the room quieted immediately. I may have been the youngest but I was the alpha and outranked both of them—not that I liked to use that to my advantage usually.

I just…

I didn't have room in my head for this right now. Not when my thoughts were spinning back to Jeffrey. To the appointment I'd overheard. To the magic of his singing voice. The way he'd smelled and tasted when I'd had him in the shower. And his mouth…god, his mouth.

I could dedicate hours to thinking about his mouth alone. All slick and pink.

But most of all, I couldn't help but wonder when I could see him again—not as his dog, but as me. Which was…weird.

Weird to think about.

All my life, I'd preferred my wolfskin to my humanskin. It felt more natural. More right. And yet, when I was with Jeffrey there was this itch beneath my skin to touch, not with my paws or snout, but with my hands. To feel the warmth of his skin beneath my palms, to hold, to kiss, to cover every inch of his body with mine until we were sweaty soft and he was safe-safe-safe.

Both omegas frowned at me, not cowed.

I didn't know what my scent was telling them, but it couldn't be good.

My cheeks heated.

Their expressions were comically similar, though Harry and Butters were about as different as could be. Harry was lithe with dark hair and severe features. Butters was thick as a slab of toast with margarine colored hair and leagues of tan muscle. He preferred to be naked when he was two-legged, and I didn't blame him. There was a reason I was pilfering clothing from him, after all. And it was because I hated them so damn much that I didn't own any. I hadn't needed them—at least until now.

Still, it wasn't fair that both of them were ganging up on me like this. Nosy bastards.

I am not a grumpy person. I am not mean. I am not impatient. Or at least, I *wasn't*. Not until now. We were only two months into this and I was already at my wit's end, caught, because of a secret I didn't want to keep.

Lying was…exhausting.

For a second, I was tempted to spill everything.

Harry would probably freak out. Stalk Jeffrey himself. Research him. Tell me off for being stupid and blah, blah, blah. There'd be no going back. No quiet slivers of peace anymore. Because Harry would tell everyone, and then my nosy-ass brothers would poke their slimy snouts into our business.

Telling all my brothers would certainly mean drama.

Theo would ply Jeffrey with pastries.

Butters would try to wrestle him—to welcome him into the pack— and probably hurt him, on account of being butter-fingered, like his nickname suggested.

And Jules would force him to join his book club and make him read all sorts of the weird crap he liked—to the point that Jeffrey wouldn't have time for me at all. And don't even get me started on Mom and Dad— because if my brothers knew, so would my parents—well…

Fuck.

They'd fly all the way out from Colorado.

They'd try to get Jeffrey to understand why our time together was temporary. They'd turn this thing—this *thing* that I had been doing my damndest to keep casual for both our sakes'—into something that hurt.

They'd tear Jeffrey apart, however unintentional it would be.

Our remaining few months of happiness would be soured.

And I'd become…not a pleasant memory—a seasonal lover—but another in a long list of the tragedies that made up Jeffrey Prince's life.

I wasn't willing to let myself become a bad memory.

That's asking too much.

Too much.

So, I refused to speak. At least not now. Even though they'd both clearly already cottoned on—at least a little as to what was going on. My growls quieted, and both my brothers continued to stare at me like they didn't recognize me at all.

I swallowed the Pop Tart, even though it felt like wet sand. It scraped down my throat, choking me a little as Butters and Harry kept waiting for answers—scents…*contrite.*

I was doing my best not to feel guilty for snapping at them.

Even without the secret keeping, if I was being honest, Harry had every right to be annoyed with me. They all did. I mean, we were only in Maine because of me. Because I'd stood in front of Dad, the Pack Alpha, and quite literally *begged* him to let us set up a new compound here.

Things had gotten far more complicated after we'd arrived. After I'd begun following Jeffrey, from the shadows, and been unable to help myself when he'd been in danger. I'd stepped in because it was the right thing to do.

And everything that had happened since had been my fault.

Because I had very little self-control when it came to him.

And that had been before I knew anything about what he'd been through.

Before he'd caught me guarding him, and instead of smelling frightened, invited me into his home. Before he'd torn apart his hands when I'd run from him. So broken and lost and lonely. Before we'd had cheeseburgers together, shared laughter, and I'd returned to his home, because I couldn't leave him again.

I couldn't do it.

I couldn't, I couldn't, I couldn't.

And he was so happy when he saw my wolfskin waiting on his doorstep. He was so happy-happy-*happy* I was there.

So despite how out of character all of this was for me, I couldn't seem to stop.

I couldn't just *leave* him. What kind of alpha would I be?

He *needed* me.

He needed me and it hurt so bad—so, so bad that this couldn't be forever. It was tearing me apart from the inside out and I could hardly breathe because of it. He deserved so much better than what I could give him. He deserved so much better than a half-mate and deception.

But it was all I had.

It was all I had.

Wearing my wolfskin, I dropped him off at work every day. I guarded him from outside the front door, listened to him charm the customers, competent as ever, his walls back in place. And when his shift was over I accompanied him home, and watched after him, because it was all I could do.

Sometimes Jeffrey pet me, other days he'd bury his face in my hair and hum beneath his breath. The same song he'd sang for open mic night. Voice angelic and sweet.

On the occasions when I had to leave while wearing my wolfskin, I would scratch at the door till he let me out. Since the first time I'd run off, Jeffrey always trusted me to return.

And any time I thought about leaving for good, I simply…couldn't.

Because I'd remember his face every time he stepped out of the small shop on Main Street after his shifts were over. The same face, every damn time. So…*hopeful.* His copper hair would glint, and the broad span of his shoulders would sink, his head dropping infinitesimally as sad-loss-lonely-scent filled the air any time he didn't see me immediately. He'd look both ways down the street, searching for me, and the scent only grew stronger as the seconds ticked by.

Until he'd see me again, waiting for him, and the air would fill with light again.

All my life I'd dreamed of the day I'd find my fated mate. The day I'd meet my perfect person, the other half of my heart's duet. Only it didn't take long to realize fated mates were a rare thing indeed, and I'd more than likely never meet mine. Most people didn't.

So I'd decided to settle, when the time came. When the moon betrayed me and I had no choice but to take a mate.

Because though my head was full of the fairy tales I'd grown up watching on my parents tiny TV, I knew I needed to be realistic. I'd choose a wolf just like my father had, and his father before him. I'd bite the back of their neck and we'd bond, and I'd stop myself from going permanently feral.

Still young, and clumsy pawed, Dad and Mom would show me the mating catalog and I'd wag my tail and picture happily ever afters with the wolves inside it. I pictured frolicking in the woods, tasting cool stream water, pups. So *many* pups. I imagined feeling whole for the first time in my life. The gaping, gnawing emptiness inside me sated. I'd daydreamed and fantasized. It had been something I was excited for.

But now, the thought filled me with dread.

Jeffrey was human, not a wolf, and he couldn't be what I needed, despite being the one my moon mother had decided was my fated mate.

It was a cruel joke, really.

Jeffrey was everything I had ever wanted, but I couldn't choose him without losing myself.

Harry and Butters were still staring at me—waiting for an answer. They could probably smell my emotions. Sad-loss-sad, and as much as I wished I could cover up my own scent, I knew that was impossible.

I took a steadying breath, lashes fluttering at the thought of all of Jeffrey's creamy, freckled skin, trying to think happy thoughts and not about the tragedy that awaited me at the end of my stay in Elmwood.

Colorado had always been home, but now it felt like a death sentence.

"Matthew…" Harry frowned at me, reaching out for me. I side-stepped his touch. I shook my head, my tongue tasting like ash. Harry backed off.

Butters made a confused sound, his tail thwacking against the couch as the ears on his head flattened. He glanced between me and Harry, like he was about to say something—but Harry growled softly and Butter's mouth clicked shut.

"Silas says he's happy you could make today's meeting," Harry said, offering me an olive branch. I nodded, my own ears flattened to my scalp. I preferred having them out, even in humanskin, as losing all of my true form felt uncomfortable. Butters was the same, he often decorated himself with his ears and tail, using them to emote in a way wolves better understood, especially wolves like us who preferred our wolfskin.

I nodded, trying not to huff in annoyance at the mention of Silas. He was alpha of the pack that resided on the outskirts of Elmwood. Tall and as severe as Harry but with a look on his face that made his mouth twist like he'd gotten a pine needle stuck in his paw.

He was a stick in the mud. And he wasn't my brother, so I didn't feel bad about saying that. So far, he'd been very specific about only ever wanting me, Theo, or Harry involved in negotiations. And he'd been a real prick about allowing Harry to come in the first place. The ass apparently hadn't wanted a foreign omega on his pack grounds.

Harry had quickly shown him how idiotic that was.

And to Silas's credit, he'd realized his error and no longer pushed for Harry's silence.

But still, I didn't like him.

"Don't flash your teeth like that," Theo said, entering through the front door and blocking the only exit with his bulk. I scowled at him, and he laughed good-naturedly. Of my brothers, Theo was the largest. Beneath his dark skin, his pearly grin, and his gold-beta-eyes, Theo was the sweetest of all my siblings. A gentle giant who was more bake than bark—on account of the amount of time he spent in front of a mixer covered in icing.

"What's gotten into you?" Theo asked, concerned. He petted my head as he passed, the gentle way he always did, but it did nothing for my agitation. For a second, I debated diving for the exit now that it was free again—but thought better of it.

It was late. Far too late to be going out, but Silas—because he was Silas—often held meetings at this time. Probably so the head of SAC could attend as well, as he was a fanged-one and could not go out when the sun was up.

"He's been running off a lot lately," Harry sighed, annoyed—unaware that Theo knew this already. In fact, he was the only person who knew who I had been running off with—even though he'd been kind enough not to ask too many questions when he'd offered his help.

"Probably pissing on trees," Butters snorted where he sat sprawled on the couch, the app on his phone pulled up again, his thick fingers swiping the screen, pink tongue poking out of the corner of his mouth while he concentrated.

None of them mentioned the sex scent again.

I'm sure they could smell my relief.

Harry handed Theo the notes he'd been drafting up at the dining table, and Theo accepted them with a grateful hum.

"Projecting much?" Jules teased. The smooth cadence of his voice wafted in from the hallway as he entered the living room from the other end, flipping the page in his book without looking up. A lock of dark hair fell across his brow. He was barely half Butter's size and his hair was as dark as Butters's was light. Yin and Yang. If I didn't know any better, I'd think he and Harry were blood-related, they looked so similar. Though Jules was slighter and shorter, and had a lock of white hair right at the front of his hair that made him look like a skunk more often than not.

A skunk that read books.

"Fair," Butters laughed, holding a hand out for a high-five that Jules returned as he walked past him without looking up.

Butters then turned to Theo, his hand cupping his mouth as he angled his body toward him. "What does "projecting" mean?"

Jules snorted out a laugh, "Why did you high-five me if you didn't even know what I said?"

"I dunno, seemed like a good diss."

"Jesus Christ," Harry pinched the bridge of his nose from where he still stood inside the archway that led to the kitchen and Theo gently patted him on the back in a soothing manner before turning back to Butters.

"When someone unconsciously attributes their thoughts, feelings, or behaviors to another person, they are projecting."

"I don't understand half of what you just said," Butters smiled serenely then turned back to his game. Swipe, swipe, swipe. "But thanks for trying."

"You're welcome," Theo pressed his lips together to hide his smile, shaking his head as he started reviewing his notes.

"I think we should ask for more land," Harry said, ducking his head so he and Theo were whispering. It was easy enough to catch every word, so there was no need for him to raise his voice. We all had superior hearing. "This isn't nearly enough for what they're asking us to pay. Besides, we need room for full moon runs without bumping into each other's packs."

"Unless they want to run together?"

"Oh. Well that's an idea."

And so it began.

Again.

Yay.

Instead of paying attention like I probably should have while we prepped for visiting the Elmwood Pack, I thought about Jeffrey again. I thought about the precious time I was missing out on. I may not have intended on staying at first, but now that I was stuck, I couldn't help but dive in headfirst.

We didn't have much time—and I intended on savoring it as much as I possibly could.

And I wouldn't let anyone stop me. Not my brothers. Not my duty to the pack. Not the full moon. Nothing.

Chapter Eleven

Jeffrey

THE PARTY RAGED around us. Couples pressed against the walls, hidden in seedy corners with their hands down each other's pants and their tongues tangled. I had hickeys all over my neck, and my red solo cup had been filled four different times—but somehow still was empty.

When I spotted Blair's fuzzy black head, I relaxed, wandering toward him.

"Yo!" Trevor, our left fielder interrupted me, reaching out and latching onto my shoulder. His hand was sweaty and he smelled like tequila and something fruity—probably the jello shots Becky, his girlfriend had made for the party.

We'd just won the state championship and all of us were on cloud nine. Becky and Martha were friends—Martha being head cheerleader, and my at-the-time girlfriend. Like a sweaty, web, we were all tangled together.

It was all very…exhausting, if I'm being honest.

It was hard enough keeping up the front at home—and out here it got even more difficult. Especially at times like this, when the alcohol was flowing in my veins and I was seventeen with a cross to bear.

"Fuck off," I managed, words slurred. I tried to shove Trevor off of me, but failed. He just laughed.

"Dude you're fucked up," he snorted, like that was funny.

It didn't feel funny.

None of this did.

"Need…" I wasn't sure what I needed. I'd forgotten. What had I been about to do? It felt important.

"Martha's over by the stairs."

"By the stairs," I repeated, squinting and looking around. Trevor latched onto my other shoulder and spun me, pointing me in the correct direction. "Just don't fuck on Becky's bed," he said cheerfully before shoving me off.

I stumbled a little.

"Where are my shoes?" I frowned down at my bare feet, and where the sticky tile clung to them. "And my socks." I frowned even more, wandering the direction Trevor had pointed me. "Someone stole my socks," I muttered to myself, annoyed. "Who does that?"

"Who does what?" Seth, our shortstop, asked me as I squeezed by him. He had his hand on his phone, and the other was holding a half-empty beer. I wasn't sure where he'd gotten the bottle. No one had given me a bottle. I'd just had cups. I frowned at my cup next, betrayed.

"Uhhh shit," I hit the corner of the door and Seth laughed, smacking me on the ass and causing me to stumble. "I dunno. I forgot."

That was true.

I had.

By the time I reached the stairs I'd been slapped, prodded, and pushed by half the baseball team. I couldn't remember why I'd come to the stairs in the first place—and when I discovered they were empty, I felt kinda…relieved if I'm being honest.

So I sat down, heavily, on my ass.

"Oof." My cup spilled, and I stared at it—flabbergasted. Could've sworn the fucking thing was empty—but, hey. Maybe someone had filled it for me? In fact…I was pretty sure Seth had. Or maybe that had been Rodney? Fuck.

Didn't matter anyway.

This was my party.

If I wanted to get fucked up, I'd get fucked up.

I deserved this.

I deserved this.

I just wanted…

I just wanted to forget.

Let me forget.

Please, please, please.

Let me just—

I downed the cup in a few, painful sips. The acrid alcohol burned on its way down, lighting my veins up from the inside out as the room spun and spun and spun. I pressed my forehead to the bannister, trying to catch my breath.

And when I closed my eyes all I saw was it.

The thing.

The big, bulbous thing—with warts and—fuck. The way it'd popped. The wheezing hiss sound it'd made when I'd sunk my knife into its neck and blood had spilled up my forearm. It'd scratched at me, scratched, and scratched, and scratched. Its claws tore into my arms but still, I pushed. Pushed deep past the fat layer beneath its skin. Into muscle. Into warm, slippery heat.

Its heart had bumped my fingers as my knife slid inside it.

And it'd gasped—this awful-awful-awful-awful sound as it died.

As it died beneath my hand.

And I just—

"Need more…drink."

Trevor was passing by again, this time with a six-pack under his arm. He must've heard me, because he handed me a new beer and I grinned up at him, thankful. He looked blurry. But that was okay. I didn't mind.

I didn't mind much right now.

Things were soft and fuzzy—and they didn't hurt so much.

There were no monsters.

There was only this beer and—oh. Wow. It felt so good pressed to my forehead. So so good. Yes. I liked that. I liked that even more than drinking it. I chugged the remainder of my solo cup then tossed it to the side, beer still in hand.

"Jeffrey," Blair's voice broke through the fog in my head. At first, I thought I imagined it. Because Blair shouldn't be here. This was a party. Blair didn't go to these—he hated my friends. If I was being honest, I hated them too. They were dumb and vapid and they thought high school was forever.

They thought any of this mattered.

But it didn't.

It didn't, it didn't, it didn't.

Not when there was blood out there. Blood and knives—and monsters—and the sounds they made when they died.

"Jeffrey," Blair tried again. And this time I felt his hand on my shoulder. I flinched away, eyes fluttering open, my beer falling to the ground with an annoying clink. "I think you've had enough, man."

"Fuck off," I reached for the beer, but Blair beat me to it. He curled his fingers around the neck, pulling it away.

"Stop being a bitch," I huffed out, flapping my hand out for the beer again, and missing—spectacularly. Which was not like me. I had impeccable aim. If I didn't, I'd be dead. The scratches on my torso itched, scabs barely healing over.

"I'm not being a bitch," Blair laughed, though he had this judgy look on his face that pissed me off. Like he was looking down on me or something. Like I was pathetic.

Hell, I knew I was.

But I didn't need him to look at me like that.

"Just let me—"I reached for it again, and he batted my hand away.

"No."

"Fuck." I glared at him, struggling to my feet, though I stumbled a little and hit the bannister. A pained hiss escaped, one of the scratches on my torso pulling to the point of blistering—white hot pain. Fuck. Ow. Fuck. "Ow—" I gasped, wheezing as I held onto the railing, eyes pinched shut.

"Are you—"

"I'm fine—" I managed, somehow holding on long enough to get the words out. "Fuck off."

"No."

"I'm fine—" my voice didn't sound like my own. It was manic, and high, and twitchy. "I'm fine, I'm fine, I'm fine."

"You're not fine." Blair frowned at me. I could hear it in his voice. Didn't even need to look at him to know what his face looked like. He was in this annoying phase lately. Seemed to think if he did whatever Lydia wanted him to, things would get better. That she'd change. That we'd be a happy fucking family and la-dee-dah.

Fat chance of that.

She was just biding her time.

Because she was evil, she was evil fucking incarnate. It was like he'd forgotten all the shit she'd done to him. All the times she'd locked him up. The violence. The nasty words. The cuts and bruises—the night terrors—

The—

The—

Everything—

"Lydia's not gonna like it if you show up at home like this," Blair said gently. But it felt like a slap to the face, hearing her name out loud. In a place like this, where things were supposed to be bright and I was, for once in my fucking life, something other than her secret protege.

Blair didn't know.

It wasn't his fault.

I knew that.

He didn't know what she made me do. The creatures I'd killed. The blood on my hands. The places she'd hole us up in—just the two of us. He didn't know about the days spent training, the blisters on my hands, the scars, the gun I shouldn't know how to use. Didn't know about the way I'd lie in my bed, pretending to sleep, because there was no way I could actually rest with her lying three feet from me.

No way I could rest when I knew the pain that waited for me the second the sun rose.

The guilt.

The terror.

The blood.

The monsters.

The way I couldn't breathe most of the time, but I breathed anyway. Always trying to be strong because if I failed even **once**, *it was Blair who took the brunt of Lydia's fury. He was her bargaining chip, and maybe he knew it— maybe he didn't. But that didn't make it any less true.*

The sun would rise and the torture would start all over.

"Again," she'd say, watching me—her eyes green as the money she coveted, when they might as well have been red. She never got dirty. Never touched a corpse, or held a gun herself. Making me repeat the drills she'd arranged over and over and over till they became so second-nature, I barely had to think about them at all.

"Again," she'd say as she forced me to shoot targets in proxy of living creatures.

"Again," she'd say, holding me steady, her nails biting into my shoulder, her breath hot on my back.

Then later, just as I'd suspected, on the day my gun wavered, the beast it was pointed toward staring at me, terrified, its heart thumping, its eyes wide with fear. There would be no sympathy from Lydia.

"I can't, I can't–"

"You're a coward, Jeffrey. Take the fucking shot."

Bodies, bodies, bodies. Hairy, scaly, wet with blood.

Over and over and over—

Dead dead dead.

Because of me.

Because I didn't say no.

Because I was—

You're a coward, Jeffrey.

You're a coward, you're a coward, you're a coward.

You'reacowardyou'reacowardyou'rea—you'rea—you're—

Nononononono.

*I didn't want to be there anymore. Trapped inside my head. The alcohol was supposed to help. It was supposed to **help**—I was supposed to be able to breathe here, at this party, with my friends. I wanted to celebrate—I just wanted… I just wanted—*

God.

I just wanted to be seventeen.

*I just wanted to be **normal**.*

I just wanted to make stupid mistakes like everyone else. Mistakes that wouldn't get me killed. Mistakes that didn't make me a murderer. Mistakes that didn't haunt me, hanging like a noose around my neck. Scars made into weapons so I could never forget where they came from.

"She's gonna be pissed," Blair was still talking. Talking. Like he could convince me to come home. To come to heel. To be her loyal dog, even now. It wasn't fair, it wasn't fair—

"You're a coward, Blair," I hissed out, and then jolted, the words falling like an anvil between us.

Blair flinched.

What little was left of my heart broke then, the second I realized what I'd just done. Because Lydia may have taught me how to load a gun, but I'd never pointed one at Blair before.

I'm sorry, I'm sorry. Fuck, fuck, fuck.

I was…fuck.

I'm no better than Lydia.

"I'm sorry—" I managed, but Blair was already pulling away. He let go of my shoulder, his expression pinched. His dark hair fell across his brow, and I couldn't breathe—couldn't breathe—couldn't breathe—"I didn't mean it—"

"I'm gonna go home."

"I'll go with you—"

"Don't."

Blair left.

Blair left and he took my beer with him.

And I…watched him go. Because my dumb legs were too wobbly and wouldn't work—and I felt heavy and scared and shaky and I just…I just…

I hated myself.

I hated myself so much.

So I drank and drank and drank. Until I emptied my stomach into Martha's bathtub and half the baseball team crowded in the bathroom to make sure I wasn't dying. I wasn't—somehow—alcohol poisoning aside. But I wished I was.

I wished I was.

Because living hurt, and this was all my fault—and I hurt Blair and I—

And I—

And I—

I was a monster.

Chapter Twelve

Jeffrey

Blair: SOS.

Me: ?

Blair: So

Me: ?????

Blair: Remember how I asked for your help with a shipment? Well it came early.

Me: oh shit

Blair: I won't make you watch Dracula ever again if you can help me pick it up.

Me: I like Dracula

Blair: I know, fuck. I don't have many bargaining chips, okay?

Me: I'll help. Of course I'll help. Don't take Bella Lugosi away from me. I already said I would.

Blair: I love you

Blair: have I told you that I love you?

Blair: Because I love you.

Blair: best brother ever.

BLAIR'S SOS CAME at the worst time possible. Because I'd been three fingers deep in my own ass and five minutes from hopping on the silicone dick I'd ordered online. It'd been taunting me. Sitting in my nightstand, hidden away—out of sight, but not out of mind.

Especially after Mutt had practically made out with my asshole—I just…yeah. I couldn't get the idea of getting fucked for real out of my head. Which was…weird. I'd never been attracted to the idea before. Never looked at a guy and thought, *Oh yeah, I wanna ride that dick.*

But with Mutt, thoughts like that were only the tip of the iceberg.

And he was going slow, and part of me could only guess it was because of my own inexperience. Maybe he could smell it on me like he could smell my emotions—or hear it in my heartbeat, like he read my lies. Or maybe it was because he'd never done this either. He hadn't outright admitted to being a virgin, but he had made it clear our first time together that he'd never been anywhere near another man's ass before.

Either way—I was gonna be ready.

I was gonna be so fucking ready, and when we finally got to that point—because lets be honest, after the second time we'd had sex, I'd accepted it was only inevitable—I wanted to be a goddamn pro.

Therefore: dildo, ass, alone time.

I probably shouldn't have checked my phone, but old habits die hard.

Ever since the day I'd come home and found Blair missing, and received *nothing* but radio silence from Blair to indicate he was okay, I'd become hardwired to react to the ping of text tones like they were goddamn tornado warnings.

For *so long* I'd waited for him to text me.

To call me.

Something.

Something to indicate he wasn't dead.

Lydia had been no help. She probably thought it was funny how concerned I was. And now that I knew she'd been trying to take his life that entire time—I understood that she would've been happy had he ended up dead after all.

She liked leaving me to squirm.

It made it easier to control me.

I wasn't sure what she'd expected to happen. If she'd succeeded in killing him, did she really think she'd come home and all would be well? That I wouldn't put a bullet right in her head, and be done with her forever?

Because I would have. She'd have been dead instead of in prison.

I may not have been a born killer, but she'd made me into one. Despite my usual squeamish nature, I would've killed her. I wouldn't have hesitated.

And I wouldn't have felt guilty.

Because she would have deserved it.

My phone rang, and I gasped out a horrified sound as I pulled my fingers from my ass and fumbled the damn thing on. "Hello?"

Fuck, this is so fucking embarrassing.

Why did I answer it?

"Hi, Jeffrey." Richard's voice was low and gentle like it always was. Not that I knew him all that well—at least not as an adult. Sure, I'd seen him in passing since I moved back, usually when he was with Blair, but I'd so far successfully avoided any and all alone time with him.

I just…

I guess I didn't know what to say.

We'd been close once—but that felt like a lifetime ago. And now he was a vampire. Which was so freaking weird.

"Sup?" I replied, trying to keep my tone casual like the dildo I'd bought wasn't staring at me from the nightstand. Like my fingers weren't sticky. Like my ass wasn't twitching and empty, hungry for werewolf cock.

"I sent you the address for the furniture place," Richard said. "It'll take an hour and twenty five minutes to drive there."

"Cool."

"I also sent you the order confirmation number."

"Dope."

"It's under Blair Evans, but I told them to expect you, so feel free to use either your name or his." My heart thumped unsteadily. What name did he put for me? It was such a dumb question, but it meant kinda…a lot to me.

"Right," I said, hands shaking a little.

Did he put Markus or Jeffrey?

Markus Prince?

Jeffrey Evans?

Jeffrey Prince?

Every name meant something different. Markus was the boy who'd died, the naive fool—the one everyone missed but me. Jeffrey Evans was a puppet—even less real than Markus was. And Jeffrey Prince…he was a messed up, twisted fuck-up who didn't know who he was anymore.

The name Richard picked for me would make it obvious how he felt about me. How he saw me. Was I the fuckup who had returned? Would he accept that? Or was I Markus, dead and gone, with no room to move on. No room for who I was in his life now that I wasn't who I used to be.

Richard continued to give me details about the order but my head was spinning. I lost track of a lot of them, but figured…how hard could it be? It was just a few fucking chairs. I could handle that.

"What name?" I blurted, weirdly late. "I mean. For me." I cleared my throat. "What name did you—"

"Jeffrey Prince," Richard sounded confused, like that had been the only answer that made sense. And my heart fluttered as I realized what that meant. It was the best-case scenario. I wasn't used to those.

Richard said something about sending help for me, but I was too twisted up inside to really understand what he meant.

At least…

Until I was climbing into my truck a while later and there was a gentle rap at the passenger-side window. A familiar freckled face peered at me, dark eyes glinting as Collin yanked the door open and slid into the seat. He folded his gangly legs up, shoving the seat back with an annoyed huff. "Blair been in here?" he said in greeting. Probably because the leg room was abysmal.

"Uh, yeah." I stared at him, not really sure what the fuck was happening. *Jesus, god. Why must you punish me?*

Collin was the last person I wanted to be stuck alone in a car with for three plus hours.

"There," the seat whirred as it moved back into place. Collin grinned, very pointedly not buckling himself up—probably to test me.

I may be trying to come across as the "cool big brother" but I wasn't an idiot.

"Buckle up, man," I said, doing up my own buckle pointedly. "The fuck aren't you in school?"

"I'm sick," Collin fake coughed like Karen from *Mean Girls*.

"The fuck you are."

"Dammit," Collin huffed, throwing his hands up. "Aren't you supposed to be the cool brother?"

His thoughts so perfectly mirrored my own, I couldn't help but laugh. "You know what's not cool?"

"If you say 'not putting your seatbelt on' I'm going to scream."

"Not putting your seatbelt on."

"Fuck."

"Richard know you're not in school?"

"Yes, Mom." Collin huffed, annoyed. "I checked with all my teachers. I'm not missing classes. I'm all caught up. Now will you get off my ass?" Blair had mentioned that this was Collin's first year at public school and that he'd been more than a little excited to attend. I wasn't so sure about that, judging by his current mood.

I shrugged, ignoring his swearing with a snort as it finally hit me what Richard had meant when he'd said he was going to send me help. Collin was…*apparently* my help. I wasn't sure how much he'd be able to lift, but now that he was in my truck I couldn't just kick him out.

Especially when it looked like—based on the bike parked on the curb in front of my parking spot—he'd biked all the way here. I had no doubt that Richard would find a way to pick it up for him, because he was just perfect like that.

Collin was sweaty, like the second Richard had called in the calvary he'd pedaled his scrawny ass over here like there was a fire lit under it. I could respect that. Seeing as I'd dropped everything to help Blair the second he asked too. Everything, as in my dildo plans. My ass still felt twitchy and loose, and that was not a feeling I liked at all when I was sitting alone with my kid-brother-stranger.

As much as I hated being stuck alone with him though, I warmed a little.

Because maybe Collin and I weren't that different after all.

We both cared about Blair.

And that was a good fucking start.

Pulling out onto Spruce, checking for wayward wolves and the very few pedestrians that populated the streets during daylight, I headed toward the highway that would lead out of town. I was quiet as I turned the music up so Collin wouldn't be tempted to talk to me, and rolled the window down so the wind would make that even more difficult.

It wasn't that I didn't want to get to know him.

I was just…scared of what he might ask.

He saw through me.

I could tell.

Saw through my cracks.

Collin took pity on me for the first ten minutes of the drive. Let me drop my guard and everything, my head bobbing to the beat as I sang under my breath, the weight of the guitar pick in my pocket centering me.

And then, music and windows be damned, he ambushed me.

Collin's silence broke as he twisted to look at me, face all screwed up tight like he'd been sucking on a lemon. I wanted to ignore him, so I pretended I hadn't seen him very obviously trying to get my attention. Or at least… *tried* to pretend. Because the longer I went without acknowledging him, the more obviously he stared at me—and the more his face scrunched up.

"For fuck's sake." I turned the volume down, my heart in my throat. "*What?*"

"What's your deal?" Collin asked without preamble. It was our first time alone together, and I suppose I couldn't blame him. He'd patiently been biding his time, waiting for this moment.

"My deal?" I played dumb.

"Yeah," Collin buckled down, crossing his arms.

"I don't have one."

"Everyone has one," he countered. "Like me." He pointed to himself. "My deal is that Mom and Dad want me to turn. I don't want to. It's shitty and annoying—but ever since they found out you're alive they've backed off."

I'd been in town for over a month and hadn't seen either of my parents, if that was any indication of how much they actually cared. "They're dicks," I said softly, my heart thumping.

"Yeah," Collin shrugged. "But I'm not." He glared at me. "So what gives? Why're you always looking at me like I slit your tires?"

"I'm not—I don't—"

"Yeah, you do," Collin huffed. "Look, I get it's weird. You've been gone. Things are weird. I'm new and you don't know me." His long fingers tapped his biceps. "But I'm not gonna bite your head off. And I may not know you either, but you're still my brother. And maybe…I dunno. Maybe I *want* to know you."

"You don't want to know me," I countered, glaring out at the road so I wouldn't have to look at him. He was naive if he thought that.

"I do."

"No, you don't."

"I do," Collin glared at me.

"No, you don't," I repeated, harder this time. This was juvenile. And it was too hard to focus on the road when we were arguing. So I pulled over to the side, a splattering of tree shadows hitting the front dash as I twisted to look at him. "You want Markus. You all fucking want Markus. Hate to break it to you but he's dead. I'm sorry, but he is."

"Markus." Collin repeated the name like it was a swear word. "Markus is a fucking ghost, man."

"I know."

"I don't want *him*." Collin stared at me. He stared at me for a long time. My heart was pounding, my palms were slick. I couldn't breathe—I couldn't. "I want *you.*"

"You don't," my voice broke.

He has no idea what he's talking about.

"I do," he argued again, softer this time. "Look…" Collin sucked in a breath, shifting to face me better. He crossed one leg over the other, his ankle hanging over his knee as he stared me down. "My whole life I had to live inside your shadow. You know…Mom and Dad only had me because you died, right? I'm like…the replacement for you. Except the second they had me they forgot why they'd wanted me in the first place."

"What the fuck?"

"I know," Collin gestured at himself. "It's gross, right? But, I mean— look at me? Do I look sad?"

I stared at him, like…*really* stared.

His eyes were bright, his body was relaxed, and his expressive mouth was twisted into a sunny grin. He didn't look sad. At all. In fact he looked like he was eating this shit up.

"I mean, yeah, they piss me off and the whole 'turn with us, you li'l bitch' thing bothers me. But I'm me, and I like me—and I'm fine." Collin stared at me. "And I'll *be* fine. No matter how often they bug me."

I wasn't sure why he was telling me this.

"Which is why I don't get you," Collin said, tone softening. "You're so fake man. Everyone can see it. We've all been through enough shit that we recognize the signs. You think we don't get it? Because we do."

"Get what?" My voice cracked a little.

"That you've seen shit." Collin's fingers tapped against his biceps as he stared me down—so fucking brave, and so little—and so…naive. "That you're drowning."

That I'm drowning.

A wet laugh escaped me, and once I started I couldn't seem to stop.

I turned away from him, not sure what the look on my face was—only that I didn't want him to see. It was *ugly, ugly, ugly.* And I knew that. *I* was ugly. Not my outsides, but the inner bits. Burnt black and charred, and withered after years held above flame.

"We're your family," Collin said, like it was that simple. "We *wanted* you to come back."

"You wanted Markus," I repeated, because that was what I'd thought—that was what I'd feared, all along. And even though he'd already said that wasn't the case, I figured he just genuinely didn't get it. Maybe he needed it spelled out. "Not me."

"You're stupid if you think that," Collin replied immediately. "And also don't know how to fucking listen."

Maybe I was stupid.

Maybe he was right, because I couldn't stop laughing.

"Are you…are you *okay?*" His hand hovered over my shoulder now and the hesitance there hurt more than his words did. "Like I get that you're *not.* I mean…you got kidnapped and like—this all has to be so weird. Coming back here. Living here. Meeting us—*me. But are you okay?*"

Another laugh escaped me, and I wished I could take it back. "I'm fine." I tried to wave him off.

Collin didn't even justify *that* with a response. He simply laid his palm on my shoulder, the warmth bleeding into me as I sucked in a fortifying breath.

"I'm fine," I repeated, because I had to be.

Because I had no choice.

"It's okay if you're not," he said gently, like I hadn't said anything at all. "Do you…maybe want to talk?" Collin asked, his voice gentle. "I know I'm probably the last person you want to open up to. But like…I want to know you, you know? Even though you're a shit liar—and you give me stank face all the time. I'm at least better at listening than you are."

"*You're* the one that gives *me* weird looks!" I snorted, more amused this time.

"Only because you started it."

"I did not."

"You did."

"Fuck." I sucked in a breath, trying not to laugh. "Look, I just…" I guess I kinda had been the first one. "It's just…like you said. It's weird…being here. It's good but it hurts too, you know? I don't…I don't know who I am, or what you want from me. What *anyone* wants from me."

"What if we don't want anything?" Collin countered.

"Everyone always wants something."

"That's fucking sad, dude." Collin frowned. "And not true."

"I dunno."

"You're…" I sucked in another breath, the truth spilling free. "You're what I should've been, you know?"

"And you're who I was born to replace," Collin countered. "At least… if you listen to *idiots*."

"I don't know how to talk to you."

"Ditto, man."

"I don't know how to talk to anyone." I squeezed the steering wheel tight enough it creaked. *You're talking to Collin,* my brain unhelpfully pointed out. "I think I'm broken."

"That's okay."

"Is it?" It didn't feel okay.

"Sure it is." Collin shrugged. "Richard once almost hit me with his car and I still love him."

"Wait, what?"

"He didn't see me. To be fair, I was going really fast, and kinda jumped in front of the car to see if he'd stop. But still. The point still stands. Family is family, man. Some people suck, but we don't."

"You jumped in front of his car?" I stared at him, horrified.

"Intrusive thoughts, dude." Collin shrugged. "Not my fault."

"That was totally your fucking fault."

"Still." Collin grinned, eyes dancing.

"You're so happy," I blurted, accidentally, my brain to mouth filter apparently broken. "And very…*you*. You—I mean…" I tried again. "You know who you are." This conversation had only solidified that fact in my mind. "I'm not like that."

Why keep me around when I didn't provide any value?

"*I* didn't get kidnapped, or raised by a murderous bitch," Collin countered, his voice just the right amount of sarcastic for his words to strike me where I needed them. Where I was gooey and soft and vulnerable. "I feel like…considering what happened to you, you're doing pretty damn good. Cut yourself some fucking slack. And damaged or not, I know for a fact that Richard, Blair, and I just want you to be our fucking brother, dude. Wow. That sounds so weird. I mean—it's complicated? Because Blair and Richard…and yeah. Whatever. You know what I mean."

I couldn't breathe.

I couldn't breathe—

I couldn't—

You deserve to be happy.

Don't you think it's time to move on?

You know I don't blame you, right?

"Okay. Let's be done with the dramatics. I reached my quota for the day," Collin replied, gently rubbing my shoulder, earlier hesitance gone. "But for the the third fucking time—I *do* want to know you. So if you change your mind about talking more…I'm *here*. Not like, *here* here, because obviously I'll have to go home at some point—but yeah."

"Right," I echoed, melting a little beneath the touch, because I couldn't help it. He could see my cracks. He could see them and yet he wasn't…he wasn't *running*. I didn't get it. I didn't get any of this.

"So," Collin said, and I feared for my sanity that he'd start questioning me again. "I heard you got a dog?"

Apparently mercy was something even nosy teenagers could offer.

Collin was surprisingly good company when I wasn't actively self-sabotaging our relationship. He knew all the Taylor Swift songs that mattered, he ate more food than I did, and when we finally arrived at our destination, he made quick work of loading all the chairs into the truck.

He was so distracting with his chipper attitude and his loud personality I almost forgot about the weird conversation we'd had in the car.

Almost.

But for the most part, I was kinda content to get to know my little brother.

It didn't hurt the way it had before. He wasn't my replacement—despite what my parents had intended. He was brilliant and sunny, and his snarky tongue reminded me a lot of Blair. Our whole relationship reminded me of my relationship with Blair actually.

It's strange.

Because this felt…easy.

Maybe…it could've been this easy the whole time? And I'd made things harder for myself than they needed to be.

"So. How do you feel about sporks?" Collin asked as we pulled onto the ramp that led back into Elmwood.

"Sporks?" I snorted, brow furrowing. "The…utensil?"

"Obviously."

"I guess…they're useful?"

"And an abomination," Collin added with a wicked grin, putting his feet up on my dash and cackling to himself. "*Both*."

"Right." I guess I'd never cared enough about sporks to have an opinion on them.

"Don't you find it weird that Blair and Richard are dating?" he asked me, jumping topics like a hyperactive frog. "I mean it's not weird for me, because Blair is Blair—and I never knew him. But *you* grew up with him."

"Yeah," I shrugged. "It's pretty fucking weird."

"Cool though, yeah?"

"Yeah." It *was* cool. Maybe it had taken a little while for me to get used to the idea of my blood brother dating my adoptive brother, but…they were so sickeningly cute together it hadn't taken much effort after all.

"They're…"

"Gross?"

"Definitely gross," I laughed, fingers tapping at the steering wheel as pop music blasted through the car and the scent of French fries filled the air.

"They stare at each other like allll the time. Blair will go take a piss, and he'll walk back in the room, and Richard gives him these eyes, like he's been gone for a zillion years and not five fucking minutes."

"They really like each other," I snorted. "You know they invited me to the movies?"

"Oh god."

"I was like, fuck no. I don't want to watch you make out."

"Good call." Collin grinned at me. "I walked in on them once. And can I just say? Ew. Like. I wanted to bleach my eyeballs. Their tongues were touching. Touching!"

"Disgusting," I agreed, and Collin beamed. Kinda felt like I'd won an award.

He ranted more about Blair and Richard for a bit. And then our mom—and then his classes at school, in particular the ones he was dreading. And then he talked about fish sticks, High-Chew gummies, and why red was the superior choice for Converse sneakers—a fact I totally agreed with.

I reached for my drink and took a long sip.

"So," Collin said, tone still light. "You ever sucked a dick?"

I choked, spluttering as I shoved the cup back in the cupholder. My other hand held tight to the steering wheel so I wouldn't swerve and get us in a wreck. "W-What?"

"I'm just wondering, you know. For science." Collin bobbed his head. "I've thought about it. Kinda a lot. And it seems fun? But it also seems like it'd be annoying, you know? A whole-ass mouthful." He frowned. "Whole dick mouthful?" He shrugged. "You know what I mean."

I kinda wanted to cut him off, but then again…I'd been fifteen once too. And I wasn't sure what about me screamed "I'm a sex-pert" but I figured, compared to Blair, I kinda was. Collin wasn't the first to ask for my advice.

Besides…after my freakout earlier it'd be nice to feel kinda…cool?

"I have," I shrugged, cheeks hot. "I like it."

"Huh." Collin's face scrunched up. "What about…you know—girls?" He tapped his fingers on his knees. "Not that I plan on getting laid, because duh, fifteen. But I'm just curious. Blair mentioned you're kinda a…man slut."

"The fuck," I snorted out, cheeks hot.

"He didn't say those *exact* words. I'm paraphrasing—but still."

"I guess I am," I shrugged, embarrassed. "I've been with a lot of people, yeah."

"Blair only mentioned girls."

"Which is why you asked about the dicks." Sneaky fuck.

"I guess I'm just…" Collin hummed thoughtfully. "I dunno. I feel like I give off bi-wife energy, you know?"

"Are you the wife in this scenario? Or do you have a bi-wife?"

"Both? IDK." Collin shrugged. "I guess I just don't really want to pick. And since Blair and Richard are gay-as-fuck, I wanted to talk to someone who maybe wasn't? Not that they can't give advice. Because they can—I just… you know."

"Wanted to talk to someone else who gives off bi-wife energy," I couldn't help but grin. Sure my bisexuality was newly discovered—but that didn't mean I wasn't excited about it. And I hadn't even gotten the chance to tell Blair, so it was kinda nice…to test it out in a safe environment. "I've only been with one man," I said, pulling onto Spruce. "And for the record? You never have to fucking pick."

The conversation was about to be cut short, so I slowed down to prolong it. I had a feeling Collin needed this. Hell, I would've killed to have an older brother at his age. That's why I'd made sure to be the best big brother I possibly could for Blair. Because it had been my fault we were alone in the first place.

"Did you like it?" Collin asked curiously. "As much as sex with girls?"

"More probably," I shrugged, cheeks hot. "Not that I didn't like that too—I just…I guess for me it's about the kind of connection. And he's…" Thinking about Mutt made me feel hot all over, embarrassed and happy and fizzy from the inside out. "Um."

It wasn't a feeling I'd had before about anyone.

Or anything.

It was safety, and warmth, and youth—youth I'd never had.

"He's…?" Collin stared at me, waiting expectantly. "What, super hot?" He was teasing, and I still couldn't help but flush.

"Yeah. Super fucking hot," I agreed, embarrassed. "And he's sweet, you know? Different. He…" This was embarrassing as hell. "He takes really good care of me."

"Which is good, you know. Cuz you're kinda fucked up."

"Right." I laughed. No one had just outright said that to my face, but I kinda liked it. It was refreshing not to be tiptoed around. I'd thought I'd hate that, but I didn't. "I think I need someone who's soft."

"I am thiiiiis close to making a dick joke," Collin held up his fingers in a pinching motion. "But since we're having a bi-bro moment, I'll hold back."

"A bi-bro moment," I repeated, oddly delighted by this.

"A bro-ment, if you will," Collin agreed in his poshest voice.

"Fuck," I laughed, sad when we pulled into the parking lot behind Blair's pizzeria. Avery's shop where I worked was just across the street, and it felt weird to be over here—and not there, but I pushed that feeling aside. "You're cute."

"Dawww," Collin waved me off, batting his lashes. "*Thanks!*"

"Collin?" I felt lighter than I had in years as I put the truck into park and twisted to look at him. "I'm sorry, for before. For treating you weird."

"I'm sorry too," Collin shrugged. "I could've been nicer."

"Me too." I smacked his shoulder, and he squawked, then smacked me back.

"Dickhead."

I shoved him against the window and he flapped his arms at me, smacking me in the face as we wrestled for a solid thirty seconds till I won. Easily. Because he may be nearly as tall as I was, but I was way fucking stronger.

When I settled back onto my side of the truck, I was a little sweaty, and my grin was genuine. "If you ever need to talk to someone about…you know, whatever—I'm here too," I offered, his own sweet words echoing around inside my head.

"Sounds good." Collin beamed at me, his copper hair flopping all over the place, eyes as bright as mine were. "Are you gonna be less awkward around me now?"

"I hope so."

"Cool."

And then he was sliding out of the car and heading around to the back to help unload. I followed after him, and for the first time since I'd come back to Elmwood, I felt like…part of my own family.

And that was…

That was…

Kinda perfect.

Chapter Thirteen

Mutt

THE SECOND JEFFREY left for work the following day, I knew what I had to do. Maybe it wasn't normal protocol for humans, but it felt right to me as I shifted to open the window, then shifted back into my wolfskin to take to the dirt toward my temporary home.

It was a wonder he hadn't figured out what I was yet, but I was grateful.

Because it meant I was able to spend every minute I could spare with him.

Still though…I craved the closeness of skin, and today, I planned to talk to him again, fur be damned.

The little house we'd rented was technically still in town, though it was on the border between Silas's pack grounds and Elmwood. They'd placed us there on purpose because Dad had no choice but to warn both officials of my condition. And everyone figured it was safer.

That wasn't the only thing in place for everyone's safety, however.

There was a number on the fridge.

A number we were supposed to call should I lose myself.

It was supposed to be a last resort—but with both the local pack and SAC's awareness of my moonsickness, there was very little room for error. If we called that number, the hunters would swarm in, and it'd inevitably end in my death.

Which was…scary.

I can admit that.

It was fucking scary.

And it wasn't fair.

I hadn't asked for this. I hadn't been asked to be born this way. Hadn't asked to be betrayed by my moon mother so early. Most alphas had plenty of time before they picked their mate. As per law, we had to wait till we were twenty years old. In the old days, before SAC had officially come to be, some packs would marry their alphas off as early as twelve. So it made sense to have regulations.

And in most cases, twenty was plenty early.

Yeah.

I was just unlucky.

But…I wasn't the only unlucky one. Because while I was dealing with the side-effects of my nature, Jeffrey had been through far worse.

I'd bided my time, patient as I soaked up Jeffrey's attention in my wolfskin and did my best not to want more. Touching him was nice, smelling his scent, listening to the sweet croon of his voice as he strummed the instrument his scent told me he loved. But it wasn't *enough*. Because I knew what he tasted like. I knew what noises he made when he was aroused. I knew what his cum tasted like—and I…well…

I was greedy.

Apparently.

I had never been a greedy person before, so this came as a surprise.

Because after a couple weeks of pretending to be his pet, existing beside him wasn't enough anymore. I knew the more time we spent together when I was in my humanskin, the more dangerous those interactions became. Soon I'd become something *more* than a man he found pleasure with, even though I'd been honest about what time we had together—and that would hurt him inevitably when I left.

But I *needed* more.

I needed it like I needed air, or water—or the moon's gentle caress.

I needed to talk to him, to *know* him. To listen to his laugh, to see him smile and know I was the cause of it. To know what it felt like to mount him fully. To hold him together when he threatened to fall apart. To right the wrongs that had been done to him when he'd been nothing but a pup.

To show him not everyone was bad, and that I would keep him safe, just like I'd promised.

Jeffrey hardly ever smiled, and when he did it was brittle.

Like he was porous and rough.

It was a smile I was after today, as I bounded over a log and decided to throw away my worries for now and focus on Jeffrey.

Trees in Maine were just as tall as the trees back home. Though *my* woods were dotted with the pale white bark of aspens, Elmwood's forests consisted primarily of densely packed pine and maple trees. With full, fat leaves that waved in the breeze. Pretty as a watercolor painting.

I knew what watercolors were because Mama taught me. She painted sometimes, on the rare occasion she adopted her humanskin. When I was a pup, I'd watch her, sitting at her feet, the gentle strokes of her brush wooshing through my ears as she created masterpieces out of thin air.

The walls of our childhood den were coated in haphazardly placed art pieces she'd made. The canvases varied in shape and size, all colorful, depicting visions of water that stretched far enough the world ended, and deserts so vast just looking at them made me feel small. In some rooms, even the walls were decorated. Altered into landscapes that made you feel like you were traveling the world, even when you weren't.

I'd been a homebody since birth.

I rarely left the pack grounds—and when I did, it was to hunt or forage. To visit with the trees, to dip inside the sparkling rivers, to stretch out my legs for as long as I could before Dad's howls ultimately called me back. As I'd gotten older he'd let me stay out longer and longer. I'd ran farther and farther. Especially after the day the moon turned her back on me, and I knew my time was limited.

All alphas went through this. Dad told me it was normal, but there was an ache in me hollow and dark that I knew wasn't right, no matter how often he told me it was.

After my eighteenth birthday I could manage several weeks alone without anyone thinking something was amiss, lurking between the trees and listening to the birds, content to gorge myself on nature's treasures when I was hungry, and not a moment before.

I'd hunt for prey and bring it home, leaving it on the edges of the compound to help sustain us.

Other than that, the full moon was the only thing that forced me to return to pack grounds now. The woods became my home as much as the cottage we grew up in and the compound our pack resided inside. A giant reserve off the beaten path with a crystalline lake and buildings that grew more crowded with every passing year.

I knew the compound like the back of my hand.

Knew the fastest way to get to the creek. Knew which roads to avoid and when. Knew every flavor the local and only ice cream shop served. Knew every nook and cranny, every crack and crevice, every tree and flower.

It was comfortable.

Safe.

My brothers had been surprised when I'd suggested we go to Maine. Shocked even. It was far away. Way farther than anyone had expected someone to suggest—least of all me. Before that moment I'd had no interest in leaving. I'd always thought Mama's paintings were enough— that I could travel the world through them and be content.

When I stood in front of Dad, the Pack Alpha, I felt every inch of my frame. Silence filled the room the moment I took my humanskin, and I could feel the weight of every single wolf present as I opened my mouth and begged.

"This is what you want?" Dad asked, his eyes soft, lips thin as always. He was a kind man, though quiet. "Maine?"

"Yes," my hands shook, because I had no idea what I'd do if he said no. I'd have to leave, at least temporarily. My heart was calling me from across the country, after all. I'd have to come back, I knew that. I had no choice. "I want to set up a new branch for the compound in Maine," My heart pounded. "It is the perfect spot. Similar in climate to home, but far enough away for growth and to strengthen the pack. There is a town—" my throat clicked. "It is a sanctuary. We would be safe beside it. There is a broad stretch of land up for sale that I know would work perfectly, and it is well within the budget you proposed. The local pack is friendly, and open to us expanding."

"You've researched this," Dad had said, talking slow and even, like always. His blue eyes flickered—the same shade as mine—a sad twist to his lips. "And you'll be back?" He watched me knowingly.

"Yes," I nodded. "I just…I need this. Please." Though the moons hurt, I knew I had at least a few in me before I fully fell beneath the weight of my wolf. There would be plenty of time to return home to bond before I went fully feral. "I'll be back, as promised. Right on time."

"I just want you safe," Dad said, his gray hair glinting. He had furs from my kills all over his chair, and was nursing a giant mug of cocoa, his massive frame making the cup appear normal-sized. I'd inherited his size, much like I'd inherited his eyes. Though sometimes, they felt like a curse, rather than a blessing.

"I know."

He stared at me for what felt like a century before he nodded, lifted his mug to his lips, and took a languorous sip. "Maine," he repeated, rolling the word around in his mouth. "Maine sounds nice. Fun. You'll enjoy it." Whipped cream decorated his silver mustache as he hummed thoughtfully.

I knew why Dad had said yes. It wasn't because of the pack overflow problem, or the location, or the strong SAC associated town next to the land I'd told him I wanted us to purchase.

No.

It was the fact I'd shifted to humanskin.

The fact I'd spoken up at all.

Mama pulled me aside after the meeting was over. Her eyes sparkled, pine needles in her hair, a smudge of dirt across her cheek. There were creases by her eyes. *Wrinkles.* I was certain they hadn't been there the last time that I'd seen her humanskin. She told me about autumn. About gold, orange, and fiery red. About the pale blue of the crisp sky and the smear of white snow that decorated the mountains.

She told me she was glad I was spreading my wings before I was stuck home for good. That it was good to explore while I was young.

I'd smiled, and it felt like a lie. But I couldn't bring myself to care, because I was protecting something precious. Something special. Something mine, mine, mine.

Something I'd have to give up—because fate dictated I did.

But something mine all the same.

Wasn't even sure I could last the full six months. Though the last moon had been surprisingly forgiving, that was not the norm. With every moon that passed, my shift got harder and harder. Longer and longer. Sometimes I'd remain shifted for days after the full moon rose—feral, trapped in alphaskin and locked away in the basement, only manacles and bruises for company.

"So…lemme get this straight," Butters hummed. "You wanna make a 'thanks for letting me sex you up' gift basket for a human—who you love—but can't bond with, *because* he's human?"

"Right."

"But Mom and Dad said you can bond with anyone." Butters frowned. "You just have to choose them."

I stared at him like he was stupid, because he was. "Have you ever heard of a human and a wolf mating?"

Butters frowned harder. Wrinkles multiplied. A car passed by on the street. The clock at the end of the hallway tick tick ticked away.

"No," he shrugged. "I guess not."

I wasn't sure what I was hoping for? Maybe that Butters would tell me I was wrong. And that he'd seen it happen after all. Because if it had happened once it could happen again, right? For me?

But no, I wasn't that lucky.

"I'm still going back home. I just…for now…let me have this." I'd never been more disappointed to be right. Sulking, I sighed, scrubbing a hand over my hair, my lips wobbling. "Basket," I said, a little hoarse. "Basket. I want to make…him a basket."

"And you want to put scentless soap in it?" Butters smiled sunnily, taking pity on me because he could scent my sadness as easily as he saw it. He was half-naked, his hand scratching his belly as he lay sprawled across the sofa in our temporary den, his brow lowered thoughtfully. "Like the one Dad buys us back home?"

"Yes."

"And you want *my* help?"

"Yes."

"But why…*me?*" Butters squinted. "Why not Harry? Or Theo? Or even Jules? They'd be better."

"No," I shook my head. "I want *you.*" It made me a little sad how surprised Butters was that I would choose him, of all my older brothers, to go to for help. He may have been…not the brightest star in the sky, but he was still my big brother. Made me glad I'd trusted him first. Well, second. Seeing as Theo had known about Jeffrey since the vet debacle.

"Your funeral, man," Butters blinked again, eyes narrowed thoughtfully. "I wonder if you could get it from the grocery store. Pretty sure he special orders it back at home, but…" he shrugged and scratched his belly again. His ears flickered as he thought, long and hard. His tail was thumping, betraying his excitement at having been chosen.

Butters was…for lack of a better word—obtuse.

But he was the brother I usually went to for help because what he lacked in cleverness, he made up for with loyalty. I was sure he'd keep his mouth shut. He was just that kinda guy, and I had a human to woo— and soap to find.

"Where is the 'grocery' store?" I asked, suddenly regretting not going with my brothers on the tour they'd taken the first night we'd come to town and Harry had offered to drive us around till we knew where everything important was.

"Uhhhh," Butters pursed his lips, eyes narrowed thoughtfully. He hadn't gone on the tour either. "Not sure?" He shrugged. "Betcha I could sniff it out though."

Sniff it out.

Yes.

That was a great idea.

"Or Google it." He scrounged around in the couch cushions for a couple minutes, grunting and groaning, his blond tail swaying with his movements where it poked out of the hole he'd cut in his sweatpants. Butters, like me, didn't like losing all of his senses when he was in his two-legged form. "Dropped my phone on my face earlier," he explained. "And it pissed me off. So when it fell, I didn't pick it up again."

Butters crowed in triumph, happiness permeating the room as he found his phone inside a crevice in the couch. He held it out to me, waggling his eyebrows as he tapped a few buttons and the screen turned white as what looked like a…map? showed up.

"Hey Siri. Find. Me. The. Nearest. Grocery. Store," Butters enunciated nice and slow.

"Finding the nearest grocery store." The phone chirped back in what was supposed to be a woman's voice but sounded all sorts of wrong. I stared at the device in horror, terrified to know the damn thing could not only hear me—apparently—but talk to me too.

"If you're making a sex basket, you should put snacks in it." Butters hummed helpfully as the screen changed, and I processed this new information. "Oh. And lube."

"Lube?"

"You know, the slippery shit that comes in a tube." Oh yes. That stuff Jeffrey had made me put on my fingers in the shower. "Don't tell me you've been jerkin' it dry this whole time?" Butters looked horrified.

My cheeks flushed.

"Oh man," he sighed, like finding out I hadn't known what lube was, was the worst thing ever. "Your poor dick. RIP."

Butters tapped a few things into his phone and then headed for the front door. Halfway through it, he seemed to remember he needed to put a shirt on. Annoyed, he huffed and turned back around. I frowned, commiserating—because I too hated clothing.

It was the stupidest invention humans had come up with.

I followed him into his bedroom, grimacing as the stench of virile-brother-sweat filled my nose. I hated going in there. It was way less palatable than the mixed scent of pack-pack-pack. This was a lot more…concentrated.

"Ha!" Butters found what he was looking for, yanking a t-shirt over his head with a happy hum, before he turned back to face me.

I hated to be a jerk, but…I just…

I did have a few worries.

My scent was worry-concern-anxiety as I spoke. "Will you be able to keep this secret?" I asked, grateful the rest of my brothers were elsewhere. Butters perked up immediately. Then he wilted.

"Well…I dunno." He bit his lip. "I'm not the best with secrets." He frowned. "Remember last year?"

"That was different."

"I told Mama what we got her for her birthday."

"That wasn't an important secret." I wasn't sure why I was being so stubborn about this, but I was. I needed an ally. Needed someone who understood humans better than I did. Who could help me.

I hated asking for help, but I'd do anything to make Jeffrey smile.

"And this one is." Butters cocked his head to the side, his ears flattening. They flickered as he thought, chewing on his lip. "Then yeah. I got you."

I perked up, my own tail wagging happily as I nodded. "Good."

I knew he'd pull through.

"So tell me about your human," Butters said as we headed out of his room, through the house, past the door that led to the basement cell, and out the front door. The woods greeted us, pine cones snapping beneath our feet as we followed the directions on his phone.

By the time I got done explaining the majesty that was Jeffrey, Butters eyes were wide and his mouth was hanging open. "No way," he said, tail thumping against his thighs as it wagged. "No. Freaking. Way."

"He is *lovely*," I explained with a proud huff. "He has hair like autumn and spots all over."

"A ginger!" Butters cackled. "That's so sick."

"He is not sick." I glared at him.

"Sorry. My bad. I forgot you were dumb. Lemme educate you." *You're the dumb one,* I thought but didn't say. "Sick means good in humanspeak."

"Oh."

"Therefore, calling your ginger sick was a compliment." Still though, it was funny how Jeffrey's hair color was the part he latched onto, but I wasn't going to complain. "It's a good thing you came to me." Butters led us through the woods, phone held high, all earlier insecurity forgotten. "Leave it to your big bro, I got this."

Forty minutes later I had lost all confidence in both of us. But me especially. If there was such a thing as the opposite of the woods back home, it would be *this* place.

The lights were so bright.

And there were so *many…things*.

Things everywhere. Small things, large things. Things in weird packages. Things covered in plastic and painted bright, overwhelming colors.

Sights. Smells. *People*.

The sheer amount of objects polluted my senses as I squinted down the length of what Butters had told me was the "*cosme-something*" aisle, and did my best not to panic. How was I going to find soap with no scent in a place like this? All I could smell was plastic, chemicals, and people.

No.

No.

I was a hunter.

I could do this.

I wanted to surprise Jeffrey, dammit.

I wanted to make him smile.

And I was going to fucking nail this.

I rolled my shoulders back, cracked my knuckles, and glared at the brightly packaged mystery objects. I was grateful I'd memorized the size and shape of the bottles, as I was sure that would help. Half the words on the labels I didn't understand. Acetone, for one. It looked like soap but when I opened the bottle, leaned in and *sniffed*, the rankest, *nastiest* smell assaulted my senses.

I dropped the bottle immediately, clawing at my eyes as they burned and more of the foul smelling liquid spilled across my feet. My nose ran a little and even though I was overwhelmed and a little in pain, I pressed onward. I got the lid back on, replaced it on the shelf, and wheezed my way down the aisle.

But a good hunter doesn't give up.

I had learned that lesson the hard way.

The human clothes I'd borrowed from Butters clung to my form and I plucked at them absentmindedly. My ears flattened against my head to block out the sound of those awful things Butters had called "shopping carts" as their squeaky wheels wailed down the aisles.

Butters appeared a few minutes later, his arms full of ice cream containers, his violet eyes soft. "Need help?" he asked, juggling a carton of rocky road so he had a free arm. His tanned bicep flexed and I scowled at him, though it didn't take long for me to relent.

"*Please.*"

Butters grinned before taking a few steps down the aisle and stood in front of what I now recognized to be an entire section of soap. *How had I missed that?*

My head hurt.

"Now we just gotta find which one it is." Butters set his ice creams down, his hands on his hips as he hummed. "Do you remember the brand?"

"The what?"

"Never mind." Butters shook his head, frowning thoughtfully. "You can read, right?"

"Of course I can read," I growled. He cackled. I *could* read. I wasn't good at it, or fast. But I could read. Kind of.

"Hey! No shame," he shrugged. "I just figured since you're usually... hairier than you are right now...you might not be able to."

"Can *you* read?" I countered, crossing my arms and feeling entirely out of my depth.

"Not really," Butters shrugged again—like that didn't bother him at all. "Never liked it. Never felt like I needed to. Mom tried to teach me but—" If Butters was telling the truth he was lucky. As an omega there were less expectations of him. Even though, as he'd so eloquently put it, I preferred my "hairier" form, I had never been allowed to skip reading lessons.

One day, if I survived, I'd take over the pack from Dad and that meant I had more training than Butters did. Though I could admit, I'd maybe need to brush up on my schooling again to do it.

"How did you pick your ice cream then?" I challenged, sure he was shitting me.

"There's a picture, *duh*." Butters shrugged a third time, tapping his chin thoughtfully before glancing at me with a frown. "So how are we going to tell if it's the right one? If you don't know what it's called, and I can't read."

"I could read the bottles." I winced, knowing that could take hours. Just looking at them now, it was hard to tell what was what. The text was tiny, and there were a lot of words I didn't recognize or understand. And everything was in different colors and different fonts, and that only made things worse.

"That would take like a million years, dude." At least I didn't have to explain to him why this wouldn't work.

"What if we sniff them?" I didn't want to risk it, because my nose was still burning from the acetone incident, but…soon it would be too late to hunt Jeffrey down. He had work in the morning. And I had a plan. A big plan. That involved baskets, and sex—and spending a few more good nights with him before I needed to be tied up for the moon.

"Good idea!" Butters said, even though it was a terrible idea. A bit better than reading the bottles, but terrible all the same. By the time we found the only scentless soap in the entire store I felt like my nose was broken.

"What else should I get?" I asked, clutching the bottle to my chest triumphantly, my tail thumping happily.

"Uhhhh," Butters scratched the side of his head, scooping ice cream with his other hand, and shoveling it into his mouth. Both cartons had started to melt, and he ate enough to feed an entire country most days, so he'd decided to finish the cartons and pay for them at the end—rather than waste them. "Snacks. Lube. Like I mentioned before."

"What else?"

"What does he like?"

"He likes…" Hmm. *What did he like?* He liked music. That was one of the first things I'd learned about him. He had the voice of an angel. "Music? Cheeseburgers." I racked my brain, trying to remember what I'd seen Jeffrey do over the last couple months. "Movies?"

"Yeah, we're not going to find anything music or movie related here."

"Why not?"

"Cuz this is a grocery store."

"I don't understand."

Butters continued to scratch at his head as he thought. "Wait. Except… Oh. Oh yeah. That's totally going to work."

Thirty minutes later, I regretted all my life choices.

Butters and I sat on the curb outside the grocery store, our wolf ears missing, our scents contrite.

"You guys are so lucky I had my phone on me," Harry glared down at us, his hands on his hips. "Assholes."

"*Sorry.*" Shame crawled beneath my skin—not because of my nudity, but because of the lingering embarrassment left behind from the grocery store. When Butters had pulled chocolate-coated money out of his wallet, I had felt more out of place than I ever had in my entire life. I didn't belong here, in Elmwood. The trees may be familiar, but that was where the similarities ended. To her credit, the cashier had just smiled at the both of us, unaffected, but I'd felt all of two inches tall as Butters counted out the rectangles to pay for his two empty cartons of ice cream, and my gifts.

Only…he hadn't had enough money.

Which was why we'd been forced to call for help.

"What happened to your allowance?" Harry huffed at Butters. "I sent you fifty bucks last week." Butters shrugged, just as embarrassed as I was. "If you spent it on that dumb app again, I am going to scream."

"You gave me digital money," he explained, annoyed. "It's not like it was real."

"Oh my god."

"How am I supposed to use it?" Butters huffed out, annoyed.

"Just because you can't smell it doesn't make it not real." Harry's voice was practically hysterical. "Please tell me you didn't lose your card?"

"What card?"

"The card you've been using to buy the dumb app shit? You know. *That* card."

"Oh. Oops."

"Jesus Christ." Harry pinched the bridge of his nose, then turned on me, violet eyes flaming. "You know what? Never mind." I flinched beneath his attention. "And you! Why the hell don't you have a phone? Do you have any idea how panicked I was when Butters phone died mid-call? I had to fucking *hunt* you guys down. I know you hate human shit, and technology and blah, blah, blah but at this point it's just absolutely idiotic to not be able to contact you when I need to. You can't be stubborn about this. Not anymore. It's a safety issue now."

I whined, embarrassed all over again. Because he was right.

I'd been far too stubborn about this.

"You don't have clothes. You are constantly stealing Butters stuff. You don't have a phone. You can't drive. You can barely read. And that's all fine and good and whatever. I don't want you to change. Of course I don't! It's fine for you to be the way you are—I just. I am this close to having a mental breakdown at any given time. Between the negotiatons—that you don't fucking come to—worrying about you because you're off getting your dick wet half the week and completely incommunicado, babysitting the blond-haired himbo with a CandyCrush addiction, and Jules and his erotica obsession, I am going to fucking break. *Something* needs to give." I hadn't considered how much pressure Harry was under, and immediately I felt bad. "I mean…what if something *happens* to you?" His eyes were wild. "*What if you get stuck?*" I knew what he meant. Stuck in my wolfskin. Unable to shift. It was the first sign of going fully feral. And the reason there was a number on the fridge in the first place.

"Because if you get stuck I only have twelve fucking hours. Twelve hours before you're put down. Twelve hours, Mutt! And I've got a whole plan. A whole fucking plan, but what use is it, if you can't call me?" Harry continued.

He was right.

Even though I wasn't sure how he expected me to call him if I *did* get stuck. But still.

I'd been stubborn.

Too stubborn.

My whole life I'd been adamant I didn't want any of the "human" things my brothers liked. I hadn't understood the appeal, or their necessity. But now I just…I *hated* the look on Harry's face.

I hadn't realized how stressed out he was.

I knew he was doing his best, and I…well…

I'd been selfish.

Been focused on myself and my struggles and hadn't seen that my older brother was breaking. I needed to do better. Besides, lately I could actually see the appeal of a phone. Jeffrey used his a lot and I wanted…well, I wanted to be able to talk to him. There'd be times when I was locked up before the shift hit, and I'd be lonely and alone—and I just…I may not have been able to write all that well, but I could try, couldn't I?

"At this point—I don't even—I just—" Harry pulled at his hair. "Aaughh!"

"Harry." It felt weird talking to him. Not because we weren't close, but because I'd never really used my words with him before. *"Harry—"*

Harry's ranting softened, as did his posture. He sighed, flopping down onto the curb beside us, his scent no longer so acrid. "What?"

"You're right," I said simply.

"I…am?" He blinked, surprised.

"You are," I leaned against him, soaking up his warmth in a way I hadn't in months. Maybe years. Not since his scent had stopped working, and the call of family didn't soften the ache of the moon. Harry whined, a low, needy sound, turning into me and flinging his arms around me. He was leaner than I was, all his bony limbs jabbing into mine as he snuggled in close.

Butters piled on, smashing into us, the scent of chocolate on his breath. *Ew.*

The warmth of pack filled my heart. It'd been weeks since I let myself have this. Hell, if I was being honest, it had been a lot longer than that. Even before I'd found Jeffrey and followed him home. Even before I'd returned and asked to be sent here. Maybe since the last time the moon had felt like a friend, and her light had been kind and not an omen.

"I'll do better," I promised, huffing softly into Harry's hair.

"Okay," he said, wilting like he'd lost all his steam. He didn't question our purchases, just simply clung close.

"Now let's go get a phone."

Chapter Fourteen

Jeffrey

I ALMOST HIT Mutt with my car. It was an accident—and to be fair, it was dark as fuck out by the time I pulled onto the street to head home from Blair's half-finished restaurant. I'd gone over to help them set up after my shift at the magic shop had ended, and I was still reeling from the conversation I'd overheard at the end of the night.

"Do you think it worked?" Blair had said, voice low. He and Richard had been in the back room unpacking some of the boxes that had arrived.

"I think so," Richard replied, rustling around like he'd just cut through tape. "He seems happier."

"My therapist says it might help, you know. To give him something to do." Blair's voice was quiet, muted, like all the life had been sucked out of it and replaced with anxiety. "I mean…this is weird for him."

"It's weird for everyone."

"But him especially." More rustling.

Weird was officially becoming my least favorite word.

I held my breath, holding incredibly still. It was a wonder Richard hadn't said anything about me still being here. I'd always just assumed vampires could hear heartbeats like wolves could. But maybe their senses were more muted?

Still, I should go.

I knew I should go.

Because I had a feeling I knew who they were talking about—and that this conversation was not for me.

"You know…I walked in on him—uh." Blair's voice grew even quieter. Difficult to hear. It was a wonder I could eavesdrop at all. "I dunno. It was his first week in town? When he was still job hunting. And he didn't see me—and he was just…he was just—"

"What?"

"He was shaking, and curled up in this awful little ball and he looked like total dogshit. Like he was crying—" I could remember that day with sickening clarity. I'd just finished applying to Avery's shop. It'd been the first night I felt like I was being watched, and the walls had closed in on me, Elmwood too small—too much—too familiar. I felt like a ghost here, surrounded by people who knew me but didn't, by places that had been home once but weren't.

It'd felt like I was dying. I couldn't get a single breath in. Everything was too bright, too loud, too much. No tears had been shed but it felt like they needed to. Like even my eyes were broken, and my goddamn body was betraying me.

I couldn't breathe, couldn't—

I'd been tempted to call Blair for help, but…hadn't known how.

Hadn't known how to be this much of a mess when he was around.

Hadn't wanted to show him my cracks.

Apparently he'd seen them anyway. Which was something I'd suspected, if his thinly veiled questions about therapy were anything to go by. I just…I guess it hadn't occurred to me that he'd actually seen me mid-panic attack.

"I was just trying to check in on him, you know? And I should've gone in there…but I—" Blair's voice was hollow. "I didn't know what to do. Because I'd never seen him *do* that. And I got the feeling he wouldn't want me there, not while he was hurting."

He was right.

It was why I hadn't ended up calling him.

I wouldn't have wanted that.

And I hated that he knew that.

I hated that he knew me well enough that he understood as much as I loved him—and I did, more than anything—sometimes looking at him reminded me of the worst times of my life. He was a walking trigger, sending me spinning and quaking, like a colt on new, wobbly legs.

"He does better when he feels important, you know?" Blair's voice was gruff.

"I'm not sure lying about the chairs was the best way to go about that," Richard said gently. "I get what you were trying to do—and I'm proud of you for that. But…" Richard had always been a serious kid. He'd been grown up before he even knew how to walk. Intelligent. Type A. Bad with people—except for Blair, apparently. "Maybe moving forward we'd be better off not lying."

Lying.

"I know," Blair sighed. "But you—I mean. Did you see his face? He looked so happy when he was bringing the chairs in yesterday."

"Sure," Richard agreed gently. "But how many deliveries can you cancel like that, Blair, before he finds out? There's gotta be a limit. Maybe some honesty would help him more than trying to trick him into feeling useful."

"I don't know how to be honest with him," Blair's voice wavered. "He just smiles, and lies—and—and he never fucking breaks. He's like a puppet person. Which is so fucking shitty, because you'd think out of everyone in the world, I'd be the one to understand. *I was there.* I was there the whole fucking time. It was always us against the world—and now it feels like him against me, and I don't know how to fix it."

"I know, baby." There was more rustling, this time less boxes—and more clothing. I could so easily imagine my giant blond brother pulling Blair into his lap. The two of them were inseparable. And…good for each other. They were happy.

It was part of why I felt so…lost.

Blair didn't need me anymore. Not really.

And I didn't know how to exist with him without Lydia hanging over us. She'd always been our shared demon. And now she was gone, and I was just me. There were no tasks for me to accomplish, and the lies I kept from Blair to protect him didn't feel noble anymore. They just felt like lies.

And that…hurt.

That hurt, and I didn't know what to do.

I felt betrayed, I could admit that. Betrayed by him, and the fact he was happy. The fact he moved on so easily and I couldn't. Betrayed because he didn't need me like I needed him. Betrayed because he'd lied to me.

He'd tricked me.

And I knew it was because he loved me—because he wanted to help, but I hated that he thought I was too weak to take the truth, even though I was. He was supposed to think the world of me. He was the only person who ever had.

"Maybe he can't open up to you *because* you were there," Richard added, voice low and rough. "Maybe he needs…space from what happened."

"I don't want to give him space."

"And that's because you're…" Richard struggled for words. "You're a good brother."

"Right."

"But if you want to be there for him," Richard said softly. "Maybe he needs to come to you. And maybe don't—"

"Lie." Blair sighed.

Richard was quiet, like he didn't know what to say.

And it hurt.

It hurt so much that both of them thought I was falling apart—even though I was.

That they'd apparently orchestrated this entire thing so that I would feel useful.

Which was why I was distracted as I drove. Why I was shaking, and sick, and my vision was blurry even though tears refused to fall. I'd gotten the fuck out of there, as quietly as I could—escaping to my truck and onto the street with my heart pounding and a sick churning in my stomach.

"Oh my fuck." I slammed on the breaks, the car swerving a little and hitting the curb as I sucked in a panicked breath, and Mutt's familiar broad frame popped into view. He crossed to the side of the car, face pressed right up against the glass of my window.

That shit was diabolical. I couldn't believe Collin had done this to Richard on purpose.

"Jeffrey!" he yelled in excitement. His blue eyes were bright, and I didn't need to see it to know his tail was wagging.

I rolled the window down, and then jolted when Mutt reached inside and immediately yanked me close enough he could push his face into my neck. He snuffled happily, his hot breath tickling my throat as he inhaled my scent greedily.

"Mmm," he sighed, teeth nicking my skin as he opened his mouth and gave my throat a single, sharp suck, before pulling back. "You are *distressed*," he frowned, brow furrowing, like my distress was ruining his whole-ass day. I was surprised it had taken him this long to figure that out—considering the fact that usually he read me like a book.

Apparently he was distracted too.

"I'm fine," I lied.

"Lie," he called me out immediately, though his expression softened. "May I come into your metal box now?"

"The truck?" I snorted, "Yeah, man. No one's stopping you."

Mutt bobbed his head, obviously still distracted as he zoomed around the car again—far faster than any human would be able to. He pulled the passenger-side door open, his tail thumping against the metal as he slid in unceremoniously. "You are correct," he agreed, like I was an absolute genius and should win a fucking award. "No one *is* stopping me."

"Right." It was just a phrase, but I didn't say that. Instead, I turned to face him.

Act normal.

Focus.

Don't freak out.

Who cares if Blair knows you're a nutcase?

You're fine.

Mutt couldn't have shown up at a worse time. I was not in the mood to be sexed up right now. Well…that was a lie. I was always in the mood to be sexed up by him. Exhibit A: my hard cock, and the tingles running up and down my spine because of the kiss he'd left on my neck.

But still.

The reason Mutt was so distracted quickly became clear when he shoved something into my hands. It took me a second to realize what it was, my brow furrowing as I stared down at an…*Easter basket?*

"What is—"

"You will no longer be distressed when you see what I have picked for you." Tail thumping, Mutt leaned into my space nosily. "Open, open, open."

"You…got me this…Easter basket?"

"I do not know what an Easter is," Mutt's tail continued to beat a steady drum behind him. "But yes. It is a basket. A sex basket. Because we had sex. And you are so sweet, and pretty—and good. And your hand is the perfect size to hold my knot. And you smell like oranges. And you are sad—and deserve good things. And I woke up today, and all I wanted was to make you smile."

I woke up today, and all I wanted was to make you smile.

"Right." That was the sweetest shit anyone had ever said to me. I didn't want to be rude—even though I felt like I was falling apart—so I began to pluck at the…newspaper that covered the top of the basket. Some of my nerves began to melt away, excitement taking their place.

"I used the fanciest paper I could find," Mutt declared proudly. "Lots of pictures and designs." He pointed at an article that talked about global warming. "That is the earth."

"Yeah," I agreed, because it was.

"Over here is a guitar," Mutt tugged the paper over and showed me an ad for the open-mic night I often attended in Ridgefield. "You *love* guitars." He looked so fucking proud that he knew the name of the instrument. Like he'd solved world hunger, or some shit.

So fucking cute.

Fuck.

"I do." My heart fluttered as I finished pulling the rest of the paper away, and then just…

Stared.

Because…fuck.

No one had ever gotten me a gift basket before. Let alone *hand picked* and decorated one for me. And that was what this was—the sloppy paper and haphazard way it was put together proving that Mutt had done it himself. He'd clearly put a lot of thought into the basket.

"You got me soap?" I asked, my heart my throat as I pulled out the bottle.

"I said I would," Mutt agreed, eyes bright. "It is better. Then I can smell you more clearly."

"Right." My palms were still slick with anxious sweat, but my nerves were fading away for the moment as I stared down at the other gifts that were shoved tightly together inside the basket. "Um. Is this—"

"A tunes." Mutt declared proudly as I pulled out a handful of iTunes gift cards. "Butters said that if you like music you would like to buy a tunes."

He said "a tunes" like it was the title of the card, and I couldn't help but find that absolutely fucking charming.

"Thank you," I said, voice wobbling a little. I wasn't sure what about scentless soap and gift cards screamed "sex basket" but I appreciated it. I'd kinda expected sex toys or some shit. Not something innocent and sweet like this.

"I bought you many lubes," Mutt added as I pulled out several unopened bottles. *I stand corrected.* "So that I may fuck you." Mutt held up his fingers and wiggled them at me in a frankly obscene way. "Press against that spot inside that makes you whine."

"Right," I laughed, unable to help myself. My cheeks were hot.

Visions of just that assaulted me. What it would feel like to have Mutt on top of me, his weight pressing me into the bed, his teeth at the back of my neck, his fingers in my ass again.

Fuck.

Okay.

Yes.

That sounded amazing.

"What else did you get me, big guy?" I hummed, unable to bite back my grin. Mutt continued to wag his tail, leaning into my space as he happily poked through the basket with me, explaining each item with enthusiasm.

There was chocolate, because I got sad sometimes, and he'd seen a billboard once that one of his brothers had told him said chocolate was the perfect treat when one was down. Then he tried to force feed me the bar—until I gave in and began to munch on it while he showed me the rest.

A pencil, because I always broke mine.

Which he only knew because he'd seen the stack of snapped ones on the counter. Or maybe, because he'd been there in dog form three days ago when I was writing a song, broke one, called it a bitch, and threw it at the wall.

Mutt may have been a hunter, but he was not sneaky at fucking all.

There was a fuzzy wash cloth, because Mutt said it was the color of my eyes. A half-eaten bag of Cheetos that he'd gotten for "us to share." A bouquet of flowers that he'd tried to make into a crown—and failed spectacularly. A new guitar pick that looked like an acorn—so I'd remember him while I was writing. And a dog toy—a fat little squirrel stuffed animal that squeaked when I pinched it. It was furry and soft, and the perfect size to fit in my palm.

"It makes lovely sounds," Mutt told me proudly as I rubbed its fuzzy head. "Like when prey is dying."

"Super lovely," I agreed, not even lying—because there wasn't a single thing about this basket that wasn't lovely.

"Last but not least," Mutt plucked a little scrap of paper out. It looked like he'd torn it from the newspapers, and there was a hastily sketched out marker on it. "Harry helped."

"Harry is…?"

"Another brother," he hummed. "I have four. Harry, Theo, Jules, and Butters."

"Big family," I replied, eager to have learned something new about him as I stared down at the scrap of paper. It took me a second to figure out what it was.

"Very big. The biggest. And it will only grow bigger soon," Mutt declared proudly. "There are always pups in search of homes, and Mama is looking."

"Is this your phone number?" I blurted out, brow scrunched. "I just…I mean, I assumed you didn't have a phone." Mutt often acted like he'd never spoken to a human before he'd met me. I guess I just figured, based on how frequently he talked about squirrels, he wasn't the kinda dude to buy the latest iPhone.

I was apparently wrong, because that's what he pulled out of his pocket, showing it to me proudly. "It is," he said, flashing me a sunny, adorable grin. He looked so young. There was a weariness to him usually, but it was hidden, forgotten, like he didn't know it was there at all. "So that you may talk to me."

"Okay," I said, heart thumping. "Yeah. That's…I mean… That would be nice."

"Here," Mutt handed me his phone, waiting expectantly. "Butters told me that I will need your number too."

The idea of texting Mutt quickly became my favorite thing ever. I bit my lip, buzzing happily as I typed in my name, and then my number, and shot myself a text. I tucked the paper with his number into my phone case for safe keeping, then handed him back his phone, suddenly shy.

I didn't know what we'd even talk about.

But I was kinda excited to find out.

There wasn't a lot in my life I was excited about right now.

My phone began to buzz in my hand, and I frowned—for all of two seconds before I realized who was calling me. "I'm right here," I laughed, though I swiped the call through and shook my head in amusement.

Mutt held his phone in front of his mouth like a microphone, and even though I felt stupid as hell, I brought my phone to my ear. I was grinning, and I couldn't seem to stop.

"This is my first phone call," Mutt declared, way too fucking loud, right in my ear. I flinched, and then snorted, shaking my head in amusement.

"Hi."

"Hello." Mutt was grinning at me, and he looked like sunshine.

"Thank you for the basket," I said, still holding the phone to my ear, my cheeks flushed.

"Did you love it?"

"I did," I said, my heart thumping. "I do."

His eyes were so bright, and warm, and he was just…god. He was the nicest person I'd ever met. He filled up the passenger seat like a good-natured giant, his ears pricked forward, eyes full of life. He wasn't broken like I was. Hollow.

He was life incarnate, and looking at him made me feel normal for the first time in my life.

"Hey, Mutt?" I said, palms slick with sweat, my earlier upset forgotten.

"Yes?" Mutt's tail continued to thump.

"You're a fucking sweetheart."

Mutt's grin only grew wider, probably because I'd just given him the smile he'd said he wanted. He looked at me like I was the prettiest thing he'd fucking seen, and my stomach filled with butterflies.

"Hey, Jeffrey?" he countered, one hand reaching out for me. I tipped into it, pressing into his palm, my phone still clutched tightly.

"Yeah?"

"Did I cheer you up?"

My heart hurt.

It hurt and hurt and hurt.

"You did," I said, shifting to press a little kiss into his palm. And then I did something I'd never done before. Instead of wallowing in the past, thinking about the conversation that had sent me into a tailspin in the first place, I moved forward. "Are you busy right now?"

"Busy?" Mutt blinked, an odd look crossing his face for a moment before he shook his head. "I am not busy."

"How would you feel about going on an adventure?"

"I love adventures."

"Yeah?" I grinned, nuzzling into his palm. The look Mutt leveled me with was needy and warm, and hungry. My belly flipped. "Me too."

Chapter Fifteen

Jeffrey

YOU KNOW WHAT'S wild? Falling in love. I hadn't thought I could do it. Hadn't thought my heart could fit someone else inside it, with all its cracks. But apparently I was wrong. Because as Mutt and I splashed around in the ocean, icy water soaking us through to our bones, I realized I had room after all.

Mutt was strange.

He spoke oddly, he didn't understand social cues, he was awkward and clumsy, and had no idea what personal space was. But he was also…kind. Kinder than anyone I'd met. He was thoughtful and sweet. He made me feel real.

When he was with me there were no demons lurking in the back of my mind. And even if there had been, I knew he'd chase them off. Probably by calling me pretty again—or telling me he'd protect me.

Before he had come into my life, no one had ever kept me safe.

No one had watched over me.

No one had saved me, not when I was small, and not when I was big either.

When Lydia had complimented me it was because she was manipulating me. I'd been wary of sweet words ever since the day I realized her love was a weapon, and her words were chains. Trapped in her web, I saw the spider that hung above me, always hungry, dripping venom—ready to bite.

Mutt's compliments weren't weapons. They had no ulterior motive. There was no manipulation, no darkness. When Mutt called me pretty, it was simply because he thought I was. When he bought me gifts, it was because he wanted me to be happy. When he touched me, it was because he wanted to. And when I melted for him, it was because he made me feel safe.

Because he made me happy.

I hadn't known I could be happy either, but apparently I could.

"Don't shake," I warned him, pointing a finger at him threateningly. "Don't do it—"

Mutt's long dark hair stuck to his back and shoulders, his eyes bright— flashing in the dark like a predator's.

"Don't you fucking do it—"

His grin was wolfish.

Delighted.

Wicked.

This was a new side to him, playful and frisky—and unafraid of me. Unafraid of my emotions. He didn't treat me like I was covered in bubble wrap, fragile and easily broken. But like I was hardy enough to withstand the frost. There was respect in his gaze. The kind of respect only an animal who has survived the cold dark nights can have for another.

The wounded sometimes recognize each other.

But I didn't feel wounded when I was with him.

"Oh my fuck—" I gasped out, as Mutt giggled like a rabid hyena and began to shake his glorious mane. Water splattered all over me, and I blocked my face with a squawk. "You motherfucker—"

"You say angry things!" Mutt cackled some more, dunking his head like a fucking lunatic in the inky black waves, before shaking it at me again. "But you smell happy-happy-happy!"

Calling me out.

The fucker.

I splashed him back, my boxers clinging to my skin as I tried to distract him for long enough I could get away.

I should've known he'd chase.

Because he did. I awkwardly waddle-leapt through the water, trying to get away—but only because I wanted him to follow. The hot brush of his breath on the back of my neck lit me up from the inside out.

Warm arms wrapped around me, yanking me against him as he caught up. He was laughing, and I could feel it. I could feel it as his chest shook and his lips vibrated against the side of my neck.

And then he yanked me down into the water with him, and it was cold-cold-cold, but somehow I was warm.

"My truck is going to smell like fish." I snorted as I wrung the water out of my long-sleeved shirt, stationed inside the open driver's side door. There was sand clinging to my legs, and thighs. And though my pants were dry—because they were the only thing I'd taken off—I didn't bother pulling them back on.

I was too salt-sticky and cold.

"You have such pretty nipples," Mutt informed me randomly. He was just as wet as I was, but didn't seem to mind. In fact, he was distracted as he reached for the hem of my shirt and yanked it up into my armpits.

"They're cold," I complained. My nipples were shivery and peaked, salt glistening on my chest as Mutt bent his head down and lapped at the perky buds. "Fuck," I hissed out, grabbing onto his head with a quiet groan.

"There," Mutt moved to the other side, sucking and rubbing his tongue along it for a few blissful seconds before he pulled back. "Better?"

"Y-yeah," I shivered, even though they weren't any warmer. In fact, after having the wet hot heat of his mouth on them, the chilly night air was only worse.

"Why do you lie?" Mutt laughed, crowding into my space, all that wet, golden muscle on full display. Not that it was really gold. Not anymore— not beneath the pale caress of moonlight. His eyes flickered, and I knew he could smell my arousal, and that only made it feel sweeter.

"It feels more natural to lie than to tell the truth," I admitted, surprised by how easy it was to tell him the truth.

"Why?" Mutt asked, and I figured that was fair.

I knew I had a fucked up past. But he…maybe didn't. For a second, I debated blowing him off. Or lying again. But…there was something about the way he was looking at me that made that impossible.

His eyes said, *you're safe.*

They said, *I'm here.*

They said, *I will love you no matter what you say.*

"Sometimes I don't even know I'm lying," I admitted, voice hoarse. "Not until after the words come out. I guess I just…got so used to trying to please everyone, I forgot it was a choice." Mutt was quiet, patient. One of his hands moved to the nape of my neck, squeezing tight.

It felt different to be on the receiving end of that strength.

But good too.

I melted, lashes fluttering, and my truths came spilling out—falling like dominos. Like it didn't hurt at all. Because it didn't. Because Mutt was a safe space. It'd just taken me a while to realize that, because I'd never had one before.

"My parents were self-proclaimed martyrs with enough money, they never learned how to be real people," I said softly. "We were props," I added, voice quiet. "The only way to get attention was to do what they wanted. I was so…so *hungry* I just…"

"Hungry?"

"Not for food."

"I understand," he said softly. "There are two kinds of hunger."

"Exactly." The warm grip of his hand soothed me. "I was always nervous, scared," I admitted. "And they didn't like that—so I hid, and hid. Pretended to be someone I'm not so they'd like me more. But it didn't work. And the hunger only got worse. And then I made a mistake—" My voice cracked. "I trusted the wrong person. I thought she could love me the way they didn't—and because of me, people got hurt, and I got… even more lost."

"Everyone gets lost sometimes," Mutt said softly, dipping his head down, his lovely dark lashes kissing his cheeks. "And everyone makes mistakes."

"Yeah but mine were really bad," I admitted, my voice shaking. "And I'm still paying for them."

"Who?"

"What do you mean?" I didn't understand.

"Who are you paying for them?"

I blinked.

I blinked again, confused—my jaw fell open, then shut again with a click. "I…don't…know."

"It is okay to feel confused." Mutt said softly. "It is okay to have regrets. But who is benefiting from your kill?" He was picking his words very carefully and I could tell, his focus written all over his face. "*Who* are you feeding? It is not you. Regret does not feed your soul. And the only people who benefit from what you continue to pay are the people who hurt you." Theo had said Mutt wasn't much of a talker. And that made his words even sweeter. They carried weight with them that lingered even after he'd stopped speaking. "Maybe it is time to stop hunting. Maybe it is time to find your way home. Maybe you have punished yourself long enough."

"What if I can't stop? What if I'm always lost?"

"Then I will come to you." Mutt replied immediately. "Until I breathe my last breath, I will chase you. We can be lost together."

It was an odd declaration, especially from a man I barely knew. A man that wasn't supposed to mean as much to me as he did. A man that was a liar, just like I was—but that I couldn't blame, because his intentions had been pure.

Mutt may have originally been a one-night stand, but he wasn't anymore. And I could admit now, under the light of the moon, with salt water drying on my skin, that maybe he never had been.

Everything spun. My brain hurt. My lungs wheezed. It was black and painful and—ow, ow, ow.

"Jeffrey—" Mutt's voice was a distant echo, panicked and full of fear. "Jeffrey!"

"Fuck," I managed, voice hoarse. I opened my eyes and immediately regretted it because it hurt. It hurt so fucking bad. And my head was throbbing—and fuck-ow-fuck.

"Shhh," Mutt was warm, but I could barely feel where he was wrapped around me, the pain in my head was so all-encompassing. "Shhh, it is okay. I have called for help. It's okay."

It took me a second to remember what had happened.

And when I did, my panic only rose.

We'd been driving back from the beach.

We'd pulled onto the ramp that led back into Elmwood. It'd been dark out and we hadn't crossed into city limits yet so there were no street lamps to light the way. Rain had begun to fall halfway back home and I'd been distracted driving—not because I'd been upset this time, but because Mutt had been growling at the radio and it'd been fucking hilarious.

I'd made the mistake of telling him I loved the singer of the song playing, and he'd immediately gone all macho man on me.

And I'd been laughing—

And the rain had been falling—

And there'd been a figure in front of the car. A blond, hairy figure. Four-legged and massive. And I hadn't seen it and I'd—

Fuck.

I'd crashed the truck.

Right into a fucking tree.

I could vaguely remember the panic. The way my headlights had swerved when I'd jerked the steering wheel. The jolt of the seatbelt as I slammed into it, and Mutt launched himself across the console to block me from the shattering glass as a branch plowed right through the windshield.

I could smell blood.

So much blood.

And I could hardly breathe—could hardly breathe because—oh fuck.

Oh fuck.

"Are you okay?" I gasped out, trying to see through the pain as Mutt hovered over me. He was still sandwiched between the console and my body, the worst of the glass having hit him. There were a few wayward pieces that had hit my cheeks, but otherwise I was fine.

I was fine.

I think.

Except.

My head was cold.

And wet—and.

"Shhhh," Mutt soothed. "I'm okay, sweet one. I'm okay." His palms were warm, I could feel their heat, even though he didn't touch me. Like he was scared he'd hurt me. "Help is coming. It's okay. You're okay."

"W-what?" I reached for him, my panic apparent as I saw the blood that was staining his shirt. His damp shirt. His damp shirt that had been white and now was red.

"Shhh," Mutt rumbled, a delicious purring sound filling the car. It calmed me. Made the twitch and burn of acid in my body soften. Made my hands stop shaking quite so much, and my spinning head still. "Alpha has you, sweet one. Everything is okay."

"I'm sorry," I gasped out, fingers tangling in his shirt. "I'm sorry—there was a wolf—and I—"

"No apologies necessary," Mutt said softly, nuzzling my cheek, that delicious purring sound vibrating even louder. "*Calm.*" It was a command, and one I didn't think I'd be able to heed. And yet…somehow I did.

All the tension in my body bled away, the snap of Mutt's voice echoing around inside my head.

My eyes felt heavy.

So heavy.

"Jeffrey—"

I just wanted to nap.

Just…a little—

Nap.

I was *warm*.

So warm.

And my head was slick but that was okay. It was all okay. Because Mutt was here. And he was Alpha. Because Alpha had me. Alpha had me and I was calm—and everything was okay.

Everything…was…

Okay.

Apparently Theo was not only an unofficial vet but a people doctor too. Which I only discovered, because after he'd shown up to pick us up in a shitty mom-van, he'd brought Mutt and I back to the house that all the wolf-brothers occupied and stitched me the fuck up.

But not before Mutt carried me around like a broken koala, and whined any time my scent "spiked with pain."

"What is stitches?!" He'd stressed as he curled his arms protectively around me. We were sitting in the living room of his house. It smelled like man sweat, expensive cologne, and cookies. Which was a weird combo, but also kinda soothing.

It was a small house. Old. Homey. With paintings on the walls and a giant ratty couch that looked like it had seen better days. Despite its age, however, the space was immaculately clean. As though one of Mutt's brothers actively vacuumed up the wolf hair everyday.

"I'm just going to sew his head up," Theo said gently, holding his arms out placatingly.

"No."

"It'll help," he promised, voice deep and soothing. His gold eyes flashed, and I kinda wanted to keep looking at them—beta, my mind supplied— but keeping my eyes open hurt. "We need to stop the blood flow and tie up the wound before it gets infected. Head wounds bleed a lot. Which means he needs stitches."

Mutt was clearly freaked out by the concept. Which…considering the fact his back had been torn the fuck up and was already healed—probably meant he'd never had a stitch in his goddamn life. I would bet my left nut he'd never even been to the doctor.

"It's okay," I reassured, fingers finding Mutt's wrist. His arms were wrapped tightly around me, his thick thighs beneath my body. His scent cocooned me, soothing and tantalizing at the same time. No one had ever held me like this, so it felt strange.

But it felt nice…too.

That pretty much summed up every interaction I had with him. Strange but nice.

He'd even made sure that Theo grabbed my basket for me, because he'd somehow known I wouldn't be willing to leave it behind.

"I've had tons of stitches before," I reassured, my filter apparently broken. "Hundreds, probably. And I'm fine."

Mutt did not look soothed. "*Hundreds?*" he asked, the panic in his voice morphing into something low and dangerous. "I will kill whoever is responsible. *Names.* Give me names, pretty one—of all the people that—"

"Fuck." I hadn't meant to upset him even more. "It's not a who, so much as a *what*—" Kinda. "Hard to explain. I just…fuck. Just let Theo do the stitches, please? I promise it'll be fine."

Mutt's eyes flashed, brilliantly blue, bright as sapphires. They seemed to glow, predatory and feral as he bobbed his head reluctantly. His claws pricked at my hip where they dug in, and his fangs flickered—half shifted in his mouth.

"C'mon, Doc," I urged, tilting my head back to rest it against Mutt's sternum for support. "I just bought us a few minutes before he freaks out again."

Theo laughed, shaking his head at the both of us as he pulled out his first aid kit and got to work. I spaced out for most of it, my eyes drifting shut, Mutt's heart thumping against my back, erratic and worried.

Mutt babied me.

There was no other way to describe it. It should've bothered me, being coddled. But it didn't. He plied me with kisses. Kept me tucked inside his bed covered in blankets that smelled like him. He brought me food, stroked my hair, and growled at anyone that walked by the door.

My head hurt too much to really do much, so I mostly slept.

Eventually the pounding faded some, and when I woke I took the opportunity to inspect Mutt's room. It was…weird being in here. Felt personal in a way we hadn't gotten till that night. In a good way.

I'd been curious about Mutt, and I could admit that.

At first I'd told myself it was because he was a werewolf, and Lydia's teaching hadn't prepared me for that. But…that was a lie. The truth was he fascinated me. How was it possible that someone could be so full of life, so absolutely *filthy*, and yet…innocent too?

Mutt saw the world with rose-colored glasses on.

And I was starting to hope they were dark enough he wouldn't see my blood stains.

"I have brought you Pop Tarts," Mutt declared the morning after I'd spent the night in his bed. "They are like food," he promised, like I didn't know what a fucking Pop Tart was. "But better."

"Thanks," I laughed, and then regretted it, because laughing made my head hurt.

Mutt helped me sit up, and I snuggled in against him, surprised by how easy it was to lean on him. "I didn't know you could have chocolate," I teased, enjoying the steady rise and fall of his chest as he breathed, and the thump, thump of his heart.

"What do you mean?" Mutt asked curiously, his fingers gently carding through the hair at my nape. He plucked at the curls, and I sighed, eyes drifting shut.

Of course he didn't get the joke.

"You know, because dogs can't have chocolate?"

"I am not a dog," Mutt scoffed, sounding incredibly fucking guilty. "Oh, look! There's a…" Mutt looked around the room for a distraction. "A tree! Outside the window."

"A tree."

"A very good tree," he agreed, his heart thumping erratically beneath my cheek. "So very good. The best tree."

You're not sneaky at all.

"Uh huh." I agreed, cracking an eye open as I picked up my Pop Tart and nibbled on it. "And you're not trying to distract me at all."

"Ha-ha! *No*. Distract you? Never."

"Mhm."

I didn't know why he was pretending but…I figured he had his reasons, and at this point…I supposed he'd earned some trust. So I let him off the hook for now and ate my Pop Tart like a good boy.

No one bothered us.

Even though I could hear Theo rustling around outside the bedroom, it was quiet in here. An oasis really. Didn't feel real. When I was here, it was like all the shitty stuff out there didn't matter.

Mutt's bed was piled high with pillows and blankets. Clearly comfort was important to him. The mattress sat on the floor in the back corner of the room, facing the door and window—which suited me just fine.

I liked to be able to see all the entrances and exits at the same time.

It felt safer that way.

However, the mattress on the floor was not the weirdest part of the room. Mutt's personality bled into everything here. Hand picked, just like a professional interior designer would do—only instead of cheesy posters, designer portraits, curtains, and decor—Mutt's room was full of wild things.

There were pine cones lining the back wall.

A giant orange maple leaf was taped to the door.

Several of my t-shirts were scattered across the floor. T-shirts I'd been certain I'd lost. And apparently hadn't, because they'd been stolen. A giant cement garden gnome sat in one corner of the room, glaring at me grumpily. I could only assume he'd stolen it, or bought it from a yard sale, it was so beat up.

"Nice gnome," I complimented. Mutt made a confused sound, and when I gestured toward the statue he brightened. His tail beat the mattress.

"You like my tiny angry man?" he said happily. "I *knew* you were perfect."

I laughed, unable to help myself. I'd finished my Pop Tart, and as I tipped my head up to look at him better, I grimaced. The stitches tugged.

"Did you steal him?" I asked, lips twisting into a smile I couldn't swallow, even if I wanted to.

"Steal him?" Mutt cupped my face with one hand, thumb stroking below my eye. He stared at me. Stared and stared and stared. Like I was a pretty sunset. Something magnificent, and meant to be admired. "I did not *steal*." His lips twisted up into a mischievous smirk, the boy who'd dunked me into the ocean like a total shithead coming to the surface. "Is it stealing if they did not want him? No. It is not."

"How do you know they didn't want him?" I had no idea who "they" was, but I was suddenly desperate to find out.

"He was sitting out on the lawn," Mutt huffed in disappointment. "Abandoned."

I didn't have the heart to tell him that that was where lawn gnomes were supposed to go. So I just grinned and prayed to whatever god was listening, that Mutt would get away with his petty crime.

Mutt and I spent the entire weekend together. I told him about Blair, and the conversation I'd overheard—because he was annoying as hell and would not stop asking me why I'd been sad when I'd picked him up.

At one point, I sent Mutt to my apartment for my laptop—and when I'd given him a key to get in he acted appropriately honored.

Not even Blair had a key to my house.

I guess Mutt was just…the right kind of threatening. Because his strength was used to protect me, and not used against me. And it wasn't that I didn't trust Blair—because I did. It was just…well…

It was my special space. The only place that had ever been my own. And apparently there was a Mutt-sized space left open. Maybe because I knew he'd seen behind my walls. Maybe because when he looked at me I didn't feel broken, I felt…well.

I felt like one of those weeds that breaks through cement.

Like maybe I hadn't grown where I was supposed to. Maybe it'd been hard, and hurt. But I was blossoming either way. And when Mutt saw me, waving in the wind, out of place, he smiled, charmed by my resilience.

I wasn't *wrong*, I was beautiful.

Mutt brought me my laptop, my phone charger, and my favorite blanket. I had to explain what the chargers looked like, and where they were—but I hadn't minded. And we holed up in his room for days, snuggled up under the blankets, watching movies and taking turns sucking each other off.

Watching movies wasn't something I'd done with anyone but Blair, so it felt kinda monumental. Like I'd truly accepted Mutt into my little bubble where he belonged. He laughed at all the wrong spots, and very obviously copied me sometimes so it would look like he knew what was happening when he didn't. But there was no hiding how absolutely stoked he was to be in bed with me, and that felt really fucking good. Mutt made me feel valued, even when I was at my shittiest.

Mutt liked dumb cartoons, probably because he didn't get the more complicated shit. So we took turns picking to make it fair.

At one point, after we'd finished watching *Lady and the Tramp*, Mutt got me on all fours. And with the ferocity of an animal in heat, he ate my ass till it was achy and wet and loose—and then finger fucked me with the lube from my basket till I came all over the sheets.

I liked his knot.

Liked toying with it. Playing with it. Squeezing and flicking it, as he humped my grip and bore his fangs at me. He was feral in the sheets, this hungry, needy twist to his expression that was ridiculously attractive.

He liked to bite.

Liked to bite and suck, and leave bruises. Liked to play with my hair, to grip and slap my ass. Liked to rake his claws down my thighs, and up my back, and over my nipples till I was shaky and quivery and needy—and the only word I remembered was, "please."

He was soft too.

Kind.

He looked after my stitches with dogged determination. He counted my freckles one by one, and told me they were *marvelous*. He kissed my fingers, my toes, the backs of my knees, and the dimples above my ass.

He asked me about my scars.

"Chupacabra," I explained, his warm calloused fingers dragging across my sternum. They skipped to a small nick on my neck. "Boggart," I shivered. He flattened his palm, sliding it over my pec, his thumb scrubbing over yet another mark of my violent upbringing. "Imp."

He didn't ask me why I'd been near so many creatures, and for that I was grateful.

Because I wasn't ready.

And talking about the scars was already more than I'd ever done.

Blair didn't even know I had them. I meticulously wore long-sleeved shirts to cover them. And even when we'd lived together in our tiny condo in Oregon—after Lydia had "graciously" allowed us to move out—I'd been incredibly careful never to shower when he was awake, for fear that he'd stumble upon me changing clothes.

There'd been locks on my door then too, but I wasn't the only one who had a key.

Lydia hadn't allowed true privacy.

She'd watched us from the cameras, always hunting for reasons to be angry.

And we'd given her plenty.

Mutt wasn't like that. He watched, not because he was looking for flaws to correct, but because he saw beauty in them. He was soft and sweet and caring. And he was fascinated by me—not because he wanted to corrupt or use me. Not because we'd been through hell together. But simply because…

Because he *liked* me.

"Why are you so nice to me?" I'd asked after our first movie marathon. I'd yet to go to the bathroom on my own, and Mutt had blocked the mirror every time. I knew why. I probably looked like shit, and all he'd had to do was smell my anxiety whenever I glanced toward it to know.

It was weird peeing with another dude nearby. Especially a dude that I wanted to ride, but hey.

It was kinda oddly romantic too.

Intimate.

"Why wouldn't I be nice to you?" Mutt asked back, confused. "You are the most wonderful person in the world."

I shook my dick off, wiped myself clean, and stared at my hands as I washed them so that Mutt would let me have access to the sink.

"I'm not going to die if I see my reflection," I told him, the suds rinsing down the drain.

"Why do you care how you look right now?" he countered. "What about seeing your reflection will help you?"

"I have stitches in my head, I kinda wanna see."

"Lie." Mutt laid a hand on my chest, right above where my heart lay.

"Okay fine. So I wanna see if I look like shit or not—since we're… you know…" I flushed, my cheeks hot. "We're *hanging out.*"

"You look beautiful," Mutt said softly, like it was a fact. I swallowed the lump in my head.

"I probably look like shit."

"Impossible."

"Can I just…please?" I begged softly, shoulders drawn up. "I wanna see." I'd never admired this insecurity before, and it felt weirdly…good. "I like you. I wanna look good for you. So if you could *pretty please* move that big gorgeous ass over and let me see the mirror so I can clean myself up—I'd appreciate it."

Mutt growled, not pleased.

Fuck.

Didn't work.

I must've smelled disappointed, because it didn't take long for him to give in. He was just a softie like that. He sighed, shoulders slumping. "You will not take my word for it?"

"Please?"

"Fine," reluctantly Mutt moved out of the way. I lifted my head to see my reflection, and immediately wished I hadn't. "You're a fucking liar," I said, jaw dropping. Because I looked like shit.

Worse than shit.

There were bags under my eyes—that wasn't new—but the hair right at the front of my head that had been shaved down to fuzz was. I literally had a massive bald spot. That alone sucked balls, but paired with the dark bruises all over my face, I looked like I'd been through a fucking meat grinder.

The stitches were probably the cleanest part of me. Everything else was just...

"I look like a wreck." I blinked. "A car wreck," I added, because it was funny, even though it wasn't.

Mutt growled.

"Dude." I couldn't stop staring. Horrified, I turned to look at him. "Dude *my hair.*"

"Had to shave it so we could do stitches."

"I literally do not even remember this." I'd been pretty out of it though—so I suppose I wasn't surprised. I just...fuck. Fuck. Fuck. "You are *such* a liar. You said I looked beautiful."

"I wasn't lying."

"Fuck you. The front of my hair is fucking gone, man. I look horrible."
And I did. And it was awful. And oh fuck. Fuck. Fuck. "I look like ginger
Homer Simpson."

"Jeffrey." Mutt caught my wrist, dragging it up to his chest. My palm lay
flat across his heart, and he ducked his head to meet my gaze. "I *wasn't* lying."

I knew what he was trying to say. That all I had to do was listen to his
heart to know he was telling the truth. But I didn't speak wolf-boy-heart-
magic, and therefore couldn't believe him.

"Jeffrey," Mutt said again, dipping low enough our noses brushed. He
blinked those ridiculously long lashes at me, and my heart thumped
unsteadily. His warm breath brushed against my lips and I was lost all
over again—but this time I was lost inside his eyes. "Sometimes I wish
you were a wolf. Not because you aren't perfect the way you are—because
you are. But because I think…if you could scent how I feel about you—if
you could feel the way my heart beats when you're around. If you could
hear my truths, I could make you happy."

My heart hurt.

"You do make me happy," I said, surprised that it was true. Mutt was too,
apparently, because his eyebrows shot up, and the cockiest, happiest grin
I'd ever seen spread across his face. His tail thumped against the cabinets.

"And you *are* beautiful," he said softly, his heart thumping beneath my
palm.

I swallowed the lump in my throat, eyes burning a little.

For the first time in months, I almost cried. Sure my body had done the
motions, the shaking, the anxiety, the aching throb of too sharp breaths.
But no tears had spilled. Not for a long, long time.

"I wish I could tell too," I admitted, and it hurt. It hurt so bad.

"I know," Mutt bent down, lacing a gentle kiss against my fuzzy temple.

"Will you help me shave the rest of my hair?" I asked, voice hoarse. "I don't think I can."

I looked fucking weird with only the front of my hair short.

"Of course."

Mutt set us up in the kitchen. Theo was nowhere to be seen, probably because he was nosy as hell and overheard our entire conversation in the bathroom. Mutt sat me down on a chair, and helped me pull my shirt over my head so it wouldn't catch on the stitches.

He grimaced, frowning at the bruises that blossomed across my chest.

He'd made that face every time I got naked over the last two days.

Like it physically pained him to see me hurt.

"I'm fine," I promised—and for the first time since I could remember I wasn't lying.

Even though this was going to suck, majorly.

And then I did something I didn't know I could—I opened my mouth, and opened up, completely unprompted. "Lydia hated when my hair was long," I said, heart thumping. I hadn't told him who Lydia was—and I wasn't sure I could right now. Or ever. I didn't have words for her. "She made me cut it…all the time. She'd bring out a ruler and if it was past what she deemed was an acceptable length, off it would go."

Everything felt far away all of a sudden. My limbs were cold and my hands tingled weakly. "The second she got locked up last spring, I started growing it out. It felt like…I dunno. Felt like I was trying to recognize myself again, you know?"

Mutt made a soft sound in affirmation. He struggled figuring out how to plug the buzzers into the wall, but eventually managed with a triumphant huff of breath. He turned back to me, clippers held aloft, waiting patiently.

"Just do it," I said, ducking my head a little. I stared at my bare knees. There were less scars on my legs, only smatterings of copper leg hair. I was glad. Because summers got fucking hot, no matter where we went, and I could get away with long sleeves—because I was fair skinned and could claim I was hiding from the sun—but pants would've been too suspicious.

Mutt had seen it all though.

He'd seen it all and he still called me beautiful.

"Hair grows," he said softly, giving me another minute to change my mind as the whirr of the blade echoed through the room.

"It does," I agreed, because he was right.

Hair grows.

And time heals all wounds.

And maybe I had to shave it now—but that didn't mean I couldn't just grow it out again. It hurt, yes, because most things I'd done because of Lydia did. But somehow…it didn't hurt as much as I'd expected.

Mutt laid a hand on my shoulder, keeping me steady as he took the clippers to the back of my hair first.

He was awful.

So fucking awful. He kept bonking me, and apologizing, and then bonking me again. But it was…kinda the best haircut I'd ever had? Regardless. Normally when people touched me like this, my skin would crawl, and I'd hold impossibly still, careful not to flinch. There was nothing professional about any of this, but the brush of Mutt's warm fingers was soothing, rather than abrasive.

And I melted into the gentle buzz as my eyes drifted shut and he worked his way through my hair, clumps of auburn falling to the floor.

By the time he was done, I'd been lulled into a sense of calm that I'd rarely felt. I tipped my head up, head lighter now, the fuzziness prickling at my neck. "Can I use your shower?" I asked, because thanking him felt…like too much.

I needed to get my skin the right size again first.

"You can't get the stitches wet," he said, parroting back Theo's warning immediately.

"I won't," I promised. "I'll call you when it's time to do my head."

Mutt looked worried, but he nodded anyway. The muscle at the corner of his jaw jumped as he helped me to my feet—not because I needed help walking, but because he wanted to touch me. I found it kinda ridiculous that there were five werewolves living in this tiny ass house sharing a single bathroom, but…whatever.

Maybe they pissed in the trees? That would make a weird amount of sense.

Also, Mutt was pretty much a permanent fixture at my apartment, so there was that to consider too.

Mutt made sure the water wasn't too hot, fretting to himself about making everything perfect. I heard him muttering under his breath about the temperature–terrified he'd injure my fragile human body more.

And I just…stared at his back, and tried not to fall in love.

And failed.

Miserably.

The hot water was soothing as it pelted my back and the sore muscles there. It washed away the last of the blood, and the sharp bristles from my haircut. And by the time I'd finished scrubbing myself liberally, I felt about a thousand percent better, even sans hair.

The bathroom door opened with a click, letting in a breeze and I snorted out a laugh, not at all surprised when the shower door opened next, and leagues of warm, sweaty muscle pushed against my back.

"Thanks," I said, because it was easier now. Because I could breathe.

Mutt didn't seem offended that it had taken me as long as it had to say the words. He just rumbled, pleased, his thick chest brushing against my back as he reached for the soap and began gingerly running his fingers through my hair. He didn't have the best motor control—probably because he was normally in dog form, but he did well enough.

It wasn't until we'd rinsed out the soap, and I turned around to return the favor that I saw what he'd done.

"You—" My words dried up, my eyes burning as I stared up at him. The stitches on my head tugged a little as I moved, but I barely felt a thing.

How could I?

When Mutt was towering over me, and there were hair shavings on his shoulders—and he'd—he'd—

"You shaved your head," I said, voice cracking.

"Hair grows," he repeated, eyes dancing. "We can grow together."

I kissed him then.

I kissed him and he tasted like forgiveness. He was warm, and lovely— and tingles zapped up and down my spine as our tongues met. His kiss was sloppy and wet, like he'd never done it before, even though I knew he had. He licked behind my teeth and along my palate, just to feel me— and I groaned, fingers biting into his hips for stability.

Lydia had taught me that compliments were only used to manipulate.

She'd taught me that there was no such thing as a white knight.

She'd conditioned me to expect punishment for failure.

She proved that people were bad, and shouldn't be trusted.

She'd shown me a dark, ugly side to the world.

And Mutt…beautiful, sweet, lovely Mutt, was making her into a liar.

Chapter Sixteen

Jeffrey

UNFORTUNATELY, I HAD to go home at some point. I took my laptop, my phone, and my heart with me. Mutt kissed me at the door to my apartment. Theo had dropped us off on his way to a pack meeting—because he was a total sweetheart. Mutt's other brothers had been away over the entire weekend, and even though I was kinda disappointed I hadn't met them, I was relieved too.

Mutt had informed me that Butters had been the one who had accidentally spooked me in the road, looking torn, like half of him wanted to beat his brother up because he'd gotten me hurt, and the other half of him recognized that it had been an accident.

I told him not to worry about it, and that had been that.

As Mutt loped down the steps, I didn't mention the fact that I knew he was pretending to be my dog. Didn't mention the fact that I remembered him. That I remembered stopping for gas in Colorado and feeding a stray dog. Didn't mention the fact that I knew he'd followed me all the way to Elmwood. Didn't do anything other than lean against the doorway, lovesick, watching him walk down the steps—barefoot—while he bolted into the woods.

It was a full moon.

I knew that.

So I wasn't worried.

I knew he'd be back. I didn't need to know everything about werewolves to understand that he'd need some time for the moon. That was common knowledge. So after a fitful night full of nightmares, I went to work as usual the next day. With dark circles and a churning stomach, I fielded off Avery's worried glances and covertly tried to find books about werewolves and their mating habits when I wasn't busy working the cash register.

"Yes, Mrs. Dougal," I hummed into my work phone, flipping through the books we had stocked in the front. I was the one that had stocked them, which was why they had any semblance of order at all.

Avery's shop was all dark purples and reds, draped curtains, and black wood. I hadn't even known black wood was a thing until I worked here. There were plants shoved in every corner that could fit them, and it'd taken me weeks to get the storefront in order so customers could even find anything.

We mostly sold over-the-counter magic ingredients, basic spell and charm books, and supplies for the familiars that Avery rehabilitated and adopted out. My job was talking to customers and smoothing ruffled feathers—like now.

"No one told me there was an expiration date," Mrs. Dougal's voice was grating on the best of days.

"I am so sorry," I hummed softly. "If you'd like to bring it in I am more than happy to get you a new bottle."

"Really?"

"Absolutely!" I flipped through one of the books I'd grabbed from one of the tables, searching through the index. "If we're selling products that are not clearly labeled, that is one hundred percent on us."

She made a quiet sound in agreement.

I knew for a damn fact that the bottle of age-be-gone was freshly brewed and perfectly labeled. It only lasted a month and a half, and I could still remember the day she'd come in. I had very specifically told her all of this. But…sometimes you caught more flies with honey, and if there was one thing Lydia's training was good for, it was dealing with assholes over the phone.

"Weren't you…" I trailed off playfully. "Oh my god! Yes. You were wearing paisley when you came in." I flipped another page, humming thoughtfully under my breath.

"You remember me?" she sounded surprised. Mrs. Dougal was a five-foot ball of stress. Probably a hundred years old, and always wore colorful patterns.

"Of course I do," I flirted. "I never forget a pretty face."

"A pretty…" she trailed off shocked.

"You have the bluest eyes!" I hummed. "Never seen anything like them."

The thing about Mrs. Dougal was that she was a grouch, but a sucker for a good compliment. And I knew the best way to smooth her feathers was to poke where she was weakest.

"Really?" she sounded so damn pleased I could picture her grin already.

"Absolutely." Another page flip. "Why don't you come in later this week, hmm? I can take a look at that bottle for you and get you all sorted out."

"You know…" she trailed off, rustling around a little more. "I think I must've been mistaken! How embarrassing. I just turned my bottle around and look at that! A label right there."

"Ah! I'm so glad to hear that."

"I must've not seen it!"

"Happens to the best of us."

"Well, aren't you just the nicest young man!"

"I do my best."

Feathers officially smoothed, I parroted a few more niceties, said my goodbyes, and then groaned when I got to the end of the book because it was full of a whole lot of nothing.

The next book didn't do me any good either.

Or the next.

When I couldn't find anything up front, I resorted to drastic measures, and hunted Avery down in the back of the shop. I heard him before I saw him. His voice was muffled through the large black door that covered the hellhole of his office, so I knew he was home.

Covertly, I sent Mutt a text before I raised a fist to rap on Avery's office door.

Play it cool, I reminded myself. *Cool as a cucumber.*

Me: I hope you're feeling okay.

Me: How are you doing?

Me: How did last night go?

Me: Thank you for this weekend.

Me: It was honestly the best days of my life.

Texts now sent, I knocked twice.

"Come in!" Avery's voice sounded muffled through the wood. I stepped inside, and immediately was assaulted with the furry scent of animals, and the thick perfume of magic.

"Oh, Gregory, you frisky little thing," Avery cooed at his newest familiar, a fat crow that sat on the top of his head, its beady black eyes blinking. He didn't look at me, far too focused on the creature perched on glittery black claws.

Nail polish, I distantly recognized.

The bird is wearing nail polish.

I had no doubt if Avery was to blame, it was because the damn beast had asked for it.

"He's going to shit on you," I pointed out with a grin that Avery did not return.

He huffed, hands on his hips, his violet eyes flashing as he finally turned his attention to me. "Gregory is a gentleman, he would not—"

The bird shat on his head.

"Oh–" Avery squawked, alarmed and indignant, his whole face bright red. Cheeks puffing out, eyes wide, he gingerly reached up to grab Gregory and set him down on his over-cluttered desk. As white bird shit clung to his bangs, I wheezed so hard I saw stars. I had to lean against the door frame, afraid I'd fall over as my laughter choked its way out almost violently.

"It's not *that* funny!" Avery hissed at me, clearly embarrassed as he waved a hand over his head, uttered a quiet incantation, and the bird shit disappeared. Fucking witches. His hair was three or four shades darker than mine, almost magenta where mine was fiery orange. The bird shit had been a nice touch.

It had *real* contrast.

Damn, I cracked myself up sometimes.

I sobered up rather quickly though, thoughts of Mutt plaguing me as I sucked on my lip. "Hey, Avery?"

"Yes?" Avery smiled at me, his tiny head bobbing.

"You got any books on werewolves?"

Forty minutes later, I found out that Avery had…pretty much nothing. We spent nearly half an hour hunting through the archives in the back only to come up with diddly squat. As he bent over the book-filled cabinets and shelves, he mentioned something offhand about alphas though that made me feel anxious. Something about the moon being…*stronger* for them, or something.

It was hard to tell what he meant.

And then we'd spent another half hour hunting through the books in his office to, again, find jack shit.

Exhausted and disappointed, I peeled my ass out of the chair I'd sat down in while he hunted. I wasn't much help. Despite having worked there since June, I still had no fucking idea how the hell things were organized. There were thousands of books between the two rooms and Avery seemed to have all of them memorized. Eyeing the door hopefully, I shuffled toward it.

"You still cool if I head out early?" I asked, now that the only reason I'd braved his office in the first place when I usually avoided it like the plague had proved fruitless. "I need to figure out what to do with my truck." It wasn't all that early. Usually I got off at six, but I figured everything would be closed by then. Businesses in Elmwood had weird-as-hell hours, due to the large vampire population—and anything that was open during the day tended to have shortened hours to accommodate for the late night schedule.

I wanted to head home and see if I would have any luck calling the mechanic.

And see if Mutt is back, I added privately.

My need to get the fuck out of Avery's office wasn't because of the mess. Well. Mostly. I wasn't the kinda guy who judged a little clutter. In fact, I loved a sprinkle of trash here and there, you know, like seasoning. It made the world less bland. Only fake people had perfect houses. Perfect offices. My aversion to order probably came from my shitty childhood. Yay for strict "shoes at the door", "no nonsense" kinda households.

Buuuut Avery's office wasn't messy so much as it was actually hell on earth.

There were thousands of books, scrolls, and letters shoved haphazardly onto the floor-to-ceiling shelves that lined all the walls. Between books were cages of all sorts, perches, and scratching posts. And the towering ceiling was always full of a menagerie of animals flapping their wings and squawking back and forth. There were raccoons that sat in the arm chairs at his desk, playing cards, and lizards that scuttled across his paperwork leaving it in disarray.

Potions, spell books, and weeks-old take-out containers covered every surface an animal or cat scratching post did not.

My very first week at the shop, a fucking rat had burst from beneath his desk and ran between my legs. I'd been so startled I'd tripped and smashed my hand in a take-out container of pasta. My new boss had looked nothing but serene, sitting his tiny ass down inside his frankly massive and garish armchair, his eyes full of warmth. All Avery had said in response to the "incident" was—"Ahhh, Beatrice. What a free spirit."

And then, after the look I'd given him, "Don't worry, Jeffrey. She'll be back."

As if *that* was the thing I'd been concerned about.

I'd started cleaning out the take-out for him after that, but the rats returned anyway.

So yeah.

Bird shit on Avery's head was probably the funniest thing that had happened to me in my entire fucking life, and I was going to enjoy that shit. Literally. For as long as possible. Served him right for being an actual animal whisperer or some shit.

Karma.

And I needed something to feel good about, considering how disappointed and in pain I currently felt. The ibuprofen I'd taken had worn off like an hour ago, and my head was throbbing, and I genuinely just wanted to go back to this weekend.

Back to Mutt's bed.

Our nest.

The perfectly reasonable amount of clutter in his bedroom, and the cute angry gnome that decorated it.

Back to when I was happy and whole and curled up with someone that made me forget my mistakes. Someone who made me feel like it was okay that I'd made them in the first place.

I wasn't sure what I brought to the table for Mutt. I was more surly than he was. I didn't have his sunny disposition—when I wasn't faking it—and I couldn't run with him, not like his brothers could. I couldn't shift.

Which was part of why I'd so badly hoped Avery would have some books about wolves. I'd thought…maybe if I researched enough, I could figure out how to make myself useful to Mutt. So that he'd need me like I needed him.

"Shoo, shoo," Avery flicked his hand at me in dismissal, huffing in exasperation down at Gregory like he expected to get shat on again. "I'll see what I can find and get it in for you."

Avery was the fucking best!

He turned his back to me, a clear dismissal. His little vest was cinched up in the back, his dress pants clinging to his legs in the way they always did. Despite working for himself, Avery liked to dress to impress. You couldn't catch him dead at work outside of his little suits, bowties, vests, and slick little dress shoes.

I didn't have the clearance to order books like Avery did, so I appreciated him even more now.

"Thanks, Avery! See you later."

He waved me off. Earlier, he'd been concerned when he'd seen my face. He'd tried to send me home, and I had quickly declined. Now, however, I was more than ready to be done for the day.

Luckily for me, my apartment was just off of Spruce, not far from the shop so I had plenty of time to daydream as I made the walk back home.

There were no texts waiting on my phone from Mutt, but I figured that wasn't all that weird. Last night had been the full moon, after all.

He'll text soon.

Unless…

I knew today was a bust in general…but maybe Mutt would even be waiting for me when I got home? *Furry or not, I don't really care at this point.*

That's a nice thought.

That someone would be there waiting for me when I came home.

Someone to tell about the bird shit on Avery's head. Someone to laugh with. To smoke with. To share shitty take-out with, to watch movies with, and to fall asleep with only to start the pattern all over again the next day.

Someone who woke up and wanted to make me smile. Someone who told me I was beautiful when I looked like a train wreck. Someone who said "hair grows" and "wounds heal" and "you are the most wonderful person in the world."

Blair had found Elmwood. He'd found a place to belong. A place he could move on and be happy. And I'd resented him for it. I'd resented the fact that he could move forward when I couldn't. And now that I'd taken that first shaky step on my own toward the future, I knew how unfair that had been.

Mutt shared his rose-colored glasses, even if he didn't mean to.

Even if he was nosy, handsy, and stupid enough to pretend to be a dog.

He felt like he was mine, when nothing else did.

Chapter Seventeen

Jeffrey

MUTT WASN'T WAITING for me at home.

He hadn't texted.

Simply put, it was fucking radio silence, man.

Instead of thinking about Mutt—and the lack of Mutt in my life—I decided to shift my focus. *It isn't all that weird that he's missing, right? I mean… Maybe he needs time to recuperate?* I'd tried to figure that out at Avery's but he'd been no help. And though there were local hunting lodges—two of them, to be exact—I didn't feel comfortable going over there to ask.

Especially as it had been less than twenty-four hours since I'd last seen him.

I didn't want to step back into those shoes.

I didn't want to be Jeffrey Evans anymore.

Focus on your truck.

One thing at a time.

Numb, I pulled my phone out.

The local mechanic offered tows. And they'd been closed over the weekend—that was the only call that Mutt had allowed—as I was supposed to be "resting." So I tried again, the acorn-shaped guitar pick in my pocket biting into my thumb hard enough to leave the skin white.

"Magical Mechanics, this is Joe speaking," a tinny, grouchy voice echoed as the line connected.

"Hey, Joe!" I grinned, immediately falling back into the persona that had become second nature most of my life. "Hope you had a great weekend."

"It sucked, but thanks. What do you need?" Rustling sounded, a clang and then a muffled, "Wallace, get your ass in here, the damn coffee machine stopped working!"

An even more muffled, "Fuck you, old man," sounded in the background.

"I don't pay you to listen to your fucking lip," Joe snapped, though there was obvious affection in his tone, even as he uttered, "*Kids.*"

Then, Joe's voice grew clear again as he spoke into the phone and addressed me. "I don't got all day. Hurry the fuck up."

I laughed awkwardly, because I wasn't sure what the fuck else to do, cheeks flushed. Apparently Lydia's training did not work on Joe the mechanic. "Uh. Right. Yes, sir." I took a breath.

"Get to the point. Jesus."

"I have a truck I was hoping you could tow and take a look at for me?" I blurted.

"A truck?" He sounded skeptical. I explained the situation, trying not to think too hard about the crash—and the pain—and the—No, *no*. Jeffrey. *Stop it.* I listed the make and model of the vehicle and listened to him rattle around for a minute before he grunted.

"I already got one of those here," he said, annoyed. "Is this a prank call?"

"What? No." I frowned, confused. "You already have a red truck…that has a tree trunk through the windshield there?"

"Well, we took the trunk out," he huffed, annoyed. "But yeah."

"Oh."

This was either a freaky coincidence or there was some fuckery afoot. Immediately, my thoughts fled to Lydia. *This is a total Lydia move. Taking my truck from me like this—just to make me feel confused, and worried, and like I'd fucked up.*

"Who called it in?" I asked, heart pounding. "Was it a woman?"

Was she out of prison?

Had she broken out?

Had she come for me?

Had she sent one of her friends after me?

Had she—

"Richard Prince," he said easily. And then he hung up the phone, and I sat there staring blankly at the wall for all of two seconds before I was ringing Richard with a fire lit under my ass. Lydia's ghost hung over me, casting shadows in my head.

How fucking *dare* he?

Like.

Who does that?

He took my fucking truck—and didn't *tell* me?

What…the *fuck*.

What the fuck, what the fuck, what the fuck.

"Answer, you dickhead," I hissed at my phone, pacing my front hall, guitar pick painfully digging in. I was still sweaty from work, still antsy and anxious—the Mutt-sized hole in my apartment glaringly obvious as I panicked.

Ring, ring—

"This is Richard," Richard's low, quiet voice came on the line.

"The fuck is your problem?" I hissed out. My vision was red, my head spinning as I burned holes in the carpet with my feet.

"What?" Richard made a confused sound. "*Jeffrey?*"

I'd never called him before, so I figured it was fair he was confused.

I was too fucking mad to care right now though.

Distantly I recognized that I was taking my anxiety out on him, but I couldn't seem to stop. The shaking had begun, and my throat was tight, and I just…I felt so fucking powerless and he—

Why had he done this?

Why hadn't he told me?

*Was he **fucking** with me?*

"You had my car towed?" I spat. "And you didn't tell me? The fuck, dude. The actual fuck."

"Jeffrey—"

"You fucking asshole." My head wasn't screwed on straight. Everything hurt, and my thoughts were jumbled. "You saw the fucking tree trunk through the windshield—and you didn't even *see* if I was okay? And then you moved the fucking truck—and like." Oh fuck. There was a pit in my stomach, and my body ached, bruises that were still vivid and dark burning where the seat belt had slammed into me. "Did it ever occur to you that I could be hurt? Or that the truck is the only fucking thing in the world that's mine—and it maybe means a *lot* to me?"

"Jeffrey—"

"*Why are you messing with me?*" My voice broke.

"I'm not," Richard made a panicked sound, and I felt bad immediately. He was a slow talker. It always took him a bit to figure out what to say, and I wasn't giving him time to explain himself. But I was just…I was just so *mad.*

And Mutt wasn't here—and I'd hoped he would be.

And everything sucked—and I just—

Does Richard not care about me?

That thought kept playing over and over and over again.

I hadn't realized till that moment just how upset the idea that Richard didn't care about me made me feel.

"Explain," I demanded.

"I'll explain—" he promised, alarmed. "Where are you? I can come to you." There was a clicking sound, like he'd just unlocked his car.

"Just use the phone, old man."

"Where are you?"

"Jesus fucking fuck, fuckchard. I'm at my house." *You're being mean. Stop it. He probably didn't mean to upset you. Calm down. Calm down.*

I wished Mutt was here to tell me *"calm"* like he had the other day. Because telling myself to calm down did not fucking work. It only made me angrier, and more bitter.

He doesn't care about you.

Why would he?

You left.

You left and now he's getting back at you.

It wasn't my voice, it wasn't mine but it hurt all the same. The barbs of Lydia's claws digging in a way they hadn't in weeks.

"I'm on my way."

Richard hung up the phone. I called him back, but it went straight to voicemail and I got one of those annoying automated texts that said "this person is currently operating a vehicle." So I swiped it away and continued to angrily pace my front hallway, my head burning—my heart aching.

Why would he do this?

Why would he—

I didn't get it.

I didn't get it.

Where is Mutt?

I want Mutt.

I want Mutt. I want Mutt. I need—

I need Mutt.

By the time Richard knocked on the front door I'd shoved the guitar pick so hard into my finger that I'd made it bleed. Richard's nostrils flared, alarmed, when I pushed the door open and yanked him inside unceremoniously. It almost clicked shut, but not quite—but I was too pissed to care as the open crack sent a beam of light into the gloom.

The hallway was still dark.

Despite the sun having gone down on my way home, I hadn't thought to flip the light switch. Something I hadn't even noticed until I had someone else in my space and realized how weird I looked. Just standing here in the shadows, fuming and panicking.

I looked unstable.

Just like Blair had pretty much told him I was.

"You have two minutes," I said, trying to seem more calm than I had on the phone and failing.

Richard wasted no time.

"I got a call that there had been a wreck after you left Blair's shop. I called around and found out you were staying with the new pack we've been negotiating with at work. They are good men, and I've been working extensively with all of them—Theo especially, and he assured me that you were being taken care of and would appreciate some space."

Okay…that made sense.

I squinted at him.

"I thought you might be overwhelmed and want some help. So I called in a favor at Joe's and they towed your truck to the shop."

"And *why* didn't you text me?" I hissed out, trying to stay angry, though it was hard when he was being so…so…*reasonable.*

"I did." Richard looked confused. "Did you not get it?"

"Of course I didn't fucking get it." I yanked my phone out of my pocket, pulled it open, and showed him my inbox to demonstrate.

"Oh," Richard said, frowning. "But it's…I mean. It's right here?" He pushed my phone back toward me, tapping at the screen.

"What do you mean it's—" I blinked, then frowned, face scrunching up. Because there was a text from Richard. Sitting right there. Already opened. Right above the automated one I'd just received.

"But I—" I pulled it closer, confused. "But I don't…I didn't—"

And then I remembered. Because of fucking course. Mutt and I had been trying to watch something on my phone and I'd kept getting texts— so I'd swiped them all away and I just…fuck. Fuck. *Okay.*

Okay, this was my fault.

This was totally my fault.

Because of course it was.

It always was.

Everything was always my fucking fault.

And here I was screaming at Richard when his only sin was doing the right thing—and I was just—I was just—

I couldn't breathe.

I'm a bad person.

I'm a bad person.

This is like the party all over again.

"Are you okay?" Richard asked, because he was a fucking saint. He looked so ridiculously concerned, standing next to me, his pale hair glinting. We looked like idiots just standing here without the light on.

At least, I did.

It weirdly…suited him now that he was all fangy and could see in the dark.

It didn't escape my notice that this was the first time Richard and I had been alone since I'd come back to Elmwood. But my head was spinning too hard to properly react.

Before, having him here would've made me nervous and anxious— terrified he'd see the five bolt locks on my door and know just how paranoid I really was. That I wasn't right in the head—because I *wasn't*. But…weirdly enough, I couldn't muster up the energy to be upset. Or to hide. Or to push him out.

Couldn't even lie.

I just…sagged.

Numb for all of two seconds before ice filled my veins.

I need Mutt.

I need Mutt.

"No," I admitted. "I'm not fucking okay."

"Okay." Richard stared at me, eyes wide—like he hadn't expected me to say that. I must've looked absolutely crazy, judging by the look on his face, but I couldn't seem to stop shaking. Couldn't get my thoughts in order. Couldn't breathe.

I broke.

"My…my head hurts," I admitted, my hands falling to my sides. "And I–I–I cut my thumb on my fucking guitar pick on accident." It hadn't been an accident, not really, but I wasn't about to confess that too. "I'm a fucking chronic pessimist. I don't know how to breathe ninety percent of the time."

My eyes pinched shut as I sucked in a broken breath. Too tired to do anything but tell the truth. Angry, and hurt, but mostly…mostly mad at myself.

Because once again, I'd caused problems.

Once again, I'd fucked shit up.

And I didn't have my wolf to make it better.

He could be hurt somewhere for all I knew, lost…or, or injured by the local hunters. Realistically, I knew I wasn't being rational. That Mutt could heal faster than I could say my own name. That hunters weren't allowed to hurt wolves unprovoked—but that didn't stop my head from reliving the nightmares I'd survived, and replacing the creatures I'd killed with Mutt.

"Mutt isn't here—and I thought he would be. Avery got bird shit on his head, and I was gonna tell him about it, but now I can't." My chin wobbled. "He's not answering my texts. And I'm worried, and mad at myself for being worried, because I *know* I'm being paranoid but I can't fucking stop." I could hardly breathe. My chin wouldn't stop moving, and it was making me irrationally angry—but that was a distant, far-off emotion.

Because once I started talking…I couldn't seem to stop.

Words spilled free.

A whole torrent of awful, mushy truths. Like sludge and muck. The truths that had clogged my system for years, along with ones I'd just collected. It should've felt good. It should've.

But at that moment, it only hurt.

My cracks had finally snapped.

"What if something's wrong? I mean… I don't know enough about werewolves. I keep telling myself to stop freaking out, but *that* doesn't help. I keep replaying my stupid therapist's advice in my head, but that's not helping either—"

Focus on the positive, Jeffrey.

"And I'm pretty sure I'm in love with him, which is terrifying—" It really fucking was. *The most terrifying thing I've ever experienced.* "And *how* am I even supposed to know if I'm in love when all of this is new? I've never even been with a dude. I've never had real feelings for someone in general. So I'm like, the least qualified person ever to say they love someone."

And wasn't that just the icing on the shit-cake?

"Plus! Blair doesn't know about him—and I *can't* tell him, because I don't know how to talk to him anymore. He's like all at peace or whatever, living his best gay life with you and your fucking cat and your life-sized

Dracula cardboard cutouts. And I'm happy for him—of course I am, because no one deserves happiness more than him—but I resent him too. Because he's moved on, and I haven't, and it's not fucking fair. We were supposed to move on together but I can't—and I'm stuck. And everything is fucking spinning all the time, and no one notices I'm drowning—or they do and look at me like I'm a basket case—like you are right now."

The words kept coming.

Things I hadn't meant to say spilling free, the drain unclogging.

"But I can't even be mad because it's my fault. It's all my fault anyway—*all* of this is. I made this mess. I fucking *made* it. I left. I tore our family apart. I abandoned you. I got Blair kidnapped. Every time *Lydia* hurt him it was because of me. Because I was a coward. Because I am so inherently fucked in the head that I thought a monster could love me.

"I owe everyone a big ass apology, you especially. I'm a shit brother. I yelled at you—because I'm stupid—and instead of thinking you were doing something nice for me, I immediately jumped to the worst possible conclusion. My truck was missing—and I got scared that Lydia was fucking with me. And then she wasn't—and it turns out it was just you. Being perfect. As per fucking usual."

Richard stared at me.

He stared and stared and stared.

"And I'm so fucking mad at you. Because you're *nice* to me. And I don't get it." I sucked in a ragged breath. "I don't. Get. It. I don't. I don't-I don't-I don't. *How can you be nice to me after what I've done?* How can any of you welcome me back at all? How can Blair forgive me? When everything shitty that's ever happened to him is my fault."

I fell to my knees, the carpet biting into them as I whined, low and hurt. Blood dripped down my finger from the jagged cut I'd made. My bruises should've ached, but they didn't. Because my heart hurt more. This gaping, awful hole. Empty and hollow and aching. "It's my fault, it's my fault, it's my fault."

I couldn't breathe—

It's my fault—It's my fault—It's my—

Drowning, drowning, drowning.

Richard's hand was on the back of my neck. And it was cool, and solid, and sure. He smelled like pine cones and cocoa, and his leather jacket rustled as he sunk to his knees beside me. And then he pulled me into a hug—and I just…I just caved in.

I shook and shook and shook, and my lungs wheezed—but no tears came.

They couldn't, they wouldn't.

"I'm sorry," I gasped out. "I'm so, so sorry."

"It's okay," Richard replied, holding me tight—like he had the day Mom had told me the truth and I'd learned the monsters I'd been frightened of were real.

"I'm sorry," I gasped again. "I'm so—I'm so—"

"Shhhh, no. It's fine. It's fine." Richard squeezed me tighter. "No one blames you."

"They should—" It hurt. Everything hurt. "You should—"

"You were nine."

"I was stupid—"

"You were a kid."

"I fucked up."

"You did," Richard agreed, slicing me in two. "But if you think you're the only person who's fucked up, you're dead wrong. And if you think you won't again, you're wrong about that too." Richard clutched me tighter. "Everyone fucks up."

"You don't."

"Yeah, I do," Richard laughed, breath leaving him in a tight gust. "I do all the fucking time. Why do you think I'm so anal retentive?"

I frowned, twisting to look at him. His eyes were red. They weren't brown like I remembered, but everything about him was the same—just bigger, broader, and paler. He may have been a vampire, but he was still the kid I'd wasted summers with. Still the kid who'd made me breakfast because I was scared of the flame. Still my brother.

"We're *brothers*," Richard said, pretty much reading my mind, even though he probably didn't mean to. He pulled his hand from my neck, and I missed it immediately, watching him blearily, my chest heaving with each ragged breath as he spat in his palm and held it out to me. The same fucking spit shake we'd done when we were little.

A pact.

"Blood is blood," Richard said, waiting patiently, his red eyes serious. "And I'll always love you."

"Even when I suck?"

"Especially then." I stared at him blankly for a second as memories of our childhood—however short-lived it had been—assaulted my senses.

My heart ached for what we'd lost.

But I could see in his eyes that there was no anger there.

Only relief.

Only warmth.

I looked for a lie, but there was none.

Maybe Richard understood what it felt like to drown better than I'd thought.

So I spat in my palm too, my heart skittering as I stared at him—really fucking stared. The same way I'd looked at Collin. Like I was seeing him for the first time.

I spat in my palm.

When we pressed our hands together, some of the weight on my shoulders fell away. I could breathe a little. And the tension that had sat like a wall between us since I'd moved back into town, finally disappeared.

And then the still partially open front door parted wider, and a familiar head popped through the crack. Blair's messy mop of black hair flopped in his face, and his eyes were wet as he stared at me.

A beat passed.

"Can I come in now?" Blair asked, voice low. "Or do you guys need more time to be gross?" I released Richard's hand as quickly as I'd grabbed it. Then wiped it off on my pants, heart thumping erratically.

If being numb had been awful, this was worse.

Fire burned through my body, my eyes wide, my heart skittering to life again as I stared up at Blair, horrified.

It felt like the world was ending all over again. *He overheard. There's no way he didn't. He fucking overheard. What did I say?*

Oh fuck. What did I say?

The peace I'd just found disappeared as quickly as it had come.

My words disappeared. My throat was dry—and I just—I didn't…I didn't know what to do.

"Did you…?" My voice cracked.

"Hear?" Blair pushed the rest of the way into the room, nodding, his eyes searching mine. "Yeah. I did."

"Oh." My head was spinning all over again. "All of it?"

"Yeah."

I didn't think I'd ever felt more off-kilter. I hadn't meant for him to hear. Hadn't meant to spill my truths like that. But now that they were out I couldn't bring myself to deny them. Mutt asked me why I lie, and I used to think it was because my lies protected the people I cared about most.

But as Blair fell to his knees beside us and wrapped his arms around me tight, I realized I'd been wrong. Because all I felt was warm as his tiny body tucked against mine. I wasn't sure what I expected. Judgment maybe? Anger? Rejection?

But I got none of that.

Instead, I got squeezed by a fucking half-pint, and was given the greatest gift of all, not arguments, not platitudes, not promises—but acceptance. The silence was full of love. It was fluttery soft and closed in around us as I slowly…slowly softened. Richard patted my back awkwardly as Blair squeezed me even tighter.

"You know," Blair said, crackly soft, voice as rough as my own. "If I knew you were that jealous of my Dracula cutout I would've bought one for you too."

I snorted, sagging into him as I nodded. "You were a stingy fuck."

"I was," Blair agreed, his arms solid and sure as we huddled in a sad little pile on the floor.

You deserve to be happy.

It's time to move on.

You know I don't blame you, right?

Blair had said those words weeks ago, but it wasn't till this moment that

I actually believed him. Till I realized he'd been telling the truth, and not trying to placate me.

In a way, I was glad things had ended up this way. Sure, I should've told Blair how I felt a long time ago. Should've spoken my truths and made the choice to break down the wall between us. But that could've taken years—and I…

Well…

I needed my brother.

"I'm sorry," I said to him, because he deserved it most of all. "I didn't mean to cut you out." It was exactly what Blair had done to me, months ago. I could still remember getting mad at him on the phone when he'd finally fucking called me and let me know he was okay. And here I was, doing the same exact fucking thing.

I guess we weren't all that different.

"Oh fuck off," Blair laughed, slapping my back and making me wince. I was still bruised, after all. "Alright. Disgusting sappy moment over. God, gives me the fucking heebie-jeebies," Blair shivered like he was disgusted, pulling back and away, though he offered me a hand to help me up. "The fuck's with your hair, dude?"

I snorted out a laugh.

"A werewolf gave me a haircut," I shrugged, accepting his help, making sure to use the hand that wasn't spit-covered.

"That's…" Blair shook his head, and then he cracked a grin, eyes crinkling with amusement. "That tracks."

He eyed my stitches with concern, but didn't say anything, once again offering me mercy. I had no doubt Richard had already filled him in. And while I knew it was probably killing him not to mother hen me, he could see how badly I needed to feel normal, so stayed silent anyway.

Richard rose on his own, liquid quick, the affection in his eyes apparent as he stared at the both of us. I'd thought he'd resent our relationship, as Blair had replaced him for most of my life. But he didn't. There was nothing but acceptance in his gaze as he offered me a little grin.

I may not have found my werewolf when I got home.

But I did find my brothers.

And that was…*well…*

That was pretty fucking sweet too.

Shitty haircut aside.

Chapter Eighteen

Mutt

BLACK.

Everything was black. Empty, cold, excruciating—hurt-hurt-hurt.

It seared me from the inside out like wildfire injected directly in my veins, riotous and wicked, destined to leave nothing but ash and memories behind. Between the gaps in the bars on the window, pale moonlight slipped across my cell floor, creeping toward me. Extending its cool caress my way like it hadn't forsaken me. I howled, and that only made me hurt more. *Because why—why had this happened? Why had my moon mother turned her back on me?* It wasn't fair, it wasn't fair, it wasn't—

Black, nothing.

Nothing, nothing.

There was nothing but the wet slick slide of blood as my manacles caught in my fur. Matted, clotted, as tangled as my thoughts. I was forgetting something. I knew I was—but all I could feel was the painful ache in my belly. Cavernous, gaping, open.

Free.

I wanted to be *free*.

Hungry. I just—I needed. I needed to hunt.

Something familiar tickled at my senses. Something bright like oranges. Like summer days. It cried, mate-mate-mate, but it was faded and faint and the moon was so strong and I—

Ah.

What was that?

Footsteps. Yes. Above me. The *thud, thunk* of feet across the floor.

There were others upstairs. I could *hear* them. Hear as they rustled and moved. *Prey.* Because everything with a pulse was prey. I could taste them already—the snap crunch of bone, the bite of coppery blood. The way their flesh would feel, parting beneath my teeth and claws.

Free, I needed free.

Needed to hunt and bite and *kill.*

The prey was so close.

So close. When I lifted my snout I could scent them on the air. One, two, three, four—yes, yes, yes. Food. Food. Hungry, hungry, hungry—

And then…the scent teased me once more. Summers, laughter, mate-mate-mate. I howled again, tearing at the manacles, desperate to be free. I needed, I needed, I need-need-need-need—

The prey spoke and it was sharp and panicked, the fearscent bright enough I could smell it from here. *"You have to go. Right now."*

"Where's Mutt? Is he okay?" a distant voice echoed when I strained. It was

hard when I was like this, my senses murky but sharp. The world flooded my mind with sensation so rapidly it was hard to process all at once. But I recognized the voice anyway. Because it was the only thing that felt right in all the world. Not the moon, not my fur, not the blood that seeped into the concrete floor. Old stains mixing with the new.

"He's gone. Home," that was the prey. "Now go. Please." That was the prey and it was wrong, wrong, wrong.

I just wanted—I just wanted the voice back. The sweet-summer-sun. The music. I huffed a few greedy breaths, trying to taste my mate even though I could hear him leaving. Hear the crackle of feet on gravel, hear the rumble of an engine driving away.

And there was only prey again.

Prey, prey, prey.

And what sanity I'd managed slipped away as quickly as it had come.

I needed *free*.

Needed *out* of these chains.

I was hungry, hungry, hungry. The prey was so close. So close. I could taste them already. Imagine the chase, the thunder of our feet, the fearscent that would only make their deaths more delicious.

They *should* be frightened.

Because I was Alpha.

It was *all* I was.

And they were nothing but *food*.

I'd fill my belly. I'd glut on them. Enjoy every last, slippery morsel. And then I'd hunt again. Again, again, again.

There was no pack. There was no moon. There was only the gnawing, aching gape of my empty stomach. There was only the jut of my cock.

Only the phantom scent of mate-mate-mate, but it was wrong. It was wrong, because it wasn't wolf.

It wasn't wolf.

And I was…

I was hungry, hungry, *hungry*.

I needed—needed-needed.

And then I was…nothing.

Nothing at all.

And it was black all over again.

Chapter Nineteen

Jeffrey

I GAVE MUTT three days. Three days of texting him with no answer, calling him with my calls going straight to voicemail, and casually hunting for him after work in all the spots I'd seen him in the past—before I decided it was time to actually look in earnest. Richard and Blair had offered to help when they'd been at my place, but I'd declined at first, because even I knew I was being paranoid.

He'll be at open-mic night.

That's what I told myself. It was at the end of the week, and Mutt had never missed one before. I had no doubt that he'd be back—from wherever he'd gone. Because at this point, there was no way his absence was because of the moon.

Right?

I mean, Richard had mentioned that Mutt might be a "special" case, but after scouring the internet and all the books Avery had ordered in for me, I couldn't find any mention of a moon lasting more than a day. A week was just…just…bizarre.

Which meant something was wrong.

When I'd gone to Mutt's house looking for him, I'd been quite literally kicked the fuck out. Theo's expression had been contrite, but he'd had a wild glint in his eyes that I didn't like.

"You have to go," he'd spat out, unusually manic. "Right now."

"Where's Mutt? Is he okay?"

"He's…fine. He went home." He urged me back down the driveway, but he looked guilty as hell.

"Okay, well, is he coming back—?"

"*Yes*. Now go. Please."

Okay. Rude.

Fuck.

In a daze, I made my way toward Richard's car. I knew Theo had been acting weird as hell, but I did as I was told anyway, because what the fuck else was I supposed to do? Wasn't like I could storm a house full of werewolves. I'd start an interspecies incident. And even if I could, what was the point? I didn't even have my weapons with me, as my truck was still in the shop.

I knew Theo had said Mutt had gone home…but…sitting still made me feel like I was going crazy.

So instead of biding my time, waiting patiently, I enlisted the help of my favorite goth-twink and his golden-retriever-gigantor vampire boyfriend, and we continued searching for Mutt anyway. With every day that passed without word from my wolf, I felt like I sunk just a little deeper. I understood Lydia in a way now, because I'd never felt insane till Mutt disappeared.

We searched and searched and searched.

Searched downtown Elmwood.

Searched inside the club where I'd met him in his humanskin for the first time.

Searched the woods around Mutt's house, and gotten chased off by Theo.

Searched Benji's, where we'd had our first unofficial date.

Searched the beach where we'd played the night that changed everything. I even knocked on the door of the nearest house, despite how manic and unhinged I was certain I looked. Though, calling it a *house* was kinda a stretch. More like huge-fucking-mansion.

When a familiar-looking, tattoo-covered asshole opened the door and pretty much immediately slammed it in my face, I wasn't even mad. Because this had been a long shot. *All* of this had been.

But still, I couldn't settle.

"He's probably home like his brother said," Blair tried to reassure, his painted fingers tapping on the back of the seat as he swiveled around to face me.

"Yeah," I replied, because he probably was.

Just…

Something just…*didn't feel right.*

I could sense it.

Like there was an empty Mutt-sized hole inside me that hadn't been there before.

I was so obviously out of it, that I didn't even notice when Richard started driving. I just kinda sat there, shaking, and trying to figure out how to breathe again. Blair had twisted around to face the front again, his feet on the dash—the same way Collin had put his feet up in my truck when we'd had our little talk, and he and Richard chatted in low tones.

Familiar with each other in a way that ached.

I pressed my forehead to the cold glass, and pinched my eyes shut as the skies opened up above us and water spilled down the chilled glass. Fog trickled across the mountaintops, decorating the roads much the same as it had the night I'd crashed.

And I ached.

And ached.

And ached.

The party was loud. Bright. Crowded.

Blair and Richard had roped me into attending because apparently I "looked like a kicked puppy" and "needed to get my head out of my ass and do something fun." I knew the choice to attend was for my benefit, as Blair had never been big on parties, and I doubted Richard was either.

I didn't have the heart to tell Blair I hated parties. That I'd hated them ever since high school. But I'd gone to them anyway, because it was expected of me. No, no. That wasn't really true. No…if I was being honest—and I was trying to do that more nowadays, fuck you therapy…

The real reason I hated them was because in a lot of ways, they were an easy way to hurt myself. Lots of booze, lots of hands—becoming the person I only was when I hit rock bottom. Self-harm in the form of harmful decisions.

Even though Mutt was gone, and I felt more unanchored than I ever had before—I had at least made enough progress to know I didn't want to be *that* person anymore. Not the kinda man who punched brick walls, or cut his fingers on guitar picks. Or the kind of man who played his guitar till his fingers bled because sometimes the pain felt better than the ache in my heart.

I wasn't stupid enough to think I'd never relapse, but I was proud that I'd come far enough to recognize I was moving forward. Away from the backpedaling. Away from the merry-go-round and its traps. I didn't want to be life-of-the-party Jeffrey anymore. Golden-boy Jeffrey. Lydia's Jeffrey.

He was sunny, happy, and *funny*.

But he was fake as hell.

And I was starting to learn that the people who cared about me didn't want him around. Which was…weird but awesome too. That despite my surliness and general grumpy disposition, all my brothers seemed to prefer me this way.

"Drink?" Blair offered, holding out a beer bottle. I declined, because my stomach was already churning and I didn't really need to add alcohol into the mix. "You wanna dance?" His voice was louder than usual so I could hear it over the blare of the speakers.

I didn't get why we were here, at Vanity's party of all places. As the oldest daughter of the Rain family, Vanity and her sister Chastity were well known around these parts. Their fortune rivaled my parents', and Richard and I had grown up playing with the two sisters, often babysat by the same brother this party was being held in honor of.

Blair was way more forgiving than I was.

Even if this was a party for Vanity's brother and his fiancé to celebrate their engagement, and not for her at all. If I had my way, she'd be halfway down a ditch by now, but since Blair was better than me, we were here anyway.

After we'd discovered Lydia had been blackmailing Vanity, things had been strained. Her attempts on my brother's life, while fruitless and obviously coerced, would not be easily forgotten by me. Blair seemed to be at peace with how his life was though. And Elmwood was a small town, with an even smaller population of humans, so I guess I understood why he'd opted to exist peacefully rather than go down the murder route like I wanted to.

That didn't mean we were all buddy-buddy though.

It was a mutual avoidance.

Though Blair and I did say hi to Chastity—who just so happened to be both Blair's best friend, aside from Collin, and the blue-haired girl who had helped Mutt buy me dinner at the diner.

Pink and indigo lights flickered, blaring across Blair's pale cheeks and making him look kinda fucking ridiculous. Like Frodo Baggins or some shit, except wearing platforms and a t-shirt that said Bite Me on it. Blair had hickeys on his neck—courtesy of Richard—and I grimaced, disgusted when I thought about the two of them making out. It was hard not to stare at them, especially when his skin was pastier than an uncooked pancake.

Not that my skin was any better, but still.

Collin was right.

They were gross.

"Go have fun," I waved him off. Blair huffed, annoyed.

And then he pulled me to the dance floor anyway.

He was a horrible dancer. All jerky awkward limbs, like a five-foot

robot. And somehow…Richard was *worse*. He moved like he had

at all, and yet—they were the happiest fucking couple at the whol

Hopping and jerking and wiggling like fucking weirdos. Despite l

like a fucking train wreck the whole time.

It was…contagious.

"How the hell are you doing that?" Blair yell-asked, staring at n

like I was fucking writing morse code or some shit. I was bruised

still, though they were healing, and wasn't even operating at my

hip-gyrating level.

"Just copy me!" I yelled back, snorting out a laugh. He tried to

me but ended up looking like a horny penguin, and it was the fu

shit I'd seen in forever. When he nearly toppled over, I grabbed

righting him before he started humping the air again.

"You trying to get the air pregnant?" I asked, unable to help myse

"Fuck off, dick."

Gleefully, I enjoyed how dumb he looked for as long as possible.

Except Richard ruined it pretty quickly, because his gaze was *hun*

of all things—as he dragged it over Blair's body, like he wasn't actin

a total fucking loser and was actually gigantor-catnip.

"Oh my fuck. Stop eye-fucking or I'm going to leave," I gagged, th

there was no true ire in my voice. Somewhere around the third weir

hump I'd forgotten all about how miserable I was and how much

body hurt, and started focusing on the present.

"Eye-fucking?" Blair frowned, then twisted to look at Richard. His

widened. Then a wolfish grin split his face and he did the awful peng

hip-jerk again. "Damn. This does it for you?"

More air humping.

Fucking Christ.

"Stop being gross!" I shoved at his shoulder and Blair fell over with a squawk. When he shoved me back, I cackled, letting him think he'd gotten the upper hand for just a second before I wrapped an arm around his neck and gave him a wet willy.

"Fuck-fuck!" He screeched like a tiny pterodactyl trying desperately to get free. "Let me go you freckled-fuckface."

I grinned, dragging him around the dance floor by the neck while Richard laughed his ass off behind us.

After we'd done a round, and I'd caught a glimpse of the guests of honor—a tall pink-haired twunk and the same asshole who'd slammed the door in my face—huh—I paraded Blair back to the spot we'd abandoned near the back of the dance floor.

Then I spent the next half hour trying to teach both of them how to move their hips.

Blair did not catch on.

Richard though?

Yeah.

He was a fucking natural.

By the time I decided I did actually need a drink—and maybe some fresh air—he'd graduated from an awkward robot, to somewhat passable at grinding. He looked ridiculously proud of himself, and the second I walked away I saw Blair grab him by the hips—and nope.

Ew.

PDA.

No thank you.

I snagged a water bottle and headed out into the hallway. And then

when it was still too fucking hot out there—and there were way too many couples making out against the walls, I left the building entirely.

The moon had risen high in the sky, waning now that the full moon had passed. The stars winked between dark, drifting clouds. It was chilly out, the cool October breeze caressed my overheated skin as I hopped down the steps and headed toward the woods at the back of the apartment complex.

I wasn't sure what I was looking for.

Something was calling me.

Something that ached and burned deep inside me.

Pine cones cracked beneath my feet as I stepped beneath the shadows of the tree line, and took a sip of my water. It went easily down my throat, calming the heat in my body from the inside out as I sucked in a deep breath and tried to think.

I missed Mutt.

It had been a week now. A week without him. A week since he'd shaved his head for me, and told me I was wonderful. A week since I'd felt like the sun had shined.

I'd missed Blair when he had disappeared, but it had been a different kind of loss. This was…well…

This felt like one of my limbs was missing. I could feel Mutt's phantom everywhere I went, and it sucked. It sucked so hard. Because I barely knew him. And I knew I was acting irrational, and crazy, and obsessive—

And I'd never been that kinda guy.

But there was something about the way his eyes followed me no matter what room we were in that made me feel like I wasn't invisible. I'd never known someone else's smile could make me feel whole. Never known I could crave the sound of laughter, or the thump of a tail just as greedily as I craved water.

I'd always wondered if you could be broken from birth, or if cracks were something that had to happen to you. Because I'd always felt like my edges were brittle, and I had holes on holes and holes.

I'd chased affection desperately, trying to fill the gaps. Pitiful, and weak, and broken.

Never enough for anyone.

Perpetually unlucky.

This was different.

Mutt was different.

He was the first person who had chased me.

And though it was weird not to be the desperate one, it made me feel settled in a way I never had before. And I missed his attention, even though sometimes I didn't know what to do with it. Even though sometimes he was so nice I felt like I was dying—because kindness felt like lies, and it was the one thing I'd never been able to stomach.

Maybe one day…if he came back—fuck, the idea of him not coming back was enough to make me sick—I'd stop second-guessing his warmth.

I'd be able to tip into it.

Because I could see webs now, see traps and monsters—and Mutt may have been a werewolf, but he would never hurt me.

The hair on the back of my neck stood on end.

Snap, a twig broke somewhere behind me, and I twisted, alarmed. *This is what I get for spacing out and not paying attention to where I'm going.* The woods were dark and vacant. Stars dripped in the indigo night above. Trees stretched high, high, high toward the waning moon, half covered by rain-heavy clouds. The creak of the branches whistled overhead, and I was alone.

I was alone.

But I could feel eyes anyway.

Stop being paranoid, I scolded myself.

Stop it.

But I couldn't.

I couldn't.

More rustling.

Heavy breathing.

Even the crickets were silent.

I had no weapons on me. No way to protect myself. My phone was in my pocket but there wasn't any service out here—and fuck. Fuck. Fuck. I was so screwed.

"It's not real," I promised myself. But it was a lie and I knew it.

So I bolted.

The wind whipped my face, branches swiping at my arms and legs as I tore deeper into the forest, away, away, away from whatever creature had stalked me there. *The fuck is following me?* I could hear the steady thump of footsteps now. Closer and closer.

And I knew, for once, I hadn't been acting paranoid.

There was a log up ahead and I launched myself over it, swearing softly under my breath as my knee skimmed its surface.

"It's fine, it's fine," I muttered, trying to self-soothe so I wouldn't full-blown panic. *Why the fuck didn't I bring a weapon with me?* I should have. Lydia had taught me to be prepared. *Why did I go into the woods on my own?* I hadn't even told Blair where I was going. Rookie move. Rookie fucking move.

I was good at fighting, but even I knew my chances alone out here in the dark with no weapon and no idea how to get home were slim.

I'm fucked.

I'm fucking fucked.

A tree loomed ahead, dark enough I barely saw it, its trunk thick enough to block out the gaps between the trees. Ferns brushed against my ankles, the damp scent of wet dirt filling my nose as I dodged around it. Moss brushed against my fingertips, cold, damp from the earlier rainstorm, and cushiony soft.

Breathing.

I could hear breathing still.

Behind me.

It was getting closer—closer—closer—

Don't look. It'll only slow you down. Don't do it—don't—

I looked.

Andddd immediately regretted it.

Because the second I stopped watching where I was going the whole forest decided to fuck me over. I tripped over a tree root and just barely managed to catch my fall. On my hands and knees now, with the wind knocked out of me, and my head spinning, I twisted my head around. Slowly, slowly, my heart racing–I finally caught sight of what had been following me—wait—*wait.*

Was that—?

Oh my god.

"Mutt?" My voice cracked, acid burning in my veins as I stared at the very large, very beautiful man, loping along behind me. He paused, waiting, his head cocked to the side. And as I scrambled to my feet, I couldn't help but stare.

Mutt was wearing clothes that didn't fully fit again—I'd learned that he often borrowed from Butters and could only assume this was another stolen set. His eyes were luminescent in the dark, and though I knew he wouldn't hurt me, the part of me that recognized him for the predator that he was, shivered.

Trained on me hungrily, his blue eyes glowed, feral.

There was something…off about him tonight.

Something foggy and needy and wild. His fangs were showing, for one thing, his breath coming in needy pants as he stared at me from several yards away like I wasn't the man he'd been fucking—and instead, was a rather tasty rabbit.

I probably shouldn't have started running again.

But I did.

My legs burned, eating up the distance as I ran away from him, gooseflesh traveling up my arms, the steady beat of his feet on the damp ground making me ache for more.

Something awoke inside me as Mutt gave me what I craved.

Something primal and needy.

A little voice that whispered, *maybe he's fast enough to catch you.*

Maybe you want him to.

It was funny. Not even ten minutes ago I had been thinking about the fact that Mutt was the only person who had ever chased me—and here we were. Instead of fear, excitement settled over me. Fizzy and bright, electric in my veins.

A grin spread across my lips, my cock perking up as I watched him with open desire, running easily beside me, dodging between tree trunks, his eyes never leaving my face. His gaze was ravenous, swallowing me whole from several yards away, like he'd been starved without me.

As starved as I'd been without him.

"Hi, big guy," I managed, voice throaty, breathless, because we were still running. He gracefully loped along beside me, ducking behind, then to the left, around the front, and to the right again. Racing circles. Playing with me. His eyes flickering in the dark like a cat's.

Mutt made running look easy. All that muscle flexing as he leapt over logs, his eyes flooded with heat. There was a playful twist to his lips though, like he recognized I was enjoying this as much as he was. Like he could smell my stiff cock in my pants and the damp precum that slicked my boxers as my monster gave hunt.

Mutt didn't speak.

And I didn't expect him to.

I didn't know much about wolves, but even I could see that something was happening here. The way Mutt was watching me made me feel like a juicy steak. Wonderous and tasty, a morsel for him to devour. The hungry way his eyes dragged over my body made my cock twitch and my nipples stiffen up, tingling and almost painful as they pushed against the fabric of my now sweaty shirt.

I'd never seen Mutt more wild than he was then.

A beast in search of prey.

A hunter.

Just like Theo had warned me he was.

I hadn't realized till that moment what being a hunter might mean for a wolf like Mutt. And now that I knew, I didn't think I'd ever be able to get it out of my head. The way his pecs flexed and bounced. The shape of his cock, hard and trapped against his leg, the shape of it obvious even in the dark.

So I picked up the pace, and decided to give him something more fun to catch.

I ducked around a tree trunk, grinning as I felt the air rustle as he whooshed by, before I swiveled and headed back the way I'd come.

Leaping, ducking, running.

We ran laps through the woods.

My face was hot, my pulse pounding, my cock straining against my jeans. At one point, Mutt slowed beside me, only a few trees between us. I was close enough to see his nostrils flare and those dark eyes drag down to my cock.

A slow, wicked grin spread across his lips, his mouth full of razor-sharp teeth.

Fuuuuck *that's hot.*

I licked my lips and picked up the pace again, but I knew it was futile. There was no fucking way I'd be able to outrun him. That thought should've terrified me, especially with a past like mine. But it didn't.

Instead…it made me feel safe.

Because if I couldn't outrun him, no one else could.

And I had no doubt Mutt would go to great lengths to protect me. Hell, he already had.

Eventually, my body decided enough was enough.

Or maybe it was the log that decided that for me.

Because I leapt over it, a grin on my face, and my shoelace caught and I was…fuck.

Falling, falling, falling.

The cold hard ground smacked against my knees, causing my breath to rush out of me in a panicked gust. Goddammit. *My foot's stuck. My foot is*— My pulse raced and I scrambled to get free, the steady *thump* of Mutt's feet louder and louder as he neared, circling me like a shark.

"Fuck, fuck," I kicked my foot out, my bruises aching, my lungs burning. "Fuck."

There! Yes!

I got my foot free, already ready to begin the chase again—

But apparently my hunter had had enough.

Because the second I tried to rise, there were teeth at the back of my neck and a hand snaking down to grip my cock between my legs, and I was—oh *fuck, fuck, fuck.* Yes. Yes yes yes. I jerked into the large, molten hot palm with a needy gasp.

Leagues of warm, sweaty werewolf crowded against me, teeth sinking deeper into my nape and turning me into putty.

The whine that escaped me was barely human, the sticky spot in my underwear steadily growing as I wheezed and melted. I knew he probably wanted a fight—that he craved it—but I couldn't…I just…

I wanted him so fucking bad.

I'd missed him.

I'd missed him, missed him, missed him.

The chase had been enough.

And now, I just—

Docile and sweet, I pressed my face into the dirt, arched my back, and shoved my ass against his crotch. Mutt was hard. Because of course he was. He'd probably been hard since the moment he'd caught my scent. I'd been able to see his dick as we ran, but *feeling* it was different.

The thick, meaty length of him shoved against my ass. Greedy. Because he was *always* greedy when I was involved. He'd swallow me whole if he could.

"Good bitch," Mutt growled, voice low and throaty. "What a good bitch. So good."

They were the first words he'd spoken to me since he'd found me in the woods, and I shuddered, head spinning. All my thoughts fled at once. My cock ached and my hole clenched—still slick from earlier when I'd fucked myself on my dildo while I was waiting to be picked up for the party.

Fuck.

Fuck.

I felt *empty*.

So fucking empty.

I'd never wanted another man's dick like this before, but I found myself craving it now. *Would it be warm?* That was my main complaint with dildos. Took them a while to warm up. *Would it feel as good as I hoped?* Thick and velvety slick, hard—pounding into the places inside me that made my eyes roll back and my balls tingle.

"Please," I managed, voice rough. My nails bit into the dirt, the scent of earth clogging my nose. I wished then that I was a wolf. If I was a wolf I'd be able to hear Mutt's heartbeat, to smell him, to sense him with every fiber of my being.

There wouldn't be a single part of me that wasn't full of him.

My mind, my heart, my lungs, my ass.

Mutt growled, a low threatening sound when I started to wiggle. His hands were possessive as they bit into my hips, his teeth gnawing at the back of my neck as if to say "hold still." With a jerky thrust, he rutted against me, the full length of him pushing against my clothed ass.

I sagged again, though I ached to reach between my legs and get my pants open. I missed the hand on my cock the second it was gone, but hip-grabbing was good too. As was this, the steady needy twitch of his hips, like he just couldn't help himself.

Like he needed me.

Like his mind was so far gone he couldn't even figure out how pants worked.

I could admit I had a thing for his particular brand of manhandling.

"Please," I gasped out again.

Mutt, despite being half-feral, took pity on me. Because the hands on my hips, holding me still as he rutted against me, slid around to the front. Halle-fucking-lujah. Clumsy fingers tore at the button on my jeans. His claws pricked my skin—not hard enough to hurt, but enough to make me shiver.

And then my jeans were being pushed down, and my ass was exposed— still slick—and Mutt was whining against the back of my neck like a man possessed. The wet hot crown of his cock pushed against my asshole, slip-sliding through my sweaty crease as he panted, needy and desperate—the same way I'd felt all week without him.

Before, if you'd asked me if I wanted my first time getting fucked to be in the middle of the woods with a werewolf, I would've told you to fuck the fuck off. But apparently…I hadn't known myself at all, because I found myself aching, greedy, *desperate* as Mutt rutted against me.

Every sweaty push of his cock inside my crack shoved his crown against my entrance. Kissing it. *Teasing.* Because I wanted it in, in, in, and he did too.

"C'mon, c'mon—" I gasped out, spreading my legs wider, as wide as I could with my jeans still half on. I wasn't sure when he'd gotten his pants down too but it didn't matter. Didn't matter as he grabbed my hips again and his rutting grew less controlled. Twigs dug into my knees, and the woods rustled around us, peaceful and quiet, as I sobbed, empty-empty-empty. "I'm ready," I begged, hole clenching. "I'm ready. I want you in. Please, please, Alpha. I need it—I need—"

"Jeffrey," Mutt's voice was a low crackling warning, muffled because he refused to let loose the back of my neck.

"Please, baby. I need it. I need it—"

"Just a little," Mutt finally conceded, muffled and slick. It wasn't much of a sacrifice, because it didn't take a genius to know that he wanted this as badly as I did. Little animal-like grunts and whimpers escaped him. And his breath was liquid hot against the back of my neck as his claws scraped over my ass, sliding back to where I was wet-loose-empty.

I could feel the chill of where the wind cooled his saliva on the back of my neck, but that only heightened the heat of where we pressed tightly together.

And then the crown of Mutt's dick was pressing against my hole—on purpose this time—and it slipped in just a little and I just—

"Hhaaa," I sobbed, cumming into the dirt like a filthy animal. My dick jerked, and my orgasm was never-ending. No fucking stimulation needed at all, just the scrape of my zipper, and the way my hole spread wide and almost painful for the fat head of Mutt's cock.

Desperately, and because I was a good bitch, I reached back—fumbling—and found the root of his dick. His knot had already swollen, the skin tight-hot-hard as I squeezed around it like he'd taught me to do. Mutt released a sound even more pitiful than mine had been. And then he was biting me again.

Tighter, tighter his teeth sunk in.

Pain-pleasure zinged down my spine. And Mutt's cock pushed in a little further.

Full. So full. He was barely inside and I just—

"Good boy," I gasped out, "Good boy, Mutt." He growled, the sound muffled. His hips jerked forward, inching in just a little more as the back of my neck tingled. And then he came inside me. Wet, hot, the mess filled my ass, making it sloppy-slick and stuffed white as he came and came and *came*. I squeezed his knot the whole while, felt the throb-ache of it, and imagined what that would feel like one day when it was fully inside me.

Part of me wished he'd push in deeper. Wished he'd shove all the way inside and take me for real. Not the sexy, aborted little thrusts he'd just done, still somehow managing self control. I wanted him to lose it entirely. To use me like the cock sleeve I wanted to be—at least…for him.

But…another part of me, the part that was human and needy, and had never been loved the way I needed—was grateful. Because Mutt was gentle, even now. And he didn't take more than I was ready to give. Like he could smell in my scent that I wasn't ready. That I needed more time, even though I wanted him just as desperately as he wanted me.

I'd missed him.

I'd missed him so much.

And I was so mad at him for leaving me—but at the same time… It was really hard to be pissed off when a dude had the tip of his dick in my ass. Especially when he released my neck, but only so he could lave it with sloppy, happy licks. Running his tongue over my skin and swiping up sweat behind my ears, and down my throat, and beneath my collar.

"Fuck," I sighed happily, ass clenching around him as I finally released his knot. The last pulsing splashes of his cum had slowed, so I figured I could now.

"So good," Mutt murmured, licking up my throat and into my ear, like there wasn't a single part of me he didn't want to taste. "So pretty, so good." His voice was low, his breath was hot, and I sobbed, never wanting this moment to end. He sounded as drunk as I felt. As drunk as Blair probably was, back at the party.

"I missed you," I admitted, voice cracking. "I missed you so much."

"Missed you too." His tongue slid across my cheek then to my lips. He claimed them in the sloppy, uncoordinated make out he favored. I didn't even mind. Just opened my mouth and let him taste the way he wanted to. "Pretty, lovely, Jeffrey."

By the time Mutt was done grooming and scenting me, I was a shivery, chilly mess. The licking was nice, soothing even. Especially when he'd flipped me over and licked all around my groin and up my crease to my still sloppy hole. But his warm spit quickly dried cold on my skin, and by the time my tongue bath was over, I was more than ready for a nice toasty nap, safe at home in my bed.

Mutt helped me up, still more quiet than usual. He looked exhausted. There were dark circles beneath his eyes and his normally bright skin was sallow. I found his hand, fingers tangling, my heart thumping erratically as without a word he began walking us back the way we'd come.

Because of fucking course he knew the way home, even when I didn't.

My compass north.

His cum slipped from my hole as we walked. There was so much of it, my underwear was slick and cold. *Do I like this?* I took a moment to debate. And ultimately decided I did.

Huh.

We were quiet the first half of the walk. I'd had to fight Mutt's dick back into his pants because he hadn't wanted to get dressed, and I was more than a little glad that I had, because we needed to talk and I…well…

I couldn't really do that with his dick hanging out.

You're a coward.

You're a coward.

You're a coward.

Lydia's words rattled around inside my head as we broke through the tree line.

I didn't ask Mutt why he'd been gone as long as he had.

And he didn't tell me.

Chapter Twenty

Mutt

I HATED CLOTHING. I always had. It was a silly, pointless human invention. Clothes made it hard to transform effortlessly, and I didn't understand why people were so offended by nudity when possessing a body was the one thing all creatures had in common.

That was all true still, but…as I walked Jeffrey up the steps to his apartment and the wounds on my chest tugged raw, covered and out of sight, I had a newfound appreciation for the fabric I usually abhorred.

Jeffrey was sleepy, soft, and quiet as he fished his phone out of his pocket and shot off a few texts, leaning against his still-locked front door.

Unable to help myself, I nuzzled against his throat, inhaling him greedily, and scenting up behind his ear, my lips brushing the downy fuzz hair there.

More tapping, more texts.

I growled at him, and he just laughed.

"Tickles!" Jeffrey snorted out, then added. "It's just my brothers," he said softly. "Wanted to make sure they knew I got home safe." He gave me a pointed look that I didn't understand. "Unlike some people," he joked.

I frowned, curiously.

"You didn't text me," he complained softly, though I could tell he was only teasing.

"I…" My cheeks were hot. I'd had my phone after I'd left the basement because I'd been inputting a number into it. And I'd seen his texts, I just–"I can't read."

Jeffrey blinked, surprised. "You can't—"

"Read." My cheeks were hot. "At least…not well."

"Oh." Jeffrey smiled at me, his eyes softening. "Um," he licked his lips. "Pictures are good too?"

"Pictures?"

"Yeah," his smile softened even more. "You can send me pictures. And I'll send you some back. I just…I just wanna talk to you when you're not here, you know? I'll show you how later."

My heart swelled with so much love for him in that moment that I could hardly breathe.

"You are a genius," I declared, because it was true.

"I dunno about that." Jeffrey scratched the back of his fuzzy head shyly, and quickly flipped around to face the door so he could get it open. I could see his blush though. See how his cheeks pinkened in the dark. His scent was pleased-embarrassed-happy.

My tail thumped happily.

I supposed it made sense that he'd want to text his family, so I didn't argue, even though I was tired and more irritable than usual, and my head hurt. I huffed against him, nuzzling around his throat to the other side of his neck. The bite I'd left along the back was raised and red, though I hadn't broken the skin. Seeing it there made something possessive and greedy flare up inside me.

I wanted to cover him with my marks.

Wanted him to reek of me.

But…even my possessiveness felt dulled in light of the post-moon exhaustion I was still suffering with. If I was being honest, my *everything* hurt. Except my heart. It was light, lighter than it had been in days. Because Jeffrey was here, and whole, and he wanted me inside his den again.

"You hungry?" Jeffrey hummed the second he pushed the front door open.

"I am always hungry," I replied immediately, because it was true.

"I don't have squirrel," Jeffrey joked. "But I do have pizza if you want some. And snacks."

I nodded, too tired to do much more than wag my tail and follow after him dutifully. He ducked into the kitchen and I wandered in after him, following his directions when he pulled my chair out for me and gestured for me to take a seat at the small rickety dining room table settled in the corner of the room. It wheezed beneath my weight, but held firm.

Jeffrey had all the markers of a wolf without being one. He was hardy, strong. He was protective. He *provided*. He was a caregiver. He believed in family, in pack. Loyal to a fault.

This meal was a prime example of that.

Wolves provided for one another. It was our way. Not that I'd been all that good at doing that for my brothers lately. Not when my focus was divided.

It wasn't fair that he couldn't be my mate.

And it *hurt*.

It hurt because I knew, without a doubt in my mind, that I wasn't going to make it to my twentieth birthday—to the mating ceremony my Dad was planning. That was a choice I could no longer make. Not when I knew what Jeffrey felt like. Not now that I'd cradled his heart in my hand. Not after holding him through his nightmares and hearing what he'd been through.

I had…maybe one moon left—two, if I was being optimistic.

And then I'd be…

I'd be…

"Hey," Jeffrey's voice was quiet, soft. The scent of cheese filled the air, the plate he was pushing toward me piled high with slices. The cheese melded them together, but I didn't mind, ravenous as I always was after the moon. I knew I didn't look my best. That I was emaciated. That my ribs were showing and my eyes were sunken.

I'd looked this way when we'd first met too—but I'd been in my wolfskin, and the fur had covered some of the imperfections.

Now there was nothing to hide behind. The clothes covered up the worst of my still healing wounds, but there was no denying that I had been through hell—and Jeffrey could see that.

He pulled a chair out next to mine, sliding into it, and offering me the plate of pizza again, brow cocked expectantly. I took the plate but set it on the table, suddenly not sure if I could stomach a single bite, even though my stomach was an empty cavern.

I'd had pizza a few times, courtesy of Harry and something he called "door dish" or something like that. It was delicious. I loved it. But I just…

I just…wanted Jeffrey.

Simple as that.

It was the second kind of hunger that plagued me at the moment, not the first.

"You okay?" Jeffrey's hand was warm. Calloused. He cupped my cheek, and I bent into the pressure with a needy sigh. He scooted our chairs closer together, our knees bumping then sliding as our legs tangled.

He didn't know.

He didn't know what was happening.

And he wasn't *supposed* to. He was never supposed to. I was supposed to be a happy memory—a lover that he could move on from. I wasn't supposed to lose myself in him. I wasn't supposed to do this to him.

He'd been hurt enough.

It wasn't fair.

I hadn't planned on telling him the truth.

But…I couldn't lie to him either.

And I just…

I was so tired.

I couldn't even muster the energy to smile.

"Mutt." Jeffrey's expression shuttered. And then he did something he'd never done before. He rose from his chair, and climbed into my lap, folding his long, muscular body across my thighs, his fingers still curled around my cheeks. His eyes were dark with concern, and so warm. So so warm. "What's wrong, big guy?"

Of course he'd noticed how off I was.

Jeffrey was observant.

It was one of the first things I'd appreciated about him. He saw things most humans wouldn't. Aware in a way I had thought only wolves were.

I sucked in a breath—stealing Jeffrey's signature move—doing my best not to fall apart as those warm, *warm* hands skimmed my cheekbones and my eyes pinched shut.

"Talk to me." Jeffrey's voice wobbled. "Where were you? What happened? You left without a word. I've been…so fucking worried."

"I…" my voice broke. I curled my arms around him, burying my face in his neck and inhaling him greedily, because I didn't know if this would be the last time. I never did, anymore. My time was so close to up. "I…" I didn't know what to say.

And sometimes…*showing* was easier.

So I reached for the hem of my shirt and lifted it, shame coloring my scent as Jeffrey stared at the bare, scarred flesh of my abdomen. Long ropey wounds severed the flesh, pink and healing, but slowly as only alpha wounds did.

"What…the fuck," he said, voice cracking. "Is that?"

I didn't tell him everything.

Because I couldn't.

Some words just…wouldn't come out.

But I did my best.

By the time I got done explaining, Jeffrey had sobered even more. His eyes were far away, and his thumbs stroked gently over my cheekbones as he processed what I'd said. "So…the moons are getting harder?" he confirmed. "And they're just gonna get *worse*?"

"Yes."

"You were gone for a week, Mutt. A week."

"I know."

"And these wounds…" Jeffrey fanned his hand along my torso, his scent soured with sadness. "This was *you*?"

"Yes."

"They'll go away, won't they?" His voice cracked. "You heal. I've seen it."

I knew he had his own scars, both physical and mental. I knew that his wounds had never healed the way mine would, marks on his body that would forever remind him of his dark past. And because of this, his concern for me was even more precious. He didn't want me to have reminders of the pain I'd been through, like he did.

"They will. It will take longer," I warned quietly. "But they will."

"Do they hurt?"

"Not anymore."

"But they did."

"Yes."

Jeffrey sucked in a breath. And then he jerked his hands from my cheeks, dragging them over the fabric that bunched around my chest, down my pecs, till he could lay them across the still healing flesh. "What could be worse than this?" he asked, and his scent was hurt-hurt-hurt.

Living without you.

That's worse.

He slid to his knees on the cold floor, settled between my thighs, his eyes full of concern.

Like he was hurting for me.

Because he was.

And then he pressed a kiss to my abdomen, and I stared down at him, enraptured.

"I could lose myself entirely," I admitted. I tried to smile, to reassure him—but the smile wouldn't come. I was just…too damn exhausted. I probably should've waited to find him, but the second I'd managed to shift back to my humanskin I'd begged Theo to let me go. Because I'd needed Jeffrey. Needed to hear his heartbeat and know he was safe—for as long as I still could.

"I'll fix this," he promised, murmuring against my flayed torso. "I don't know how, but I will."

He couldn't.

But I didn't tell him that.

I had already made my choice.

His eyes said, *I'm sorry.*

They said, *you deserve better.*

They said, *don't be scared.*

"I'm sorry," Jeffrey said, tipping his head up, his lips still pressed to my sternum. I shuddered, my eyes burning as I stared down at him. "I'm so sorry you were hurt."

I shook my head, my eyes pinching shut.

This was more painful than the wounds.

Keeping the full truth from him.

If he could smell my scent or hear my heart he'd know. He'd know I was withholding something. But he couldn't, and he didn't.

It seemed fate was offering me some mercy today.

"Come back up here," I commanded, heart aching, tail thumping. Jeffrey complied, climbing my legs with his hands and sliding into my lap with a quiet little oomph. "Jeffrey." I stroked a hand over his cheek, running my fingers across the fuzzy fur on his head, and near the half-healed cut on his brow.

"Yeah?"

"I'm also sorry you were hurt," I said, watching his pale lashes flutter, and his whole body begin to quake.

"Yeah," Jeffrey's voice cracked. And this time when he looked at me there was strength in his dark, lovely gaze. "Me too." His hands were shaking, shaking—but they stilled as our eyes met and a soft, lovely little smile wobbled across his lips. "It sucks."

"It does."

He'd told me things. Things I got the feeling he'd never shared with anyone else. About his childhood, about the woman who had stolen it from him. I couldn't understand, not fully. And I wouldn't insult him by pretending I could. But I could love him anyway. Could admire him. Because there was nothing stronger than surviving, and Jeffrey had done just that.

I'd offered to kill Lydia for him—as we lay curled up beneath my blankets in my bed. And he'd laughed, like he thought I was joking. When I'd doubled down, he'd simply shaken his head and told me, "She isn't worth it."

He was the bravest, strongest person I'd ever met.

And that was only proven even more true as Jeffrey spoke again, his hands finding my cheeks for the second time, all that lovely lanky muscle settled in my lap where it was meant to be.

"It sucks," he repeated, "But..." his smile grew stronger, his dark eyes brighter. "Things get better."

My heart thumped, my hand suddenly sweaty. That look was just... wow. He looked so sure. So...confident. And the comfort was appreciated, more than he knew. I had only given him the tip of the iceberg but...I could admit I needed his warmth more than ever right now. The silvery threads of our incomplete bond throbbed and flickered, and I grasped onto them, starved, begging whatever gods were listening that Jeffrey would be an exception.

That he'd be able to reach back, that we'd twine together the way we were supposed to. That I'd know I could keep him, before I was forced to step away.

That peace I'd felt was gone as quickly as it had come. The flickering twists of the bond I'd felt fell away. Because I knew it was false. Reality was a cold, bitter thing.

I couldn't pick Jeffrey.

He wasn't a wolf.

Even if he made my heart sing, and my body light up.

"They do?" My heart ached. It ached for all that Jeffrey had been through. The fact that he'd suffered enough that he could confidently say that there was light at the end of the tunnel.

"They do," Jeffrey nodded, stronger now. "Shit happens, you know?" he offered. "And it hurts. And it haunts you. But…it always gets better." He pressed a kiss to my lips and it tasted like relief. "Just like hair grows."

"And wounds heal," I echoed, my voice rough.

"It's hard." Jeffrey's voice was full of emotion. It wasn't until he spoke again that I understood why he was so affected by his own words. Because they weren't his. They were mine—from weeks ago. "But one day it won't be." My heart hurt. "There will be a day when you forget the pain. When it is simply a memory."

"Wise words." My eyes burned. There wouldn't be time for me to move on, but again, I didn't say that. Because this felt pivotal, and I was honored to be here for such a precious moment.

"Some guy told me that," Jeffrey shrugged. "I've thought about it a lot."

"You have?" It was silly, but the fact that my comfort had so affected him meant more than I cared to admit.

"Every day," Jeffrey admitted. "He's pretty smart."

"He is?" No one had ever called me smart before.

"Hot too."

I jolted, a laugh bubbling up. I wasn't sure if he was trying to cheer me up or not, but he certainly was. "Really?" My tail thumped against the chair.

"Really, really."

"He's kinda perfect actually," Jeffrey added, his voice tight. "If dopey himbo werewolves are your type."

"Are they yours?" I didn't know what *himbo* was. I only knew dopey because of the dwarf from *Snow White*, but I got the sense that Jeffrey didn't mean it as an insult. In fact…if I listened to the *thump, thump* of his heart and the fizzy brightness of his scent, I knew it had been a compliment.

"Yeah," Jeffrey bumped our noses together, and my heart jerked in my chest. "They are."

My body hurt and my mind was a mess—but Jeffrey was right. Already, I felt better.

"You know…" Jeffrey trailed off, his eyes dark and searching. "Sometimes there are burdens that are too heavy for one person to carry." I had no doubt that it was hard for him to admit that. "You taught me that." He swallowed. "Because every time I open up to you, I feel lighter."

This wasn't the same kind of wound that left him aching, but still…his comfort meant the world. Wolves were tactile creatures. I couldn't count the amount of times my brothers and I had flopped together in a puppy pile as kids just because it felt right to do so. We craved warmth and pack and a sense of belonging.

Since the day I'd begun to go feral it had felt like the ties that connected me to my pack had begun to fade. They grew fainter and fainter, until one day they would simply snap. When Jeffrey touched me, I didn't feel that aching loss anymore. New ties formed, reaching for him, tangling around his heart where it beat strong and sure.

He couldn't be my mate.

He couldn't save my life.

But that didn't mean he hadn't saved me.

I grinned.

"You are so lovely," I said honestly, the ache in my body fading away as I curled tightly around him, tugging him in close. "The loveliest."

"Yeah, okay, Casanova." It was the second time he'd called me that.

"So smart, so brave, so strong—" I squeezed him and he was solid, and warm, and home. "You have healed my heart."

He felt like home.

"Ouch, easy on the goods—" Jeffrey cackled but his scent wasn't hurt. It was *sunshine. He* was sunshine. I squeezed him harder, hard enough I wished he'd leave an imprint on my body.

I got the feeling this was the first time Jeffrey had ever sympathized with himself.

And it was beautiful and humbling and wonderful all at once.

"You want some food now? Cold pizzas are still good. And the shit Blair makes is like…top tier," he offered, voice light. "How about a movie? I can give you a back rub. You look like you need it." Jeffrey smacked a kiss on my cheek and my head spun as I realized how different he was already. "I bought those bacon things you told me you like. And Pop Tarts. Chocolate ones."

"Chocolate?" I perked up. "I love chocolate."

"I know you do, big guy." Jeffrey slid off my lap and padded across the kitchen toward the cupboard. Jeffrey reached into the top cupboard, the hem of his shirt sliding up. There were finger-shaped bruises on his hips, and scratches from my claws. I groaned, immediately distracted, my heart settled once again.

He grabbed the box down and turned back around, leaning against the counter with a cocked eyebrow and a sexy smirk. Beautiful and bruised, both. "See something you like?"

"Everything," I replied immediately. Jeffrey laughed.

"Dork." Then he handed me the Pop Tarts and wandered off into the living room to set up the TV for a movie party. I watched him move around, my heart settled, the box he'd given me clutched gingerly in my grip. "Hey, I talked to Blair," Jeffrey said—scrounging around in the couch cushions for the remote. "Richard too. You know…about shit."

"You did?" I shoveled pizza into my mouth—figuring I'd save the treats for later.

Jeffrey kept talking, and the more he told me, the more proud of him I became. He was moving forward. No longer stuck. And the lost-lost-lost scent that had exuded from him when we'd first met was long gone.

It would take a while to heal.

Some wounds took longer than others.

But I had no doubt that one day Jeffrey would.

And the things that had felt impossible before would become as easy as breathing.

I hadn't been lying when I told him he was the most wonderful person I'd ever met. And every day I spent with him, that only became more apparent. I just wished…we had more time. Our clock had begun ticking the moment I'd followed him home. And I knew that. But that didn't mean it didn't hurt.

If all I got was one more smile, my choice would be worth every sacrifice.

There was no escaping the hurt now, and I may not have been a human like he was, but even I knew we'd crossed that line long ago.

Chapter Twenty-One

Jeffrey

MUTT'S SCARS HAUNTED me. They took a good week to heal, and all the while, I did my damndest to find a solution to the pesky-moon problem. I had less than a month before the next moon, which meant I didn't have all that much time.

I buckled down.

And between my hunts for information, Mutt sent me texts. Cute pictures. Images of squirrels he found out and about. Of gnomes he'd been tempted to steal, probably. Of his hand, holding a broken Pop Tart. Of his bed, empty without us in it. Of each of his brothers, with no captions, though I could feel the love he felt for them without words needed at all.

It was a chilly, stormy day when I stumbled upon a lead that made my stomach churn.

"Do you know anything about mates?" I asked Avery, jerking my way into his office. He'd just finished up with a client, a nice lady who'd been cursed to speak backwards. Avery's eyes narrowed in thought as he tapped his lip, then made a startled face when he realized he'd been elbows deep in a vat of frog warts and hadn't taken off his gloves.

He gagged, bolted away, and returned five minutes later scrubbed clean, his hair a spiky mess.

"Sorry. What were you asking me?"

"Mates?" My heart pounded. It hadn't stopped pounding. Not since I'd opened one of the new books he'd gotten me and stumbled upon a page that talked about them. "Do you know—"

"Werewolf mates?" Avery frowned, twisting to look at me. "I know a little, yes."

And then we just kinda stared at each other. Avery blinked, long lashes fluttering, and I made a sound like a kettle reaching a boil. I was normally a pretty patient person, but even I had my limits.

"Are you gonna fucking tell me? Or just keep jerking my dick off, or what?" I didn't mean to be rude, but fuck. I felt like I was going to die.

Avery snorted out an amused laugh. "You remind me of my sister," he said fondly, and then his frown returned. "What do you want to know?"

"Let's start with everything."

Apparently he'd been doing some reading of his own, because he sure as shit knew a lot more today than he had when I'd first asked him for information.

According to Avery, because Mutt was an alpha, he needed a mate. An official one. Someone who would keep his wolf under wraps. It was a soul bond. Something that couldn't be constructed with artificial magic, and something so ancient even the witches hardly knew anything about it. There was a ceremony that Avery didn't know the details of, only that it was important, and something only wolfkind shared.

The most important thing I learned about mates, however, was the fact that humans couldn't be one. At least, according to Avery.

We didn't have a wolf inside to bond with.

Which was just…fuck.

Fuck fuck fuck.

That night when I went home I curled up with Mutt-the-dog in bed, his fur tickling my nose, and tried not to die. I hadn't felt this helpless since that day when I was a kid and I'd watched Blair scarf down the rolls I'd stolen for him and knew there was nothing I could do to stop him from getting locked up again.

Avery helped where he could. I spent way too fucking long on the dark web. Before, I'd avoided the local hunting lodges and libraries like the plague because of their association with Lydia, and the fear that I'd run into some of our old colleagues. But the second I'd learned about Mutt's condition, all those anxieties flew out the window, and I found myself planning trips out to visit local hunters to see what they knew.

Eventually I'd try the two big lodges, but for now, I avoided them. I didn't necessarily want to draw a whole bunch of attention to us, because even though I didn't know much about the moons and their pull—I did know about hunting laws.

And hunting laws dictated that a feral alpha werewolf was fair game. The second they got stuck in their wolfskin they had twelve hours to be claimed by a Pack Alpha who was willing to be responsible for them or… they'd get killed.

Blair helped where he could, Richard did too.

Even Collin helped—though his help was kinda more of a hindrance than anything else, because he was always fucking hungry and had the attention span of a goldfish.

I learned a lot that first week. More of the books I'd asked Avery for came in, and I pulled two all-nighters in a row pouring over the information in them. Mutt kept having to remind me to eat, and neither of us mentioned the fact that my "dog" never showed up when he was around.

I wanted to save him.

And I thought…maybe if I searched long and hard enough, I'd find a way for us to get around the whole pesky humans-can't-bond-with-wolves thing.

Because even though I'd told my therapist I wasn't ready for a relationship, I'd realized how fucking wrong that was. And I wanted to keep Mutt. I wanted to keep him. To make him happy. To give him all the smiles he asked for. And my only shot at that was if I could figure this shit out before he had to go home in January.

At one point, sleep deprived and staring blankly at the last page of the last book Avery had ordered in for me, I wondered why fate was a cruel heartless bitch. Because wolves weren't like vampires. I couldn't just fill out a paper and ask the council for permission to become one. Wolves were born, not turned.

And these books were fucking useless.

When I wasn't searching for answers, I spent all the time I could with Mutt.

And he was as adorable as ever.

After our intense, awful, horrible conversation in my kitchen, Mutt pretended as though nothing was wrong. He watched a shitty horror movie with me, asked me about a zillion questions—because he didn't understand half of it—and snuggled with me on the couch till well after three, stroking fingers beside my stitches like he was still worried. Mutt rumbled and purred, nuzzling into my throat, behind my ears, back down my spine and to my ass.

He pulled my pants down and licked me clean, running his tongue over my hole over and over and over till I was twitchy and wet and humping the couch cushions. He fucked my thighs—aided by the lube he'd given me, which I procured from "sex basket". And as he fucked me in earnest, his grunts and growly voice rumbled against the back of my neck. "Lube is the best invention ever."

And he was right.

After Mutt "left for the night" he'd even went as far as to show up to my front door in his wolfskin pretending to be my dog again. I pretended too—letting him in with a big grin and a pet to his furry head.

He looked…emaciated. Weak. The same way his human form had. But he was chipper as ever, woofing at me happily as he padded into our bedroom and curled up on our bed to wait for me while I brushed my teeth and stripped down for bed.

So many times I was tempted to tell him I knew.

But I didn't.

Because at the end of the day, if he needed this distance—I figured the least I could do was let him keep it. At least…for now. Besides, I didn't have it in me to confront him right now. Not when every spare ounce of energy I possessed was spent on trying to fix this shitty, awful situation.

I'd *promised.*

I wasn't even sure Mutt knew how much danger he was in. If the moons were getting stronger, and more painful—that only really meant one thing. I couldn't stomach the idea that one day he'd get stuck. That he'd be put down.

And I just…

When I thought about a world without Mutt in it, I just—*no.*

No, no, no.

Sleepless nights. Manic days. I did my best not to break. I even considered calling Lydia at one point—which…as you can guess was a clear indicator that I'd hit rock bottom.

"No fucking way," had been Blair's response when I brought it up to him. "*No.*"

"No," Mutt had echoed when I'd mentioned it to him afterward. "No."

"No," Richard had said, when I'd gone to him after talking to Mutt.

But still, I considered it.

I considered it long and hard.

I considered it long enough to buy plane tickets to Oregon, to the airport nearest to the prison where she was being held.

Unfortunately for all of us, Mutt still had to work on negotiations. He told me he was already doing the bare minimum, and while that was fine and dandy, I still hated any second he was away from me. Though, we did spend as much time together as we possibly could. Going on adventures, trying new things I'd never done before because my therapist had suggested it, eating cheeseburgers, and splashing around in the icy-as-fuck ocean.

Mutt came to every single one of my open-mic nights.

He sat in the front row and cheered loudly—no longer lurking in the back like the creepy stalker he'd been. He brought me flowers every time. Flowers I wasn't sure he hadn't stolen, but appreciated all the same.

But still…the impending moon hung over our heads.

And by the time it rolled around, and Mutt disappeared again, I hadn't come up with jack shit to help with anything.

Miserable, annoyed, and defeated, I lay alone in my bed, staring up at the popcorn ceiling. Across town, Mutt was tied up in the basement of the little cottage he and his brothers had rented from the local pack. He was hurting. He was lost.

And I couldn't…I couldn't do *anything* about it.

Couldn't mate with him.

Couldn't ease his pain.

Because I'd rather be high than deal with the turmoil of my thoughts, I lay in my bed and contemplated my options. It'd been a long day of a whole lot of nothing. Thanksgiving was only a couple weeks away now—the first snowfalls had already begun—and my thoughts were spinning. The wrapper of the joint in my hand crinkled as I pinched it and sighed.

The merry-go-round spun and spun and spun.

I thought about white sneakers.

About mistakes.

About forgiveness.

And then I lit up and blew my worries away. The weed helped me straighten out the tangles in my head. Helped me reach clarity. Helped me make sense of the things that eluded me.

It centered me.

Reminded me to breathe.

To relax.

To be present.

It also made me horny.

Super fucking horny.

By the time I'd finished my joint and snuffed out its withered remains I was floating. Sometimes it took a while to kick in fully, but I'd taken my sweet time with every puff, and so I was fully sunk in foggy bliss as I lay back on the mattress and let my mind—and hands—wander.

Like my thoughts always did lately, they found their way back to Mutt.

To his stupid sunny smile.

To his stupid floppy hair.

To his hands.

A man's hands.

Veiny, big, scratchy. And those claws—holy fuck. There was nothing human about those fucking claws. Even though I had limited hunting knowledge when it came to werewolves, I'd met enough of them working at Avery's shop that I knew Mutt's partially shifted appearance was abnormal.

More comfortable as a wolf than he was as a man—to the point that he almost never fully shifted into human form. Always some sort of hybrid mix. Hairy. Claw-y. Fang-y.

It shouldn't have turned me on the way it did.

Especially since, by all accounts, I'd never been attracted to a man before I'd met him. Not the way I was with him. This weird fucking itch beneath my skin every time I saw him and he wasn't touching me.

I pushed away thoughts of the future, too stressed and high to think about anything other than fuzzy happy trails and Mutt's knot.

I groaned, threading my fingers in my short hair as my free hand slid down my torso. As high as I was, my wandering thoughts were more tantalizing than frustrating. They slipped away as quickly as they'd come as I focused on the brush of my palm, the tickle of my fingertips as I pushed beneath the waistband of my boxers and reached for my dick.

The skin was soft and dry after my shower, almost velvety to the touch as I curled my fingers around the base of my dick and held it snug, lashes fluttering. Sometimes I liked to do that. Just hold it. Feel my dick grow hard in my grasp. Feel the veins twitch, my cock flex.

I bit my lip to hold in any sound, a habit I'd learned young.

"Fuck," I hissed quietly through my teeth as I pictured what might happen if Mutt came home now. If he saw me. Saw my hand between my legs, my head tossed back, my eyes flooded with heat. Would he like what he saw? I hoped so.

God.

I really, really did.

I spread my legs wider, my imagination running wild. Mutt would growl. I knew he would. That sexy little rumble he did when he got turned on. Low and sweet. His eyes would be black with lust. His thick chest would heave. And if I looked between his legs I'd see the shape of his cock, hard and needy, listing to the left like it was doing its best to point at me despite its fabric prison.

My cock jerked and I gave it a tight squeeze, nipples tingling.

Mutt would say something stupid. Something sweet. Something about how pretty I looked with my legs spread—about how much he liked my dick when it was hard—even though he couldn't see it.

He'd crawl across the bed.

He'd beg to touch.

Beg to taste.

Beg to feel me.

Call me his bitch and try to mount me.

And when I pinched his knot he'd sob the way he always did, knot-drunk and horny, tucked tight inside my body.

I came with a stuttered gasp, hot and wet across my fingers. My lashes fluttered and I sighed blissfully, letting the rest of my fantasy play behind my lids. Mutt would lick me clean. He'd suck the sweat from my skin, lap up the cum like it was a treat. My cock jerked pitifully in response.

And then he'd spoon me.

Hold me close.

Nuzzle the back of my neck and whisper pretty words in my ear.

He'd make me feel special. *Me.* Not the golden boy. Not the kidnapped kid who had no choice but to be perfect. Just me. Terrified, bitter, ugly me. Made beautiful, when he looked my way.

I'd sleep.

I'd sleep and there would be no more nightmares.

There'd be no need for bolts on the door.

No need for wolves and mates and Lydia.

I'd be his forever.

I'd be safe.

When I woke up my mouth was dry as hell and my head hurt. Water. I needed water. I stumbled groggily to my feet, grimaced at the state of my hand, and promptly went into the bathroom to shower.

Then I chugged what felt like a gallon of water before stumbling back to bed in a daze.

I'd missed Blair when he was gone. Missed him desperately, especially for those few months I'd thought I'd never see him again. But this was a different kind of ache. It burned me from the inside out. Made my eyes burn, and my teeth itch.

A week passed and it felt like hell.

My brothers did their best to distract me, but even they gave up after a while, because I was a miserable, awful grouch. Scrooge on crack, really. Werewolf-loving scrooge McAsshole. Blair did give me another baggie of bud though—because he was the best—so at least I had that.

On the seventh Mutt-less day, Avery—because he was Avery—sent me home with a pat on the back and a box of tea. "You're driving me insane," he said gently, looking cheerful as always with a lizard sitting on his shoulder. "Go home. You're done for the day."

Banished, I did as I was told.

Though I wasn't happy about it.

I was exhausted and overworked—and there was no end in sight. Because no matter how hard and long I looked, I never found the answers I wanted. Mutt still needed a wolf for a mate. And I couldn't find any information that pointed otherwise.

I couldn't be what he needed me to be.

Even though I would in a heartbeat if I could.

I missed him.

I missed him so fucking much.

So I stomped all the way home in a huff, ignoring the buzzing in my pocket and the barrage of texts I had yet to answer. Probably Blair asking how I was doing again—or Collin telling me about the episode of *Drag Race* he was watching, or Richard telling me it'd take another fucking week to fix my truck—I was starting to wonder if Joe had even fucking worked on the damn thing. Or the random plethora of people from Oregon I still needed to fucking block.

If I could burn the fucking device, I would. But then I wouldn't see pictures of Blair's cat anymore, or those weird jokes he kept sending me. And what if Mutt texted me—what if he woke up and he couldn't move and he needed me? What if he found another squirrel and I fucking missed it because I was too busy angsting?

No.

No.

I kinda needed my phone.

Was it unrealistic to contemplate blocking everyone I had in my phone besides Mutt and my family? Maybe. But it made my cold, black heart warm just thinking about it. I'd delete everyone on Facebook. Block all the assholes. Erase the people from my life systematically that had always made me feel like I had to put up a front.

I ate dinner in silence.

Again.

And even playing the guitar didn't help my foul mood. I'd been plunking around writing a new song lately—with my new pencil—and I was nearly done with it. I could admit that I was more than a little excited to show Mutt, as he was kinda my biggest fan. But even the daydream of his reaction wasn't enough to cheer me up. So… After showering and crawling into bed I lit up another joint and let my thoughts wander. It was easier to control the darkness that lurked beneath my skin like this.

Pleasure was an excellent distraction.

The only thing that worked, honestly.

My cock was ready before I even touched it, like it sensed what we were about to do. Where my mind was about to wander.

Big hands.

Brilliant blue eyes.

A fat fucking cock, all flushed and hard.

Would he fuck my fist?

Would he fuck my mouth?

Would he fuck my—

"Ohhhh," a deep, needy growl echoed through the room, and I was jolted out of my fantasy. My eyes flashed open, immediately clocking the open window, and the dark figure that loomed in front of it. Triangular ears flattened along the top of the wolf-man's head, his tail wagging, his eyes glowing sapphire in the dark.

"Mutt," I gasped, surprised, pissed, and pleased all at once.

He's okay.

He's here.

He came.

My toes curled and my cock leaked against my palm as I gave it a squeeze and tipped my head to face him better. Even hidden in the shadows I could make out his shape, his shoulders and hips, his legs parted to accommodate the thick cock that nestled between them.

He rumbled hungrily.

Like a predator.

And I couldn't help but preen.

Mutt looked exhausted. Worse than the last moon. But beautiful all the same. The bruises beneath his eyes only served to make them somehow brighter. And though he was thinner than usual, he was still massive, crowding in front of the window like a fucking creeper—like he didn't have a key to the front door at all.

"You forget about doors?" I teased. I hardly recognized my own voice; it was so hoarse.

"This was easier." Mutt's tone was gravelly low. It lit me up from the inside out, heat pooling low in my belly. I'd never asked for my key back, and I never intended to. He wore it around his neck on a string, and that made me way too fucking happy.

"*Liar*," I taunted him, the way he always taunted me. A fresh drop of precum slicked the inside of my palm as I rubbed it in a gentle circle along the top of my cock. "You knew what I was doing." I bit my lip and Mutt growled softly, his fangs flashing. "Probably watched me from the fucking window before you came in."

"You are right," he admitted, hands twitching at his sides. His claws flashed as he clenched his hands into fists. Probably so he didn't reach out and touch without permission. "I knew. I could smell how much you wanted me. Your mouth is full of lies, but your scent betrays you. I can practically taste how needy you are." Mutt's nostrils flared and he sucked in a deep, greedy breath.

"Fuck, that's hot." The idea that Mutt had been chasing the scent of my arousal was just…fuuuck yes. Made me feel needy and hot. My hole clenched and I stared at him, unable to help myself.

I missed you.

I missed you, I missed you, I missed you.

Stared at the shadows beneath his eyes. The luminous flicker of his familiar gaze. The way he stared at me like I was something worth staring at, scars and all. I spread my legs wider, lashes fluttering as I met his gaze. I'd wanted him here. I'd wanted him here so very badly—and…here he was. It was odd.

I'd never been a lucky person, but Mutt made me feel like I was.

Maybe I'd saved all my luck for the day he found me.

I licked my lips, my hips jerked, cock flexing toward him like it was magnetized. I wanted him inside me. Wanted to feel more than just the thick tip of his cock. Wanted to submit to him so badly I ached for it. But I didn't know how to ask.

"I wanted to see you," Mutt admitted. The dirty fucking perv. "To touch you."

"Of course you did," my balls were literally tingling. "Probably wanted to stick your greedy tongue in my ass again, huh, big guy?"

"*Yes,*" Mutt hissed, his fangs flashing again. He was trembling with the effort of holding back. That huge fucking body, and he was entirely at my mercy.

"Wanted to get inside me in whatever way you can."

Mutt nodded, jerky and happy. His tail wagged, appearing out of nowhere, his wolf ears flicking toward me, eyes dark with lust.

God.

This was trippy.

Really fucking trippy.

And relieving. Because Mutt being here meant he'd survived another moon. And I figured…we both deserved some much-needed relaxation. I had never in all my life wanted something more than I wanted that goddamn stupid wolf in my bed. And now I had him, I intended to make the most of it.

Chapter Twenty-Two

Mutt

FUUUUUCK. MY BALLS ached. My head was spinning. My cock had never been harder in my entire fucking life. The scent of Jeffrey's arousal in the air was making me turn inside out with the need to touch him. To taste him. To feel all that hot, sweat-sticky skin against my own.

I could taste the salt of his precum in the air and my hips jerked with the need to bury my dick inside him. That was the one thing we hadn't done. Full-on fucking. After I'd shown him my scars, I hadn't felt like I could ask—even though it was the thing I wanted most in the world. I'd already asked too much of him, I couldn't take that too.

I hadn't had to try this hard to control myself since my first shift, and god—I wasn't sure how much more of this I could take.

He was teasing me.

There was a cocky, confident glint in his eyes that made me want to roll over and show him my belly—even though I was his alpha, goddammit. I wanted to please him so fucking bad I could hardly breathe. He was an entirely different man than he'd been when we'd first met.

Or maybe that was just his scent in the air. Spicy sweet. Citrusy bursts of flavor. My nostrils flared as I flexed my hands, then clenched them into fists again, my claws severing flesh. The pain helped ground me as Jeffrey spread his legs and I watched, enraptured, as he pulled the hem of his underwear down low enough the crown of his cock flashed at me.

Pink. So pretty. Leaking slick. Desperate to be touched.

I licked my lips.

Jeffrey's smile was downright evil.

"You look hungry, Mutt," Jeffrey purred, his legs splayed wide, those freckled calves taunting me as he hitched one leg higher than the other and swiveled his body so that I had a front row view to the show. He shifted around, wiggling so that his back was against the wall and his legs hung off the side of the bed, facing where I stood stock-still just inside the window.

The moonlight painted him pale blue, making his freckles stand out stark on his creamy skin. My cock flexed, knot tingling as it began to form.

"I'm *always* hungry." I murmured, mirroring the words I'd spoken to him just a short month ago. Only this time I wasn't talking about pizza. "For you," I added, shivering when Jeffrey sucked in a sharp, overwhelmed breath.

Fuck, my cock hurts.

It took every ounce of control I had not to stride across the room, pin Jeffrey to the mattress, and force my dick inside whatever hole was closest. I wanted to show him who was boss. Who was the alpha here. The moon still aching beneath my skin.

This moon had been painful. They all were. But this had been…

It had…

I didn't want to think about it.

Didn't want to think about the way my wolf had torn at the manacles, severing tendons and flesh in an attempt to get free. To chase the shivery bright orange of a scent I didn't recognize, but needed all the same.

I'd gone under quickly, and come out exhausted. Though my memory was black, the blood on the floor, the scars on my body, and the faces my brothers had leveled me with as they'd released me from my shackles had clued me into just how bad it had been.

"You wouldn't stop whining," Theo had said, keeping his touch gentle as he slipped the key into the lock wrapped around my ankle. "Howling."

"I'm sorry." My voice was hoarse.

He'd looked at me then, gold eyes lost, and I could see he was hurting for me. I'd decided then that I'd do my best to spend some more time with him, and all of my brothers, before I…

Before I took matters into my own hands.

Before I was lost entirely.

The second I'd showered off the blood and pulled on my clothing— apparently my brothers had gone shopping at some point and bought me clothes that actually fit—I'd said my goodbyes and immediately leapt out the door in search of Jeffrey.

I still needed to tell Jeffrey the truth about myself—about my wolfskin— and the fact that I'd been pretending to be his dog. But I just…I didn't know how. I'd never been good at words.

How do you tell the person you love that you've been lying to them?

I didn't want to hurt him.

I didn't—and I already knew I was.

It was as inevitable as the next rise of the moon.

Now…however, was not the time to be worrying or reminiscing. Because Jeffrey was here, and he was beautiful, and he was putting on a show for me, my perfect mate-mate-mate.

The sweet scent of sex filled my nostrils as a slick drop of precum slipped down Jeffrey's cock, disappearing beneath the dark fabric of his boxers as his hand slid up his length, blocked by fabric. I wanted to lick. I wanted to inhale him. To chase that sweet droplet down his shaft and stick my nose behind his balls to where his scent was headiest.

"I deserve an apology," Jeffrey said, almost conversationally as his pelvis twitched toward his fingers and his lashes fluttered. He was glorious like this. Flushed from head to toe, his chest heaving with stuttered breaths. His nipples were rosy and peaked. His eyes were half-mast. His lips, bitten raw. "You left me alone."

It was a game.

We both knew I'd had no choice, but pretending as though I had… softened things. Made everything less dire. Made my tail wag and my heart burn with warmth for this resilient, lovely man and the little mercies he bestowed upon me.

"I'm sorry," I replied automatically, because it was true. I was sorry about a lot of things. But I wasn't sorry about this. About him. I couldn't regret him, even if I tried.

Broad shoulders flexed as Jeffrey slowed his movements, glacially so. Watching me watch him, like my micro-expressions were what was getting him off. Every time my brow twitched or my nostrils flared his cock would leak again. His gaze was dark as he watched the tick of my jaw, and my mouth, his expression hungry. Always hungry. Always aching for touch.

"You're not forgiven." Jeffrey's voice was gravelly soft.

I whined, low and unhappy. We were playing, but I still hated the idea of disappointing him.

He laughed.

My cock jerked.

God. I liked this side of him. I liked it a lot. I liked it just as much as every other side to his personality that I'd discovered. For once, he was being honest with his emotions. For once—he wasn't holding back. There were no demons in his gaze. He was quaky, hungry, and masculine need.

"Please," I begged, aching to touch, my body trembling. "Please can I touch now?" I wanted to pin him so fucking bad. To mount him till he cried. To knot him. To breed him till he was full of my cum. Wanted to impregnate him, to fill him full of my pups, even though I knew that wasn't something he could do.

I wanted to try anyway.

Don't.

Don't.

Don't.

You'll scare him.

My wolf howled at me to move closer. To take what was ours. To respond to Jeffrey's teasing and taunts the way an alpha should. With absolute dominance.

Don't scare him.

My hands flexed at my sides, the bones creaking.

"No," Jeffrey twisted his fingers around the crown of his cock and I strained to catch a glimpse of it again. The damn fabric kept covering it. "Only good boys get treats."

I whined again, falling into our game with gusto. "I'll be good," I promised, my cock flexing. It tented the front of the silky shorts Harry had bought me, pointing obscenely toward him. Jeffrey's gaze snapped down to it liquid-quick, and my hips jerked. My knot ached. "I'll be good. I'll make it up to you."

"Are you willing to work for it?"

"Yes. Yes. *Yes*." A million times yes. I would do *anything* to be in his favor again.

I would burn the world for him if he asked.

But he didn't.

No.

No.

Instead, he decided to torture me some more.

Jeffrey flipped around. The perky cheeks of his ass were on full display as he slid onto his knees. I stared. Because what else was I supposed to do? That sweet little hole was there, just hiding behind fabric, begging to be fucked.

Legs splayed wide, Jeffrey reached back, long dexterous fingers putting on quite a show as he pulled his boxers down inch by inch till they sat just below his bare cock and balls. All that creamy skin on display.

I licked my lips.

Jeffrey's cock was glorious. Red, flushed. Lean and freckled like the rest of him. The head was rosy and slick. It hung between his legs, swinging a little as he shifted, twisting his upper body enough that I could see the corner of one dark, lust-filled eye. He crooked a finger at me, his balls, cock, and sweet little hole begging for kisses.

Oh thank God.

I took a step forward, more than a little eager.

"No," Jeffrey shook his head, and I froze. His eyes were black with lust as he stared at me, tracing over my body like he needed me as much as I needed him. I wanted to preen, but I didn't dare. Didn't want to break the spell. To spook him before he let me touch. "Crawl." *Crawl?* "Like a dog."

I growled, a low noise that rumbled deep inside me. Rage, anger, frustration burned beneath the surface of my skin. Alphas did not submit like this. We didn't. But for him…for him I would throw away everything—even my pride.

I fell to my knees.

The alpha in me howled its fury but I ignored it. Instead, I shifted forward on my hands and knees. Slow and steady, I stalked across the carpet, crossing the distance between us without ever taking my eyes off of the gorgeous man above me.

He shuddered, something flickering in his eyes as he reacted to my approach.

Something primal.

Something sweet.

Sweet, sweet *Jeffrey*, hiding behind his games, scared to be vulnerable but knowing I'd take care of him anyway. Knowing I wouldn't hurt him, even when he teased. There was trust between us now. Trust I didn't know if I deserved, but I was going to do my damndest to earn.

Jeffrey needed his alpha.

Needed me.

I would play his games.

I would do as he asked.

His cock dripped onto the duvet. He arched his back, his sweet little hole winking at me as I continued to approach. One of his hands moved, and his breath left him in a ragged gasp the moment I finally reached my destination. There were a scant few inches between my mouth and his dick and I burned to reach out to taste him. To suck him inside my mouth. To please him.

He twitched when he felt my breath tickle over where he was red-hot and achy.

"You want me," Jeffrey accused, his voice reedy soft, thick with emotion. Like this was the first time he was really allowing himself to accept that.

"I do." I nodded, shaking all over. "Always."

The scent of blood filled my nose—my own, as I'd pricked my palms to keep myself in check—but I shoved it aside. Greedily, I pressed my face against Jeffrey's thigh and inhaled. *God, he's delicious.* Just smelling wasn't enough, so I moved, running my mouth along the soft skin. Tasting the auburn hairs on his legs with my tongue, enjoying the prickle of them as he shuddered.

"You'd do anything for me," Jeffrey's voice wobbled, like he wasn't sure if he was right—but he wanted to be.

"Yes," I agreed, leashed to him by choice.

And then—because while I loved my current view, I desperately needed to see his face, I grabbed his hips and flipped him over. He gasped, body jerking, a needy whine escaping as the breath whooshed out of his lungs.

"Wh—"

"There." I grabbed his legs, forcing them up toward his chest, his boxers still trapping them together. This way I could see his face and his cock and hole at the same time. I licked my lips, eyeing him greedily. Admiring the way his chest twitched with each panted breath. Admiring the way his cock jerked, his balls drawing up tight like simply being manhandled into place was enough to make him nearly cum.

Satisfied, I settled back into my rightful place between his legs.

Skimming my nose along the edge of where his boxers met his thigh, I stared up at him, enraptured. He looked like royalty above me like that, eyes dark with lust, his broad shoulders trembling with the effort of holding back. This was better. This was way better.

Up close like this, I could smell his cum even better. It blocked out the distracting scents of the woods outside the still open window, and the detergent he used. Stronger even, than the blood on my palms.

I licked my lips and he bit his lip in response, eyes pinched shut, before they opened again. Flooded black. Dazed. He faltered.

"Tell me what you want, my prince," I murmured.

Jeffrey gasped, his cock jerking as the nickname fell from my lips without thought. It'd been a while since I used it, but it felt even more accurate now. Because he was my everything, and I'd serve him the way only I could.

All my life I'd wanted to be the prince from a fairy tale. The one who saved the day. The hero. I'd thought I'd find my mate and yank them right off their feet—or sweep? I couldn't remember which word was supposed to be more romantic. Yanked seemed accurate though.

I realized now, however, I'd gotten that all wrong. Jeffrey was the prince in this scenario. He was the one who left me weak-kneed.

Like now.

Lying between his thighs, my cock left a sticky wet patch against my new shorts, reminding me how badly it needed to be buried inside him.

"Suck me," Jeffrey commanded, straightening his shoulders as his breath wobbled. Trying to go back to being in charge, despite the fact my manhandling had clearly affected him. That fuzziness in his gaze was back—the kind he only got when he felt safe and warm and cared for. If I had my way I'd keep him like this always. Sated and docile. My pretty, pretty bitch.

"Suck me and I'll forgive you," he tried to sound tough, and failed rather spectacularly, his voice was so hoarse.

I didn't need to be told twice. I'd been gagging to get my mouth on his dick from the moment I'd caught his scent in the woods. This was no hardship. He was hot and warm as I sunk him down my throat in one fluid movement. It was much easier now than it had been before. My muscles remembered just what to do, how to relax, how to suck and suck and suck.

I grabbed his hips, careful of my claws. The scratches that I'd left on my palms had already healed, though a smudge of my blood smeared across his milky flesh. I willed the claws away so I could dig my fingers into the meat of his ass and urge him deeper down my throat.

"Uhhhh," Jeffrey whined, clutching at my head, all his bravado wavering as I slurped around him. He was delicious. Everything I'd ever wanted. Thighs trapped, he had nowhere to go. Couldn't even wriggle free. "F-Fuck." He gave his hips an experimental flex, pushing into my mouth, and I growled, sucking harder to tell him it was okay.

If he wanted to fuck me he could. I'd let him.

Slurp, slick, slurp.

"F-fuck," Jeffrey repeated, taking my swallowing as the permission it was. And then his hips smacked against my face again. And again. And again. He ground his cock against me, my saliva making a mess down my chin. "Jesus fuck, you're so fucking good." His voice was low and breathless. "I'm gonna—gonna—"

I smacked his ass cheek hard enough he howled, giddy when I felt it jiggle. I'd wanted to do that for so long, it felt unreal that I just had. So I did it again. Enjoying the sharp sting of impact as a red mark formed beneath my hand. Jeffrey seemed to like it just as much as I did, because the second my palm met his ass a second time he spilled on my tongue, sated and breathless, still clutching hard at my hair. His fingers brushed over my wolf ears as he pulled me off of him, slowly, inch by inch.

Huffing hot against his pelvis, I ignored his whining, and forced his now-softening cock back into my mouth.

"What are you—oh."

I sucked every last drop of cum from his dick, my own cock straining toward him as I pressed a parting kiss against his crown and tilted my head to look up at him.

Jeffrey was a *mess*.

There were tears smudged down his cheeks, his lips were swollen from biting them, his cheeks were splotchy red, and his eyes were nearly black with lust. "Good boy," he gasped out, shuddering, his hard nipples taunting me.

Good boy. My skin buzzed.

I leaned up to bite one, because I could, and he shuddered, clutching his hands in my hair and forcing me to the other side.

"Fuck," he gasped again, entire body trembling.

He had just come, yes. But all it took was one look to know that he was far from satisfied. My mate needed more. Jeffrey pushed me away from his chest before I could suck any more hickeys against it, his hands shaking as he pulled hard at my shoulders.

"You did so good," he shuddered. "You were such a good boy—" My tail wagged. I couldn't help it. He grinned, and it was soft again—though an edge remained. "Do you want a treat?"

A treat?

I did not want a treat.

I just wanted him.

"I want *you*," I gasped out, gaze zeroing in on his pink little hole and where it winked between his legs.

And then he rolled over onto his belly again. His elbows took his weight. His legs spread wide as he reached back with one hand and pulled his boxers down his bouncy, freckled ass, inch by inch. I growled, claws popping free once more as I gripped the edge of the mattress, immediately shoving my face toward his ass. His hole was pink and innocent between the curve of his cheeks.

I wanted to bury myself inside it.

Suck and lick.

Fuck it till it was loose and open, dripping white with my cum.

Maybe I could put the tip inside again?

Just a little—

Just…just—

Jeffrey shimmied his hips away before I could connect with that sweet little hole and I whined in complaint, lips bumping against one of his fleshy ass cheeks instead.

"Beg," Jeffrey demanded. He wagged his ass in my face and I whined, low and plaintive. Like a goddamn puppy.

"Please," I gasped out, shuddering with desire as his hole clenched. I wanted in. I wanted in—I wanted— "Please, please, please, please, please—"

"Okay." Jeffrey gasped out a little laugh, tugging his boxers the rest of the way down and leaning on both elbows again. His hole twitched at me and I whined, opening my mouth, ready to plead some more. "I'm sorry. That was mean—" He was trembling. His freckled thighs were pulled tight with tension. "You can—"

I didn't need to be told twice.

I yanked him up onto his knees again, enjoying his happy little gasp.

And then my mouth descended on his hole before he could finish his sentence. He howled, bucking away from me in surprise as I slicked my tongue around the twitching entrance and tore holes in his mattress trying to force myself deeper.

"Shit," he gasped out. "Oh shit." His hips circled back a little as I speared my tongue, his hole wet and soft when I finally was able to push my way inside. "Fuuuuuck." He humped my tongue, the tension in his body slipping away as he grew lax and obedient. "Fuck, buddy."

"You missed me," I murmured against his entrance, speaking to it directly. "Your greedy hole needed fucked." I pulled my tongue out so I could swirl it around the twitchy entrance before I pushed back inside the tight clutch of his body. He was just as sweet here as he was everywhere else. Calm, unlike anything I'd ever known, settled over my body.

"Fuck," Jeffrey gasped out. "Yes—I…I did."

"You missed…" I murmured, rubbing my lips around the tightly clenched hole. "*This*." I flattened my tongue, dragging it over his hole to demonstrate.

The weakness I usually felt after a full moon melted away. Till I was simply a toy. A toy for my mate's pleasure as he circled his hips, back and forth, back and forth, and rode my tongue. The deeper I pushed inside him the harder he fucked himself, these broken little "uh, uh, uh" sounds escaping him every time I wriggled deeper.

I wanted to grab his hips.

Wanted to force him to ride me harder.

Wanted him to sit on my goddamn face.

But I wasn't in control right now, and I was terrified of hurting his fragile human flesh. So I settled for fucking him as well as I could without it. My hand fell to my cock, even though what I really wanted was to climb on top of him and force it inside him. My nails pricked my own flesh as I rutted into my tight grip at the same time my saliva dripped down the crack of his ass and my tongue wriggled deeper.

When Jeffrey came for the second time that night he clenched around me. A pitiful, overwhelmed little sob escaped him. His scent was needy-soft-overstimulated. This flicker of twitches that had my head spinning and my cock drooling. I came all over my fist only seconds later, unable to help myself, my fingers twisted tight around the base of my knot to prolong the pleasure. His sticky hole clung to my tongue, sucking at me.

Jeffrey circled his hips, once, twice, three more times before he wiggled off my tongue, and fell to his belly onto the mattress with an exhausted groan. His legs were sprawled wide, hole gaping at me. I grinned, unable to help myself as I leaned forward and buried my face between his cheeks again to suck a few more kisses against it.

"Jesus Christ," Jeffrey trembled, reaching back to tangle his fingers in my hair as my tongue slipped inside the tight clutch of his body again. "Fuck. You can't—"

"I can," I argued, though I had a face full of ass so it wasn't very articulate.

"Fuck." Jeffrey didn't argue again. My fangs dug into his sweat damp skin but he didn't seem to mind. He let me suck kisses against his pretty hole. Let me lick the crease at the back of his thighs, even though he claimed it tickled. He let me suck hickeys along the tops of his ass cheeks. In the dimples there. Up his spine. Along the back of his neck. Let me lick his armpits, down his arms, and the insides of his wrists. Let me snuffle and skim my nose behind his balls, and across them, let me taste and taste and taste. He let me rub my cum onto his ass, the backs of his thighs.

Let me kiss and bite my way down his hamstrings, suck the backs of his knees till he kicked, then down to his angular, gorgeous feet. I gave each toe a lingering suck before he finally, dazedly, pushed me off, with a sweet little whimpery complaint.

He stunk of me.

Reeked of me.

My mate.

My pretty, pretty mate. With all his speckles. And his clever games. And his hole that begged to be bred.

I curled around his back after arranging him beneath the blankets, my teeth held snug but gently around the back of his neck—like he was a pup in need of punishment. And we fell asleep like that. Together.

Sated.

Sticky.

The way we were supposed to be.

The way I knew we wouldn't be for long.

Chapter Twenty-Three

Jeffrey

IT SHOULD'VE FELT weird to have someone else in my space. Like a violation. But it didn't.

Because I wanted Mutt with me always, and I was coming to terms with that fact. Which was why it wasn't fucking fair. None of this was.

A week had passed since Mutt's return and I was no closer to answers. Every day the moon loomed high in the sky, and my resentment for it grew.

Today I'd convinced Avery to take me to a town on the outskirts of Ridgefield, looking for answers from one of the local hunters. His name was Allen. He'd been kind, worked at a crematory, and was soft spoken. But he'd been unable to help me. He even directed me to one of the main lodges in the area, as there were two, but I wasn't ready for that yet.

Wasn't ready to mingle with the people Lydia had raised me to fear.

I was supposed to be one of them but I wasn't.

And every day, I considered calling Lydia.

Considered facing my monster so I could save Mutt.

The tickets I'd bought burned a hole in the back of my mind. The knowledge that I was only a plane ride away from her, hanging like a cloud over my head. It was a last resort. A last resort that grew more tempting with every day that passed.

Only…deep down I knew even if she could help me she wouldn't.

And I didn't want to waste any of the time I had with Mutt.

But still…memories assaulted me as they often did when I thought of Lydia.

The weight of a gun in my hand. The scent of blood in the air. The laughter as bodies fell and hunters celebrated their deaths like it was an accomplishment and not murder. I'd done my best to block them out, but there was only so much I could do.

Memories twisted like a noose around my neck, flickering behind my eyelids.

Copper, copper, copper.

All day I'd caught myself wondering what *she'd* think. What *she* would do.

The answer had sent me running to the bathroom to throw up.

Because Lydia was not a savior. And I knew her solution to this problem would be to put a silver bullet in Mutt's head.

Lydia had stuck her talons so deep inside my brain, even if I pulled them out splinters would be left behind. It was ridiculous to think I should ask her for help. She'd never helped me. Not a single day in my entire fucking life.

All she'd done was hurt me.

She'd peeled my skin from muscle, and beat every bone in my body till I was shattered and easy to rebuild.

"You're a natural," one man had said, a grizzled hunter with a handlebar mustache and too much chest hair. The woods creaked, the stars high above, darkness creeping around us. A group of ten or so hunters gathered, all staring at Lydia like she shined sun out of her asshole. But they weren't here for Lydia today.

No.

They were here for me.

My first time as head hunter.

My initiation.

He'd slapped my shoulder, and I'd laughed—because that was the person I was supposed to be. My character would be happy. He'd be thrilled. He'd just killed a wendigo.

"I learned from the best," I grinned, jerking my head toward Lydia.

"You're lucky," the man's hand lingered on my shoulder and I hated the fact that it felt good. Kind touch had always been the surest way to tear me apart.

"I am," I agreed. Inside I shriveled up, a withered husk.

"Your aim was a little off. But overall it was a good hunt. You did our name proud," Lydia had said later that night as we'd fallen into our matching twin beds. She spoke like she'd just handed me a zillion dollars, a puppy, and a truckload of cocaine. Like I was supposed to fall to my knees in gratitude that she'd offered me a single shitty compliment. But I wasn't phased. Because at age eighteen, I'd been with her for nearly ten years now, and I knew how to play her like a fiddle.

I still didn't understand why we had to share a room. I'd won her trust. It had taken years, but I'd done it. You'd think that would come with a little freedom.

But the leash I was on was as short as ever.

"Thank you," I'd smiled at her, fluffing my pillow and pulling my blankets high so she couldn't see any part of my body.

"I think you're ready," she'd said, turning to look at me. I glanced over, because it was what she wanted, and I immediately regretted that choice. The way she was staring at me was…unsettling. Her tiny, compact body lay still as a corpse in her bed, her bleach blonde hair slicked back tight. And I knew then, that something was…off. Her eyes were manic, *bright*. Her painted lips were pulled into a grin that sent a chill down my spine.

"Ready?" I echoed, keeping my tone light even though I was terrified.

"For the anchor that's been holding you down to be cut," she'd hummed, like I didn't know exactly what and who she was talking about. Like she hadn't just talked about separating me from the only person that gave my life any meaning.

Blair.

"Lydia—" Panic. Panic zinged through my body, made me feel sick and small, off-kilter. I shouldn't have gotten cocky. I should've never thought I could predict her, that I'd gotten a handle on this after all.

"Mommy," she corrected me, and I flinched. Fuck. I hadn't slipped up like that in years. *What was I doing?*

"Mommy," I said, tone soft and careful. Careful not to show weakness. "What do you…I mean—*What do you mean?*"

"You'll see." Her reply was cryptic. And it…haunted me. Haunted me all night as I stared unseeingly up at the ceiling, a gun beneath my pillow, and my mind a million miles away. She turned her back to me, and for a single—solitary second, I debated killing her. But I lost my nerve.

I hadn't known then what exactly she was planning, but in hindsight, I'd simply been blind. It felt so…obvious now. The papers she'd placed in her husband's desk for us to find. The trap laid for Blair to come to Elmwood where she could take care of him once and for all.

The fortune she thought she was owed.

The sister she'd killed to get it.

I should've killed her, I knew that now.

What was one more stain? It wasn't like I'd ever been clean.

So many…so many people had died because I was a stupid kid. And I knew that. All my life I'd known that. I'd carried that burden with me every goddamn day. Felt its shackles around my wrists and its weight on my shoulders. It altered the way I thought, the way I breathed, this ever-present ache that never lightened. Like walking on a bed of nails.

The only time I'd ever managed to truly forget was when I was with Mutt.

When he dragged me into his—or my—bed. When he jerked me over the long line of his body, let me lay my head on his pillowy chest, and listen to the steady thump of his heartbeat. When he held me close and tight, grabbed the back of my neck, and pinned me where I was safe and happy and cared for.

Where I belonged.

Not because I had to—but because he simply…wanted me.

Wanted me the way no one ever had.

"Sometimes I wish you were a wolf," Mutt had said once. "Not because you aren't perfect the way you are—because you are. But because I think…if you could scent how I feel about you—if you could feel the way my heart beats when you're around. If you could hear my truths, I could make you happy."

Mutt was safe. He was warm.

He was bright enough to chase away my shadows.

And I…trusted him.

I trusted him to keep me safe. From everything that haunted and hurt me—and from myself too. He'd saved me more times than I could count.

And now I wanted to save him.

I wanted to keep him.

I wanted to live for a future I'd never known I'd have.

But that didn't mean I wasn't terrified.

Because now…now there was something new to lose. *Someone* new. And part of me condemned myself for allowing these feelings to grow at all—but I…I couldn't regret him. Even if this hurt. Even if I failed. Even if all I had were memories.

At least now I had good ones.

Feeling sick and sluggish, I tore my clothes off and slid inside the shower stall. Nightmares still festered in the back of my mind. Nightmares of a world where there was no more cuddling, no more laughter, no more wagging tails.

Nightmares about losing Mutt entirely.

Nightmares about living a life without him.

I hadn't had time to settle yet. Usually the hot water helped, but right now it just…hurt. I couldn't seem to get my hands to stop shaking while I gingerly twisted the shower knob and squeezed my eyes shut tight as the pipes wheezed into action. You had to baby the damn thing. Pull too hard and the handle would pop right off.

The pipes sputtered, and with a rush of heat, a torrent of water was let loose. It pounded harshly against my body, boiling my skin as water drops skittered across my shoulders. I hissed out a breath, focusing on the bright bursts of pain. They grounded me enough in the present that Lydia's voice didn't feel quite so loud as I clenched my teeth tight and willed the panic that had been stalking me all day to subside.

Think about something else.

I needed a distraction, and my bacon-chip-eating house guest was the perfect candidate. Werewolves kept their secrets close. And I'd yet to find one fucking usable thing that would work to give Mutt more time.

One of Lydia's buddies had once told me that werewolves peed on their mates to mark their territory. I really, *really* hoped that wasn't true. The same guy had gotten himself killed trying to lure a group of goblins out of a cave using a pack of firecrackers and imitation gold, so really—it was probably wise to ignore anything he'd said.

It was unfortunate that I knew more about their peeing habits than how to save Mutt.

Lydia's training forced the monsters under my bed in front of my bullets. And yet nothing I'd been through could help me now. Not when I needed it.

There was no escaping my past today.

I couldn't breathe.

I couldn't breathe.

I couldn't—

Gasping like a fish out of water, I jerked the dial on the shower as hot as it would go, hoping the pain would be enough to distract me again. Thankfully, it cooperated instead of breaking. *Woosh,* it rained down, baptizing me of my thoughts.

Breathe, breathe, breathe.

Think about something else, anything else.

I was glad that water had decided to be blistering today.

The more it burned, the more centered I felt.

My teeth started to chatter, my heart racing as my jaw clenched tight. It stayed just as unforgivingly hot as when I'd first gotten in, but I welcomed the pain. I let it assault my back, familiar numbness settling into place. I shut my eyes and the world went dark. My teeth ached. My hands were shaking.

I reached for the bar of soap and—grabbed the scentless bottle Mutt had bought me instead. And then I sat on the shower floor and cried. At least, until Mutt's furry head pushed through the bathroom door, and the big hairy beast crawled into the shower beside me. His fur became matted and soaked, but he didn't mind.

And as I buried my face in his fur, my thoughts spin-spin-spinning, I tried to figure out what the fuck I was going to do.

Because I'd been wrong when I'd thought I was lost before.

How could I have been lost when I'd never known where I was in the first place?

And now I did. I did know. I knew happiness. I knew who and what I was. And I just…I didn't want to lose him. Blair had said I deserved to be happy. I'd thought it an empty platitude. Hadn't believed him or trusted it.

But I was starting to think…that maybe…if someone as sweet and loyal as Mutt wanted me. Maybe if my brothers were so doggedly determined to keep me in their lives. Maybe the fact I'd survived at all meant I was stronger, better, more loved than I thought.

They say it's better to have loved and lost than to never have loved at all.

And they were right.

Because I'd bear this pain gladly if it meant I got to keep Mutt for as long as possible.

Chapter Twenty-Four

Jeffrey

"YOU WANT...DATING advice?" Blair slurped his orange soda, brow quirked. "From...me?"

"Yes." My cheeks were hot and my hands felt sweaty. Blair was driving. We were on our way to check out another lead for my ongoing hunt for answers to help Mutt, and we'd just stopped at a shitty Mexican food place that had surprisingly good burritos for lunch.

Blair had plowed through his in record time. Swear to God he'd only taken two fucking bites of the thing, and happy-food-danced the whole time. And now we were on the road again, and I was still nursing my own burrito.

Truth was...I wasn't all that hungry.

Talking to hunters made me nervous. And though I'd told Blair this wasn't all that new to me, he still didn't know the full truth. Not about what Lydia had put me through. Not about my training.

My therapist had said that sharing the truth might help me feel less like I was drowning, and I wanted that…I really fucking did. But the words just…didn't want to come out. They felt stuck and clogged and every time I tried to open my mouth to tell him something else came out.

Like now.

I also hadn't meant to ask for dating advice. Well…I had. Just…not this very second. That was gonna be after I told him the truth. He was probably wondering, if I'm being honest. It was a giant fucking red flag that I already knew as much about the supernatural as I did.

Blair seemed to assume it was because I remembered growing up in Elmwood, and I'd let him.

But…

Fuck.

I was so tired of hiding.

And I just…I wanted my brother back. Maybe I'd never truly had him at all. Because I'd been a liar from the start—but I wanted to try. I wanted to give us a fighting chance to be what we should be. Maybe without the trauma-based codependency—as that hadn't served either of us.

I knew that now.

I'd craved it when I first moved here.

I'd resented Richard and Collin in a way because it had felt like they'd replaced me.

But…that was a good thing. I realized that now. Blair needed support just like I did, and he'd found that. After he'd overheard my angst-riddled freak out he'd been softer somehow. It was weird. Before he'd looked at me like I was going to break. Like I was fragile. Like I was two seconds from blowing myself up.

But that had relaxed.

And fuuuuck.

Okay.

That meant my therapist was right.

The truth really had helped.

"I have a boyfriend," I said, awkwardly.

"Yeah, I know," Blair snorted. He slurped at his drink again.

"And that's not…weird to you?"

"Weird why?" He frowned at me as he pushed his cup back into the cupholder and both his hands tapped at the steering wheel. Taylor Swift was blasting, and we were vibing to the beat, Blair's black chipped nail polish flashing.

"You know because he's like…a dude."

Blair looked at me like I was stupid, which I suppose was fair. And then, like he was talking to a toddler he very slowly said, "You are aware that I'm gay, right?"

I glared at him, because he was being an asshole, then soldiered onward, not dignifying that with a response. I'd been the one that fucking brought him to his first gay bar, of course I fucking knew. "He's a dude. *And* a werewolf."

"And I'm dating a vampire." Blair cocked his brow at me pointedly. "What's your point?"

"Touche." I relaxed a little, and Blair did too—almost like we were telepathically connected like freaky circus twins. At an impasse, we both remained quiet for a solid five seconds before I broke again. "So."

"So," Blair echoed.

"Boys?"

"Boys." Blair snorted, shaking his shaggy mane like I was being an idiot. Which I guess I was? So I laughed too.

Just ask him.

Rip off the Band-Aid.

"How do you like…woo a dude?" I asked, cheeks flushed. "I mean. With girls I always just told them their hair was pretty, and like…listened to what they said and repeated it back to them." This was such a weird parallel. We'd had a conversation so similar to this, not all that long ago, only it had been Blair asking me for advice, and not the other way around.

It was a testament to how much I'd changed that I could ask for help at all.

"*Woah.*" Blair twisted to look at me. "Asshole much?"

I grimaced. "I didn't—I mean. Fuck. You're right." Damn. I hadn't really thought of it that way. My cheeks flushed with humiliation I definitely deserved. "I just."

Trees whirred by the windows, painting the horizon black as the wheels stuttered over murky, mushy fallen leaves. Above, dark gray storm clouds climbed across the sun, blocking it from view for a moment before splitting apart once again.

"Why exactly did you do that?" Blair called me out after a beat of silence. "I always thought you were like…I dunno–"

"What?"

"Perfect?" Blair shrugged a shoulder. "But if you were perfect, why secretly act like such a dick?"

"I…" I wasn't even sure how to answer that. With Martha I'd been better. I'd cared about her. But not the way I was supposed to. We'd dated for a while, off and on, and it'd been great for appearances. Lydia had liked it, and it took the attention off of Blair and his gay-scapades. Which he'd thought Lydia didn't know about but she usually did. "I guess I didn't realize I was being a dick," I admitted, cheeks hot. "Fuck." My stomach churned.

"And now you do?"

Did I ever love Martha?

No.

The answer came quickly enough I immediately felt sick.

"Yeah." I picked at my seatbelt, wondering how the hell this had gotten so turned around. "Mutt is…different. But I'm different now too."

"No shit."

"*No*, I mean…" Man. *Just how many lies am I fucking keeping?* "Before I dated mostly to keep Lydia off my back—and to keep her attention away from you." Blair made a wheezy sound.

"*What?*" his voice was flat.

"Whenever I had a girlfriend she'd get so sucked up into schmoozing her family, she'd lay off you for a while, you know? And it just…felt *easier*. Made me what she wanted me to be. I was…desirable or whatever. When I had a lot of attention it meant she did too. She liked that." God, this was harder than I thought. "Plus the girls didn't mind. Most of them only dated me because they wanted to brag about fucking me."

"That is so fucked up I don't even know what to say," Blair pulled over to the side of the road. The same way I'd pulled to the side for Collin when we'd had our little heart to heart. "Give me a second to think. Because what the fuck, Jeffrey."

"Right."

I stared at the clouds some more. Stared at the shadowy gaps between the trees and the mountains that flickered behind them, fog colored and smoky with the late autumn chill. The window was cold to the touch, and it soothed my feverish skin as I pressed against it, leaving a streak of clear glass within the condensation.

"Let's start with the obvious. You…" Blair shook his head, staring resolutely forward as he formed the words rattling inside his head. "You *didn't* like the attention?" When he twisted to look at me, his pale green eyes were wide and hurt. The *but you said you did,* was implied. He didn't need to say it for me to know what he was thinking.

I wanted to lie.

I wanted to pretend like I hadn't just blown the top off Pandora's fucking box.

But…

Blair was strong enough for the truth now. Maybe he hadn't been before, but he was a different person now, just like I was. Maybe eight-year-old Blair couldn't have handled this. Or sixteen-year-old Blair. Or even twenty-year-old Blair. But the Blair in front of me wasn't the same person he'd been back then—angry, bitter, always scared.

This Blair had decided to live. He'd taken his first steps on his own, and he'd found who he was—through trial and error—but still.

He was strong enough.

And maybe…just maybe, I was strong enough too.

If I didn't end this torture who would? This was a prison of my own making. I was a guard as well as an inmate, and it was finally time I felt some peace.

So I tapped into my inner Mutt and told the truth. *Bluntly.* To the point.

"No." My heart skittered. "I hated the fucking attention."

"You hated the—"

"All the eyes, and the—the fucking…false niceties. No one fucking liked me. They didn't. How could they? I wasn't even a person. Just a fucking puppet Lydia made. A card trick to impress her friends. Stupid and fragile, and fake."

Blair's eyes were wide and alarmed. "You know how I love guitar? And music?" I added.

"Yeah?" Blair kept staring at me. He was looking at me like he didn't recognize who the fuck I was, and that was fair. I'd never actually let him know me.

"The part I hate the most about it is the fact I have to sing in front of other people. I only do it now to remind myself that it's different. That I'm not a party trick anymore, and that I'm doing it on my own terms."

"But you…" Blair shook his head. "But you always loved that shit. The parties. The medals. The—the—*you know what I mean.*"

"No," I shook my head. "I didn't love it. I *don't.*" I bit my lip, and my heart hurt. "I just…I just wanted to survive, you know? And if I became who Lydia wanted me to be then she…" I trailed off.

"Then she?" Blair prompted.

"She would stop hurting you."

"What the fuck." Blair was shaking, and I was too. "What the actual fuck." And then he was pulling me into an apple-scented hug, and his arms were wrapping tight around me—and I just…fuck. I could breathe again. "What the fuck." He repeated a broken, jittery record.

"I hate baseball," I admitted, unable to hug him back because it didn't feel like I deserved it. "I hate parties." I sucked in a breath. "And those baseball retreats Lydia and I always went to? Yeah. They weren't fucking sports related.”

My heart hurt.

“Unless you count hunting monsters as a sport. Which I guess…some people probably do.”

“What—” Blair pulled back and I groaned, dragging a hand through my hair, my voice wobbling.

“Look. It’s probably easier if I just show you.”

So I grabbed the hem of my shirt, and even though I was terrified—yanked it up.

Blair stared at my torso like his brain had completely broken.

“What—” His hand hovered, like he wanted to touch the jagged myriad of scars on my skin, but didn’t know if it would hurt me. “Fuck.” He sucked in a breath, eyes wet, and I just… “Why didn’t you tell me?”

Fuck.

“Because it was my fault we were in that mess,” I said, voice cracking. “And I just…”

“No it wasn’t.” Blair shook his head, then pulled me into another awkward hug. “It wasn’t. It wasn’t your fucking fault.” The gear shift dug into my ribs but I ignored it.

This time I hugged back.

And it was good and right and warm.

“I don’t think I ever felt safe a day in my life,” I admitted, one last final truth, “Until I met Mutt.”

Blair shook as he squeezed me closer. We were a jittery, quivery mess.

And then we both jerked away at the same time—because that was enough of that—and coughed awkwardly. “Okay, so.” My cheeks were still hot, my shirt officially back into place. “Boys?”

"Boys," he agreed for the second time that day.

Apparently Blair's advice for dating men was to:

"Get sloppy when you give head."

"Care about what they have to say."

"Use a lot of tongue."

Advice one and three were pretty much the same fucking thing—and self-explanatory, so they didn't really help. He did, however, give me some solid date ideas. And after I'd told him how obsessed with Disney movies Mutt was—*Lady and the Tramp* in particular—we came up with the most genius idea for a first official date.

I just…needed to actually ask Mutt out first.

Because Blair had been incredibly unhelpful, and I was curious, I texted Richard for advice too. He, at least, didn't talk about blowjobs.

Me: Do you have any advice for dating men?

Richard: Why are you asking me this?

Me: Just answer the question, asshole

Richard: I am not qualified.

Me: Not qualified my ass. You literally have a boyfriend.

He didn't reply, so I sighed and texted him again.

Me: Why aren't you qualified?

Richard: I've only dated one person. Blair.

Me: Yeah, I know.

Richard: I imagine every person is different. And as I only know how to date Blair, I don't think the information I've learned is relevant to you.

I was two seconds from giving up, but decided I'd give it one last shot—because I was stubborn and also…maybe it was my turn to need a big brother right now. Richard must've known that, because he stopped fucking with me and gave in pretty immediately.

Me: Can you just…try? Jesus fuck. It's like pulling teeth.

Richard: Give me a minute.

It took Richard half an hour to reply again, and this time he had a comprehensive list.

Richard: Romantic gestures are always appreciated. Quality time. Listening when they talk. Little gifts that remind you of a person, simply because you'd think they'd like them. Try

to understand where they're coming from, especially when you're arguing. Don't keep secrets. They have a way of getting out, and all they do is hurt the people you care about.

It was weird. Everything Richard had just listed was stuff I could recall Mutt doing for me. He was just…naturally good at dating, I guess. Even though he was an overgrown puppy with a constant hard-on.

When Blair dropped me off at home, Mutt was waiting for me like usual. In dog form today. Now that I was on a roll telling people the truth, I was half-tempted to straight-up call him out. But…the silence was nice too. And I figured if Mutt was in this form today it meant he needed it.

"You wanna go for a ride?" I offered, because I wanted to get my mind off the weird car conversation with Blair, the dead end with the hunter, and the date I was planning.

Mutt wagged his tail happily, and that was that.

I fed him cheeseburgers again, this time sitting in the back of my pickup truck. And I plucked away at the strings of my guitar, working on the song I was writing with my back to the cabin, and my head tipped up toward the stars. Mutt wagged his tail lazily, keeping my legs warm, his big head settled on my thighs.

It was nice.

Easy.

The perfect end to a difficult day.

"I hate talking to people," I told him, still strumming away. "I wish I could be like you," I shrugged a shoulder, staring into his bottomless blue eyes. Mutt woofed softly and I grinned, cheeks hot. "You wouldn't believe the day I had," I admitted, uncharacteristically chatty now that I was with him. It was a little awkward at first, because I'd never been all that open with my feelings. But the second I started I couldn't seem to stop.

I told him everything. Told him about the bird shit on Avery's head—Gregory was a serial shitter now. Told him about my fears and my worries. Told him about Blair's dating advice, and how he looked happy, and it didn't hurt anymore.

Told him about Lydia.

About some of what I'd been through.

An hour passed.

I was chilly and shaky, and wished I'd thought to bring heated blankets for us so we wouldn't have to go back. But I felt better.

Because I may be shit at dating, but Mutt wasn't.

And this had been a pretty damn good date.

Chapter Twenty-Five

Mutt

"MUTT," JEFFREY'S VOICE cracked, needy soft, helpless, tinny through my phone's speakers. I jerked up from where I'd been nestled in his bed. My phone only had a few batteries left, and I scrambled around for a charger, suddenly cursing myself for not thinking to charge it.

I knew he was out running around today. I'd tried to invite myself along but he'd been cagey about it and his scent had been sneaky-happy-excited, so I figured there was a reason he hadn't wanted to include me.

"What is wrong?" I jabbed the charging string into the hole on my device, growling down at it. "What has happened? Where are you?" I could and would hunt him by scent if necessary. But if I could get a location that would make things quicker. "Are you hurt?"

"My—" Jeffrey sucked in a breath. "I'm stuck. And my truck broke down again, cuz the thing's a piece of shit and probably didn't get fixed right the first time—and I can't get home. And I would've called Blair, I *should've* called Blair or Richard but I just…" His voice cracked. "I just wanted *you*."

My heart throbbed erratically.

"Tell me where you are. I'll fix it."

"Okay." Jeffrey's voice was soft, meek. He rattled off a bunch of words I didn't understand, but I committed them to memory immediately. "You…you'll come?"

"Yes." My heart lurched. "I'll come."

"Okay." Jeffrey sounded relieved, and that hurt. Because he shouldn't have been scared at all. I should've been there. I should've been protecting him. I knew what asking for help meant to him, and I was so incredibly proud of him.

"Stay put."

"I will."

"How old are you?" Harry's voice was flat and nasally, his hands on the steering wheel as he glared into the rearview mirror at the both of us. I'd insisted on sitting in the back with Jeffrey, and Harry had let me, even though he mumbled something biting about being a show-fer, whatever that was.

"Twenty-five," Jeffrey replied. His scent was worry-relief-grateful. I soaked it up, nuzzling against his throat, more than a little thankful that I'd bit back my own pride and asked for help. As always, he was a good example.

"How did you and Mutt meet?" Harry asked, body stiff, his eyes narrowed.

"He…" Jeffrey's gaze skipped to my face, then my hands, his scent souring for a second before it cleared. "He saved me."

"Right." Harry hadn't been expecting that, obviously. I preened, huffing at his throat happily, one of my hands curled around his hip to hold him still. He was used to my touch by now. At first he'd flinch a little, and then melt—almost like he wanted it, but didn't think he was allowed.

Now he simply softened, tipping into me obediently the second I was near, submissive, his dark eyes full of need.

"What's his favorite food?" Harry quizzed again. I wasn't sure what he was doing. Interrogating Jeffrey like this. But I didn't like it.

"Squirrel?" Jeffrey joked, eyes dancing.

"Lucky guess." Harry's grip on the steering wheel tightened till it squeaked. "What's his favorite color?"

Jeffrey blinked, stumped for a second. "Um." He glanced at me, his cheeks flooding pretty-pink.

"Brown," I mouthed, staring into his eyes pointedly. His flush only blossomed brighter and he sucked in a startled little breath. Pleased-pleased-pleased.

"Brown," he hummed. Then he mouthed "dork" at me, clearly embarrassed. Harry made a sound, though his gaze flickered to me, then Jeffrey in the rearview mirror like he was assessing us. I didn't know why he'd asked *that* question. It wasn't like he knew my favorite color either.

But I trusted that he knew what he was doing.

He and Jules were the last to know about Jeffrey, and I figured it was time. Even though there was bound to be fall out because of this.

"Who is Lydia Evans?" Harry's voice was mild but his scent betrayed his anxiety. I jerked a little, especially when Jeffrey flinched. I felt it. The twitch of his body, the way he stiffened, turning to ice in my arms.

"I…what—"

"I looked into you," Harry said, not balking. I jolted, shocked. "Mutt is not exactly sneaky." *I am plenty sneaky!* "And your name is always right beside hers."

"I…" Jeffrey trembled.

I had no doubt that Harry already knew the answer to this question. He was just testing Jeffrey, and while earlier I'd found his questions harmless, now I felt the need to step in.

I growled, low and dangerous. My eyes flashed, the scent of my anger filling the car. And yet…Harry held his ground. I squeezed Jeffrey tight enough his bones creaked, my ire pointed toward my annoying-ass-older-brother. "*Shut up,* Harry," I hissed out, half-tempted to climb between the seats and shut him up myself—moving van be damned. He was pack— but that didn't excuse him for being an asshole. "Or I'll make you."

"No." Jeffrey squeezed me back, gently pushing me aside so I wasn't blocking him from view anymore. "*No,* it's cool." He flashed me a reassuring grin, though it wobbled. "It's…I mean. It's not like it's a secret. I should get used to talking about it, right?"

I don't know about that.

I growled at Harry again, and Jeffrey shoved at my shoulder. The silly human wasn't strong enough to move me on his own, but I shifted out of the way as guided anyway, trusting him to know his own limits.

Jeffrey flashed me a grateful smile, obviously realizing what I'd done.

"Lydia kidnapped me when I was nine," Jeffrey said easily—like it didn't hurt, even though I could smell how much it did. My heart thumped erratically. Harry's eyes widened a little, his own scent growing sharp.

"She faked my death. Stole me away. Made my life a living hell for like… years and fucking years. She only recently got locked up–and I came *here* right after." He trembled, but he met Harry's gaze through the mirror unflinchingly.

Brave as always.

"Are you aware of what she was?" Harry asked, though even I could hear his tone was softer.

"I mean…" Jeffrey sucked in a breath. *Don't lie,* I begged, though I wouldn't blame him if he did. This was his trauma to tell, and I hated that Harry was forcing it out of him like this.

But at the same time…I was grateful.

Because now I wouldn't be the only person who realized just how brave Jeffrey was. Who respected him. Because that was what he deserved. With every new detail I learned about his past that respect only grew.

"Of course I am," he admitted, and his heart rang true. His eyes were cloudy and far away, like his nightmares played in front of them even now. "I did a lot of shit I'm not proud of when I lived with Lydia. I…hurt people." Jeffrey's voice was rough. "And I understand if that makes you nervous—because of what you both are."

"Of course it does." Harry's eyes narrowed again. "How do I know you're not going to turn around and shoot one of us the second our backs are turned?"

"Because I'm not…I mean." Jeffrey closed his eyes, sucking in a fortifying breath. And when his eyes opened again there was confidence in them. Strength. It made me shiver, my body burning bright with the need to own the beautiful, resilient man beside me. To keep his light within reach. "I'm not a bad person," Jeffrey admitted. "I've done bad things. But I was just surviving—and I'm past that."

The fact he realized that was frankly amazing. I was so fucking proud of the progress he'd made.

"If you're past that part of your life then why are you out talking to local hunters, hmm?" Harry hissed out, betraying himself and the fact he'd apparently been *following* my mate.

Angry again, the rumble in my chest started up again.

How dare he.

How dare he follow my mate.

"Because—" Jeffrey looked at me, confused. His brow furrowed. "You…"

"Because he's trying to *help* me," I snapped, angry that Harry was bringing this up when we were both doing our best to ignore it whenever possible. "Because it's getting worse."

"What do you mean it's getting worse?"

"I *mean,* it's getting *worse.*" I hadn't actually admitted this to him. Not out loud. I knew my brothers suspected, and that there were physical signs. But this was the first time I was openly acknowledging it. I ducked my head and buried it in Jeffrey's neck to leech his strength, suddenly exhausted.

"Oh."

Harry called my dad. Because of course he fucking did. Tattletaled on me immediately. And Jeffrey got to be privy to that entire conversation as we rode the rest of the way to his apartment in Elmwood.

Ignoring Harry's protests, I followed Jeffrey up the steps to his apartment, crowding him against the front door with my face at the back of his throat as he fumbled with his key. The plastic bag he carried rustled. "You should probably…you know—damage control?" Jeffrey offered, twisting a little.

"No." I nipped at his shoulder and he laughed, shivering.

"Mutt." When he flipped around to face me, he blocked the doorway, hand at the handle. His tone was serious.

"You need me. You *called* me—"

"I know." Jeffrey's smile was soft. His scent was sure. "But your brother is freaking out," he reached up, gently stroking over my cheek. "And he needs you too."

"But—"

Jeffrey kissed me, fingers twisting into my t-shirt, his tongue pressing against the seam of my lips. He rubbed and licked, lighting me up from the inside out as I groaned and pressed back against him. Too soon the kiss ended.

When Jeffrey pulled back his lips were swollen pink, and his eyes were at half-mast.

"I'll be waiting for you when you're done," he said softly. "But you need time with your family. And if things are as bad as you say they are…maybe you guys need to have a game plan. Besides, I've been monopolizing you."

"I…don't know what that means."

Jeffrey's scent was amused-amused-amused.

"It *means* I want you here all the fucking time, every fucking day," he admitted, releasing my shirt. "But I think you need to go talk to your family."

"I…"

"Trust me," his eyes were full of monsters all over again. "I…for a long fucking time I was quiet. I avoided my brothers because I was scared facing the truth would make it hurt more." He shook his head, his lips twisting. "But it doesn't. It's the lies that fucking suck. And maybe you're not like me—maybe you're not outright withholding the truth." *I kinda was—*

from him too. "But you owe it to them, and yourself, to have a clean slate."

"Jeffrey—"

"Don't be like me," Jeffrey's eyes were dark. "Don't repeat my mistakes."

A car passed by on the street, the sun sinking low, the creak of one of Jeffrey's neighbors opening and shutting their door echoing inside my head. Despite this, I narrowed my focus, centering myself in him as I met his gaze and fell even more, helplessly in love with him.

Jeffrey was no wilting flower.

He may have been stomped on but his petals remained firm. What had once withered had fallen free and grown anew. Ever enduring. Solid and sure.

Not at all like I was. Telling him there was no need to lie when here I was, a fucking liar. Afraid to be vulnerable with the people that loved me because I didn't trust them not to take him away from me.

"I wish I was like you," I admitted, voice rough. "You are..." I leaned down and kissed him again, sweetly. "You are the most resilient person I know. Like a flower that survives the frost. If I have even an ounce of your strength I will survive."

"You can't say cheesy shit like that to me," Jeffrey laughed, but his voice was wet. "Fuck. That should be on a Hallmark card or some shit."

Cheesy?

"What about what I just said inspired thoughts of cheese?"

"Shut up." Jeffrey yanked me into another kiss. And then he pushed me away, and I went, once again allowing him to move me when we both knew he couldn't. "Come back when you're done. I've got more...*research* to do."

"Okay, my prince," I grinned, even though I ached to follow him inside and finish what we'd started.

"God, I hate that nickname."

"Lie," I laughed, because it was. He loved it, and he knew it.

Jeffrey must've recognized the look on my face, because before I could ignore his words and shoulder my way inside he shut the door in my face. Which was probably good, because I had very little self-control as it was.

I stared at the chipped wood for a beat, whining softly under my breath before I forced my feet to move away from him even though it felt *wrong*.

The car ride back to our house was awkward as hell. Harry asked me a million and a half questions. I had to force myself not to ignore them or bite his head off. And by the time we reached the house I felt drained. But…better too.

Is this how Silas feels after a meeting with Harry?

My sympathies went out to Elmwood's Pack Alpha.

"Thank you for your help," I managed as we climbed up the steps.

"You're welcome." Harry shoved the front door open, holding it for me to go through first. "I…" His voice wavered. For the last two minutes he'd been eerily silent and I knew it was because he was mulling over what I'd said. His white button-up was ironed to perfection as always, but there was something unkempt about him.

Harry would be hard to win over. He was picky. Loyal. But prickly.

I tried to tell myself that his opinion of Jeffrey didn't matter, but it did. Because he was *pack*. He was mine. And I just…I felt pulled in too many directions at once. It would be nice not to feel so untethered. To have support, when for months I'd let my lies get between me and my family.

Jeffrey hadn't asked that of me, but I hadn't known what else to do.

"I see why you like him," Harry finally said and his tone was surprisingly gentle as he let the door fall shut with a quiet click. None of his usual ice remained. When I scented the air all I felt was *calm*. The lights were off, but my other brothers' heartbeats sounded down the hall. "I mean…I think it's *stupid* that you're fucking a human before you're going to have to go home and find a mate—but."

Harry said the word "but" like it was its own sentence entirely.

"But?" I repeated, aching anew.

"But he's…*sweet,*" Harry shrugged. "I heard him, you know." *Because of course he did.* "He made you talk to me. You didn't want to." I nodded, because he had. "I know…words are hard for you. I don't know why. That's never been a problem I have but I can understand that we're different. I just… I mean—you…you don't *talk* to me. Or us. How are we supposed to help you if you don't tell us what's going on?" he shook his head.

"Words are…" I lowered my head, standing in the doorway feeling small. "Words are easy to mess up. I do not have your gift with them. I am too awkward. Too honest. I can not spin them like webs the way you do. It is better to be quiet, than to say the wrong thing."

"That's stupid," Harry's eyes burned. "But yeah. Okay. I get that."

"Jeffrey is…" Jeffrey was a lot of things. But most of all, "he is *good.*" My heart hurt. "He is a good person. A good person who has had very bad things happen to him. I could not protect him from them because I was not there. And I am doing my best now, but I know I don't have much time left."

I'd already made my choice.

Not that Harry knew that.

"When I am gone I was hoping that you…" I trailed off, heart thumping.

Harry's brow scrunched. "That I what?"

"That you will look after him?" I said softly, my heart hurting. "That all of you will. He is precious, and sweet—and the best thing that has ever happened to me. But I am not the only one who sees his softness. He is so desperate to be loved he becomes blind to the vultures. Trouble can scent him as prey from miles away. And I need to know someone will protect him when I can't anymore."

Harry was silent.

"Please just…*please say yes.*" My heart thumped erratically.

Arms enveloped me.

It was an odd sensation—because I was still looking at Harry, and he wasn't the one hugging me. But then Butters scent hit. And Theo's. And Jules's. And I realized—belatedly—that I'd walked into our home and spoken loud enough for all of them to hear.

"Of course we'll take care of him," Harry said, staring at me like I'd grown a second tail. Theo huffed into my hair in agreement and I melted, heart fluttering as I finally let myself relax around my brothers the way I should've all along.

I would miss them.

I would miss this.

But I knew, in my heart, that I could not regret my decision. Because to live without Jeffrey was torture—and I had less time than any of them realized.

Jules's fluffy head tickled my nose as he shuffled around to my front. He was the smallest of my brothers and barely came to my chest, the lock of white hair at the front of his head sticking straight up. He smelled like the books he loved so much, and his lavender eyes were wet.

"I'm so pissed at you," he admitted as Harry squeezed around me, finally crowding in, his head leaning on my shoulder. Butters huffed at the back of my neck and I grinned, warm in a way I hadn't been in years.

"Pissed at me?"

"Why am I the last to know you're dating someone?" Jules glared up at me. "I'm like the only person here who is qualified to help you."

"To help…me?"

"Impress a human, obviously."

"Oh."

I held him close. I held all of them close, my eyes pinched shut. "It's not too late," I said, because it wasn't.

Not…yet.

"Okay," he said, content.

"Okay," I agreed, warm, warm, warm.

Wishing Jeffrey was here.

Because the only thing that would make this cuddle pile better would be if he was right in the middle beside me.

Chapter Twenty-Six

Mutt

WHEN I RETURNED to Jeffrey's apartment later that night there was a strange sound coming from his bedroom. Immediately alarmed, I yanked the window open and launched myself into the space. Jeffrey was on the bed, his hand down his pants, his laptop in front of him.

He stared at me, eyes wide—scent suprised-alarmed-sheepish.

The weird sound kept squeaking from his headphones, and I stalked forward, yanking them off of him carefully, sniffing at them as I tried to figure out what the fuck was happening.

"Mutt—"

"What is—" I glanced down at his computer screen, then balked, shocked when I saw the naked bodies there. Naked bodies having sex. On camera.

What…the fuck.

I climbed onto Jeffrey's bed, pulling the headphones on myself, my gaze zeroing in on the screen with fascination. "What is…" I blinked. "This?"

"Porn?" Jeffrey flushed. I could hear him over the little whines and grunts from the headphones, and Jeffrey, because he was the smartest person in the world, unplugged the headphones so we could both hear.

"Porn," I repeated.

"You know…" he flushed. "To like…"

"To?"

"Get off?"

I scowled at him. "You do not need porn to get off. You have me."

"Okay, Mr. Possessive." He snorted, hitting pause on the video. "Yeah. But I was…you know," he licked his lips. "Doing *research*. Like I said."

"Research?"

"Yeah." Jeffrey's eyes were dark, his arousal apparent. "I mean…" He slid a hand down my chest, slow and deliberate. When he cupped my cock I groaned. "You're uncut."

"I am what?" I had no idea what that was. Though I was no stranger to nudity, the concept of watching sex on video was foreign. It was impossible to be a prude when you lived in a pack like mine. During the full moon we all stripped down and shifted together—so I'd seen my fair share of cocks.

"You know, *uncut*." Jeffrey gave my cock another squeeze, his long fingers dipping low enough to brush my balls. "You have foreskin."

It took my brain a second to work again—because he was talking nonsense, and also his hand was on my dick. But then it clicked, and I nodded jerkily, breath coming out in a tight hiss. "You don't," I said, voice low.

Jeffrey laughed, cheeks flushed. "Yeah," he said, obviously embarrassed. "You can blame my parents for that."

"Blame your…" I frowned at him, confused.

I didn't like that we were talking about his parents when his hand was on my dick.

"They didn't circumcise any of my brothers except me." Jeffrey's eyes were dark. "They were on a whole religious kick thing around the time I was conceived—and they…yeah. I dunno. They did a lot of weird shit when I was really little."

"Why would joining a religion cause you to cut off a part of your son's cock?" I stared at him, horrified. "What—"

"I dunno," Jeffrey gave my dick another squeeze. "It doesn't matter. What matters is that…you have foreskin, and I don't."

"Okay," I agreed, because that was true. "I wondered why your cock was missing pieces," I murmured, voice low. "I thought it was a human thing."

"Do all wolves have cocks like you?" he asked, curious.

I growled, because I didn't like him thinking about anyone's dick but mine. "Doesn't matter."

"I'm going to guess that means yes." Jeffrey grinned, eyes flooded with heat. "Which makes sense. Bet if you cut it off it'd just heal."

I grimaced, Jeffrey laughed.

He was a lot more settled than he'd been earlier today. I'd have to ask him what happened after I'd dropped him off—but I was…distracted. "I guess it is," he added, leaning into my space, his lips brushing the shell of my cheek. "A human thing, I mean."

"So you…" God, he was distracting. His scent was raspberry sweet, and when I glanced down I could see his cock tenting his sweats, pointing directly at me. "You were researching foreskin? Why?"

My cock jerked.

"Kinda." Jeffrey pulled away just as quickly as he'd pushed into my space. "I'll show you."

Five minutes later, I stared blankly at the computer screen, frowning thoughtfully.

"So…" I blinked, my dick jerking as I licked my lips. "They…*inside?*"

"Yeah," Jeffrey nuzzled against my shoulder, slow and sweet. His scent was stronger. Arousal clogged the air, making my head fuzzy and my body oversensitive. "You just…" He mimed something odd with his hand. "Slide mine right in—"

"In my foreskin," I echoed, heat pooling low in my belly.

"Yeah," Jeffrey licked his lips, nose skimming across my pec, his hot breath tickling my nipple as he rubbed up against my side. "And then we just…"

"*Oh,*" I shuddered.

Before I could think, I had him on his back, and his pants around his ankles.

"Fuck," he gasped out, his cock slapping against his belly, wet and pink and pretty. Now that I knew he'd been cut intentionally, his cock was even more foreign looking. But not in a bad way. In fact, I kinda wanted to suck on it, to roll my tongue around and feel the velvety slick of it all over again.

But I had better ideas.

"So you want to do it?" Jeffrey offered, eyes black with lust. He spread his legs, his lovely sac pulled tight, the sweaty crease between his cheeks peeking at me. His hole was my favorite place in the world. My favorite place to lick, and sniff, and slip inside. But today…I kept my gaze on his cock.

Mostly.

"I can do it better than the man on screen," I promised, shoving my shorts down and crawling between his legs. "You will never have to watch the porn again."

"'The porn was *illuminating*," Jeffrey teased, a sprinkle of amusement flickering in the overall overwhelming cloud of lust he exuded. "You should be *thanking* it. We're about to benefit greatly from it."

"The only dick I want you looking at is *mine*."

"Y-yeah," Jeffrey sucked in a breath. "That macho bullshit should not be hot. But it totally is." He licked his lips and his cock bobbed again, angry and throbbing, needy as he was. I growled. "Okay, buddy. But what about… I mean—I need like…*ideas?* Right. This is my first time dating a dude." He shivered. "I want to get it right."

It wasn't fair. That he was so damn cute, spread out, creamy speckled muscles glistening, with his hard cock on display.

"Fine," I conceded, dipping down, my teeth gnawing at one of his perky nipples the way he liked. He gasped. "For research…that's okay. So long as I get to benefit."

"C-cool," Jeffrey groaned. "Fuck that's hot. Tell me more about how I'm not allowed to look at other peo—oh fuck." Jeffrey's hips snapped up as I took him in my mouth. I willed my fangs to stay back, my tongue sliding along the slippery surface of his crown, rubbing it curiously—like it was my first time doing so even though it wasn't.

When I pulled off a slick little trail of spit connected my tongue to his dick. Jeffrey stared at it, lips parted, his sweet little tongue showing, his eyes nearly crossed. "Fucking fuck," he whispered, trembling. "Okay."

And then he was shoving at my shoulders and body, and crawling up onto his knees and into my space. The bed rocked and squeaked, and the second our cocks bumped, we both released a mutual gasp.

"Fuck," I groaned, forehead dropping to his shoulder.

"*Fuck*," Jeffrey agreed, nuzzling against my cheek till I tipped my head up and our gazes met. His eyes were black with lust, pale lashes fluttering. "I've never—I mean. I might suck at this."

"You will be perfect."

"Yeah okay, but I might mess it up."

"It will still be perfect."

"*Okay*." Jeffrey relaxed, melting as he tilted his head down to stare at us. I looked too—because it was impossible not to. His cock was shorter than mine, leaner too, freckle coated and pink. In comparison, mine was nearly purple by contrast, the difference in our skin tones absolutely fucking gorgeous. I reached down, running a single, solitary clawed finger up the length of his dick. It flexed and I groaned, my knot throbbing.

I wanted to fuck him *so badly.*

To shove him onto his belly and push inside him.

But I didn't—I didn't—

Because this was equally fascinating.

"I need to..." Jeffrey shuffled back a little, until the tips of our cocks aligned. "There. I think. I mean, in the video he made it look all...easy." He sucked in a breath, still staring at us, the heat in his eyes evident. "Can't believe I never realized I like dicks," he added, voice hoarse. "I mean...*that* is a dick." Jeffrey jerked his head to indicate my cock.

"Of course it is a dick."

"I just mean...it's..." he licked his lips, reaching out to mirror my movements, his fingers dancing up the length, toying with the stretchy foreskin at the tip. My cock flexed. "It's a *dick*. You know? All thick and... veiny and shit. And you have a knot—which is like...even dickier than a dick. And I fucking love it. I want that thing in me—like, in every hole it possibly can go."

My knot throbbed again, and I groaned, already panting after him.

"Jeffrey," my voice dropped low. "I want to play your games today—"

"Yeah?"

"Yes. But I..." My wolf clawed beneath the surface of my skin, and a fresh rush of precum flooded my foreskin, wetting it. "I *need*—please. I can't. No more waiting. I need it—" My chest heaved, my dick jerking. "I need you."

"Okay. *Okay.*" Jeffrey nodded jerkily, even more arousal flooding the room as he bit his lip and those long dexterous fingers fit around the girth of my cock. He slid them up, using his other hand to keep our tips aligned as he gently began to slide my foreskin where he wanted it. "It should stretch—I mean—*right?*"

I grunted, not sure why he was asking me when I didn't know any better than he did.

Every thought in my head fled the second our tips began to kiss. My fangs popped and my tail formed, wagging hard enough it disrupted the blankets we knelt on top of. So slick. So warm. Fuck, fuck, fuck. His tip rubbed mine.

"There—that's...just." Jeffrey lost his grip on my foreskin, swearing softly as it retracted.

I whined, and his gaze snapped from our cocks to my face, contrite.

"Sorry, big guy, I just—just let me try again, please?" He looked fucked out already and we'd barely touched. "*Please?*"

"Okay," I managed, voice husky.

And then he was gripping my cock again, more sure this time. Slowly, carefully he slid my foreskin forward, centimeter by centimeter. It hurt a little—the sensation foreign, but that quickly faded. And as the skin wrapped around the silky velvet of his tip, sliding snug, I just…

"F-fuck," my voice broke, head falling back as my eyes squeezed shut.

He was *inside* me.

That long, lovely cock was inside me.

I grit my fangs, claws biting into my palms in an effort to keep still.

"Shit," Jeffrey gasped, voice just as hoarse as mine. Suddenly desperate to see his face, I jerked my head back down, staring at him, enraptured. Staring at his black eyes, the bitten raw flush to his lips. The way he looked shaky and lost and overwhelmed. The way his lips were parted in awe, entranced as he stared down at—

Oh fuck.

Fuck, fuck, fuck.

If feeling his cock inside mine was overwhelming, looking at it was mind-boggling. It looked so wrong in the rightest way. The dusky dark of my foreskin pulled taut over the tip of his cock, held snug by his fingers. I groaned, more precum slipping free, my knot throbbing.

Unable to help myself, I reached down, rubbing my thumb over where we were connected, desperate to feel it from the outside.

"You feel so good," Jeffrey gasped out. "So warm…and tight—and I—"

I knocked his hand out of the way, taking over immediately. I started gentle, unsure if I'd accidentally hurt either of us by moving too quickly. Squeezing, rubbing, running my palm across our joined flesh, I made sure not to nick either of us with my claws.

All the while, Jeffrey stared—though his hands found my biceps, fingers biting deep as he whined and leaked inside our shared sheath.

"I'm not gonna—not gonna last—" he gasped out. "That is just fucking–woah."

My chest heaved, nostrils flaring as I rubbed and stroked, and squeezed.

"Squeeze my knot," I gasped out, voice low and gravelly. "Please—I need—"

Jeffrey's fingers curled tight around my knot, pinching it just the way I liked. His hand was hot and strong, his calluses scratching just right. My eyes rolled back and I grunted, balls drawing up. The velvety slick of his tip kissing mine made me spin. Faster, faster, I moved—until—

"Uhhhhh," Jeffrey spilled between us, his hips jerking, cum flooding and slipping free. I followed after, gently pulling my cock free, our mixed cum slicking the loose skin.

"Fuck," I hissed out, hips jerking in his fist where he still dutifully wrapped his hand around my knot. Part of the mess spilled onto the bed—and the rest I gathered onto my fingers. Jeffrey didn't even need to be asked.

When I offered them to him, he leaned forward, a dazed, foggy look in his eyes as he groaned, tongue already sticking out. Slick, wet, warm, he lapped at my palm and fingers, sliding his slippery tongue between the pads of my fingers, and up, chasing every last bit of our shared essence like he needed it.

I trained him well.

I licked him clean. Licked inside his mouth. Licked behind his ears, down his throat. Licked the sweat from the coarse hair in his armpits.

Licked across his nipples, into his belly button, across the divots of his hips. Licked the curls at the base of his cock till they lay flat. Pressed his softening cock flat to his stomach, and then lapped around the root, then his balls, then under them, and into the secret soft skin there.

I licked every drop of sweat from his skin, enjoying him the way he was meant to be enjoyed. Licked every one of his scars.

And then I flipped him over and did the same to his other side.

After I'd lapped at his ass for a while, then up the line of his spine to the back of his neck, Jeffrey huffed out an amused, aroused grunt.

"Mutt—?" His voice was low and fuzzy. He was relaxed. I could tell because all he did was twitch when I reached down and gave his hole a little rub, just because I missed the way it felt.

"Mmm?" I nuzzled behind his ears, then into his hair, enjoying the fuzzy prickles. It was longer now than it had been when we'd cut it. His stitches had healed. His bruises were gone. My hard cock flexed against his ass cheeks, slotted between them as I gave him an aborted thrust.

I didn't want to fuck again—content to groom and love him—but that didn't mean I wasn't going to enjoy pushing against him.

"Why won't you fuck me?" Jeffrey's voice was sleepy soft.

I stiffened.

"I mean…we've done pretty much everything else," he added, voice low. He twisted a little so I could see one of his dark, pretty eyes. "So what…gives?"

I licked my lips, suddenly caught out.

I should've expected this.

Really, I'd been naive not to.

"I…" I didn't know what to say.

"Is it because I haven't asked you out?" Jeffrey asked, voice soft. "Like, on an official date."

I nodded jerkily, but then immediately felt awful for lying.

"Oh, cool." His smile was sunny—none of his usual tension was present. He was sweet. And his scent was fizzy-happy. "I thought it might be something like that—I just...I guess I got worried, you know? That maybe you didn't...want to?"

"I want to." I promised immediately because that was true. "It's all I've thought about since the day I saw you."

Jeffrey laughed, his body quivering as his eyes crinkled. "Okay. So it's just...like, a formal thing then? For wolves."

I could keep lying.

He was making it easy.

But my own words came to bite me in the ass. I was already lying to him about being his dog. I was withholding the truth about him being my fated mate. And I just...I...I just knew he deserved better.

"I don't want to hurt you," I admitted, voice cracking. Jeffrey frowned, some of the buzzy light in his eyes dimming. I nuzzled the back of his neck, curled my arms around him, and squeezed him from behind like he was a large, delicious teddy bear. "I'm terrified."

"Why would you hurt me?" Jeffrey asked, voice muffled against the covers now that I'd smashed him into them again. "Does your knot hurt or something?"

"No. I mean—I don't think so." Fuck. I had no idea. "It's not that."

"Then what is it?" Jeffrey was still soft. Warm. Sated. He smelled like home. Like mate-mate-mate. "C'mon, sweetheart." Jeffrey's voice was gentle. I got the feeling he didn't often use that word. In fact, it sounded foreign, almost like he'd never used it at all. At least…not like this. To soothe someone he cared about, soft and safe in his bed. "You can tell me. I tell you shit—like…*so much shit.*"

It was true, he did.

I was pretty sure I knew most of his secrets by this point.

And I had been pretty tight-lipped.

And that wasn't fair.

But I was still terrified. Terrified we'd cross a line—and I just.

"I want to be a happy memory," my voice broke. "When I'm gone. I just…I want you to think of me and smile."

"I will," Jeffrey's voice was just as rough as mine. "Of course I will. And you're not going anywhere. Not if I can help it."

"I've taken so much from you, already," my heart hurt. My eyes burned. Jeffrey's fuzzy hair tickled my nose as I buried my face in his nape and inhaled greedily. "It's selfish."

"No, it's not." Jeffrey reached back, hand floppy and lax still, fingers curling around the back of my head to hold me still. "If I hadn't wanted it, sure. But I did. I have. I *do*. I've wanted you from the moment I saw you too."

That wasn't true.

It wasn't.

Because the first time he'd seen me hadn't been at the club in Ridgefield. Hadn't been when I tasted him for the first time and realized I could never go back. Hadn't been when I'd saved him from the man that smelled like a public restroom.

No.

It had been *way* earlier.

I didn't call him out though, because that meant betraying my secret—

and I just…I felt like this was more important. One step at a time.

"It will hurt more," I murmured, annoyed when my body began to shake. My eyes burned hotter, wetter. A few tears slipped free and I was too terrified to bring attention to them to swipe them away. *Hopefully he won't notice.* "When I'm gone. If we cross that step."

"You keep saying 'when, when, when.'" Jeffrey huffed, annoyance creeping into his tone. But…I could smell his fear. I could hear the skip of his heart beat. And I knew he was scared. As scared as I was. "I'll fix it," Jeffrey promised again, even though it wasn't in his power to do so.

"I know," I murmured, because I knew he believed that. And I believed in him. I just…knew more about this than he did. And I hadn't been entirely honest—and I'd dug this awful, horrible hole for myself to lie in. "I trust you."

"You know…" Jeffrey sucked in a breath. "We don't have to fuck if you don't want to."

"I want to," I blurted immediately, because apparently I hadn't been enthusiastic enough the first time. Jeffrey laughed.

"And *I* want to," he said softly. "So if you trust me…can't you trust me to be able to consent? Can't you trust that I know what I want? That at the end of the day—if the worst possible shit happens, I'll be happier having had you in every way I could."

"But—"

"Believe me…I know hurt. I've *been* hurt. And this isn't that."

"Oh." I melted, sniffing a little, then annoyed that I'd betrayed myself. Jeffrey petted his hand through my hair, rubbing behind my ears and making me sigh. "So you…"

"Yeah, man. I wanna go through all the bases with you."

"Okay." My cock jerked, like it had been eavesdropping on the whole conversation. Jeffrey snorted out a laugh, arching his back and rubbing against me with a sleepy hum. I had less than two weeks left with him. And he didn't know that—but I did.

I just…I'd accused myself of being selfish, and I still felt that way.

Because I was hiding the truth from everyone.

Maybe it was the alpha in me, desperate to protect the people I cared about till the day I couldn't anymore. Or maybe I was simply a coward. Too terrified to lose what I had earlier than I had to.

Selfish, cowardly, weak.

I wasn't like Jeffrey at all.

But I was going to make the best of the time we had together anyway.

Because I loved him.

I loved him so fucking much I could hardly breathe when he was around. Loved him more than I knew I was capable of loving. And that love only grew when Jeffrey spoke again and asked me a question that lit me up from the inside out.

Made me forget all about my fate.

"So…" Jeffrey blinked his lovely eye up at me again. "Can I take you on a date?"

Chapter Twenty-Seven

Jeffrey

I WAS NERVOUS.

That was the honest to God truth.

This wasn't my first date by any means, but it was the first date that really mattered. Especially because I'd already decided by the end of tonight I was going to lay everything on the line.

Blair, Richard, Collin, and even Avery had banded together to help me prepare for tonight. While Avery was off in the woods prepping his side of things, Blair and Richard were in the kitchen cooking.

"The meatballs need to be bigger," Blair coached from the sidelines, because he knew jack shit about cooking but was apparently an expert anyway.

"That's what she said," Collin hollered from out in the back of the shop where he was helping move the chairs out of the way.

"Are you sure these are gonna be fine outside for a few hours?" I yelled loud enough that Blair could hear through the open door.

"I already said yes. Shut the fuck up," Blair shouted back. I didn't question him again as Collin and I hauled everything out the back door and stacked them in neat piles.

"Tell me why we're uprooting the whole restaurant?" Collin squinted at me, sweat beaded on his temple, his auburn hair damp.

"It's more accurate."

"It would be more accurate if you were eating in an alley," Collin huffed.

"Yeah, but this is Elmwood." I dropped my pile of chairs, then carefully, systematically began stacking them to the side. "I don't wanna get rained on when I'm in the middle of wooing my man."

Wow. That was weird as fuck.

"That was weird as fuck," Collin echoed my thoughts. "Wooing my man? Lame."

"What else would you call it?"

"I dunno." Collin shrugged. "Something less…cringey?"

"Oh, fuck off." I flipped him off and he snorted, but dutifully followed me inside to grab more chairs.

"Leave that one—" I instructed him, gesturing toward the little table and chair set I'd pushed in the corner. Collin had been reaching for it, his grubby fingers ready to sabotage my plans unknowingly.

"Why that one specifically?"

"Because." I couldn't explain it. I just…liked that one. It had a little chip in the wood on the corner and it was cute. Mutt would like it too.

"Fine." Collin grabbed a different table and waddled his way down the long hallway that led out back to the parking lot again. "You know what's dumb?" He panted as I followed after him, arms equally full.

"What?"

"The fact that you're worried about rain and yet you're putting all this furniture out here."

I shrugged. "I asked and Blair told me to—"

"Shut up, I know." Collin snorted, hands on his hips. Then he shrugged. "Oh well." He twisted around to grin at me. His eyebrows raised and his lips curled into a smirk—and I knew before he opened his mouth he was about to say something dirty—or ask me about knots or some shit.

So I just turned back around and walked inside again.

Four hours later, Richard had perfected his special sauce. Ew, fuck. I did *not* mean to say that. Gross. Blair had approved the meatballs. Fuck, that was even worse. And all three of us had set up the dining area perfectly to plan.

Now I just needed to get ready.

And then Mutt was going to show up—

And it was going to be…yeah.

It was going to be real fucking good.

I crossed the street to Avery's shop and climbed the steps to his apartment above it, feeling giddy and nervous—but excited all the same. He'd given me a key and told me to make myself at home. I could've gone home to get ready, but I figured this was easier.

I…miscalculated.

Because when I pushed into Avery's apartment I was immediately assaulted with the most terrifying mess I had ever encountered. If I'd thought his office was bad, this was—no. Nope. Shit. But I was running out of time, so I braved it anyway.

A black cat skittered across the floor, leaping toward the door the second I stepped through it. I slammed it shut quickly, because today was not the fucking day to end up hunting one of his familiars down because they were escape artists.

"No way," I wagged a finger at her. "Nice try."

And then Gregory—the serial shitter—struck again.

Except his victim was me this time.

Karma…is a *bitch*.

I barely had time to clean myself up and get into my clothes. The bird shit had been a nightmare I had not been prepared for. I vowed to myself to never enter Avery's apartment again—not even if I was fucking dying. I'd rather choke on my own lung juice than trip over another pile of books and fall face first into week-old pasta take-out.

Again.

Freshly showered—at least Avery had better water pressure than I did— and dressed in a spiffy black t-shirt, my nicest blue jeans, and red Converse, I scurried down the steps and across the street to Blair's restaurant.

Blair opened the door for me and the second I saw him, I burst out laughing.

"Shut up."

"Fuck—"

"*You* did this."

"Oh my god." I bent over, snorting out my laughter as I stared at his spiffy little chef outfit.

"I hate you." Blair shoved at my shoulder and I shoved back—heart light for the first time in…forever.

"This is my new favorite look on you," I told him, plucking at his chef hat with a giggle.

"Fuck you so very much." Blair flipped me off. With both hands. Then stomped off into the kitchen.

Ten seconds later, Richard popped his head out of the back—wearing an identical chef outfit, his eyes dancing. "Ready?" he asked, because he was a sweetheart.

"So fucking ready."

"Me too." Collin slid out of the bathroom, tugging on his little bow tie, his grin wicked. He had on a pink collared shirt, a teal vest, and a white apron.

My evil plan had all come together swimmingly.

Not that it was very evil to impress the man you love—but still.

"Okay," I sucked in a breath, standing up taller. For a second...I regretted my life choices. Because I wasn't sure if this was too cheesy—or weird—or like...obscure. I wasn't sure if Mutt would get it.

I shouldn't have worried.

Mutt arrived right on time, appearing at the front door with a polite knock. I hadn't expected the knock—usually he just kinda...invaded spaces. But today I guess he was on his best behavior. It was glass so I could see him through it.

And for a second I just...stared.

Because he was dressed in a suit.

A suit.

And he looked...

Fuck.

He looked so fucking good.

The black fabric clung to his body, showing off the swell of his biceps almost obscenely. The button-up he wore beneath the fitted suit jacket was practically popping in an attempt to cling to his muscle. Slick black fabric clung to his thick thighs, and rather than wear a tie, his shirt was gaping open, his chest peeking through the gap.

"Oh my fuck," I shuddered, mouth suddenly dry.

"Woah," Collin blinked beside me, staring out at Mutt with heart eyes. "Super hot," he mouthed, amazed.

"Stop that. Right fucking now." I jabbed him with my elbow and he laughed, hopping out of the way. "Get your prepubescent ass back to work."

"Aye, aye captain Jerk-frey," he huffed, giving me a playful salute. "I'll go wait in the back."

"You do that."

"While you…" Collin waggled his eyebrows. "Enjoy all that…wow. All that—"

"Shut uuuuup." *God, please give me patience. Amen.*

"Shutting up!" Collin spun around and then with a little heel click, skipped off into the back where Blair and Richard lay waiting.

I jerked the front door open, all finesse completely fucking missing.

"You look—"

"You look—" Mutt's voice was low and rough.

"Underdressed?" I offered, shivering as his sapphire gaze dragged down my body greedily.

"What do you mean?" His hands found my hips, and he yanked me against him, face pressing to the side of my throat. His hot breath huffed over my skin as he inhaled greedily, groaning like I was a joint and he was taking a hit of me.

"Just that you…fuck. You look like sex on a stick." Damn, that sniffing thing was distracting.

"I don't know what that means."

"It means you're *sexy*," I said softly, head tipped back obediently so he had room to work. "And I'm surprised you're wearing…this." I plucked at his collar and he pulled back and grinned down at me, all sunny confidence.

"You like it?"

"Yeah. I mean—fuck. I did not expect this. I didn't even think you knew what a suit was."

"Jules said if I am to woo you I need one," Mutt declared proudly.

Apparently I wasn't the only one trying to do the wooing around here. I bit back a grin, then decided that was stupid, and grinned wide. "Yeah?" Jules was his bookish brother. He'd told me about him, just like he'd given me a rundown of all his other brothers.

Theo was the gentle one. The vet. The one that had sent me away when I'd gone looking for Mutt.

Butters was the sweet one. He'd helped Mutt make my gift basket.

Harry was the careful one. Which I knew from personal experience.

And Jules was the pretty one. The one who loved humans so much he never stopped reading about them.

"What else did he teach you?" I asked, pressing into him, the warmth of his body bleeding into mine. He always ran like a zillion degrees, and even in a suit I could feel the heat of his skin.

"He said to bring you flowers."

"You already do that."

"I know," Mutt smiled, nuzzling my cheek. "But I brought you more anyway."

"Where are—oh." I glanced at our feet and snorted out a laugh when I saw the red bouquet of roses that sat scattered on the floor. I hadn't even noticed him carrying them. Or when he'd dropped them to hold me.

Priorities.

"You smell nervous," Mutt hummed, ducking right back down again to get back to work. I shivered, tipping into the flutter of kisses and licks that he settled along the length of my neck.

"I am," I admitted, shivering. "I have a surprise for you—and I'm not sure if you'll like it."

"If you planned it I will."

"Softie," I slapped his chest playfully, then decided that was enough snuggling for now and peeled myself free. Only Mutt apparently was not done. Because he reeled me right back in, his face buried in my hair.

The next full moon was only a week away, and he'd been more and more clingy lately. I didn't mind. Hell, if I was being honest I kinda loved it. He always touched me, possessive, and all encompassing. Clinging to me, pressing me into things, crowding on top of me like I was the comfiest place in the whole world.

We snuggled in the doorway for five minutes until Collin poked his head out of the hallway to check on us.

"You done?" He called, obviously trying to hide his outfit so he wouldn't spoil the surprise.

"Fuck." I flipped him off for the second time that day and laughed. Collin disappeared, but I decided he was right. It was time to get serious. Let the wooing commence. "C'mon, big guy. Let's get you some grub."

I jerked Mutt toward the center of the room, heart in my throat.

"What is a grub?" Mutt asked eagerly, twisting to admire the room with wide, blue eyes.

I shifted to the side so he could see better, waiting half-terrified to see if he understood what I'd done.

"It's a dumb word for food."

"Oh!"

A single round table sat in the center of the room covered in a checkered tablecloth. Two chairs sat beside it. A green bottle with a dripping candle rested in the center of the table beside a vase full of breadsticks. The buttery garlicky scent filled the room as I waited—and waited, heart skittering.

Does he get it?

My palms were sweaty.

And Mutt just kept staring.

There was a frown on his face, his brow flickering as he stared at the table like he recognized it but wasn't entirely sure what was going on. So I hurried forward and pulled his chair out for him. He smiled at me, still confused. Then he moved to the other chair and sat down with a happy hum. He picked at his collar like it was itching him, and then his sleeves, staring at the candle with fascination.

"Do you…get it?" I asked, laughing a little as I slid into the chair I'd pulled out for him. Of course he didn't know about that—chivalry or whatever. He wasn't a chick.

Oh fuck.

Had I gotten this wrong?

Why wasn't he talking?

Collin had obviously been watching us, because he appeared a few seconds later before Mutt could even reply. Except he was a shit. A total fucking shit—because he had a mustache on. And that had not been an approved part of his costume.

"Now tell me what's your pleasure," Collin said in the most horrific Italian accent I had ever heard in all my life.

"Collin—" I said warningly, horrified.

"Ala carte—"

"*Collinnnnn.*" This wasn't part of the plan. He was just supposed to dress the part. Not act it! It was supposed to be the right amount of cheesy, not full-blown embarrassing.

"Oh." Mutt said. I twisted to look at him. His eyes were wide and full of wonder, his mouth dropped open as he stared at Collin, then me, then the table, then Collin again. "*Oh.*"

He gets it.

He gets it!

I stared at Collin too—realizing suddenly that he'd been helping me out, rather than fucking with me. I could kiss him, I loved him so much right then.

"You!" Mutt gripped the table tight enough it creaked. He was practically vibrating in excitement. There was an awful tearing sound and then I heard the steady *thump, thump* of his tail—and I knew...fuck.

I knew I'd done good.

"I?" I grinned, wiggling back excitedly.

"You did not!" Mutt declared, slapping the table, his hair spiking up all over as a blinding smile broke across his face.

"I did!" I grinned back. And then because I could, I leaned across the table and tasted his smile. Careful of the candle, I couldn't really make out with him—so I pulled back, way too soon, and took my seat again.

"Ew," Collin said, grinning at the both of us. And then he placed a menu on the table just like the man in *Lady and the Tramp* had—it'd taken me for-fucking-ever to make that shit—and gestured at it. "Pick what you want—but don't actually," he dropped the accent as quickly as he'd picked it up, making it even more obvious that he'd only adopted it to help me in the first place. "Because you're eating spaghetti and meatballs."

I laughed, unable to help myself, covering my mouth as I stared at Mutt and his giddy excitement. He fingered the menu with his big, tan hands, sniffing it curiously, then beaming at me the second he seemed to realize I'd made it by hand.

"I'll be back in a minute," Collin saluted me, then Mutt, then headed back down the hallway.

"He is your brother," Mutt declared.

"He is," I agreed, and claiming him came easy. "The little one I told you about. He's a shit."

"I have many shits for brothers," Mutt smiled, eyes crinkling.

"Seems like it's a requirement."

He nodded, still vibrating happily. *Thump, thump, thump* went his tail. "You did this for me," he said, and my head jerked, my cheeks hot. "Because I told you I loved the movie with the dogs who kiss."

"Yeah!" I wiggled happily, so fucking glad that I'd gotten this right. "You like it?"

"Like it?!" Mutt slapped the table, and the candle rattled. "I love it!"

"Really?"

"Really!" He beamed at me, and I beamed right back. His tail kept thumping, and I was half-tempted to ditch my chair entirely and join him in his. But…I wasn't so sure Blair's tiny dinky chairs could handle our combined weight. I wished I had a tail, so I could wag back and he'd know just how fucking happy he made me.

When Collin returned with the food my stomach gurgled.

He sat the massive plate of spaghetti between us, piled high with meatballs and red sauce. Mutt licked his lips, staring at it eagerly, his eyes bright. He plucked at his collar again, tugging at it subconsciously, like he didn't even notice he was doing it.

As sexy as he looked, he looked uncomfortable too.

We dug in. Mutt even tried to use a fork—which was fucking adorable honestly. He was very careful. Jabbing the meatballs like they were bombs about to go off, and someone had taken great pains to teach him. And every time he took a bite, he glanced down at his button-up, as if terrified he'd spilled on it.

"Hey," I said, reaching across the table to close my hand over his. He was still gripping the table, his claws having popped free in his excitement. "Why don't you take that off?"

"Take it off?" He blinked, frowning down at his suit. "You do not like it?"

"Nah, I love it," I said, my heart thumping. "But you'll be more comfortable without it."

Mutt didn't argue. Which was a testament to how uncomfortable he'd been. I had no doubt he would've stayed clothed the entire date unless I'd said something, so I was more than a little glad that I had.

He peeled the suit jacket off like it was full of ants. And then struggled with his buttons.

"Here," I got out of my seat, crossing the distance between us and helping him with the buttons so he wouldn't accidentally rip them. When his shirt hung loose and open, I couldn't help but cop a feel, my hand sliding over one of his pecs and giving it a squeeze. He laughed, like the touch was ticklish.

His eyes were bright.

"I love you," he said simply, like it was a fact and not a declaration.

I nearly stumbled. My head jerked up, and Mutt's eyes were warm. So fucking warm.

They said, *it's true.*

They said, *don't be scared of me.*

They said, *I've waited every day since I met you to tell you that I love you.*

I didn't say it back.

I didn't know how.

The words just got stuck—but he seemed to know anyway. Because he kissed me soft and sweet, and stripped out of the rest of his clothes with the enthusiasm of a man who fucking hated wearing them.

Dressed in only boxers, he climbed back into his seat. Then he dug in with gusto and I did too—far more comfortable than we'd been before.

I love you.

I love you.

I love you.

Collin did a double take when he walked back into the room and Mutt was practically naked. Which was fair. I hadn't exactly thought that part through. The music that was playing overhead—some sort of ballad or instrumental—switched to something more upbeat.

Something more…Swiftie.

"Oh shit, this is my jam," I laughed, grinning at Collin and then Mutt. Collin blinked, like he was surprised to see me so happy—and I guess… that was fair. Mutt just…brought out the best in me. Made me feel like nothing could go wrong. Made me feel whole, like my scars were beautiful, and my past was just that—the past.

"T-Swizzle, our lord and savior," Collin echoed, refilling our breadsticks and water glasses with the skills he'd picked up while working at Benji's diner.

"The love of my life," I agreed.

Mutt growled. He glared at me, then Collin. "Who is this *Swizzle?*" His eyes narrowed. "I will fight him."

"Taylor's a girl," Blair corrected him, popping his head into the room for the first time that night. He and Richard had been biding their time in the back, playing chef. The second Mutt saw their outfits he cackled, smacking the table in delight.

And then he sobered.

"I do not care if she is a girl," he said sagely. "I will still fight her."

"She's just a singer, big guy," I promised with a snort, reaching out to smooth a hand over his hand. "Not competition."

Mutt relaxed. "Good. I did not think so. But…" His face scrunched up. "There are many I want to fight for you. I am making a list." The idea of Mutt hunting down every person who'd ever flirted with me quickly became too much.

I laughed.

And I couldn't stop.

And it hurt—so good—I could hardly breathe. Mutt stared at me in wonder, like my laugh was the most amazing thing he'd fucking heard. And then he joined in, laughing just as loudly as me, pretending to get the joke because he was a solid dude, despite being obviously confused still.

"Ha Ha! Yes. Taylor." He smacked the table and I snorted into my elbow, shaking with mirth. "The singer!"

When I glanced up, Richard, Blair, and Collin were all staring at me like I'd grown a second head. Blair's expression in particular was odd. His eyes were wet, and his lips were twisted into a smile that looked fond and sad at the same time. Like he was seeing me for the first time.

"Hi," he said, offering Mutt his hand, a warm smile spreading across his face. "It's so great to finally meet you. I'm Jeffrey's brother."

"Greetings," Mutt smacked his hand into Blair's and gave it a violent shake. Which was just—so fucking cute, I started laughing again.

"We're just gonna…" Blair jerked his head back toward the kitchen, "Holler if you need anything."

"Sure—" I grinned at him, and gave him a covert thumbs up. He glanced at it, then me, and his smile softened even more. He returned my thumbs up with one of his own.

And then he yanked Collin and Richard back with him, and Mutt and I were alone again.

"Did you know your brothers are fucking?" Mutt asked me the second they were no longer in the room. He looked concerned, and I could not fucking stop laughing.

"Oh my—fuck." I snorted. "They're—I mean. It's complicated? They're not related and I—you know what. It's a long story."

"I like long stories."

And so I told him.

I managed to get a spaghetti moment with him, with the damn meatball, and didn't even care that I got sauce smeared on my nose to do it.

As far as dates went it was pretty fucking perfect.

The most perfect.

The happiest night of my life.

Which was why, of course, I had to immediately go and ruin it with the second half of the date.

Because I was a glutton for punishment apparently.

Why am I like this?

Chapter Twenty-Eight

Mutt

JEFFREY WAS QUIET as we made our way into the woods. He'd borrowed his tiny brother's car—as his truck was in the shop again. It was difficult to squash inside the vehicle, but I managed, still half-naked, my suit laid across the back seat.

The car stank like cat, and I huffed, sniffing at the fabric with a frown the second I'd climbed inside.

"Sorry about the mess—I didn't have time to clean this." I blinked around the vehicle, frowning because I could not see a mess. "The hair," Jeffrey explained. "I figured it would bug you—you know, with your super nose."

"It is alright," I told him with a sunny grin. Jeffrey grinned back, and then we were off.

It hadn't taken long to get to this spot in the woods, though we had to go down a back road. A road I knew for a fact would end—because the woods at the end of it were right on the edge of the Elmwood pack lands. I found it a little odd that we'd traveled here, but figured Jeffrey had more surprises for me, so I wasn't going to complain.

The first surprise had been…

I didn't have words.

It had been thoughtful and sweet and romantic—the way Jules had tried to coach me to be. I wasn't sure I'd managed, but Jeffrey certainly had. And that laugh…god. The laugh he'd let loose would haunt my memories for the rest of my time.

I'd replay that memory during my last moments, and it would give me comfort.

We hiked through the woods on a skinny little path that looked abandoned. Though Elmwood was full of trees just like home was, it still felt off. Wrong and right at the same time. It didn't take long to reach our destination, and when we did, I frowned, confused.

Because in front of me was a clearing.

With a treehouse—recently rebuilt.

"This place used to be my sanctuary," Jeffrey admitted, stepping to the side so I could stare. I could taste death in the air—something old and lurking—more spiritual than it was physical. With a frown, I twisted to look at him. "It's also where Lydia found me."

He cracked himself open, his ribs split wide, his heart in my hand.

He told me about the sun. The way it had shined above on the day he'd been taken. Told me about the months leading up to that day— the gifts, the affection, the lies. Told me about the pretty promises, the compliments. The seeds of doubt planted in his young mind.

And then he told me about what had happened after. The people that had died. The people that he had blamed himself for.

About Lydia and her training.

Slowly, all the pieces that made up Jeffrey Prince fell into place. The tall grass hugged my legs as we moved deeper into the meadow, the barren trees hanging dry and high in the sky. The sun was beginning to sink low, but Jeffrey didn't seem bothered.

"I'm not…" Jeffrey sucked in a breath. "I'm not weak," he said softly, like he was trying to convince himself more than me.

"You're not," I agreed, because it was true.

"It took me a long time to realize that," he admitted. And then he tangled our fingers together and tugged me toward the targets that were set up near the tree. "Just…I mean. I think part of you is worried I won't be able to help you—and I just thought…"

There was a table beside the targets, covered in weapons. I stared at them, confused. Nothing was silver—and I could only assume that was on purpose. Because every weapon on that table was well-worn and obviously used. Some were more blood-stained than others.

Jeffrey released my hand—too fast—and reached for a bow and quiver of arrows. "Come back with me," he said, jerking his head toward where we'd come. "I'll show you what I'm capable of. Why you should trust me. That I can keep you safe too."

I followed dutifully, still not sure what was happening.

But…my confusion quickly melted away.

Because as soon as Jeffrey had me a safe distance away from both him and the targets, he let loose. Arrow after arrow. Target after target. Each arrow hit its mark strategically, effortlessly. His body was coiled to strike, graceful as a panther, the brutality of each precise movement making my head spin.

Jeffrey gestured for me to wait, then headed for the table again.

This time he came back with a handful of knives.

I stared, horrified and enraptured as he let those loose as well.

Bullseye after bullseye.

Knife after knife.

And then he grabbed a gun, and let loose much the same way.

And then a crossbow.

And then an ax.

I only recognized half the weapons he used because they were standard hunting equipment. Because we'd grown up being fed nightmarish stories of the hunters that existed out there—just waiting for the moment we became feral.

Some hunters waited their entire lives to kill an alpha.

They saw it as a game.

An achievement.

When Jeffrey finished, he was sweaty and flushed. His skin glistened, and his fuzzy orange hair was damp. He set his weapons down and turned to look at me again, eyes somber.

"You officially know more about me than anyone else," he said softly, nervously reaching into his pocket to fiddle with the guitar pick he kept there. "I know it's *a lot*—and probably scary—but I promise I would never hurt you." Obviously Harry's words had snuck inside his head.

I broke then.

I'd stayed still the entire time he'd been demonstrating, flinching as each target was struck, because the sound of the weapons making impact rattled around inside my head. Reminded me of what I was about to experience. Of the decision I'd made.

Of the hunters who would find glee in my death.

I know what he wants. He wants me to trust him. To believe in him.

To believe that he is capable of finding a solution for us.

Jeffrey's eyes searched mine. I wasn't sure what he saw there, but it probably wasn't good. He wilted, his hands clenched into fists as he glared to the side. "I…" he sucked in a breath. "I *wouldn't* hurt you," he repeated, voice hoarse. "I swear. I never did any of this shit because I liked it. She… she made me. I know I had a choice. That I could've said no. But I—"

I had asked Jeffrey once, who had hurt him. And while Lydia had done a lot of damage, it had become increasingly clear over the last few months that the person who hurt him most was himself.

"No," I disagreed. "You didn't."

"I had a choice." Jeffrey wavered.

"What kind of choice was that?" My words must've struck a chord, because he stopped fiddling with his guitar pick, his entire body frozen. "Lydia does not strike me as the kind of woman who takes no lightly. You did what you had to do. You protected your family. You survived. There was no better choice you could have made."

"I wouldn't hurt you," Jeffrey repeated, like a broken record, trembling as he processed this new information.

"I know." I reached for him, my hands shaking. Desperately, I curled tightly around his body, my face pressed into his hair. He smelled like *home* and I breathed him in, my thoughts going haywire. *"I know."*

"I won't hurt you," he repeated again, still frozen. "I won't—"

"I know, sweet one." I shushed him softly, enjoying the way he sagged into me, though it took him a moment to thaw. This dangerous, wicked man. Covered in scars, and full of secrets. Secrets that I was now privy to. Every last one. "But what if I…"

My head was spinning.

Spinning.

Spinning.

Don't do it.

Don't ask.

My moon mother hadn't risen but even now I could feel the ache of her touch. Feel the wolf threatening to burst beneath my skin. Feel the hungry hollow in my belly, and the way my claws were two seconds from bursting out of my skin.

My last moon.

This would be my last.

"But what if you…?" Jeffrey trailed off, head tipping back to look at me. I cupped his cheek, stroking over it to cover his ear. When I pressed a kiss to his sweet forehead and the wrinkle there, he sighed.

And then I fell to my knees at his feet.

His scent was confused-alarmed-worried, but I spoke anyway. Spoke even though this would be the end for us, and I knew that. But I…I just…I needed him. I needed him so very badly.

Dirt clung to my bare skin, grass tickling my body as I tipped my head up.

It was my turn to be lost.

"But what if I want you to?"

Chapter Twenty-Nine

Mutt

"W-WHAT?" JEFFREY'S VOICE broke.

"Please," I said softly, grabbing his wrists, and pulling them to me so I could press a kiss to each palm. "I need you to."

"I'm not going to hurt you," Jeffrey was shaking, and I hated that it was my fault. "Why are you asking me that? I…I can't. I won't—I—I'm not a monster."

This hadn't been what he wanted.

I knew that.

But I hadn't been able to stop myself.

"I'm not asking you because I think you're a monster." My heart hurt for him. "I'm asking you because I love you." He sucked in a breath. "Because I am sick," I kissed his palm again, my body shaking. "Because I need you to put me out of my misery. Before I do something I can never come back from."

And then something spectacular and horrible happened.

Because for the first time since I'd met him Jeffrey's eyes flooded with tears. His lashes became spiky, salt dripping down his cheeks as he stared at me like I was killing him. I'd never seen him cry like this. I'd seen him shake and twitch, sure, seen him hold himself together.

But I'd never truly seen him crumble apart.

Jeffrey cried then.

He cried and cried and cried.

These great, gasping sobs. Like he'd cracked right down the middle. "No, no, no." He shook his head, trembling all over. "No. You can't—you can't ask me that."

"I'm sorry," I said, because I'd known it was selfish even before the words had escaped. "I'm sorry, sweet one." I pulled him down and into my arms, and he folded immediately, limp as a rag doll.

"No no no no."

"Shhhh, I'm sorry." I cradled him close, kissing his cheeks, and the salt, then his temples and his ears. "Shh, I know. I know. I'm sorry."

"I can't—I can't—"

"I know," I rocked him, heart aching. I knew I shouldn't have asked but I just...fuck.

It was wrong. It was so wrong. But I thought...if Jeffrey was the one to put me down, maybe it wouldn't hurt.

"I would *never* hurt you." Jeffrey sobbed, clinging to me tight. Higher than he ever had before. His grip was bruising, fingers biting into my body. "I'll fix it. I'll fix it. I swear I will. I promised I would. I just need a little more time—I'll fix it."

He couldn't.

He couldn't, but I didn't tell him that.

Because my worst fear had just come true.

I'd hurt him. I'd hurt him and I couldn't go back. I couldn't fix it. I couldn't take it back.

"I'm sorry," I murmured, nuzzling his ear, my own tears spilling into his sweat-damp hair. "I'm sorry."

"I—I—" Jeffrey hiccuped. "Don't make me. *Don't make me.*"

"I know." He was a child in my arms, quaky and scared. Looking to his alpha for guidance. I hated this. Not because I didn't want him to rely on me. But only because I knew this would be the last time he'd get to.

I could feel my wolf even now. Unanchored. Drifting. Tearing at the surface of my skin. The fear that coursed through my veins only made it worse. Soon I'd be unsafe. Soon I'd maim and murder—kill those I cared for the most.

I could kill Jeffrey.

And I'd never even know I did.

I sucked in a breath. "I'm sorry," I murmured again, fluttering kisses on his face, on his nose, down his throat. "I'm sorry." Jeffrey shuddered in my grip.

He cried for a long time.

For long enough the moon rose high and the air grew brutally cold. Half-melted snow crunched beneath our feet as I stood, carrying him in my arms. The trees waved along the path but I paid them no heed, my smile absent as I walked us back to his car before Jeffrey could catch a cold. His breath came out in foggy puffs, and he curled into me, brave even now. Letting me hold him, because he trusted me, even after what I'd just done.

Trusted me even though every person he'd ever trusted had hurt him.

Noble.

Even now.

Even when he was hurting, just as much as I was. I could smell it in the air as easily as I could smell the citrus-bright of his scent.

"I swear I will," Jeffrey promised, face buried in my chest, muffled. "*I'll fix it.*"

"You can't." I hardly recognized my own voice, it was so hoarse. When we got to the car, I pulled the door open and carefully set him down. "I'm sorry."

"Don't apologize to me." Before the door could shut, Jeffrey reached for me, curling his fingers around my wrists and tugging till I filled the gap between him and the woods. Even after he released me, I remained obediently still. Jeffrey's thumbs skimmed my cheekbones, a hot tear dashing down my cheek as I memorized the feel of them. Memorized how long they were. Memorized the brush of his palms and the scratch of the pads of his fingers. "Just…just tell me what's happening? Explain so I can understand why you would ask me something so…so awful."

He was brave.

He was so brave.

So strong.

He would survive this, I knew he would.

And I supposed…the time to protect him from the truth had already passed. There was only forward. There was only the moon and its cruel caress. There were only the handful of days I had left, and I only had one heart. One heart I'd already given him.

I'd trusted him with that.

The least I should do is trust him with the truth.

"I'm going feral," I said, and it was easy. It was easy. Like it wasn't this horrible, awful thing that had stolen my childhood from me. Like it wasn't the end of my life. Like it wasn't a nightmare only alphas had to face, one I'd been fighting for years.

"Feral?" Jeffrey made a sound. His scent was confused, and I sighed, forcing my eyes open to meet his gaze.

"I'm an alpha," I said softly.

"I know."

"How much do you know about wolves?" My hands found his hips, fingers digging in—clawless now that I'd settled. I made sure to keep my tone gentle and sweet as I spoke.

"I dunno. Not much. Lydia taught me some—" Lydia again. I hated her so fucking much. I growled, and Jeffrey laughed, smacking at my chest. The fact he could still laugh made me settle a little. He was strong. So incredibly strong. I'd always thought so. "And I've been researching on my own."

"I have three forms," I started, because it was easiest this way. Rip the Band-Aid off.

"Right," Jeffrey nodded, staring at me, his dark eyes warm and frightened.

"My wolfskin."

"The one you use when you're pretending to be my dog," Jeffrey interrupted.

I blinked, shocked.

"*What?*"

My ears rang.

"Dude, I figured that out months ago," Jeffrey laughed, but then he sobered. "Just…just keep explaining? It doesn't matter. It's water under the bridge. I don't even fucking care."

I didn't know what bridge water had to do with anything, but I didn't ask. "You're not angry?"

"No." Jeffrey shook his head. "Why would I be?"

"I lied."

"You did," he shrugged, his eyes still wet. There were tear streaks on his cheeks, and his skin was splotchy red. He was a mess. A complete mess. And he'd never been prettier. I wrestled his keys from his pocket, repeating the motion I'd seen him do a dozen times, before shoving them in the ignition. The heater blasted, and I relaxed, turning my attention back to him as he warmed up.

"Did you do it because you wanted to hurt me?" he asked softly, even though his eyes said they already knew the answer.

"No." My throat felt tight. "I just…I just wanted…to keep you safe. *I promised.*"

Jeffrey nodded, like that was all the answer he needed, and then he waited patiently for me to continue. "Your wolfskin," he repeated, to show me he'd been listening. "What else?"

"My humanskin, like I'm wearing now."

"Right."

"And my alphaskin. That's what I was…when you came to the house two moons ago." I'd remembered him, which was…odd. Normally I didn't remember anything. "That's why Theo turned you away."

"Right," Jeffrey frowned, hands impossibly warm when they moved back to clutch my cheeks.

"When an alpha starts going feral they have to find a mate," I explained, voice tight.

"I know," Jeffrey nodded. "I know. I'm trying… There's gotta be a way around it. And if not, we can find you one." I wasn't sure how he knew that, but figured I shouldn't be surprised. "I read up on it. If I can find you someone else—a wolf to mate with—you'll survive. You can bond with them. You'll be saved."

He was a clever one, so clever. And he'd been running around like crazy the last couple months trying to help me. But still…there were some things only wolves knew, and he'd sounded hopeful, and I just…I couldn't let him cling to that, not when it would only hurt him more in the long run.

He deserved the truth. I'd kept it from him long enough.

"It's not that simple," I said softly, because it wasn't. And he needed to understand. I didn't want him to mourn me before I was gone but I respected him too much to hide the truth from him any longer. "Bonding with someone else hasn't been an option for me for a long time. Not since I met you."

"I don't know what you mean."

I supposed that was fair. For so long I'd guarded this secret, and that seemed silly now, especially when I'd made my choice.

"*You're* my mate," I admitted, voice wobbling, heart cracking open.

"I'm your—but I can't—"

"Yes," I could hardly breathe. Jeffrey looked like he was going to throw up, because he knew as well as I did, apparently, what that meant.

"But I'm—I don't…*I don't understand.*" Jeffrey was quiet for what felt like an eternity. The trees rustled, and the whisper of the wind blanketed the silence. When he spoke, he looked as though he'd seen a ghost, all the color having drained from his face. "How can I be your mate? I'm not a wolf. You can't bond with me."

"That may be true, but I choose you anyway," I said simply. "I may have wondered at first why the moon mother had played a joke on the both of us, making a human my fated one, but I understand now. *I understand.* Because you are harmony. You are warmth. You are the peace I have always searched for."

"What the fuck." Jeffrey's voice was hoarse, like he was reciting something he'd read. His scent was pain-pain-pain. "What the fuck—and you—"

"Will not mate with anyone else. Will not bond with anyone else," I said, my wolf rising to the surface, my teeth snapping. "I won't. I would rather die."

"Okay," Jeffrey's lips wobbled. "*Okay.*"

"Wolves mate for life."

It was a fact. A fact I was proud of.

Even though…it meant my life might be shorter than either of us liked. It was still a source of pride.

"I chose you. I *choose* you."

"But I can find you a real mate. Someone that can stop you from going feral. I can *save* you. It doesn't have to be this way," Jeffrey's voice was hollow. "You don't have to die."

His lovely pale skin turned green, and the light in his eyes flickered out entirely, like a flame snuffed out. He looked so very far away. Like he was lost again. I didn't know what to do to make this better, because there was nothing that I could offer him but the truth now, and what little time I had left.

"And that's it? We're fucked?" Jeffrey's voice was faint, and the grip he had on my face grew slack. "You won't hear reason. You won't…" he trailed off, his focus falling away. "There's just…*nothing* that I can do?"

I shook my head.

"Fuck." Jeffrey's voice broke. "Fuck. Fuckfuckfuck."

And then because this was apparently not bad enough, I was forced to keep going. Because while Jeffrey was clever and knew many things, I had no idea how much. And I couldn't just assume.

"When I go feral, I will need to be put down," I told him even though based on what he'd just shared with me in the clearing, and the scars he'd told me about, I figured he already knew. My fingers bit crescents into his hips. Like I'd hoped, the tight grip brought him back to the present. His eyes swam into focus again, no longer dazed. He met my gaze head on, my brave, lovely mate. "I just…I should not have asked you. It was *wrong* of me. Not noble at all. Not like you are."

So perfect.

It wasn't fair.

It wasn't—

"There are rules in place," I added softly before he could interrupt. "For situations like mine." My heart hurt, and Jeffrey was shaking— and I hated this. I hated it so much. Why had I done this to him? Why had I done this? "It's why I was sent here with all of my brothers. We needed enough of our pack to be able to at least…slow me down should something happen."

Jeffrey looked sick.

"It was assumed my wolf would do better surrounded by family." Which was true. I was more than certain that had helped—though the recent moons had made it clear my alphaskin no longer recognized even my kin.

"When alphas go feral they become ravenous," I continued, because I needed to get it all out. Because for years this had been my gaping wound. An injury I shared with no one, always bleeding on my own.

It was awful, horrible, terrible.

But it felt…it felt good to share it.

Jeffrey could carry its weight better than I could.

"My first moon…the first moon I felt the shift in mother moon's favor—I stopped talking, stopped using my humanskin in general. I was younger than most alphas when I began to go feral. I should've had years—but I didn't. I was young and scared and *stupid*. I thought it was something I'd done, something I needed to be forgiven for, and that was why it took me so quickly."

Jeffrey's eyes widened. He made a sad, choked up sound.

"But it wasn't." It had taken me a long time to realize that. "I know that now. The moon takes you when it is your time to go. She makes no mistakes. She knows better than we do…and I wasted…so much time trying to save myself that I lost what little I had left." My voice broke. "I should have searched for you. I should have found you earlier.

"I don't want to hurt my family. I don't want to hurt you. It is why I'm here. Even though it is selfish to take your time like this when I know it is only temporary. From the moment I met you, I could not keep away from you. I am a bad person, I know that. I just…I just w-wanted you," my voice cracked. "Even if it was only for a little while." My lungs felt tight, my breath stuttery and cold. "And I have no regrets. If I were to die tomorrow I would be happy. Because when I close my eyes I will know that my life has not been a waste. Because I made you smile."

"Fuck."

"I did not want to hurt you," my heart cracked right down the middle. I could see on his face that he was listening, but I wasn't sure his heart was. I wasn't sure he understood what I was saying. Or how dangerous I really was, even now. "I *don't* want to hurt you."

"Mutt."

"That is why I asked you for help. Because I am selfish. Because I know I have very few choices left, and I know soon the moon will take the last of them from me." I couldn't stop my hands from shaking. My stomach churned. "I *will hurt you*. I can not control it. I am not me anymore when I am in my alphaskin—I am something else. Something evil. Something… something twisted and dark and *awful*. Like an evil villain—but worse. I recognize no one. There is no empathy within my heart. There is nothing that sates my lust. No amount of blood that will make my beast rest. There is only death, greed, and hunger."

"Like horror movies," Jeffrey echoed, terror written all over his face. It hurt. So much. That he was looking at me like that. Like he had already lost me.

"I will kill," I said softly. "I will kill and kill and kill. And it will never end. Not until someone takes me down."

"What the fuck," Jeffrey's voice cracked. "What the fuck are we supposed to do then?"

"Nothing," I said softly, hand shaking. "We can not…do anything."

"Will you…will you let me *try*?" Jeffrey's voice cracked. "Please. Will you let me try to find you a mate? I know there's not a lot of time, but I…I swear we would make it work. We'd make it work. I'll find one that's happy to let us stay together. Just…let me try."

It was futile, but the desperation on his face made me ache.

He had no idea what little time we had left. That I'd run our clock down to zero. But I couldn't deny him this. I couldn't. Not when he looked at me like that. Even though the wolf inside me screamed that it was wrong, wrong, wrong to agree.

"Fine."

Jeffrey sagged, eyes pinched shut for a moment as he sucked in a breath. "Okay. Okay. Thank you—" His eyes opened, brown as summer dirt, warm the way it felt when it squished between the pads of my paws. "Thank you."

"It may not work," I warned him, knowing fully that it wouldn't.

"I have to try," his voice shook. "Just let me please?" He glared up at me and he was so fierce and beautiful I could not help but grin, despite everything else.

"I am glad we met," I said softly, because I was. Even if our meeting had meant I would choose this fate. "If I had not met you I would have died having never lived," I told him softly.

Jeffrey's expression pinched, his shoulders drawing up tight, his breath leaving him in a ragged little sob. "No," he said, shaking. "Fuck no. Fuck. That's so fucking awful. I hate it. I don't want that. Stop acting like you're dying. I'm not going to let it happen."

I grunted, my eyes burning. He was blurry. Just a creamy smear as I blinked away the tears. "I know." This was more painful than anticipated, but I deserved it. Because if he was going to be in pain, I should be too.

Jeffrey shook his head rapidly. His sweet little bare ears stuck out, the fluffy hair on his head glinting in the light. "This is..." He was shaking. "This is so fucked."

"I know."

"How long?" Jeffrey asked, voice hoarse. "How long do I have? To find you someone."

"Two moons," I lied, even though it hurt.

Even though it hurt more than anything.

"And you're *sure?*"

"This last moon I…" Now it was my turn to tremble. "I almost didn't come back." The words were hoarse and brittle. They hurt. They hurt so much. I hadn't admitted this to my brothers. Hadn't admitted that the first thing I'd done after waking up in my humanskin, still shackled to the wall, was head upstairs and make sure that the number on the fridge was in my phone.

The number that would lead to my death.

The number we were only supposed to call in case of emergencies.

"It's not fair," Jeffrey's voice shattered. The dam broke. Like it had been cracked for years and years, and the pressure had finally grown too much. And then he started crying. Hot, salty tears smeared against my throat as Jeffrey collapsed into me like he trusted me to hold his weight. "It's not fair."

"It is not," I agreed, rocking him gently, my own heart hurting. "But I am so glad to have gotten to know you, however short our time has been." My own voice was hoarse, quaking with emotion. "Knowing you has been my greatest honor. You make me so happy. The other half of my heart's duet. The most wonderful person in the entire world. My prince, my happy ending."

"I'll fix this," Jeffrey promised, a hiccuping little sob escaping him. "I'll fix it. I know I don't have a great track record with fixing things, but I will. A month is enough. Just push through this moon and by the next I'll have figured it out, I swear."

We were caught in a negative spiral. A spiral that wouldn't end unless I put a stop to it.

So I did.

"Do you know what I want?" I said, peeling him out of my neck, the grip I had on his nape still tight enough to soothe him. His eyes were bleary with tears, his cheeks splotchy red, his lashes spiked together.

He'd never been more beautiful than he was right then.

There were no barriers between us.

Just honest heartache.

"W-what?" A tear dashed down his cheek and I leaned forward, lapping at it, before pulling back to meet his gaze again.

"I want to spend as much time with you as possible," I said honestly, heart thumping. "I want to make memories. I want to laugh with you. I want to play. To hear you sing. To see you smile. To keep you safe. To make you happy—for as long as I'm able."

"Mutt—"

"I want to be a happy memory," I told him, and I meant it with every fiber of my being. "*That* is what I want."

"Okay," Jeffrey said, his face pinched, though I could tell he was trying to be strong all over again. "Okay."

"You are a gift," I told him, in case he didn't realize. "My greatest gift."

Jeffrey leaned forward, and when our lips met they tasted like salt and sadness.

"I…" Jeffrey's voice was quaky and soft. "I…"

I knew what he was trying to say, and I wasn't angry he wasn't ready yet.

Because I loved him. And I didn't need to hear the words to know he loved me too.

Chapter Thirty

Mutt

THAT NIGHT I laid Jeffrey gently in his bed, and I took him apart bit by bit. I kissed every inch of his gorgeous body. I tasted his tears and his lips, sipped from his cock, and licked his hole till he was sloppy, wet, and open.

When I cracked open the lube—seriously best invention ever—Jeffrey groaned. He shifted onto his belly, arched his back, and wagged his ass at me, always greedy, always ready to be stuffed full of whatever I wanted.

My cock ached.

My knot throbbed.

I groaned, baring my teeth as I slid slick fingers against the tight ring of muscle and gave it a teasing rub. It gave beneath the touch, already softened. I growled low, hips jerking as he sucked me inside, my knuckles sinking deep.

He was looser than normal.

I hadn't noticed with just my tongue—but with my fingers it was obvious.

"Jeffrey?" My voice was low and rough, I hardly recognized it.

"So you finally realized." He laughed, and then gasped as I twisted my fingers, finding that spot inside him I'd discovered made him sing. "I…thought…tonight—so I prepped before."

Immediately visions of him shoving his fingers deep inside himself. Of him sitting on that damn dildo he didn't know I knew about. Of the hot pink splash of his ass giving beneath the pressure as his head tossed back and he howled, all that pale muscle clenching.

"Fuck." I jerked my fingers faster, spreading them wider, grinning when he began to sing for me all over again.

My favorite song.

Jeffrey's pert ass flexed, his cock dripping onto the mattress as I toyed with him, struggling not to throw caution to the wind and simply push my cock into him the way I wanted to.

"Why are you—" Jeffrey gasped. "I'm ready. Stop teasing— Why the hell do you think I prepped myself?" he grouched at me, twisting to glare. "You think it was for shits and giggles?"

I didn't know what that meant.

But he certainly wouldn't be laughing in a second.

"Are you sure?" I asked, hips flexing toward him, my cock dragging along the back of his thighs, leaving a sticky trail. "Are you—"

"Have at it, big guy," Jeffrey murmured, tucking his knees more fully under himself and arching his back.

That was all the encouragement I needed.

I grabbed my knot, squeezing it tight as I lined my tip up and just…

sunk right in. Wet, slick, velvety heat grabbed me, sucking me deep. My toes curled, a broken gasp escaping me. I couldn't help it.

All finesse disappeared.

I snapped forward, claws popping free, biting into Jeffrey's hips as I drove into him with single-minded need.

Please, please, please.

He felt so good—so wet—so hot—so yes, *yes.*

"That's it," Jeffrey gasped out, fingers scrabbling at the comforter, though they grew slack when I angled my pelvis higher—and then, yes, yes. There we go. He sobbed, babbling words muttered into the fabric as I found his sweet spot and pounded into it relentlessly.

Why had I waited so long for this?

I could've been fucking him all day every day.

I jerked into him, over and over, groaning, my teeth clenched, my knot throbbing.

"C'mon," I gasped out, yanking him back onto my dick, the sticky pink of his insides clinging to my crown. "Take it—"

"Fuuuuck," Jeffrey sobbed, a limp, dazed mess. His eyes were foggy again, his lips parted. Drool spilled onto the mattress as he lay docile and submissive beneath me, head tipped just enough I could see his lovely face. Taking my dick, the way he was born to do.

"Going to fill you up," I promised, lashes fluttering. "Gonna make your belly swell—" Fuck, fuck, fuck.

Slap, slap, the wet smack of our hips filled the room, filthy and beautiful.

He looked so damn pretty like that, with his ass clenching, but the rest of his body soft. All that muscle relaxed, like he'd never felt more at ease than he did now, getting speared on my dick. I growled, plowing into him harder, enjoying the little *uh, uh, uh* sounds he made every time I pushed in.

My knot tingled, this fizzy electric zing that zapped down to my toes. It inflated, growing with each eager slap of our hips. In, in, in. I wanted it in—I wanted in—

"Please," I begged, hands slipping to his ass cheeks and forcing them apart so I could watch. Could see the way my knot pushed at his hole, begging entry. "Please."

Jeffrey scratched meekly at the mattress, slutty and useless, his ass finally—blessedly giving in—and then.

Bliss.

Tight, sweet, wet, warm—fuck, fuck, fuck.

My eyes rolled back and I came. I came and came and came, claws digging into him—not hard enough to cut—but enough to bruise. I filled him up. Over and over and over, just like I'd promised. "Good bitch," I gasped, mirroring the compliment he usually gave me. "Such a good bitch," I ground into him harder, spilling for what felt like years.

"Fuck," Jeffrey moaned, voice low and fucked out. "Thank you."

I crowded against his back, teeth itching to bury in the back of his neck. To mark him as mine, mine, mine. But I couldn't do that. Not now. I sobbed instead, burying my face in the fuzz there, mouthing at his nape with need.

"Bite me," Jeffrey moaned softly, dazed and sweet. "I know you need it."

That was all it took. With my knot tucked snug inside him and his warm muscle smashed against my own I just...I lost it.

My teeth sunk hard into the back of his neck, breaking skin, the bright copper of blood bursting on my tongue. I wished then that I could turn him. But I couldn't. I couldn't.

Jeffrey sobbed, and I came again, hot spurts filling him up. Enough that it began to spill free. Growling, I dragged a hand down, scooping the cum up and rubbing it into his ass and thighs. I wanted him to stink of me. Wanted to mark him as thoroughly outside as I'd marked him inside.

After my third load, I twisted my hand around him, feeling the swell of his belly with a greedy moan. Another spurt filled him and he gasped, docile and sweet—his expression blissed-out and blank.

"Good bitch," I murmured again, holding him tight, my tongue lapping at the bite mark I'd left on the back of his neck. It was a clean bite. Straight through muscle and sinew. It would heal beautifully. A scar he'd chosen—when the rest of his scars hadn't.

If he'd been a wolf we would be bonded now. The ceremony complete.

I made Jeffrey come twice on my knot.

Twice before he whined and batted my hand away from his sweet little dick, and begged me for a nap. It was our last day together. Our last day and I wanted to make the most of it. I couldn't make him suffer with hope any longer. So instead of forcing another orgasm out of him, when my knot deflated I simply held him. Let my soft cock nestle in where he was warm and slick. Curled around him protectively one last time.

And loved him fiercely.

Because if there was anyone who deserved being loved, it was Jeffrey Prince.

The next morning I left him. I kissed his sleepy brow, his speckled shoulder, his sweet fingers.

"I love you," I told his sleeping form, before rising to my feet.

And then I went outside, dazed.

Naked.

Lost.

I pulled up the number I'd saved in my phone.

And I called.

Chapter Thirty-One

Jeffrey

WHEN I WOKE up Mutt was gone. I wasn't surprised. I knew he'd wanted to spend some time with his brothers today. So I wandered into the kitchen and chugged water from the tap to wet my dry mouth, limping all the way.

My ass twinged in an incredibly pleasant way, and I grinned to myself, more than a little excited for the next time I'd get to take his knot again.

And then…the conversation we'd had in the woods came back to me.

And I panicked.

An hour and a half later I was sitting in the parking lot of my therapist's office and I had half the country out looking for answers for me. Well…not half the country. That was an exaggeration. But definitely all my brothers.

They'd all been assigned different magic shops in the area, and I had plans after my appointment to head straight for the big hunting lodge east of Elmwood to see if I could get some answers of my own. I'd avoided it like the plague—mostly because I knew I'd get recognized there. Knew I'd have to play my part, the way I always had for Lydia.

But at this point…I didn't fucking care.

Mutt was worth it.

If I could play Jeffrey Evans for the last sixteen years—I could do it a few more times. Especially if it meant I got to keep my mate.

Because that's what he was.

Maybe there was a way to turn me? A way to work around the rules. Except that everyone knew wolves were born, not turned. And the movies, comics, and TV shows that said otherwise were full of shit.

I was giving myself today.

Today.

And then I'd give up on this and start hunting for a mate for Mutt.

I nearly canceled my therapy appointment entirely—but…for the first time in my life, I was actually ready for it. Actually ready to speak about what was happening to me. And I needed…well, I needed someone to talk to.

Which was why there was no hesitation when I pushed into the doors of the pristine white office, flopped onto the "thinking couch" and let loose.

I told Doctor Mason everything.

Once again glad that I'd opted to go with a therapist that was sanctioned by SAC as it meant I didn't have to filter most of my life. She listened, and her expression was gentle and fond. By the time I was done talking, when I glanced at the clock, I realized our time was almost up.

"Sorry," I managed, throat dry. She offered me a water bottle and shook her head with a wry grin.

"Don't apologize," she said softly. "Listening is what I'm here for."

"Right," I flushed, taking a sip of the water—and then chugging it, because why not. She'd offer me another, and I was paying her a shit ton of money, so.

"Why did you forgive him?" she asked and I frowned, confused. I crinkled the bottle up, and tossed it across the room. It hit the wall and skipped right into the trash can.

"Forgive him?"

"Mutt," she clarified softly. "Why did you forgive him for lying about being your dog?"

If she felt bad for telling me my "dog" was just a "dog" it didn't show. I suppose she did get paid the big bucks to have a pretty spectacular poker face, though. She'd make a killing in Vegas, that was for sure.

"I...I mean. Why wouldn't I?" I frowned, not sure what her point was.

"Think about it," she said softly, watching me with warmth in her eyes. I stared at her for a second, frowning deeper. I had no idea what she was on about, but...sighing, I did as I was told and closed my eyes to think.

"He wasn't trying to hurt me," I decided, because that was the first thing that came to mind.

"Right," she agreed, voice gentle. "In fact...he wanted to keep you safe."

"Yeah." I didn't really get the point of this—but she'd taught me over the last few months that she was one wise motherfucker. And she did help. Even if I hadn't wanted to admit it at first.

"Would you have forgiven him as easily if he'd lied because he had an ulterior motive?"

"Like...if he was pretending because he was working for Lydia or something?" As always, my mind went back to Lydia. "I mean. Obviously.

That would've been shitty—and a lot harder to forgive."

"So you're saying that intentions matter," she said carefully.

"Obviously."

"They're important to you."

"Of course they are," I opened my eyes and stared at her, not sure what she was getting at.

"Jeffrey." Her voice was warm, and her eyes were a little wet as she leaned forward, hands on her knees. "When you were nine—"

"Fuck." I already knew where this was going. This was how she always brought up when I'd been taken.

"Did you know what Lydia had planned?"

"What? Of course not." I stared at her, arms crossing tightly over my body. "Of fucking course not. I wouldn't—I mean. If I'd known I wouldn't have gone with her."

"Did you…*intend* for people to get hurt?" She worded that so carefully, and I appreciated it, but there was no point beating around the bush.

"Did I intend for Blair's parents to get murdered? No."

"Did you want Blair to be taken with you?"

"Fuck no. I didn't even know who he was."

"And after you were taken—when you found out what lengths Lydia was willing to go to keep you in line…did you intentionally act out to cause Blair harm?"

"What?" My head was spinning, memories assaulting my senses. The bite of blood. Dark closets. A party that made me feel hollow. Millions of tiny little transgressions. The constant fear. Adrenaline in my veins. "No."

"Would you say…your intentions have always been good?"

"I…" I stared at her. Really fucking stared. Because…that was the moment it clicked. That was the moment I realized what she was getting at and I just…

The clock on the wall *tick, ticked.*

My tongue felt like it was fuzzy, and my stomach was full of lead.

"I…" I tried again, voice cracking. "I—"

Because I understood. I *understood* now what she was trying to say.

All my life I'd held myself accountable for Lydia's actions. I'd blamed myself for the harm that had fallen on Blair and his parents. The hurt that had decimated my already broken family. I hadn't understood why they could take me back. Why they could love me—so wholly—when all I'd done was hurt them.

I was fucking poison, and I knew that.

Except…

Except…

Maybe…*this* was…why?

Maybe, the same way I'd forgiven Mutt for his lies, they'd forgiven me. Because intentions mattered. And if *they* could forgive me—if I could forgive Mutt—should I not…forgive myself?

I was nine.

Nine years old.

I was a stupid kid, yeah.

But Lydia had been a monster.

Mutt said I was the most wonderful person in the world. He thought I was strong. Resilient. And I was realizing now…he was right. Because I was. I fucking was. I'd survived. I'd survived every game Lydia had made me play, survived every weapon, every barb—every tightrope.

And all this time I'd carried the weight of my guilt like a noose around my neck.

But…

The noose fell away, as easily it had formed. Sixteen years of anguish dropping to the floor like it had never been there at all.

I sucked in a breath, and Doctor Mason grinned at me. "There," she said softly. "Congratulations, Jeffrey." My skin felt too tight, but…right all the same. Like all this time it'd been two sizes too small and now it finally fit the way it was supposed to. "You just had your first breakthrough."

"I have a lead," Avery's voice was tinny through the speaker of my phone as I sat in Blair's car—because he'd let me borrow it, solid dude that he was. Richard had not offered his Audi, and I figured that was fair, as I apparently did not have the best track record with cars.

Not that my truck breaking down recently was my fault—because it wasn't. The water pump had been loose, and it was a more extensive fix that Joe said he "did not fucking have time for right now."

Richard had used up his favor already to get my truck towed a second time, and therefore I had no choice but to wait.

"You have a lead?" My fingers gripped the steering wheel tight enough the leather squeaked. "Fuck."

"It may not help," Avery warned. "But if you head to the lodge like planned there should be a hunter there named Nieve. I was talking to my mom and she mentioned something about him having lived with a wolf pack for a few years."

"I thought they didn't do that."

"Most don't," Avery rustled around on the other end of the line. His voice grew muffled, "Betty—do not—get that out of your mouth—I swear to God."

"Avery."

"Sorry. Cats." More rustling. "Okay so. Nieve. Try to find him and get him talking—maybe you can find out something new. If there really are wolf packs out there that allow humans inside them, there might be stuff they know that other packs don't. I don't know if you'll get the answer you want, but it's a start."

"Thanks, Avery. Seriously, man."

"Don't worry about it." I was about to hang up when Avery spoke again. "Do you need backup?" I appreciated his concern, especially because he knew just how…scary entering a lodge would be for me.

"Nah, I'm good." I didn't want to wait for him to arrive—and I figured…I'd be safe.

"Are you sure?"

"I'm sure—"

Avery squeaked. "Oh! My food is here. Gotta go. Let me know what happens."

"I will," I promised, my heart in my throat, but the line was already dead. Anxiously, I pulled the address up on my phone and started the drive. Blair's little Yaris rattled around on the road—struggling with the pebbles that accosted it.

I remembered driving this car.

It'd been mine before it was his—and I'd never liked how sketchy I felt on roads just like this.

Apparently buying a truck hadn't done me any fucking good though, at least…not now.

The two hunting cabins in Maine were located forty or so miles from Elmwood. Close enough to offer SAC support when they called for it, but far enough away that the rare citizens who knew they were there often forgot about their existence.

They were a widely spread secret—but a secret all the same.

I knew the location of every lodge in North America. Courtesy of Lydia's teachings and the monsters she'd had us travel all over the country to kill. I'd never actually been to these two, but that didn't mean I didn't know where they were, or what would happen when I arrived.

So I buckled down, buckled up, and prepared for the worst.

Nieve was a dead end. I plied him with compliments, fake bonded with him over killing things, and acted starstruck. Even bringing up Lydia's name didn't garner any extra information—which meant that he knew jack shit.

She was my golden ticket.

"It's so good seeing an Evans in these parts again," he said, arm looped over my shoulder. The wooden walls of the lodge felt claustrophobic as Nieve urged me toward the massive fireplace that sat in the center back of the large visiting area. Up the steps were the bedrooms—just like the ones I'd spent my entire childhood holed up in with Lydia. "We were starting to worry—" Nieve laughed. "But it seems Lydia's boy's got a taste for something rare."

Fuck, his voice was loud.

Too loud.

The group sitting on the couches by the fire twisted to look at us. And with sinking horror, I realized I *recognized* one of them. *This is exactly why I didn't want to come here.* The pit in my stomach grew heavier, but I pasted on a smile anyway.

Smile.

Don't show them the truth.

You can do this.

"Something rare?" One of the men—the one I fucking recognized—said. He had a handlebar mustache and his dark eyes were bright, assessing as he dragged them up and down my body. My skin crawled, and I had to force myself not to flinch. Instead, I flexed a little, watching the way his gaze flooded with heat.

Maybe I could use his attraction to me to my advantage?

That was something—right?

"Our boy's asking about werewolves," Nieve laughed, like it was funny. Even though these psychopaths probably thought I was trying to kill one.

"Werewolves?" Handlebar's gaze moved from my crotch to my face and I hid my flinch. "You know, I've got a book in my room about werewolves I could let you borrow."

I had no doubt there was no fucking book in his room.

Helplessly, I glanced around the other hunters. There was a woman with dark hair and a stank face that ignored me entirely. A round man with rounder spectacles and a ketchup stain on his shirt. None of them looked particularly impressive.

Pitiful, Lydia's voice echoed around inside my head, but I forced it away.

"Nieve and I were catching up," I grinned, bumping my shoulder against the older man. "But I'd love that book if you would be willing to grab it for me—"

Handlebar's eyes narrowed.

I remembered him.

He'd been there for my first wendigo. I could remember the way he'd grabbed onto me at the end—had I not realized how creepy he was then? Fuck. There was no way in hell I was going anywhere with him.

What if he really does have a book?

I wavered.

"How about…when you're done catching up," Handlebar's lips pulled into a smirk, "You can come on up."

Goddammit.

He was stubborn.

I shouldn't have come here.

I realized that now. It was pointless. And these hunters were as likely to help me as they were to shoot me with the fucking pistols they kept strapped to their hips. The guns glinted, and I forced myself not to take an anxious step back.

I'm stuck now.

I wished I'd had the foresight to accept Avery's offer of backup. Or at the very least, let Mutt know where I was headed. Though…him walking in here as a feral alpha was a recipe for disaster.

For an hour I schmoozed, plying the group with jokes and stories of the shit Lydia and I had done. With every bloody anecdote and their resulting laughter, I hated them just a little bit more. These people were fucking evil. The way they snorted when I regaled them with my first goblin hunt was disgusting at best.

"Did they squirm?" Handlebar asked, eyes dancing. "I love when they squirm."

"Knife or gun?" the woman asked.

"I made one explode once," round glasses hummed, voice low and nasally. "Covered him in C4 then watched him go kaboom." He mimed an explosion with his hands, then frowned. "It was messier than expected."

"How can you expect anything less than a mess if you're blowing them up?" The woman rolled her eyes. "Slow and steady is the answer."

"You only say that because you like to bleed them," Nieve laughed.

I wanted to throw up.

But my smile never wavered.

Get me out of here.

Fuck fuck fuck.

I shouldn't have come.

I shouldn't have come.

A phone buzzed.

Thank fucking God.

The conversation stopped as handlebar pulled his phone out of his pocket with a grimace. A grimace that quickly morphed into something wicked. "Evans," he said, addressing me, his eyes burning. "Looks like you're about to get your wish."

"What?" My ears were ringing.

"Just got a call about a rogue alpha wolf not that far from here."

I couldn't breathe.

My smile never fell.

"A rogue alpha?" I laughed, two seconds from breaking in half. *Please don't be Mutt. Please don't be Mutt. Please don't be Mutt. Please don't be*

Mutt. "Where?"

"Found him in Elmwood. Someone called it in. Local hunter went to investigate, and fucking thing couldn't shift to talk to him."

"That's the first sign," the woman hunter grinned, leaning forward in excitement. "So he's free game?"

"The clocks ticking," round glasses added.

"You think they'll let us let him loose so we can hunt him?" Nieve asked, his voice low and crackling, his arm still tight around my shoulder. He gave me a little shake. "Aren't you a lucky one?" he purred, grinning down at me like I was supposed to be fucking elated.

I suppose I couldn't blame them for thinking this was what I wanted.

But I just…

Fuck.

Fuck.

I was so tired.

So tired of pretending.

"Fuck you." The words slipped out before I could stop them. Nieve flinched back, his arm sliding from my shoulder, his eyes narrowed.

"What?"

Fix this.

Fix this.

Fix this.

"Fuck you," I repeated, jerking out of my seat. The fireplace continued to crackle but it didn't burn nearly as bright as the hate that bubbled up inside me. "Fuck all of you. Every fucking one of you." Movements jerky, I headed toward the front door, desperate to get away before I heard another fucking word.

"Evans!" they called after me, but I was already outside.

The trees climbed high toward the sky, and my heart was pounding. Head jerking left and right, I searched for—oh fuck. There.

Hanging over the railing I threw up the remnants of my coffee, heaving, as visions of Mutt with a bullet in his brain assaulted my senses. I didn't know what his alphaskin looked like but it didn't matter. It didn't fucking matter, because no matter what shape he took, it was him—it was him—

And—

Fuck.

Fuck.

Please don't be him.

Please don't be him.

Please don't—

A warm hand settled on my shoulder. I flinched, jerking away, my fingers fumbling for my gun. I discovered, too late, that I had forgotten to arm myself before I'd left the car. *God, I was so fucking stupid.* Only—it wasn't handlebar, or Nieve, or either of the other creepy goons who was touching me.

It was a man.

A very big, very *golden* man.

With short butter blond hair, lavender eyes, and triangular ears on the top of his head.

A wolf.

A fucking wolf.

At the hunting cabin.

Do you have a fucking death wish?

"You can't be here," my breath caught. I didn't need to ask for a name to know who he was. The resemblance to Mutt was uncanny. "You can't—"

My breath reeked, and I knew that—but I just couldn't…I couldn't be fucked to care.

"It's okay," the wolf—who I could only assume was Butters, Mutt's older brother—said. He held his big hands out placatingly, his eyes soft and warm and full of understanding. "It's okay."

"It's fucking not," my voice snapped. "You have to get out of here."

"Come with me—" Butters reached for me, and I didn't push him off. I couldn't. Because visions of injured Mutt assaulted my senses again and I tipped over the side of the bannister to throw up again.

His big warm palm rubbed my back, a soothing rumble buzzing through the air. This time when I glanced up, his ears were flattened back, worried.

"Why are you—" I tried to catch my breath, spitting over the side of the bannister, before grabbing the hem of my shirt and wiping my mouth. I could hardly breathe. My knees were weak, and black spots swam around me. "Why are you here—"

I didn't want to know.

I didn't want to know.

Because I got the feeling I already did.

"I'm looking for Mutt."

"No." My voice broke. I fell to my knees on the wood, heart skittering. "*No.*"

"Theo's around back—we split with Jules and Harry."

"Fuck." I couldn't breathe. "Fuck, fuck, fuck."

"Why are *you* here?"

"I'm—"

"Jeffrey?" The front door pushed open. And within two fucking seconds—

we were fucked. Completely fucking fucked. Like a total idiot, Butters transformed, his wolfskin bursting free, his clothing tearing and falling in tatters to the floor as he jerked in front of me. Yellow fur decorated his body, his tail tucked between his legs, his ears flat. He snarled, and Nieve stumbled back inside, a wicked grin on his face.

"Fuck." He'd just bought us a minute while they gathered silver bullets—but that wasn't enough. Wasn't fucking enough. "Go, go, go, go." There wasn't time for my panic. So I shoved it aside, knees weak and wobbly as I forced myself up, grabbed a fistful of Butters's fur and yanked him toward the steps.

He made a confused sound. Probably because he was the stupidest person alive—and had no idea what he'd just done.

Werewolves were protected as a whole.

The only exception to that was feral alphas—aaaaand those who had actively attacked a human. And Butters had done just that.

This was open season.

At a fucking hunting cabin.

"Go, go, go, go—" I jerked him down the steps, and he followed, huge hairy body brushing against my belly as we stumbled. "Fuck, fuck, fuck."

I should've brought my gun inside.

Should've brought it with me—

What had I been thinking? The car beeped as I unlocked it, jerking Butters behind the bumper as I yanked the hatchback's trunk open and scrambled inside for something—anything.

There was no time to run.

No choice.

I grabbed the gun I'd placed there, checked the barrel was full, and shushed Butters's whining.

The front door to the lodge opened. A quiet creak. They couldn't see us behind the car, but that would only last for so long. All they had to do was walk across the porch and—

I only had a second to get this right.

The guilt I normally felt disappeared entirely as I took a deep breath, closed my eyes, and prepared myself for blood.

When I jerked around the side of the car I could see all four hunters lining the patio. They were looking for us. Guns in hand.

Pop, pop, pop—thump, thump, thump.

They fell like dominos with pained cries—bodies hitting the porch.

Handlebar moved behind a bannister and—fuck, fuck, fuck.

I can't get a clear shot.

"What the fuck. Are you doing?" he yelled out, but I barely heard him.

Butters was panting beside me, his massive body quaking like he was absolutely fucking terrified. Which was fair. Because he could probably smell the silver in the air.

C'mon, Jeffrey.

One more shot.

You've got this—

I jerked back behind cover for a second, biding my time. If I was silent. If I held still—I could tempt him out into the open again. I could—

A giant black wolf tore into the parking lot, gravel kicking up beneath his paws.

Theo.

Butters had said Theo was here.

That he was—

Oh no.

Oh no.

I jerked around the side of the car just in time to see handlebar raise his gun and point at Mutt's other brother. Oh fuck no. No. *Fuck.* Fucking *idiot* wolves.

I pulled my gun up—pointed—and at the last second, handlebar shifted his muzzle toward me. Good. *Good. I'm the threat here—I'm the threat—don't shoot him. Don't kill him. Don't—don't—*

There. A clear shot. I aimed my gun at his heart.

I shot off a bullet and seconds later, agony, unlike anything I'd ever felt exploded through my chest. I couldn't breathe—blood clogging up my throat as I fell to the ground with a painful grunt.

Butters whined, but my head was spinning and I just—

Fuck.

The gravel tore at my knees and cheek as I fell forward. Sticky hot, my chest—my chest felt—

"Fuck." Theo's voice was as sweet as ever. Warm hands gently latched onto my shoulder, gingerly tugging me around so I was lying on my back. Which—was a bad fucking idea, because I began to fucking choke. My eyes swam, searing pain burning through my body as I gasped and spluttered, more frothy pink liquid spilling from my lips.

"Lungs." Theo's voice was tight and panicked. "He shot him in the lung."

"Fuck." Butters's voice was shaky. "Fuck, fuck." Blearily, I recognized that I was lying on the gravel of a hunting lodge with two naked men hovering over me. Which was weird as hell, yes, but not all that weird in the grand scheme of things.

"M—" I tried to ask them about Mutt, desperately needing to know that he was going to be okay. That they'd fix this. Even though I…

Fuck.

Fuck.

I couldn't.

I couldn't.

I didn't know how much time I had, but I wasn't a fucking idiot. A human can only survive so long without oxygen and I couldn't—I couldn't—I couldn't—

"Butters—" Theo's voice quaked.

And then more pain exploded in my shoulder. Liquid hot and horrible. I couldn't even whine, coughing and shaking—and then…

Everything went black.

Chapter Thirty-Two

Mutt

SIX HOURS. THAT was how long it took for the hunters to process me into their lodge, to lock me up, and for Jules and Harry to arrive. Because they were…idiots, and wouldn't let me die. I growled, jerking in my cage, staring at the two of them as a set of hunters marched them in through the back door.

The room was fully concrete aside from the back wall that had what Harry had once described to me as a "garage door." It was like the basements I was familiar with, but different too. Colder. Larger. An open hangar full of cages and vehicles with manacles hanging from the walls.

The cage I was inside had room for me to pace back and forth—and that's what I'd been doing. Biding my time. Waiting, because soon enough it'd all be over. I'd planned this out. Planned it out specifically so that I wouldn't be at risk of hurting the people I cared about most.

They weren't supposed to be here.

So why were they—

"Fucking beasts," one of the hunters muttered, jerking Jules to his knees beside my cage. Apparently they had enough forethought not to put my brothers inside with me. Instead, they got chained to the wall to my left, both of them eerily silent as they held their hands out obediently for the manacles the hunters snapped into place.

Twin sets of violet eyes stared at me.

Stared and stared and stared.

Stared until the door fell shut with a quiet click and several long, silent minutes passed. And then—Harry, because he was Harry, chewed me the fuck out.

"What were you thinking?!" he hissed, glaring at me. "Calling them on yourself. You fucking self-sacrificing, wolf-shaped asshole." Harry sucked in a breath, face bright red before he started up again. "You were just gonna what? Let them kill you? And let us all figure that out…when exactly? When we saw your fucking corpse? Fuck you. Fuck you so fucking hard in your stupid fucking face."

Jules glared at me, but his expression softened when he looked at Harry. And then he laughed, but tried to cover it up. "Sorry— You just—"

"Fuck you."

"You just…look so stupid when you get mad."

"I hate you so much right now," Harry snapped at him, and then me. "And I hate you. And I hate everything about this."

"I read a scene in a book like this once," Jules piped in helpfully. "There was this dude who got all tied up—and then his mafia boyfriend came to the rescue. Killed all the guards or whatever. And then they fucked using the blood as lube.”

“I don’t want to know about the porn you read, Jules,” Harry’s hands twitched, like he wanted to pinch the bridge of his nose, but he couldn’t.

“It’s not porn. It’s erotica. There’s a difference, and you know it. You’re just being a bitch.”

“All I’m hearing is that you’re a slut.”

“Oh my god, you can’t just call me a slut.”

“I just did.”

Normally Harry and Jules got along. They very rarely fought. Very rarely raised their voices. Harry was prickly at best, but Jules seemed to be his exception. To see them at each other’s throats like this was sobering.

I whined, and both of them quieted, swiveling to look at me.

The scent of angry-sad-loss clogged the giant empty hangar we were stationed inside, and I knew then, that I’d fucked up. Because even though I’d been trying not to hurt them—that didn’t mean I hadn’t.

They were hurt.

And it was my fault.

I was supposed to be their alpha. I was supposed to take care of them. And I hadn’t done shit for months.

“I’m sorry.” I shifted, bones cracking, fur morphing to skin. Curled into a naked ball in the corner of my cage, my ears flattened to my head.

“I fucking *knew* it!” Harry gasped out in outrage. “You liar. You fucking *liar*. I asked and the hunter on the phone said you couldn’t shift—and you—you were *faking it*?!” He keened, low and sad, distressed. Jules leaned into his side, nuzzling at his shoulder as Harry trembled. “Why— why would you do this?”

"I…" Miserable, I sucked in a breath. There were no cameras in here. I'd looked for them when I first arrived.

"Why the fuck would you do this to us?" Harry's voice cracked. "You know I'd fix it—I fix everyone's shit. All you had to do was *ask* me."

"There's no fixing this," I said softly, feeling small and hurt—and brittle.

"I know there's not a lot of time, but one of us could've turned Jeff—"

"No," I bit out, voice low and waspish. Turned wolves were shunned. It wasn't something that was done unless in extreme duress. It was the reason omegas were looked down on. They were the only wolves that could turn humans, and if they did, they were immediately banished from their pack in retribution.

It was taboo.

Wrong.

I couldn't do that to Jeffrey.

And I couldn't ask that of my brothers—it wasn't right.

That had never even occurred to me as an option.

But apparently it had occurred to Harry.

Apparently he loved me enough to be willing to lose his home.

"Well, now I fucking can't," Harry huffed out. "Because I'm in here. With you."

"Why *are* you here?" I bit out, voice quaking. I knew my scent betrayed me. Told them exactly how needy and frightened I was. Exactly how desperately relieved I was that I wouldn't have to spend my last moments alone.

The truth was, they were chained up like I was—but at the end of the twelve hours, they'd be set free either way. Whether or not a Pack Alpha showed up to claim me. Neither of them had attacked the hunters, or they'd be dead right now. And if SAC sought justice for the lost lives of two innocent wolves—there would be no survivors.

They'd be sent home.

"We're here to rescue you."

"From yourself, apparently," Jules added, shaking his head. "Because you're stupid."

"The stupidest," Harry agreed.

"I don't want to be rescued."

"Liar," Harry accused, voice low. "You're a fucking liar." His entire body was pulled tight. "You think I can't fucking hear it? That I can't smell it? You're scared."

"Yeah," I admitted, voice breaking. "Yeah, I am." Harry obviously hadn't expected that, because his mouth clicked shut and his eyes went wide. "Every day for five fucking years I've woken up terrified." My breath hitched. "You don't get it. None of you fucking do." My eyes burned. "You've never *been* a monster."

Jeffrey had.

Jeffrey knew what this was like.

To carry power in his body—to be able to hurt and hunt and maim.

To hurt the people he cared about—not because he wanted to—but because fate decided for him that he would.

He'd survived.

He'd survived.

And I was so fucking proud—

He'd learned what he had to do and he'd done it without question. And I…was just…doing the same. Why was that so hard for everyone to understand?

"I can feel myself slipping," my voice cracked. "Sometimes I'll just be sitting and the world will fall away—and the hunger…the fucking hunger will take over and I'll think—" I sucked in a breath. "How easy it would be to act. To—to—hunt. To do what I'm meant to."

My eyes pinched shut and I scrubbed a hand over my face.

"I'm going to die," I said, voice hoarse. "You know it. I know it. Everyone knows it. I'm going to die—and I just…wanted it to be on my terms. Just wanted to do it before I did something I can't come back from."

"Mutt," Harry's voice broke. I twisted to look at him, my heart lurching when I saw the tear streaks on his face. "Why didn't you tell us? We would have sent you home early."

"Because it wouldn't have changed a thing," I said, aching. "I made my choice—and I was…*am*…so happy with that."

"Is he really worth this?" Harry's voice was hoarse.

I nodded, and he…well…

He nodded back.

"I love him," I said, because I did. "I know it's stupid. I know there were easier paths. But…" I shook my head. "He was the right choice."

"I called Dad," Harry said several long silent minutes later. Jules was silent beside him, his eyes far away, his head nestled against Harry's arm.

"You what?"

"I called him," Harry said. "You were being held in one of two places. Butters and Theo went to the other—they told me you weren't there. So I called Dad and we came here."

"Fuck."

"I know…" Harry sucked in a breath. "I know you're just trying to do the right thing. But…Mutt. Fuck. I can't let you." His eyes were swimming again. "*I can't.* So when Dad comes, I'm telling him the truth. I'm telling him that you faked it. And then I'm going to show the hunters the phone records that prove that you're the one that called them in on your fucking self. And then you're bonding to the first eligible wolf we find."

I should've resented him.

I knew that.

But I couldn't.

Because Harry may not have been an alpha but he was my big brother—and I couldn't hate him for protecting me, even though it fucking hurt.

Several more hours passed. I'm not sure how long. My stomach ached, and I'd transformed back into my wolfskin to keep up the facade. I didn't want the hunters to realize that I could shift. They'd be forced to release me—and I…just…

No.

So, stubbornly, no matter how many times Jules and Harry cursed at me, I stayed firmly put.

Nothing changed, aside from the garage door sliding open at one point for a vehicle to be parked inside, only for that same vehicle to drive back out twenty minutes later loaded with cargo.

To pass the time, Jules—because he was Jules—started regaling us with the plot from the book he was reading at home.

"Gunther was like, two seconds from confessing," he lamented. "You couldn't have waited to turn yourself in until after they'd made out?"

I grunted, and Jules laughed. He'd warmed up to me a bit over the last few hours, though Harry remained mostly icy. I couldn't blame him. I knew what I'd done was shitty but I just…I didn't know what else to do.

Maybe I really was a self-sacrificing, wolf-faced asshole.

Every so often I'd hear Harry mutter something about me being "an idiot," but I ignored him for the most part. Though my wolf ached to be with them, outside the cage, curled up like pack one last time. There were bars between us though and that felt fitting. In a way I was grateful too—because the pull of the moon was stronger than ever with my emotions so heightened, and I was dangerous.

It was why I'd called the hunters in the first place.

My skin itched. It itched and itched and itched.

That was, of course, when things got worse.

Way worse.

Because a hunter came into the room—and before I could see him, I could smell his fury-anger-frustration. He stormed across the hangar toward a large black vehicle. Harry opened his mouth—probably to try to out me as a liar to the man, but there was no time. Because just as soon as the first hunter entered, a handful of others did as well.

They smelled panicked.

Panicked.

And none of them looked at me.

So I knew it wasn't my fault.

What could be more troubling than a feral alpha?

I swiveled toward them, listening intently as they spoke.

"Four of ours are down," the man spoke almost frantically. "Fucking idiots didn't have backup."

"What happened?"

"Jeffrey Evans. That's what happened."

I jerked, slamming into the bars, my head spinning. Jeffrey Evans. Jeffrey Evans. That was—that was Jeffrey's other name wasn't it? The one he'd told me about? Why was he out on his own? What had he done?

Fuck.

This was why he needed me with him at all times.

I should be with him.

I should be protecting him.

I promised.

"Two rogue wolves loose," the guy added. "Better load up on silver bullets."

"Jeffrey Evans?" the guy echoed, jerking the front door to the vehicle open. He slid in, and the others began piling into the back. "Are we sanctioned to shoot to kill the kid?"

"No need," the first guy said.

My ears were ringing.

"No need?" guy two asked, confused as the door slid shut with finality.

"He's already dead. Nieve called it in right before he bit the bullet."

He's already dead. He's already dead.

Something broke inside me then.

My skin burned, claws severing flesh as I jerked against the bars and roared. Spittle fell onto the concrete, my form tearing liquid hot as acid burned through my veins.

He's already dead. He's already dead. He's already dead. He's already dead. He's already dead. He's already dead. He's already dead. He's already dead.

It hurt. It hurt. It hurt.

The threads I'd formed that had twined around Jeffrey from the day we'd met snapped, and what little bond I'd managed to form disappeared entirely. All that was left was black, black, black. The ache. The hunger. The bars bit into my shoulder as I slammed against them—taller now—on two legs. Over and over, I slammed against them, metal screeching as I tore at it.

"Mutt—Mutt—" Harry's voice was faint. "Mutt—"

He's already dead. He's already dead. He's already dead. He's already dead. He's already dead. He's already dead. He's already dead. He's already dead.

Claws tore at the metal, blood smearing along their surface as I slammed into them over and over and over and over and over.

He's already dead. He's already dead. He's already dead. He's already dead. He's already dead. He's already dead. He's already dead. He's already dead.

"Mutt—" Jules's voice now. "Mutt!"

"Fuck." Harry's voice was hollow. "Fuck. Fuck. He's feral. He's fucking—"

The large vehicle peeled out of the garage, the door rising and staying open, the woods outside calling my name as the prey disappeared in a cloud of crunching gravel. Hungry, hungry—so hungry.

It hurt hurt hurt.

My mate—

My mate—

He's already dead. He's already dead. He's already dead. He's already dead.

He's already dead. He's already dead. He's already dead. He's already dead.

"Mutt—Matthew—" Harry tried again.

This time I turned my ire on him, swiveling around, my hackles raised, a low rumbling snarl bubbling up inside my throat. I hit the other side of the cage, hairy arms pushing through the gaps, blood soaked claws jerking toward the two wolves chained to the wall.

I wasn't close enough.

Wasn't close enough—

I just—

I was so hungry—

I just—

He's already dead. He's already dead. He's already dead. He's already dead.

He's already dead. He's already dead. He's already dead. He's already dead.

"Fuck, fuck, fuck." Jules and Harry jerked back against the wall, flattening themselves against it as the room clouded with fearscent. "Fuck. Fuck." Harry's eyes were wide, the whites showing. Jules was quaking, skin nearly as pale as the white streak at his temple.

"We're so fucked," Jules hissed.

"No, we're not." Harry glared at him, then me. I snapped at him, and he flinched back. "We're—I mean. Oh fuck."

"Dad can only save him if he's not feral. That's pretty fucking feral."

"I know."

He's already dead. He's already dead. He's already dead. He's already dead.

He's already dead. He's already dead. He's already dead. He's already dead.

Out.

I wanted out.

I needed out.

Needed mate—needed—

"You gotta come back," Jules's voice cracked. "Mutt. C'mon." He was the quiet brother, the pretty one. He'd never been the most emotional person—not like Harry, who wore his emotions plainly. "You—"

I snapped at him and he jerked back.

"Fuck." Harry's eyes flicked between me and Jules, and I growled, backing away and then barrelling into the bars again. They creaked. "Fuck. Okay. Okay." He twitched. "Think. I gotta think. I gotta—"

"Did they bond?" Jules asked.

"Of course fucking not," Harry hissed at him. "You can't bond with a human."

"Except that you can." Jules jerked his head at me.

"What do you—"

"His mate. He *has* a mate."

"No, he—"

"Look at him. Just fucking…*look* at him." His voice was low and tight. "The second he found out Jeffrey got hurt he went ape shit—"

He's already dead. He's already dead. He's already dead. He's already dead.

He's already dead. He's already dead. He's already dead. He's already dead.

No no no no no no.

Their words filtered away, blackness clouding my vision. The hunger ached brighter, tighter. My teeth itched. Retreat, slam. Retreat, slam. Retreat, slam. Over and over I hit the bars, attempting to weaken them with every leap.

"Don't be an idiot," Jules huffed out. "Stop thinking with your textbooks and try to be a little fucking romantic for a change. Use your imagination."

"That's not how it works—"

"Freckles!" Jules screeched—loud enough he broke through the red haze in my head.

Freckles.

Spots. Speckles. Creamy skin.

My head spun.

"Uh…fuck fuck fuck," Jules muttered and my vision swam. "Freckles and uhhhh red hair!"

"What the fuck are you doing?"

"I'm anchoring him."

"That's not how that works."

"You got a better idea?"

Harry was silent…then he sucked in a breath. "An ass that won't quit!"

"Jesus, that's not what I meant." Jules laughed. "You can't just comment on another wolf's mate's ass."

"I don't know shit about him—" Harry hissed out. "I noticed his ass. That's about it—"

"Music!" Jules shouted. "Oranges. His face when he saw you in a suit!"

"Think, Mutt." Harry's voice was frantic. "Think. You're not this… you're—you're—your mate needs you. Your mate needs you. He needs you—come back."

"Jeffrey needs you."

He's already dead. He's already dead. He's already dead. He's already dead. He's already dead. He's already dead. He's already dead. He's already—

Jeffrey.

Jeffrey, Jeffrey, Jeffrey.

I jerked away from the bars, falling to my knees with a broken whine.

Jeffrey.

Jeffrey last night. The way he'd looked when he took my knot, the wet pink of his ass stretching obscenely wide.

Jeffrey and the way he'd cried for me. The way he'd hugged me. The way he'd promised he'd save me—always the savior.

Jeffrey and the way he melted beneath kind touch, like he'd never had it before.

Jeffrey and the way he opened his heart up even though he'd been hurt over and over and over again.

Jeffrey and the dark circles beneath his eyes. Dark circles because on top of fighting his own demons he'd decided to fight mine.

Jeffrey and the way he sang, musical and sweet. Prettier than bird song.

Jeffrey and how quick he was to jump to someone else's aid. Self-sacrificing, even more than I was.

Jeffrey and how easily he'd forgiven me for lying to him, even though by all rights he should hate me.

Jeffrey and his obsession with the damn guitar pick in his pocket.

Jeffrey and the fact he'd put the squirrel I'd given him on his night stand. He kissed it every night before bed, then flushed, terrified of getting caught.

Jeffrey and his loyalty—unwavering.

Jeffrey and his bloody knuckles, so distressed when I'd run that he'd punched a goddamn wall till he bled.

Jeffrey and the way he'd giggled over spaghetti, his head tossed back, throat bobbing.

Jeffrey and the ocean. The way water droplets had clung to his skin.

Jeffrey in the woods. The way his heart had raced with excitement and not fear. The way he'd run for me. The way he'd leapt over logs, effortlessly athletic. The way he'd bolted—because he craved the chase.

Jeffrey at the diner, his eyes warm, the way he'd laughed when I ordered wrong. The way he'd watched me through those pale lashes. The way our feet had bumped and he'd flushed when I glanced his way.

Jeffrey and the million wonderful, beautiful things about him.

My sweet mate.

My darling.

My prince.

The red haze bled away. The blackness faded. I curled into a ball on the floor, whining, my ears flattened, my alphaskin trembling.

"It's okay," Harry's voice echoed, scent relieved-relieved-relieved. "It's okay—"

"Fuck, can't believe that worked."

My heart, my love, my mate.

My sunshine.

And he was—

I sobbed, keening as the world spun and spun and spun.

Gone.

My sunshine was gone.

I wanted the blackness back. I wanted it back—because this…this hurt too much. It hurt it hurt it hurt it hurt it hurt.

I'd been so terrified of hurting Jeffrey—of leaving him behind—it hadn't even occurred to me that he could leave me first.

Chapter Thirty-Three

Jeffrey

I WOKE UP with a start.

Great, gasping gulps of air. My mouth tasted like ass—in a bad way. My whole body felt bubbly—electric, lighter than ever before. But I could feel the ache there too, veins full of poison, the world swimming in and out of focus. Sounds louder, the crunch of the wheels turning on the asphalt, the snap of a twig beneath the foot of a deer in the woods, the creak of tree limbs, a sparrow flapping its wings high above us. Then all at once they'd fade away again, as memories of Mutt, Mutt, Mutt assaulted me.

Mutt hurt.

Mutt captured.

Mutt dead.

That sunny smile, *gone*.

"He's awake." I didn't recognize the voice at first, the fogginess bleeding away for a moment as the world overwhelmed me once again. My eyes didn't want to open, but I forced them to anyway. My lids felt heavy—so fucking heavy. Too bright, too fucking bright. I forced them shut again with a quiet whine.

Ow.

Fucking ow.

"Drink this." Something cold pushed against my face, and I squinted, forcing my blurry gaze to focus as I grabbed weakly onto the—*oh.*

Water bottle.

I tried to jerk the cap off, but I was too weak. Too fucking weak.

The car wheels continued to crunch. Loud. Too loud. The woosh of my companions' breath going in and out. The thump of three hearts, theirs and mine.

Stay open. Stay open, I willed my eyes to cooperate.

Slowly, slowly, the blinding white settled, colors returning, though they looked duller somehow. Less vibrant.

The back of Blair's car seats were cleaner than they ever had been when I'd owned this car. And the orange soda stain from when we were kids was missing. I blamed Richard and his clean freak ways, probably.

"Here." The bottle disappeared, and when it returned the cap was off. I grabbed it, jerking it toward my mouth, sucking it down greedily, the cool liquid soothing my aching throat. The taste of blood slowly disappeared as I chugged, and by the time I finished, I felt at least…marginally better.

"Little one, you have five minutes to wake up," this voice was softer than the other one. Gentler. It hurt, but my head managed to move—at least enough that I could see the owners of the two voices. Everything came back in pieces as I stared at the back of—

Theo and Butters's heads.

Damn, had Butters's hair always been that yellow?

Right.

We'd been at the cabin—Butters had challenged the hunters—and Theo had jumped in and I'd—

Fuck.

"Did I…did I die?" I asked, voice cracking.

"No," Theo said at the same time Butters said, "Yes."

One of them was lying. I knew that. I just…wasn't really sure how I knew that. It should've been logical but it wasn't. It was something else. *Thump, thump.* There was a weird thudding sound echoing around in the back of my head.

"Five minutes…" I shook my head, attempting to sit up—and failing. "Five minutes—"

"We're going to see Silas."

I didn't know who Silas was.

But Theo did not sound excited.

"Silas?" I frowned.

"To help with Mutt," Theo explained. "If we can get a Pack Alpha to claim him we can buy him some time."

Everything came swimming back into focus.

Clarity hurt even more than the fog had.

"Harry called Dad and he's on his way—but his flight got delayed. There's a storm." Theo continued to explain. "So Silas is our best bet—if we can convince him to take on a feral alpha that isn't even from his own pack."

"We're going to have to be convincing," I struggled up, heart pounding.

Mutt. Mutt's clock was ticking.

I should've questioned why I was alive. How I was alive. But for the moment, I remained laser-focused on what was most important.

"Can we bargain?" I didn't know what I could offer. "If he says no. Do we have something we could barter?"

"Not anything that he doesn't already have," Theo grunted sadly. "It's a long shot. But since Harry and Jules got themselves captured, it's up to us."

"I better stay in the car," Butters fretted from the front seat. "I'll fuck it up."

"No, you won't." Theo moved one of his hands from the steering wheel to the back of Butters's neck. "I promise."

"Okay—but—there's a reason I haven't been to any of the other meetings. He hates omegas."

"I know."

"And I just…did the thing that makes most people hate us."

"I know."

"I'll fuck it up."

"You won't."

Gravel crunched beneath the wheels. My head was spinning, and I leaned heavily against the cool glass, watching the trees whip by, my head full of cotton.

I need to save him.

"Tell me what to do," I said, interrupting them. "Tell me and I'll do it. Anything."

"Just stand there and look pretty," Theo laughed, eyes crinkling with affection as he peered at me in the rearview mirror. We were in Blair's car. Which meant Theo and Butters's car had gotten left behind.

Cramped in the back seat, I curled in on myself, focus fizzling in and out as I reached down and laid a hand over my chest. Where the gaping hole in my t-shirt sat. My clothes were still damp with blood, though it was tacky now—like it'd been hours since I'd been put down.

"How long do we have?" I asked, heart thumping.

"Three hours max," Theo grunted.

"We had to drive around for a while to ditch the hunters."

"Fuck." I pulled the bullet hole in my t-shirt wider, staring down at my chest expecting the worst. I had no idea how I'd survived. At least—I didn't—until I moved the fabric aside and saw the smooth flesh where a fatal wound had sat.

My head jerked up and I stared at the two wolves, head spinning. "What—"

Butters smelled contrite, but proud too. "Look, I know this is gonna be super weird for you."

"What did you do?" My heart thumped. So fucking loud. A rapid fluttering sound. "What did you—"

"I didn't have a choice," Butters whined, his ears flattening. "It was turn you…or let you die."

"Turn…me?" My voice was reedy soft. "But I thought—I didn't—I mean. I didn't think wolves could do that. Wolves are born. Not made."

"Yeah…" Butters twisted to look at me, lavender eyes swimming with emotion. "It's not exactly a normal thing to do? We're not…*supposed* to do it. It's against the rules. And there will be repercussions."

"And you…" My head spun. "You did it anyway."

"You're Mutt's mate," Butters said simply, like that explained why he'd break the law for me. Why he'd betray their secret. Why he'd offer me this horrible, wonderful thing—this thing I hadn't even known was an option. "I had no choice."

I think…someone else would've been angry.

But I wasn't someone else.

And the elation that burned through my body sent me reeling all over again.

Because I'd just received the greatest gift I'd ever had.

And now…I might actually have a chance of saving Mutt, and keeping him too.

Butters had been convinced he was going to be the reason Silas turned us away. And that ended up being…entirely the opposite of what ended up happening. Theo went in alone at first. He'd thought that Silas would be more receptive that way.

He'd been wrong.

I could see why—because he smelled like sweat and desperation, and I could imagine Silas didn't want to be responsible for Mutt when his only kin were that terrified. Never mind the fact that we were terrified for him, not of him.

But yeah.

We didn't look like a solid bet.

I went in next.

Butters had offered me his shirt—which I appreciated, as mine was still blood soaked. It smelled funny. Kinda like marshmallows? And it drowned me. I used every bit of Lydia's training I could. I schmoozed, complimented, and bargained—to no avail.

Silas was an asshole.

A tall, dark-haired, blue-eyed prick. His eyes were pale where Mutt's were vibrant. He wore a suit—which seemed out of character for the leader of a pack as large as the Elmwood pack. I associated wolves with easy-to-change-out-of clothing, and shit that looked like it had been bought from a gas station gift shop.

But maybe that was just Mutt and Butters.

Silas was a lot more formal.

Butters was our last straw. And none of us were very hopeful he'd be able to help—especially Butters.

Dejected, shirtless, and needy—he wandered into the room alone.

Fifteen minutes later, Butters returned to the car.

The Elmwood pack wandered around outside, eyeing us curiously—especially when Silas exited the main hall and headed toward his own vehicle. I hadn't been able to hear shit, despite my new super hearing. Everything else was simply too loud, and I didn't have to focus to manage it.

"I gotta go." Butters jerked his shoulder.

"What do you mean you gotta—" I jolted when Theo laid a hand on my shoulder. His eyebrow arched, his head cocking as he stared at Butters.

"Did he say yes?" he asked, voice low, terrifyingly calm. Like he was expecting the worst—but hoping for the best.

"Yes," Butters nodded.

Elation, unlike anything I'd ever felt before flooded my body. Laughter bubbled out of my throat and Theo joined in. He gave Butters a happy shake, making his teeth chatter as the blond grinned, tail thumping.

"What did you do?" Theo asked, dark eyes bright.

"I dunno!" Butters admitted, tail still thwacking. "I just walked in the room—and he looked at me—and he just…kinda stared?"

"Oh shit," I gasped out, jerking back against the seat when I saw Silas approach us. He rapped on the passenger window. Butters pushed at the window button, then made an annoyed sound when it didn't roll down right away.

"You gotta push harder, it's sticky—" I explained.

He pushed harder, and with an awful whirring sound the window began to roll. Very. Very. Very. Slowly. Because it was kinda, maybe broken? And barely worked on a good day. Blair had warned me about it and said he'd been meaning to get it fixed, but Joe had been busy, and he was the only mechanic in town, so it just hadn't happened.

Whirrrrr, the window continued to roll.

Silas's scent was spicy. That was the best way to describe it. Spicy. His dark hair fell over his brow, his sharp cheekbones cutting as he ducked his head low. The look he leveled Butters was nothing short of hungry.

"Are you coming?" he asked in a low, cultured voice curling down at the end.

"Y-yeah—" Butters nodded, head jerking. "I just—I need to get the address for you."

"I know the address," Silas rose up to his full height, shiny toe tapping impatiently. "I don't have all day." The corner of his jaw jumped. "Unless you'd no longer like me to claim your brother?"

"No! I do!" Butters jerked the door open and it slammed into Silas's side. He made a soft sound. "Sorry. Sorry." Butters stumbled out of the car, clumsy and massive—towering over Silas, looking small despite his bulk.

"We'll see you soon," Theo urged. Butters nodded jerkily, then offered us a wave, before he was bolting across the parking lot to Silas's vehicle in front of him.

Someone opened their door and I flinched, glancing around, trying to figure out where that had come from. "What was—"

"Don't worry," Theo urged. "You'll get used to it."

"Get used to—"

"Come up front." His voice was soft again. "I'll debrief you while we drive. There's a lot to go through."

I did as I was told, hurrying into the passenger seat and buckling up quickly. Theo started the car—and I didn't complain. Because I didn't trust myself to drive right now. I felt half drunk, my limbs sluggish, my veins full of acid.

Theo pulled out of the pack grounds and headed onto the interstate, moving west toward our destination. The other hunting lodge was located nearly an hour away from Elmwood. Which meant we were cutting this close.

While we rode, Theo spoke.

He told me about the pack he was from. About the turned wolves he'd encountered there. About the way they were shunned in other packs—so most never left. Apparently it wasn't socially acceptable. So taboo even, that turning a wolf wasn't even something the wolf community shared with others.

"Can I—" my voice cracked. "Am I…"

"You could've always been Mutt's mate," Theo said softly. "A mate is just someone you choose. But yes. If we can get there in time there's nothing standing in your way."

"Oh." My head was spinning. "Mutt said it had to be a wolf. That there was no other option.”

“I can see why he would think that,” he said softly. “I’ve never seen anything else. And if I haven’t—he sure as hell hasn’t.”

“So why do you think it’s possible?”

“Just a hunch.” Theo shrugged, glancing at me. “He…got *better* when he met you, you know?”

“Got better?” The trees spun by on either side of the windows, a tall spindly blur. Snow had begun to fall, torrents of powdery flakes falling to the ground. It would be just my luck if we got in another fucking wreck.

At least this time I’d heal fast..right?

There was so much to unpack—there was no way I could do it all right now.

But…

I couldn’t say I regretted the way things had gone.

There was something inside me—something small and shriveled. A part of me that had always ached for connection, to be nurtured. And it was quaking, growing, extending outward. Out through the wounds, a silvery thread. It twisted, writhed—searching, searching, searching.

Searching for Mutt.

A mate is just someone you choose.

Theo’s words rattled around inside my head.

“Before,” Theo spoke again, voice low. “It was like…Mutt was fading.” His fists squeaked as he clenched the wheel. “Every day he lost more color.” His big shoulders curled in tight, blood splattered t-shirt clinging to every muscle. “I’ve seen it before—when animals get really sick. And none of us knew what to do.”

“And then one day he just…changed.” His shoulder jerked up. “I think that was the day he met you," Theo's full lips twisted into a wry smile. "He asked to come here, and we were confused—but Dad humored him anyway. Because none of us wanted to see his light go out again."

I reached into my pocket, fingers digging into my guitar pick for strength as I sucked in a breath.

"You gave me my brother back." Theo nodded. "And for that, I'll always be grateful."

My eyes burned and I nodded, chest tight.

"So if you need help—you just ask me, okay? Or any of us. We're pack. And pack is…"

"Is…?"

"Pack is a place to belong. And people to belong to."

I'd never belonged anywhere.

Not really.

Always on the outside.

Always missing pieces.

Awkwardly shaped.

The silvery string that trailed from my heart kept reaching—reaching—reaching.

Because that was a lie.

That was a lie.

I had belonged somewhere.

And I realized that now.

Because Mutt's arms were perfectly shaped, and the bow of my legs was perfectly sized to fit his hips. I belonged with him. I did.

And I only hoped I wasn't too late to tell him.

Chapter Thirty-Four

Mutt

I HAD NOT known true relief till the day I met Jeffrey. Like there had been something itching beneath my fur my entire life and I had never even known it was there. An uncomfortable ache that always burned. A thirst that couldn't be quenched.

He was tall and muscular, dressed in a hoodie and jeans that clung to his form as he ducked through the rain and hurried into the gas station.

We'd been in Colorado then, only miles away from my home. I often wandered the woods for days, even weeks at a time. Though I returned home for the full moon like clockwork, well aware of the damage I could do. The full moon had been only a few nights previously so I was feeling achy and tired as I stared at the unfamiliar figure through the glass.

He talked to the gas station attendant. He smiled, he laughed. His fingers were long and dexterous and they flickered with a flurry of movement, punctuating everything he said. He was a vision, his hair like a flame on his head as he paid, then headed out into the rain again.

There was something about him that called to me.

That pulled me closer.

Pulled me from the cover of the trees and out onto the pavement.

Pulled me between the gas pumps. Between waiting cars and their owners. I ignored the quiet call of a child saying "doggy!" Behind me as I padded forward, well aware of how intimidating my size could be.

The redhead didn't turn when I reached his vehicle. He just kept humming under his breath, his eyes shut, his finger tapping on his leg like he was playing a symphony as the steady chug of gas filled his tank.

I wasn't sure if I should leave.

There were rules against this.

I was breaking a dozen or more of them now, showing myself like this in public. Anyone who knew anything about dog breeds would understand that I wasn't a house pet. That I was meant for the woods and wilderness, for blood and pine cones. For balance.

Predator and prey.

I couldn't stop myself though. Couldn't turn away. Couldn't even bring myself to breathe for fear of missing a single beat of his sweet humming as the seconds ticked by and the gas siphoning into his car slowed.

He opened his eyes.

Warmth flooded my body as his gaze met mine.

Surprise tinged the air and I couldn't help myself, my tongue lolling happily as I stared at him, trying to make myself as small as possible to avoid intimidating him.

"Where did you come from?" he asked, his eyes wide and soft. Softening even more as he wiped his hands off on his jeans, forgetting the gas entirely, as he took a half step toward me. "Damn, buddy, you look hungry."

I always looked emaciated after a full moon. It took a lot out of me. The wounds my claws left on my body that sometimes stayed for days afterward, and the craving for hot flesh—when left unfulfilled—resulted in my body looking sickly for days till I recovered.

I was not at my best.

A thought that made me self-conscious as the tall man bent close, his hand cupped like he was waiting for me to sniff him. I didn't need to touch him to do it. I'd been inhaling his scent since the moment he parked his car—it's what had driven me closer after all, away from the hunt I'd been on.

Away from the quiet creak of trees and the rustle of wild things.

Where I belonged.

Correction.

Where I'd thought I belonged. Till that moment. Till the moment those fingers carded through my fur and that sweet voice echoed in the air. "Stay here." he'd said, and I stayed. I stayed because what else could I do?

When he'd asked so gently?

When he was everything.

So sweet. So pretty. So wonderful.

So handsome. So amazing.

When he returned with a big bag of beef jerky, a water bottle, and a paper bowl, I couldn't help the way my tail thumped happily against the ground in response. It wagged back and forth, with a mind of its own as my human's eyes grew soft and he knelt beside me.

"It's not much," he said as he filled the bowl with water and tore the pack of meat open. It smelled processed. Cooked. Not fresh at all. But I ate it obediently anyway, lapping at his fingertips every time he offered me a morsel, my heart thudding unsteadily when he laughed—finding my tongue ticklish.

He was kind.

He was kind.

So sweet.

So perfect.

So good, good, good.

My mate.

My perfect, wonderful, sweet mate.

Feeding me because he saw I needed him. Stroking those fingers through my fur till I rolled on my back and offered him my belly—something I'd never done. Not for anyone other than my father. He rubbed me gently there, humming softly under his breath like he didn't even notice as I let him touch me where I was most vulnerable.

My mate.

My mate.

My mate-mate-mate.

My prince.

My fairy tale.

I'd wanted Jeffrey to save me. I'd wanted him to save me so bad—I just hadn't let myself admit that. And maybe…that had been my folly the whole time. Because it was only after I accepted that truth that I realized the truth.

I'd gone feral.

I had.

And if the memory of him was enough to bring me back from the brink of insanity then that meant…fuck. That meant perhaps we could've bonded all along. Human or not.

For so long I'd agonized. I'd told myself it was impossible. Torn myself apart when the truth was right in front of my face.

Mom and Dad had always told me a mate was a person you chose.

I just…hadn't realized I could choose Jeffrey.

He wasn't a wolf and I'd thought…well…

I'd thought that it wasn't a possibility.

This was my fault.

All along this had been my fault. Because while I'd chosen to stay with Jeffrey, there had always been a small, shriveled part of me that knew my days would end. And that part of me—the part that resented the moon— the part that knew I wouldn't have a happy ending, was the reason our bond had never settled.

Until now.

The silvery threads of our souls twisted toward one another. My wolf stirred beneath the surface of my skin. Harry and Jules were quiet, solemn as they watched the sun sink low behind the trees.

Downy soft, pearly white snow covered the ground, sweeping in through the open garage door. Wispy and chill, it fluttered inside the garage. I was grateful for my fur then, and even more grateful to be a wolf—because we tended to run hot.

If Jeffrey had been here he would've been shivering.

As it was, however, all of us sat still, waiting for the other shoe to drop.

When the hunters returned, they'd see me—in my alphaskin. They'd remember the way I'd torn at the bars. And Harry would only have a few moments to convince them that I was back—and that this was over. I wasn't sure I had another shift in me.

My wolf surrounded me, keeping me safe, my shuddery, broken heart fluttering as weakly as the snow.

The moon rose high in the sky, not quite full, but close enough. I watched her, heart aching.

For so long I'd resented the cool blue of her caress. She'd made me a monster.

But now I…realized how wrong I'd been.

It wasn't my moon mother who had betrayed me.

It was me.

With every negative thought, with my secret surety that things would end bloody and violent. I'd stolen my life away—blaming her for my own transgressions.

For the first time since I was sixteen and lost the moon, her light felt warm.

"Time's almost up," Harry said, voice hoarse. It was the first time he'd spoken in…hours maybe? I wasn't sure. Based on the height of the moon I knew he was correct. "Where are they?"

"Where's Dad?" Jules's voice was small. I twisted to look at them for the first time since I'd fallen to the floor. Everything hurt, but the silvery threads of my bond to Jeffrey were still reaching—and I hoped…I hoped they didn't chase in vain.

"He should've been here by now," Harry chewed on his lip, a dark lock of his hair falling over his brow. He and Jules often looked like twins—though Harry was quite a bit taller than Jules was. They shared the same haunted eyes now, however, as they looked at me.

"Can you shift back?" Jules asked, his shoulders drawn tight. The sweater he was wearing had slipped over his shoulder, the enchanted tattoos that spread across his collarbone stark against his olive-toned skin.

I shook my head. And even that hurt.

It wasn't a body hurt—because that had long healed, though the blood remained clotted on my fur. It was the kind of hurt that aches deep inside your bones. That makes you feel cold even when you're warm. That reminds you of all your fuck-ups. A weight that was cruel, and hard, and unforgiving.

Is this how Jeffrey feels? I wondered to myself, my heart hurting for him anew.

I hadn't had much room in my life to regret. Not because I was perfect, but because I'd always been so frightened of stepping out of line that I hadn't truly lived. At least…not until I moved here. Not until I'd met Jeffrey. Not until I'd seen the watercolor painting that was Maine in the fall, and realized it paled in comparison to the auburn shade of Jeffrey's hair.

Regret was a horrible, awful thing.

It made my mouth dry. Made me feel weak and shaky. Made a pit in my stomach grow lead heavy, burning like silver.

I hated it.

I *hated* it.

Footsteps sounded, multiple. Muffled voices echoed behind the door that led into the lodge. The large van that had left earlier had not returned.

The hangar had been a ghost town for hours now, and the sound of hunters was as welcome as it was terrifying.

"They're coming." Harry sat up straighter, jerking to attention.

"No shit," Jules muttered to himself, like he couldn't help but snark.

"Shut up," Harry hissed back, though his lips twitched into an indulgent little smile.

All of us came to the same conclusion at the same time. I saw the light flicker in both my brothers' eyes, our gazes meeting, before they snapped back to the door.

Because if these were *new* hunters—if they hadn't seen when I'd gone feral—maybe we'd have a chance to save this. The others could've told them what happened, sure, but given how quickly they'd left to help the felled hunters the chances of that were slim.

Which just reminded me of Jeffrey again.

Beautiful, wonderful, perfect—murderous Jeffrey.

Pride bubbled up inside me, bright and effervescent as I thought about the fact he'd incapacitated not one, not two, not three, but four hunters, all on his own. *Our mate is strong, my wolf preened. He is a good choice. A good bitch and a good hunter.* He was a wonder. An absolute wonder. I'd thought so as I watched his weapons display. I'd thought so when he'd chosen to spare me. And I thought so now—aware of the blood he'd spilt, no doubt to protect my family.

Because that was just the kind of man he was.

Noble.

Ready to carve off bits of his soul if it meant protecting his kin.

The footsteps drew closer. All three of us stared at the door, waiting with anxious anticipation. I knew there was a simple solution to our problem.

A solution that was visual—and would make it impossible for the hunters to hurt us.

I just needed to shift into my humanskin.

If I could shift they'd have no choice but to acknowledge the second they entered the room that I was back. That I was fine. That they couldn't kill me after all.

But no matter how hard I focused, no matter how hard I tried—I couldn't do it.

Thud, thud came the feet.

C'mon, c'mon, c'mon.

I closed my eyes, focusing everything I had on the tingle in my body—the burn I usually felt as my fur melted away and my humanskin came back into focus. The way I shrunk, my snout shortening, my teeth flattening.

Only…still…

That didn't work.

So I changed tactics.

I used the hope I had—the little resilient sliver that was oddly Jeffrey shaped. I thought about him. I thought about the curve of his smile. Thought about the freckles that decorated the top of his ass. The way he giggled when I bit at the back of his knees. The way his sweet little toes curled when I slurped his cock down. The way his dark eyes were full of warmth. The way he made me feel—whole, strong, appreciated.

Like when he looked at me I was everything I'd always wanted to be.

When the door opened, my eyes opened too.

Harry was laughing, and the sound was relieved-happy-exhausted. And I knew then, that we would be okay. That I would survive this. That I had done what I had to do. There was no denying then, human or not, fated or not—Jeffrey was my mate.

Because my hands were human as I wrapped them around the bars, pressing against them, my heart in my throat.

I sensed him before I saw him.

The silvery threads of our bond reaching toward each other. They wound tight the moment they tapped, braided and thick, twisting, twining—until two ropes became one, and I could…fuck.

I could breathe.

Just like that, my wolf snapped back in my head, its snarling, foaming teeth softened. Gums no longer exposed. Hackles no longer raised. What had been feral grew docile, needy soft.

Because Jeffrey was here.

He was here—

He was okay—

He was.

"Hi, big guy." Jeffrey approached the cage first, his hair a blood-sticky, wild mess. Distantly I recognized that he wasn't alone. That he'd brought my brothers with him—Silas too, and my Dad. They'd all appeared at the last possible minute to save me. And I knew that—and I was grateful.

But I only had eyes for one person.

One perfect, wonderful, beautiful person.

He smelled like blood, his and others, and his eyes were bright. But they were different just like his scent was.

The brown was gone, replaced instead by—

Lavender. Like my favorite blossoms. The ones that scattered along the mountain back home in the spring.

"Jeffrey—" My voice cracked, my hand scrambling through the bars for him the second he drew close enough to touch. "Are you okay? You—they said—I—you look so beautiful. You—Butters? He—You're a wolf—he—what?" My jaw fell open, eyes wide. "What—I mean—"

"I'm okay," Jeffrey pushed up against the bars, as eager to get close to me as I was to get to him. My fingers curled in the fabric of his shirt. It smelled like Butters but I hardly cared, gulping in great, greedy lungfuls of his scent. I hadn't let myself hope that I'd ever smell it again. "I'm okay."

He smelled different but the same.

Like himself, but more concentrated.

And beneath the zing of orange, and the flavor of home there was the fizzle of magic too. His wolf, still new, hiding beneath the surface of his humanskin. I couldn't wait to see it. Couldn't wait to run with him. To chase him. To listen to the thrum of his paws hitting the dirt and know that he was mine. No injury could take him. And the moon mother would smile down kindly on us both.

My mate, my lover, my savior, my Jeffrey.

"You were hurt—" I tried to shove between the bars, and while my humanskin was smaller than my alphaskin had been, I still couldn't manage it.

Behind Jeffrey the hunters were releasing Jules and Harry into my Dad's custody. Butters was talking to Silas, tail thumping. Theo was hanging near the back, tears running down his cheeks, like now that things were finally over, he could finally let go. Dad was speaking to the head hunter—the one who'd found me in the woods—and I knew I should tune in.

They deserved an apology too, and I'd give it to them. But right now…I couldn't. I couldn't be an alpha. Couldn't be their brother. Couldn't be anything other than what I was. A scared man who had almost lost everything, but somehow gained it all instead.

I knew I should care what was happening, but I didn't.

I didn't.

Because Jeffrey was here. He was okay. He was whole and beautiful, and brighter than the moon that hung outside. Snow drifted in through the open door, scattering across the floor and sweeping across his blood-soaked sneakers.

"Butters turned me," Jeffrey said. "I know that's bad. I know he wasn't supposed to but—"

"It's okay," I shook my head. "It's okay." I would deal with this. I would fix it. If anyone mistreated him—if SAC came down on us for this, I would deal with it. "It'll be okay."

It wasn't right, and I knew our path would not be an easy one. Butters would be banished now, and Jeffrey would spend the rest of his life shunned by those that didn't know him.

But I couldn't blame Butters.

In fact…I'd never been more grateful in all my life.

I'd buy him all the rocky road he wanted. I'd even brave the grocery store to do it. But more than that, I promised that I would make this right. That Butters would not pay for his choice to save the other half of my heart.

"He didn't have a choice," Jeffrey was shaking, minute little twitches that betrayed just how stressed his sweet body was. I ached to lay him out, to climb on top of him, to protect him from the events of today. To keep him warm and safe and docile sweet.

"I know," I said, shaking. "It's good. It's good he did."

"I can be your mate now—" Jeffrey's voice was shaking, his eyes blurry with tears. "We can bond. Can't we? Officially, I mean. You don't have to leave again—you don't have to choose someone else—"

"You can—you *are*—" My voice was rough. "I won't. I don't."

"Good because you fucking…you *scared* me. You scared me so bad. And you're not supposed to." Jeffrey's words were angry but his scent was happy-sad-needy. "You're supposed to be the one who makes me feel *safe*."

I whined, even though he was right. *He was right.* Of course he was.

"I am sorry," I said, because he deserved an apology. They all did. "I am sorry. I thought there was no other way. And I just—"

"I know." Jeffrey reached through the bars, warm hands cupping my cheeks. Warm despite the chill, because he was *other* now, just like I was. My wolf spun in circles, a new kind of hunger floating to the surface. "Believe me," Jeffrey's lips tipped up into a knowing, sweet smile. "I know what it's like to be backed into a corner. We do stupid shit just to survive. And if anyone can understand being a self-sacrificing asshole, it's me," he laughed and I was…

God.

So relieved.

I wasn't sure what I'd expected. I hadn't had much time to anticipate at all. And I hadn't dared let myself hope. Maybe I should have. Because Jeffrey Prince was a good luck charm. Better than a rabbit's foot and an incantation. And he had this uncanny way of making my life better, even in the darkest of times.

I nodded jerkily, sagging into his touch. Pressing kisses against his palms, I ached for him.

"You're not angry?" I asked, my voice hoarse. "That I…left?"

"No," Jeffrey shook his head, forehead pushing against the bars. We were pressed head to toe, with the bars squashed between us. "*No.*"

"I..."

"How could I be mad at you?" His violet eyes glinted, tears swimming inside them. "When I would've done the same thing."

I had never been so happy to be understood.

When we kissed, it was awkward and disjointed. Hard to reach between the gaps, but not impossible. He tasted like freedom, like happily ever afters, like fairy tales and oranges and happy-happy-happy.

Teeth, tongue, bruising. Biting. Eager. The kiss evolved from soft to needy, to desperate. Neither of us wanted to acknowledge just how close we'd gotten to losing each other. And as the silvery threads of our bond twisted tighter, tighter, tighter, I knew we'd be fine.

I knew as surely as I knew the next moon would rise that Jeffrey Prince was my happy ending.

Only, our story wasn't over yet.

Chapter Five

Jeffrey

I HAD NEVER been as relieved as I was the moment I pushed through the doors into the hangar at the hunting lodge west of Elmwood and saw Mutt standing naked, blood soaked, and shaking inside his cage.

So much had happened before that moment.

The spinning wheels as we struggled up the snow-logged roads.

When we'd gotten stuck, Theo had suggested going the rest of the way on foot.

The blaring lights of a car behind us—a car that ended up being Silas's. Silas who had apparently picked up Mutt's Dad on the way. His pack trailed behind us in the woods, hairy bodies dipping between the trees, the steadily falling snow making them look eerie and beautiful all at the same time.

Silas told us it was for insurance.

And the sick, terrified flip in my gut I got every time I saw the hundred or so massive wolves that trailed like an army behind us was just—yeah. Okay. Yep. If I was a group of hunters I would be incredibly hesitant to fuck with us.

I wasn't sure how I was going to get away with what I'd done.

The shooting.

But I figured…if what Theo said was correct, I was pack now. Pack. And while that was difficult to wrap my head around—maybe it meant I could trust that we'd figure this out. Together.

Mutt's eyes were swimming with tears when I approached.

He looked broken in two, his ribs caved in, blood smeared over this body, fleshy chunks splattered across the floor. I wasn't sure what had happened—but I didn't question it. Not now. Not when I had the opportunity to talk to him, to kiss him, to hold him again—when I hadn't known I'd ever get to do that again.

When the hunters finally let Mutt out of the cage, my heart was in my throat.

And then he was on top of me, pushing me into the cement, his nose at my throat, snuffling loudly, happily, his bloody body smearing all over mine as his tail popped free and it *thump, thump, thumped.*

My favorite sound in the entire world.

"Matthew," Mutt's Dad's voice was gentle. He jerked his head up, body a warm blanket on top of mine. The cement had skidded across my knees, but I couldn't be assed to care—especially when I felt the weirdest fucking sensation ever as my skin began to knit back together.

"Dad," Mutt trembled. He curled around me tighter, his voice rough. I expected him to pull off of me—or something.

But he didn't.

Instead, he just squashed me tighter. "There's someone I'd like you to meet." His dad arched an eyebrow, blue eyes crinkling with amusement.

"Is there?" he hummed, waiting patiently for Mutt to get off of me.

Mutt's dad was a nice-looking man. His scent was warm and spicy, but in a different way than Silas's was. Or even Mutt's. I was starting to think that fizzle was an alpha thing. He exuded calm, casting an unworried cloud of it in the air that immediately set me at ease.

He had a mustache and wore the most adorable plaid button-up and bowtie combo. Kinda like Santa if he was hot, wore pastels, and kept his hair short.

Mutt jerked to his feet, yanking me up easily, then bundling me in front of his body with a happy hum. He nuzzled the back of my neck, then pulled back to speak. "Dad, Jeffrey. Jeffrey, Dad."

"Nice to meet you, sir," I held my hand out to him, then regretted it—because I'd been hugging Mutt, which meant that I was just as blood-soaked as he was. "Sorry." I rubbed my hand off on my pants, which did absolute shit for cleaning it off, then offered it over again.

"It's lovely to meet you, sweet one." Mutt's dad ducked his head, his eyes warm as he encased my hand in both of his, and gave it a gentle squeeze. I melted immediately, the oddest sense of safe-warm-loved flooding through me. "Thank you for looking after my son."

"He's the one that's been looking after me," I chirped back, because it was true. And maybe a bit of a joke—because of Mutt's stalking. "But uh. Yeah. You're…welcome, man." My cheeks felt hot. "It was my pleasure." I was too tired to filter my words, and I must've looked shocked as hell that that had managed to slip free, because he laughed, and just squeezed my hand tighter.

"I'm sure it was," he laughed, lingering for just a moment longer, his eyes searching mine before he gently released my hand with a soft pat, and took a half step back.

Mutt was staring at his dad with heart eyes. Like he thought the world of him. And that was such a foreign idea it took me a second to wrap my head around it. I'd never had a father figure I could look up to, or parents that cared about me.

Mutt and his father had a conversation with each other without having to share a single word. The older, silver-haired alpha leaned forward, his forehead pushing against Mutt's with a soft hum. Mutt was taller, but not by much. They shared more similarities than they didn't.

It took a solid minute for them to stop their weird telepathic heart-to-heart. A solid minute of warm silence, and the gentle thump of Mutt's tail thwacking my thigh. Without thinking, I reached back to halt it before it could hit me again—only to realize with shocked awe that it wasn't Mutt's tail smacking me at all.

It was mine.

My tail.

My fucking tail.

Because I was a wolf now—and maybe that's why talking to Mutt's dad made me feel like I was wrapped in a warm blanket. Why that empty ache that had sat hollow inside me all my life was full. It was my pack. The bond I had with Mutt—but more than that too.

Mutt's dad only confirmed that when he finally pulled back, turning his attention back to me. And then he dipped down, his forehead brushing mine and warm-happy-family-belonging burned so hot and visceral through my body for a moment I could hardly breathe.

"Welcome to the family," Mutt's dad spoke, breaking the silence.

And then he pulled back and offered us both a sunny smile.

"Dad—" Mutt's voice cracked. "I know it's not custom, but I—" Mutt sucked in a breath, chest puffing up as he stood to his full height. "I would like to bond with Jeffrey now. Officially. Please."

"Go ahead," he laughed. "With my blessing."

And then he twisted back around and headed over to his other children to do more of his alpha-werewolf-voodoo. I sagged, skin still buzzing as I tipped my head up to look at Mutt. "Bond with me?" I asked, voice low.

"Yes," Mutt murmured.

"Wolves only mate once," I echoed his earlier words, my heart thumping as erratically as my tail.

"Yes."

"And you—"

"You are my mate," Mutt's eyes were bright. His expression was solid, sure. He may not have been Pack Alpha, but that didn't mean I couldn't feel the strength behind his frame. The warmth that buzzed beneath my skin just looking at him. "You have always been my mate. And I would like to keep you. If you would let me. I know I have messed up. That I have lied, that I have been stupid and reckless, but I—"

I kissed him.

I kissed him till his words fizzled out. And when I pulled back I hoped he could see the promises in my eyes. Inside my wolf—the wolf I'd never had before, a foreign entity that felt as natural as breathing—preened.

I felt bubbly and bright.

Happy.

In a way I hadn't known I could be.

Maybe it was reckless, but I'd spent my life carefully living by a plan. I'd been meticulous. Terrified. Paranoid. There'd been an anvil over my head and chains around my ankles, pulling me deeper, deeper, deeper.

But for the first time in my life, I felt no hesitation. I felt no anxiety. Not about this. Not about Mutt.

"Forever," I murmured, voice low and soft. "This is forever isn't it?"

"It is," he agreed.

"Till the day we die." My skin felt tight, and my tail kept wagging. *Wagging, wagging, wagging.* Mutt's eyes danced. His scent was happy-love-love. I was glad then, that I'd learned to trust him before I'd had these new senses. Because there was trust between us now. Trust that never could've been built without some uncertainty first.

But that didn't mean I wasn't soothed as his scent told me exactly what I needed to know.

Mutt grabbed my hand. He pulled it over his chest, his lovely squishy pec flexing beneath my touch. His heart skipped and danced, throbbing beneath my palm. With his other hand he grabbed my chin, forcing my face up so we were staring at each other all over again.

"I love you," he said, like he thought I needed to hear it.

I'd never said it back.

And I'd regretted that, so much.

Only now I was grateful, because I couldn't think of a better time to lay my heart on the line than right now. With the snow falling in a blanket behind his head, sliding in through the open door, the crisp scent of winter in the air.

It'd been sunny the day I was taken. But the day I found my way home,

Elmwood was blanketed in pillowy snow.

I hadn't had many perfect moments in my life.

In fact, I hadn't had any—not until I'd met Mutt.

There had always been a noose around my neck, my heart heavy.

But now I was…light.

Lighter than ever before.

I heard the steady thump of his heart, and knew he was telling the truth. Before, I would've killed to have this skill. To know without a doubt in my mind whether or not someone was lying. To know if Mutt's "I love yous" were sincere.

But…I didn't need to hear the steady thrum of his heart to know that anymore.

It showed in every action he took. In the little glances, the finger brushes, the way he breathed me in like I was enough to sustain him. The way he looked at me, bright and wide, and full of affection. The way he laughed simply because he enjoyed me.

The way he'd sacrificed himself. So terrified of hurting me and the others he loved, that he'd seen no other choice.

For so long, Mutt had given me his love, I'd just been too hurt to see what was right in front of my face. To trust it. To trust him. To trust the thrum of my heart and the love I'd felt bubbling up inside me in return.

I'd thought because I'd never loved before I had to second-guess it.

But I was tired of second-guessing.

I was tired of being scared.

And I thought…if there was one person who deserved my trust, it was Mutt.

So I said the three words I'd never said before.

Said them to the person that made my heart hurt, made my skin buzz, made my belly flip and my stomach tie in knots. Said them to the person who made me feel strong. Who made me hopeful for the future. Said them to the wolf who made me feel like I was whole.

"I love you" tasted like freedom in a way nothing ever had before.

And as Mutt took my mouth with his, his heart skittering beneath my palm, my tail wagging behind me, I knew with absolute certainty that I was lucky after all.

Because while I still had my issues, and those would never go away completely, I had so much to look forward to. No longer stuck in a replay of the past, I was ready to make new memories. To move forward in a way I never knew I could. It would be difficult, I knew. And there would be days with clouds, days when the memories resurfaced and the noose felt tight once again.

But things got better.

They got brighter.

For so long my life had been a tragedy. But one day it wouldn't be. There would be a day when I forgot the pain of what I'd been through, when it would be simply another memory.

Like blood covered by snow.

Buried beneath the happy memories I was determined to make.

I had years and years and years with this perfect, silly, wonderful wolf. Years to rewrite my past, to fill my head with love and my heart with his warmth. And for once, I couldn't wait to move forward.

Because Blair was right that day we'd sat in a graveyard and he'd cracked my chest right open.

He was right.

It was time to move on.

I deserved to be happy.

And Mutt was my hairy, handsome, happy ending.

Epilogue

Jeffrey

SIX MONTHS LATER

"FUCK, FUCK, FUCK." My pulse was racing, the moon high above. It drooped between the looping twist of trees as I scurried through the woods. All four of my legs ached, but in a way that only made me burn brighter–harder–*longer*. The wind ruffled through my fur, and the cold snap that had settled now that the sun had sunk low tasted bitter-bright on my elongated, panting tongue.

Behind me, the thud of feet hitting the ground made my blood sing.

Thump, thump, thump.

I could smell him. *Need-hunt-hunger.* The spicy musk of alpha. Something sugary sweet that only Mutt possessed. Stronger today because it wasn't just the full moon, but Mutt's rut too. It'd come later this year than usual, probably because of what we'd been through last winter.

Thump, thump, thump.

Another tree to twist around, another twig to snap beneath my paws.

The stuttery beat of my heart called to my mate, beckoning him after me.

Mutt's desperation clogged my nose, made me feel fizzy and soft. Made me want to roll over and give him my belly—because he was alpha—*my alpha,* and I needed him as much as he needed me.

But first…the chase.

It was a tradition. Something we'd done for the first time that day in the blood-covered snow. Bursting through the trees and wandering far into the milky white froth of winter, desperate for heat and warmth and the slick-hot bite of his teeth in my neck and his knot in my ass.

That had been our first true chase.

Today was different for many reasons, but no less delicious. Because anytime I lost the steady beat of Mutt's feet—feet, because he was in his alphaskin tonight—I could still scent him on the wind.

Calling to me.

Begging for me.

My lungs burned, my muscles tingling as I leapt over a mossy log, the *thump, thump* of Mutt's feet getting louder. My fur stood on end, panic and desire fizzling beneath my skin as my alpha grew closer and closer. I was faster in this form than I was in my humanskin, but it still felt odd, unnatural.

One day it would be second nature, but today was not that day.

It'd only been a few months since I'd figured out how to shift, after all, and I knew it would take some getting used to. Just like my new heightened senses had.

There were still days when the new sounds and smells overwhelmed me. Made my skin feel tight and the world feel small. And all I could do was crawl beneath the blankets in our bed and nest, desperate to hide.

At those times, Mutt's scent and warmth were the only things that soothed me. His favorite blanket and mine, tangled over top of my head to block out the worst of the noise. He'd find me, because he always did, and he'd sneak beneath the covers beside me. All that hot, sticky skin pressed to mine as the gentle rumble of his purr calmed my racing thoughts.

For hours we'd nest together. It wasn't overtly sexual. Simple and soft and innocent. Until the moment it wasn't anymore, and my need burned bright. Oftentimes the moment my skin became the right size for my body again, I knew just what I wanted. Mutt was always quick to deliver, sweetheart that he was.

Sleepy and docile, I'd turn onto my belly, arch my back, and beg him to mount me till my hole was puffy and slick with his cum, and the wolf that thrummed beneath the surface of my skin was as sated as I was.

Tonight was not a night for cuddling.

No.

Because Mutt had woken up that morning with an itch beneath his skin, and his cock pointed right at me. He'd whined into my hair, huffing and shuddering, hips rubbing needily against my ass, his naked cock leaving hot smears across my skin.

I'd thought I'd been getting the handle on this whole werewolf thing. But apparently there was always something new to learn—because three knots later, when my body was trembling and twitching, and Mutt's cock was still hard, we finally figured out what was wrong.

He was in heat.

No matter how many times he sobbed and fucked into me nothing seemed to work. The itch beneath his skin only grew, his claws popping free, hair spreading across his body, tail erect.

"Please," his voice had been low and rough as he'd nuzzled into my ear. "Please— It's not enough—" His hips snapped into me harder, a pitiful whimper escaping him. "I need—I need—"

"Anything," I'd promised, because I meant it.

Which was why we'd ended up here. On a chase. With Mutt's alphaskin behind me rather than his wolf, and the anticipatory crackle of sex in the air.

The other wolves in the pack were running tonight too, like they always did on the full moon—but they kept their distance. Despite being clingy as a whole, every moon they kept a polite distance. Mutt said it was because though we were *pack* and therefore family, they knew I was still new and wouldn't appreciate voyeurs catching an eyeful of Mutt taking the moon out on my ass. Which was nice, but also super invasive.

I figured you couldn't really avoid invasiveness though. Not when you could smell sex from fifty yards away, and hear it from even farther.

Today was no different, though we had gotten a few amused catcalls before we'd split off from the group on our own. All it had taken was one whiff of Mutt when we'd stepped into the clearing we all met in for the start of the run for all of them to steer clear of us.

Thump, thump.

Another log.

My heart raced.

Fuck, fuck, fuck.

While I wanted Mutt to catch me—because of course I did—I still didn't want to make this too easy. He needed to chase as badly as I needed to be chased. So I made a beeline for the creek that spanned the chunk of land that the Rocky Mountain pack had finished negotiations on.

If I can get in the water—I can hide my scent.

I pushed harder, lungs burning, heart racing.

And then, there it was, peeking through the trees. Moonlit and beautiful, the small stream trickled loudly as I burst through the woods and raced toward it. I couldn't hear Mutt anymore, but that didn't mean he wasn't close.

He was an excellent hunter, and he could easily conceal himself even from me. When I heard him it was only because he wanted me to. Which meant…he was no doubt close, and I didn't have much time to get away before he found me.

My paws skidded over pebbles as I slid down the rocks toward the water, heart in my throat. I only had a split second to see my reflection, lavender eyes glowing softly on a furry orange face I barely recognized before—

Fuck—ow—*oh.*

Time's up.

All the air wooshed from my lungs as a heavy, furry body jerked on top of me. Mutt's black fur glinted, the water rippling, his distorted reflection flickering. The gleam of his sapphire blue eyes wavered in the water, as did the pointed ears on his head, and his long snout filled with razor-sharp, wicked teeth.

And then he was hauling me backward with his claw-tipped hands, away from the creek, onto the much softer sand. I fought back, heart thumping erratically as I struggled in his grip, putting every last ounce of fight I had left into the movements only to fail spectacularly.

Because he was simply stronger than I was.

Bigger.

Better.

A predator made to hunt other predators.

Mutt's claws bit into my furry hips, forcing me flat on my belly, pinning me into the sand as his hot breath huffed at the back of my neck. *Caught. I'm caught.* I jerked again and he growled, low and rumbling, and terrifying.

My wolf whined, melting beneath the much larger beast, giving in immediately. And the second I gave in, I shifted. It felt odd, like it always did, but right too as my fur melted away. Naked and much smaller now, my humanskin ached with need as I dug my blunt fingers into the cold, damp sand, looking for something to ground me.

God, he feels good.

So big, so fucking—

Fuck.

Mutt growled his triumph, voice rumbling through the air as the hot slick of his drool dripped on the back of my neck. His hands shifted a little, still holding tight to my hips, keeping me pinned and obedient beneath him.

"Oh shit," I whined softly, achingly hard. The brush and scratch of his coarse fur along my back made my head spin. It was so foreign and strange, and sexy as hell because beneath the teeth and the hair and the claws was my mate.

My Mutt.

My mate.

The man that owned my heart.

And he *needed* this.

He needed *me*.

So fucking bad I could taste it in the air.

My ass was slick and ready—we'd known this would happen before we'd even left our little shared apartment. Not that I'd been anything other than puffy and full of cum all day, but still.

"Fuck, Alpha," I gasped out, groaning when Mutt's hairy, claw tipped fingers dragged over my hips, forcing them up, and open, till my ass was presented and I could feel the slippery hot of his pointed, rock-hard cock pushing against my cheeks.

There was no preamble, no foreplay—and I was fine with that.

Completely fucking fine with it—because I'd been hard the entire time he'd chased me. And his scent was aroused, aroused, aroused—a plume of need and musk filling my nose. I sobbed, arching back obediently till the slick tip of his dick kissed my achingly empty hole.

We'd done a lot of experimentation since the first time we'd run together like this. I'd taken him in every one of his forms, in every one of mine—but this was…fuck. This was maybe my favorite. The way his alphaskin—a source of terror for most—became puppy-like greed, and achingly gentle as he lined his hips up and—

Ohhhh fuck yeah.

Fuck.

So fucking huge.

He filled me. He filled me and filled me and filled me. So slick and big and hard—the red of his normally sheathed cock tucked snug inside me. So deep I swear I could feel it in my throat as the damn thing pushed against every bit inside me that sent stars bursting behind my eyelids.

"Fuck yes," I moaned, hips jerking. Or, trying to. Because Mutt's hands were still on them, his claws digging in as he yanked me back, unceremoniously till he was buried to the hilt.

He fucked me, rutting into me, over and and over and over—setting a brutal animalistic pace. All I could do was drool into the dirt and whine, the intoxicating scent of his rut filling my nose and head—till all I could think about was more, more, more.

A hot tingle bubbled up in my veins as I shuddered and gasped, ass burning as Mutt forced himself inside again. Every time he pulled out, I couldn't help but clench, begging him back in, my eyes rolling back.

He snapped his teeth at me and I sobbed, nipples pebbled and hard, my cock bobbing uselessly between my legs.

Over and over, deeper and deeper, he rode me like a man possessed.

Our thighs bumped. His muscles rock hard beneath bristled fur. The thwacking wag of his tail could be heard—but only barely—over the wet slap of his balls smacking my perineum. If Mutt kissed like he had no fucks to give, he fucked like there was no tomorrow. Like he never wanted out of me.

His claws cut crescents into my ass and thighs, raking over my skin and leaving trails of raised scratches. Wounds that healed as quickly as they rose.

Mine, mine, mine—Mutt's voice echoed in the back of my head, our bond twisting tighter, brighter, lovelier.

Mine, mine, mine—

Need you.

Need you need you need you.

Needyouneedyouneedyou.

"Fuck," I sobbed, reaching down between my legs to clutch my cock. All it took was one squeeze. One single squeeze, and then the brush of Mutt's fur on my back, and his cock in my ass sent me off. Mewling weakly, I spilled into the dirt, clutching tight at his dick as it pistoned inside me, stretching me wide enough I could hardly breathe.

Take it, take it, take it.

Mutt's knot swelled, stretching the tight skin of my rim as I gasped and whimpered, and with a brutal jerk of his hips he forced it inside. It was the sweet kind of ache. The kind of pain that burned just right.

Drooling, I jerked a little, then relaxed when Mutt's teeth bit into the back of my neck, severing the skin there, the scent of blood filling the air as he marked me the way he always did when we were like this.

The way he had the first time—when we'd fucked in the snow in the middle of the woods outside the hunting cabin, and our mating had become official.

Since then, a lot had changed.

We'd moved in together, officially. Blair's restaurant had finally opened. Mutt had bonded with all of my family, and I'd bonded with his. Butters and I now competed on CandyCrush. Which he was…ridiculously good at. He'd been banished from Mutt's pack for turning me, which was fucking shitty as hell. But luckily for everyone, Silas had welcomed him into his pack with open arms, and probably an agenda. An agenda that I was pretty damn sure Butters did not mind, if the looks he shot Silas were any indication.

Theo and I spent at least an hour a week sharing stories—to Mutt's chagrin. And Harry and I had become fast friends. He'd randomly call me, rant about something I usually didn't understand—most of the time it was about Kaiju—and then he'd hang up.

Blair and I were better than ever. And while there was still some awkward moments, we were working through those. I think…what I'd needed was a breakthrough. And while it had been hard won, and we had bad days as well as good—at the end of the day, I'd never felt closer to my brother.

I'd thought he'd hate me. That they all would. That the second I dropped the act and told them the truth I'd no longer be appealing.

But they didn't.

Instead, they accepted me with open arms.

When I'd shown up at Blair's apartment covered in blood, recently turned, with Mutt in tow, I'd expected the worst. I'd wanted to see my family, to make sure they were safe—which Mutt said was normal and a wolf thing. But Blair hadn't batted an eye, he'd just nodded, squinted at me and said, "Nice."

Richard, however, had gagged. Very obviously.

"That'll take some getting used to," he muttered to himself, and then plugged his nose as he gave me an awkward, half-pat-hug—because he didn't want to get his shirt dirty.

Apparently Collin was telepathically connected to the two of them, because five seconds later the front door had banged open and he'd launched himself at me and Mutt with lanky-armed enthusiasm.

"Is this real blood?!" he'd asked, amazed. "Holy shit. That's like. So gross. But cool."

Luckily we'd mostly dried off, but he was still a little tacky by the time he peeled himself off of us and walked into the kitchen in search of food. "You never have edible fucking foo—oh." He popped his head out. "You bought Pop Tarts."

"Of course I bought Pop Tarts." Blair rolled his eyes.

"I. Love. Pop. Tarts," Mutt boomed, loud and excited, his tail wagging like crazy. "They are the best! Crunchy and wrong, because they are not real food. But very good. So much sugar! Yes."

"Yes! It's the wrongness that makes them so good," Collin agreed, wagging the box at him. "You want some?"

"Do I—" Mutt jerked his head back, eyes wide, like Collin had just offered him a trip to meet Santa, and not a shitty pastry.

Don't get me wrong, I love Pop Tarts as much as the next guy. But it wasn't like they were fucking gourmet or some shit.

"Do I want a Pop Tart?" Mutt's tail whacked me hard enough he nearly made me stumble.

"Yeah." Collin blinked, looking at me, then Mutt, then me again. Then he snorted. "They're—"

Mutt did not need convincing. He looked to me for permission and when I nodded my head he bounded across the room and slammed into the kitchen, already reaching for the box.

"Why is it every time I see you, you've just got out of trouble?" Blair asked like a long-suffering old man, and not like he was a year younger than me and made of just as much chaos.

"Says the dude who almost got killed three fucking times before noticing it was intentional."

"Touché," Blair shrugged, and then he grinned at me. "The eyes are new."

"Yeah." And then I was hugging him, and he felt good and solid and like pack. I rubbed my face against his shoulder and his throat, scenting him happily, before releasing him just as quickly as I'd grabbed him, and moving on to Richard.

Richard groaned, but let me, shoving me off by the end with a shake of his head. "You have no idea how much work you've caused me," he huffed out, but his eyes were fond. "The Council is gonna be pissed." He frowned down at the tacky blood smear on his leather jacket.

I shrugged apologetically. "We didn't have much of a choice."

"You wanna elaborate about that?"

"Right now? Nope." I gave him one last hug, really rubbing the blood in, then abandoned them both so I could go steal the last Pop Tart before Mutt ate them all. *I was fucking starving.* And also maybe to brush my scent all over the walls a bit so that Blair's place smelled right.

"Mom's going to be pissed," Richard laughed, sounding weirdly happy about that.

Mutt grinned at me when he saw what I was doing. And because he was a babe—the babest babe that ever babed, he offered me a silver packet of Pop Tarts. The last ones, because "I did not want you to go without."

A lot had changed since that day six months ago, but a lot had stayed the same too.

Mutt still enjoyed the toys I'd bought him from the pet store—which was…*hilarious.* I still coveted the squirrel dog toy that he'd bought me for my "sex basket". We were as horny as ever. And now that I'd discovered the joy of getting plowed with wolf dick, I kept my ass primed and ready like ninety percent of the time.

So that all he'd have to do when he saw me was slip my pants down and slide right in.

Just the way we liked it.

I forgot what it was like not to be covered in quick-healing hickeys and bruises. And we discovered—through trial and error—that bites from his alphaskin took the longest to heal, and those quickly became our favorite.

The bite on the back of my neck—the mating mark—never faded.

The first one. From his human teeth.

The one that had bonded us before we'd even known we could.

"Good bitch—" Mutt's voice was muffled, his teeth sliding out of my neck, the crackled growl of his alphaskin's tone buzzing through the air. He didn't like to speak like this. It was difficult and hurt—but he managed anyway sometimes, because he told me the ache to talk to me was worse than any pain.

"Pretty bitch," his voice was a low, buttery snarl.

I shuddered, moaning softly as the wet slide of his teeth leaving my skin made my nerve endings light on fire. Shivery and docile, I groaned when he shifted his hips, his knot rubbing up inside me. It couldn't move much, especially when he was in this form. It was a wonder it could fit at all, he was so fucking big.

It burned so good as he rocked it inside me, the hot spurts of his cum filling me up.

"Need you," Mutt's voice dropped even lower, and I chanced a glance back, desperate to see his face. His furry head was tossed back, his dark pelt liquid black where it cupped his shivering pecs. He was panting, snout tipped toward the sky, his powerful humanlike body shifting with every minute twitch of his hips.

Gorgeous.

So fucking gorgeous.

My ass twitched and he growled, dropping his head back down, his eyes flickering like a predator as he snarled at me. I didn't flinch, because it wasn't meant to scare me. Not really. Besides, he couldn't scare me if he tried.

He was a giant cinnamon roll, even in this form, and that was the goddamn truth.

With his wolf so close to the surface, Mutt was ravenous when he was like this. He normally had very little mind to mouth filter, and that only got worse the hairier he was. There was something primal and delicious about the way his hips continued to rut—almost like he couldn't help it—like despite the fact that he was buried as deeply inside me as he could go, he still wanted deeper.

When his knot finally softened enough he could pull out, he whined, this low needy sound, slick, pointed cock slipping free.

The bright pink flesh was still hard, flexing toward his belly, his hairy balls full and swollen with another load, despite the fact I could feel his cum dripping out of my ass. That was another new thing we'd discovered. He came a lot when he was shifted.

"Mutt," I murmured, voice low and soft. Thready sweet, the way I'd never known it could be till I met him. "*Alpha*," I twisted around, twigs digging into my bare back, my movements sluggish, my hole clenching.

"So sore and wet," Mutt rumbled, staring at my hole as I spread my legs to give him a better look. His long, textured tongue flickered out to wet his lips. And then he descended on my ass like a starving man. Dexterous and slippery, his hot tongue slid inside me, rubbing his cum deeper, then scooping it out, his fangs pushing against my most sensitive flesh.

It should not have felt as good as it did.

It shouldn't have made my skin zing and my spent cock perk up.

But it did.

The danger of it was nearly as good as the pleasure.

This looked so wrong—his wolf-like head tucked between my legs. And that little thrill only made me harder, made me clench tighter, made my head toss back and my legs spread wide enough to accommodate his massive furry head.

When Mutt pulled back—after making me cum twice more—first with his tongue on my hole and cock, and then with his cock inside me, he had a smug grin on his face.

His eyes glinted and I laughed, fucked-out and quivery, the full moon coating his fur in blue light. He was a smug bastard. More confident now than ever, as he'd had months to learn my body, and liked to use his newfound knowledge to his advantage.

I was sweat sticky, coated in my own release, and exhausted. And still, his cock rocked into me, the wet slip of his spilled cum squelching as the liquid-hot pressure pumped in over and over again.

He was a charming, smug bastard.

And apparently smug bastards were my thing.

Mutt kept releasing these lovely shallow grunting sounds, his hips snapping, his powerful body bowed over mine as he fucked and fucked and fucked, eyes pinched shut, mouth full of razor sharp teeth clenched tight.

When he came again he hissed, the hot splatter of his cum inside me painting my insides. I was so full I was surprised he could fit more inside me at all. Could feel my belly bulge when I lay a hand on it—not sure if it was in my head or not—but either way, it was hot as hell.

"Gotta breed you," Mutt murmured, voice crackly soft. "Gotta breed you—Please—I need—"

"I-I know," I gasped out, because I did. I did know. Better than anyone honestly. His need to claim and mark and mate. To fill me full enough I'd be aching and empty for days without him. To make my ass smell like his cum. To mark me inside and out.

When I squeezed his knot inside me a second time, Mutt made a garbled wet sound, pitiful and sexy all at the same time.

Hours later, after we'd calmed down and fucked like rabbits all over the woods, Mutt carried me home. I healed quickly now—quickly enough most wounds didn't bother me. But he was still a gentleman. Chivalrous as hell. And he took it upon himself to make sure I was sore enough it'd take a while to fully heal, just because he liked the way I whined.

I couldn't complain. I liked it too.

"You are happy?" Mutt asked, still in alphaskin, his fur warm and prickly soft as he carried me through the woods toward the little house we'd rented on the new pack grounds. It was kinda…the most perfect place ever. Had amazing water pressure. Never ran out of hot water. There was a cobblestone path that led up the steps, and the front was covered in ivy.

It looked nothing like anywhere I'd ever lived before, and it felt right.

It was kinda huge too—for two people, but Mutt assured me we wouldn't be alone for long. Like he'd told me long ago there were "many pups who needed homes," and while neither of us were ready for parenthood yet, one day we would be.

It showed how far I'd come, that that thought filled me with warmth and elation, and not dread.

Because I knew now, despite never having a good father myself, that I would be a fucking wonderful dad. Our kids would be safe from harm, no matter what befell them. They'd be safe from the monsters that wore human faces, and the darkness of the world. And they would be loved, as simple as that.

Mutt had taught me a lot of things.

But most of all, he'd taught me that true strength came from surviving. From enduring the cruelties of the world, and learning how to smile despite them.

As Mutt tucked me into bed, shifting with a crack-snap of bone, his fur melted away. Warm skin pushed against mine. His tongue lapped at the bite on the back of my neck, soothing and slick, the blankets pulled up snug around us. The gnome in the corner of the room sat sentinel, watching over us as our hearts beat the same lovely rhythm.

I'd been lost for so damn long.

Tired for so damn long.

And as my eyes slid shut, with my mate behind me, safe in our nest, in the home we'd made, it felt good to finally rest.

TALES FROM THE TAROT
King of
Hollywood
FAE QUIN

In the meantime, explore more of
the *Spooky* BOYS universe in......

King of
Hollywood

Acknowledgments

THANK YOU SO much to everyone who finished *Hunt Me*! I hope you enjoyed your adventure with Mutt and Jeffrey, and I can't wait to see you for my next spooky release. Special thanks to all those who made the creation of this book possible, especially Molly with her creative artsy genius, all my incredible beta readers, my writers group who sprinted toward the finish line with me, (bless you Mozz and DL who listened to my frantic rambling and helped me detangle my thoughts), and my husband, who supplied me with caffeine and motivation throughout the entire process. His love and support always keeps me going, and his endless patience has allowed me to grow and change because he catches me every time I fall.

This book will always have a special place in my heart, as it was published less than two weeks after our five year anniversary! Thank you to everyone who contributed their time, energy, and love to this project; you are all my dear friends. And most of all, thank you to the reader, because without you, the creation of this story would have been meaningless. I write the words, but you are the ones who bring the story to life. Each and every one of you is priceless. Thank you for falling in love with these characters alongside me. I love all of you so much. See you next time!

Love,

Fae

About Fae

FAE IS OBSESSED with anything romance. From a young age she realized she had a passion for falling in love over and over again. She loves to tell stories through both her art and writing. With a passion for classical monsters, meet-cutes, and contemporary romance, you can often find her with her nose stuck in a book and her pet corgi, Champa, on her lap.

She currently resides in Utah with her amazing husband and her collection of squishmallows. When you read one of her books you can expect to find love stories between humans, monsters, and loveable assholes that will make you laugh (and cry) as you get lost in their worlds for just a little. Every story comes with a happy ever after guarantee.

Find her online at:

WWW.FAELOVESART.COM